Mortal Leap

Mortal Leap
MacDonald Harris

Introduction by Jonathan Coe
Afterword by Steven G. Kellman

RECOVERED BOOKS
BOILER HOUSE PRESS

Contents

Introduction
by Jonathan Coe

.-- .... --- .- -- ..   .-- .... --- .- -- ..   .-- .... --- .- -- ..   .-- .... --- .- -- ..

MacDonald Harris was the pseudonym of Donald Heiney, an American academic who, besides holding a distinguished series of university posts for more than thirty years, published fifteen extremely diverse and well-received novels. Born in 1921, by the time of his death in 1993 he was not exactly a household name, but his books were much admired, with one of them – *The Balloonist*, published in 1976 – being nominated for the National Book Award. The fact that his fiction is now mostly forgotten is a sobering reminder to all working writers that time can be unkind even to the brightest talents, and no one can rely on a glittering afterlife.

Fortunately, in Harris's case a modest revival seems to be getting under way, and the reissue of this, his second novel, is a significant part of it. *Mortal Leap* was published in 1964, and in Britain at least did well enough to merit a mass-market paperback edition three years later. But it didn't linger in the public memory. Who knows why not? The literary marketplace was just as arbitrary and unforgiving in the 1960s as it is in the 2020s. It should surprise no one that it allowed this novel to slip through its net, even though *Mortal Leap* is, in its way, pretty much a masterpiece of existential fiction.

The novel sets out its stall in the first few pages and makes no bones about its intent or ambition. An unnamed man, the first-person narrator, is looking at his reflection in the mirror. "And with a familiar chill, like the air that sinks down at evening from the hills behind the coast, came the question: who am I?" A few paragraphs later, the narrator's speculations have already broadened out from the personal to the universal. "We are all innocent, in the end," he writes, "and all guilty. We move blindly toward our sins, and the things we do and the things we suffer for don't have much to do with each other. In the end there's no justice: the universe is not an auditing firm." And this is just page three!

Lofty though the explicit concerns of the novel may be, its tone is anything but. The reader immediately notices on those opening pages the terse precision and economy with which Harris uses words. *Mortal Leap* is a visually rich novel, full of vividly-imagined scenes, but there is nothing indulgent or flowery about its prose. Even when Harris is dealing with metaphysical concerns, his use of language is sharp, ironical, plain, and the easy yet emphatic rhythm of his sentences is matched by the beguiling rhythm of the novel itself, its succession of telling, pointed dramatic episodes.

These episodes combine into a story full of mystery, full of suspense, which is difficult to resist. It is a story of two distinct halves. The first tells of the narrator's early years, starting with his escape from a strict Mormon family as a teenager, fleeing by bus in the middle of the night. Very soon he has run away to sea, finding work on a tramp freighter, where he falls under the influence of a cynical, hardened, anti-Semitic Russian called Victor. The milieu of this first half is unremittingly grimy and affectless. The world of these merchant seamen is portrayed as a joyless battle for survival, where all human relationships are transactional, where women are seen as merely "receptacles or machines." An entirely masculine world, too, in which emotions can be processed only through reading: because our narrator turns out to be bookish – much to the derision of his shipmates – although he soon discards his early hero Conrad on the grounds that he is a "sentimentalist," has no truck with "books by tea-party fairies like Proust" and tosses a copy of *The Forsyte Saga* overboard because "I very quickly saw what was wrong with it; Galsworthy was a gentleman, and no gentleman would ever write a good book."

To avoid spoilers I will not discuss how the narrator becomes transported, after much incident and trauma, into an entirely different social universe. He finds himself moving in with what he calls "the leisure class" and builds an alternative life for himself with the help of a new accomplice. She is a woman, this time, one whom he finally understands as neither receptacle nor machine but as a human being with needs and agency, and who decides to save him and throw in her lot with him for reasons which are, at first, every bit as covert and unknowable as his own.

In its second half, then, *Mortal Leap* gradually reveals itself as a novel not just about masculinity, war and identity, but also about class. The self-annihilation and erasure of personality which the narrator embraces at the story's midpoint is pivotal in more ways than one: it buys him passage into an altogether more privileged and materially comfortable world, in a way which perhaps parallels Heiney's own journey. During the Second World War he joined the merchant marine as a cadet, was awarded a Third Mate's license and saw action in the North Atlantic and Mediterranean campaigns. The sweaty, deadpan account of life aboard ship which makes up the first half of the novel was written from lived experience. But love of literature determined the course of his post-war life, which was spent mainly on university campuses and involved writing book-length studies of "tea-party fairies" like Proust. It's inevitable that we end up reading *Mortal Leap* as a metaphorical account of his own experience: a post-traumatic attempt to make sense of his irreconcilable wartime and peace-time lives. Projecting this autobiographical dimension onto the narrative does not, however, diminish its power in any way: quite the reverse, in fact. It adds even more personal and emotional heft to a book which addresses itself, without preamble or apology, to the very fundamentals of the human condition. It's a novel which aims high and hits its target.

Mortal Leap

by MacDonald Harris

For V.J.D.
who taught me about ships and women

He who loves a person, on account of that person's beauty, does he love the person? No; for the smallpox, which kills the beauty without killing the person, will destroy the love. And if one loves me for my judgement, for my memory, does he love me? No; for I may lose those faculties without losing myself. Where, then is this ME, if it is neither in the body nor in the soul; and how love the body or the soul, except for these endowments, which are not what constitute the ME, since they are perishable? For could we love the substance of a person's soul abstractly, and without reference to its qualities? This is impossible, and would be unjust. One never loves the person, then, but only the qualities.

Pascal, *Pensees*, VI: 17

Chapter 1

.-- .... --- .- -- ..   .-- .... --- .- -- ..   .-- .... --- .- -- ..   .-- .... --- .- -- ..

I've forgotten the name of the French philosopher—or was it an Indian mystic?—who said that attention is the highest form of prayer. But I know what he meant. By paying attention to the little things we finally come to notice things that are deeper and more elusive, the things that are invisible to ordinary eyes. If you are interested in the study of what used to be called souls you have to watch carefully, for a long time, until finally you see under the surface—most people have never been trained to look and so. They see only the outsides of things. If you learn this kind of attention, you can look at the things, the objects, the people you have lived with for years and see things you never noticed before. For example, it was only recently that I discovered the furrow between my eyes. I was standing in front of the mirror in the bathroom and perhaps through some trick of the fluorescent light I happened to notice it, a small vertical crease in my forehead, like a narrow V sketched in with a pencil. Was I getting thoughtful in my old age, I wondered? That would be an irony. (I am convinced the universe is terribly ironical.) Anyhow, there I stood before the mirror with my feet sunk in the fuchsia carpet that had cost fourteen dollars and a half a yard, brooding over this shadow in my brow as though it were the mark of Cain. It was a strange thing for me to do, uncharacteristic, so to speak. What was I staring at myself for anyhow? What did I expect to find, stigmata? For that I would have to take off my shirt. Besides. I am not very religious.

All right, I thought, let's take off the shirt. Let's take off the pants too. What do we have here anyhow? Let's get down to essentials. There he was, this strange beast the I, standing there in the mirror with the scars of old agonies faintly visible through his tan, the white shadow of his swimming trunks fitting him like a garment—on the face there's another pale shadow of skin a little lighter than the rest, and a line like a fine seam starts on the forehead and follows down the cheek to the mouth. In short, a body which had been broken and then carefully put back together, with patience and skill, by hands which had left only a trace of their work. It seemed to me that of all the strange things in the world nothing was stranger to me than my own flesh. The wall beside me, the chromium fixture I touched with my hand, was hard and solid, but the rest was strange and I was unable to believe in it. In that moment it seemed that a stir of breeze could sweep it away. I thought, it is strange that it is only I who give a reality to this world, these objects that seem so solid: all that is inside me. And with a familiar chill, like the air that sinks down at evening from the hills behind the coast, came the question: who am I?

Because the secret is that I don't know the answer to the question any more than you. Behind the scars, behind the swimmer's tan, is something that even I myself have half forgotten: elusive, shadowy, the ghost of an old identity. There are times when for weeks on end I don't think of it, when everything is familiar and reassuring and I imagine I have always been as I am now. But the shadows are still there, and then I ask myself—why not? Isn't it possible to carry shadows inside you and still live, love, sleep, be happy or bored like ordinary people who are the same all the way through, like cheese?

Besides, who's made out of cheese? I never did understand them, these cheese-people. Who doesn't have a dark place somewhere inside him that comes out sometimes when he's looking in a mirror? Dark and light, we are all made out of shadows like the shapes on a motion-picture screen. A lot of people think that the function of the projector is to throw light onto the screen, just as the function of the story-teller is to stop fooling around and simply tell what happened, but the dark places must be there too, because without the dark places there would be no image and the figure on the screen would not exist. Fine, let's look at the dark places. To do this we have to roll the film back to a previous incarnation of myself: I am twenty-five years old, looking the same as I do now except a little thinner and more cocky, without the scars and the furrow between the eyes. In this somewhat faded photograph I am wearing a dirty cap with gold braid on it, the third engineer of a ship which through a piece of stupidity was sunk in the Solomon Islands in the fall of 1942. It was an event of no particular military or historical importance; a merchant ship had no business being in that part of the world in the first place and that was the year they were getting the gas ovens into high gear at Auschwitz. What possible significance can be attached to any individual fate, the things that happen to any single collection of bones, ligaments, reflexes, sensations in a time when six million people were exterminated according to the latest scientific methods? It was not an important agony, looked at objectively. What happened was simple, even banal: I became naked, died, lost parts of my flesh and most of my ego along with a few illusions such as a belief in the uniqueness of my personal scrap of consciousness and the cosmic importance thereof, and went on from there. All that was left was something inside that I don't know what to call—a soul? Even the theologians don't believe in that anymore. Maybe it's better to believe in ghosts.

That was all that was left, but it was enough; a thread to connect the past with the present, death with life. Anyhow that was what I saw, that day when I had this epiphany or satori or whatever it was, looking in the mirror: under the scars, behind the wrinkle in the forehead, there were other ghosts, deeper and more elusive. Here was the mark where I murdered and fornicated, betrayed my friends and was betrayed by them; here I slept in strange rooms, the whore's cubicle, the prison cell, the psychiatric ward. Is there anybody who would like to have written on his forehead a record of the places where he has slept? We are all innocent, in the end, and all guilty. We move blindly toward our sins, and the things we do and the things we suffer for don't have much to do with each other. In the end there's no justice: the universe is not an auditing firm. Would we like it better if it were? If we had to pay for everything, down to the last cruelty, the last fornication, the last harmless lie? Let's leave the dark places where they are.

Not that we would want to do away with them, those dark places. There's a faint odor of death everywhere, for example under the arm of the woman to whom we make love, that gives a dimension, a metaphysics, to her smile. I know this isn't scientific; the chemists are working on deodorants. I wish them luck; they're working in a good cause. But I know too that if we ever make a world without shadow, if the chemists and scientists and psychologists succeed in abolishing fear, pain, loneliness and death, some of us win find life so intolerable we will probably blow out our brains out of sheer boredom.

All right, fine, probably next I will want to revive the Inquisition and start burning people. Well, maybe so. Without shadows there is no metaphysics and without pain, no love. Don't you think they felt their aliveness with a new intensity, made love well, savored the wine at the base of their tongues, after they had lit those fires?

What do you take me for, a humanitarian? Well, no, I don't want to burn people. I've been burned too: look at my hands.

Even from the beginning I never did belong to the cheese-people and for a long time I didn't know what was the matter with me. It started in a little Utah town with the mountains all around it, where the wind came up in the morning and rustled in the poplar trees outside my bedroom window. The place I came from was good, and I understood from the start that I was the one who was wrong, for not fitting into it and being happy like the others. Maybe someday I will go back there, and stop and get gas and look around for Feigel's drugstore and Mr. Poulsen's pigeon-barn and the cafe where you catch the Greyhound bus, some time when I have a long white beard so nobody will recognize me. If you wait long enough, you don't have to put on a false mustache: time provides the disguises. It would be interesting to see what it is like, to see if it is the same as I remember it. I don't think it would have changed very much!

The people I came from were good Mormon stock, and what they lacked in knowledge of the world they made up in virtue. I respected their virtue then, as I do now. My parents conscientiously paid their tithe to the Church all through the Depression, they abstained from alcohol, coffee, and tea, and they believed with a quiet and firm conviction that people who smoked cigarettes were destined to pay for it in Hell. When I questioned any of these beliefs, like the one regarding the drinking of coffee, I was referred to the section in the *Doctrine and Covenants* known as the Word of Wisdom, which in our house was consulted in the way other people consult the encyclopedia. Some Mormons used to dispute whether the Word of Wisdom was divinely inspired or only a kind of compendium of hygiene assembled by Joseph Smith (it said tobacco was good for horse-poultices but bad for human beings) but my father was bishop of his ward and his opinion carried a certain authority. He believed it was divinely inspired. No tobacco or coffee was ever seen in our house. When I was a child a magazine like the *Saturday Evening Post*, which had pictures of people smoking and drinking coffee, had all the dark fascination of an oriental casbah and I would ponder over it wondering what these vices could be like. I imagined the pleasure of smoking as something dark, warm, and phallic, with a taste like the odor of incense. *Chesterfields—they satisfy!* intoned the radio around the time I was fourteen or fifteen and full of strange unsatisfied desires. When I heard these words, my heart would pound.

I knew even then I was different from the others, my cheerful basketball-playing cousins with names like DeWayne and Lamar and Virl who went on missions for the Church to Norway and Holland and came back and married girls they met in Mutual and got jobs as Chevrolet salesmen, and were destined someday to be the bishops of their wards. How did they do it? For them it seemed as easy as breathing, but I was queer, freakish, something was wrong with me as though I lacked some essential organ, my vocation for normality was missing. I contemplated myself, on the outside a glum thoughtful boy, silent and rather abstracted, on the inside a misshapen freak. Certainly it could not be accounted for by my ancestry. Mormons are very genealogy-conscious and I knew mine by heart. My mother's family, the Beales, were among the first settlers in the valley; there was a Beale Creek in the mountains and a town called Beale's Mill a few miles east on the road to Heber. On my father's side I was descended from the legendary Lorenzo Backus, the scholar-apostle who taught himself Persian and Hebrew, translated the Book of Mormon into Italian and carried eight hundred and fourteen books, including a complete set of Dante in calfskin bindings, from Missouri to Utah in a Conestoga wagon, killing several Indians on the way and fording three rivers without getting the books wet. The books were still preserved in the Pioneer Museum and there was a statue of my great-great-grandfather in Temple Square, in the heart of Salt

Lake City. Once in a while when I came to town with my family, I would go to look at the statue. Brother Lorenzo, a craggy giant in a greatcoat which came below his knees, was staring into a large stone book with a frown of annoyance between his eyes, perhaps pondering how to translate "Melchizedek Priesthood" into Italian. His eyes were granite spheres, as opaque as those of Greek gods, and his bearing was severe and patriarchal. Sometimes I had an impulse to climb up between the arms of the statue and see what was written in the book. Probably it would say something like "Generation of pygmies! Whence sprang you from my loins?"

And I knew he would mean me, the gloomy silent boy who needed a haircut, all neurasthenic with the pale cast of thought. It never occurred to me that there was anything in common between Brother Lorenzo's love of books and his urge to travel and my own strange restlessness—it was only years later that the thought struck me I was more like my great-great-grandfather than I thought, that he too had been a misfit when he ran away from a Tennessee farm to join the Mormons, that probably his relatives had said the same things about him that mine said about me— that he was queer as Dick's hatband, that he had bats in the belfry, that he would never amount to a hill of beans. For example, I am probably the only other Backus after my great-great-grandfather to have read Dante. But in those days, I couldn't see it that way. I didn't want to be queer as Dick's hatband. Nobody does at sixteen or seventeen. I wanted to be like the others.

Confronted with the creepy problems of adolescence, I grew queerer and queerer. I hid in Mr. Poulsen's pigeon-barn next door when it was time to go to church, and I spent my lunch money on the clandestine girlie magazines which were sold under the counter in the local drugstore. The drugstore was run by the only Jewish merchant in Spanish Creek, a lonely bespectacled Brooklyner named Feigel. I knew next to nothing about Jews and I had the vague impression that somehow Mr. Feigel had invented voluptuousness, that it was a specialty of his race. Poor soft-eyed sad Mr. Feigel! I wonder if he read the magazines too. He was a widower who had lost his wife years before and he had no children. The magazines had names like *Panty Antics* and *Nifty Pics*, and they were full of pictures of healthy girls bouncing around playing badminton and other violent games without their bras on. Whoever published them was probably only trying to earn an honest dollar and I hope he never got caught; I have a soft spot in my memory for him. The magazines, and Mr. Feigel, were my first contact with non-Mormon culture.

Then around the time I was sixteen I made another discovery. Like eighty-five percent of all other adolescents, I heard about Krafft-Ebing and I went to the library to see if I could find *Psychopathia Sexualis*. But I imagined the author's name started with C, and looking for it on the shelf I stumbled across Conrad instead. Heart of Darkness: the title leaped out at me from the row of books. I took it home and read it only half understanding, and then I went feverishly on through *Nostromo, Lord Jim, The Nigger of the Narcissus, An Outcast of the Islands*. I didn't quite understand why Conrad fascinated me, but it was probably because he was the first human being I had encountered who was like myself: this Polish boy, born in a landlocked country, who had a strange call to become two things he was not, a sailor and an Englishman. I read everything I could find about Conrad and the sea. I pored over atlases until I knew Malaya, the Dutch East Indies, the Solomon Islands better than I knew the map of Utah. Somehow I had the premonition that the books were unholy, that they had led to transgression, darkness, oblivion, the opposite of everything that was familiar and secure—my family, the warm house, my room with its neatly folded bedspread. And yet I couldn't stop. After I was supposed to be asleep, I read *Victory* under the blankets with a flashlight. I only half understood the books and I didn't understand myself at all. Nobody else I knew read Conrad under the blankets; it was like a sickness. I didn't tell anyone about it, and no one knew I read the books.

We would sit at supper, my parents and I and my sister Veronica, and there was no sound but the ticking of the kitchen clock and the click of the forks against the plates. My father was preoccupied with his wholesale hardware store and the business of the bishopric. He had three hundred souls and twenty thousand dollars' worth of doorknobs, bathroom fixtures, and square-cut shingle nails to think about and it didn't leave him very much time to think about his family. But my mother noticed; she saw that I didn't eat and that there were circles under my eyes. "Larry, your carrots. Larry, you haven't eaten a thing. Larry, if you don't eat, I'm going to see Dr. Nielssen." She stoked me with cod-liver oil and tonics that made me faintly nauseated and left me as skinny as before. She was bewildered; in her world if you took your cod-liver oil, got plenty of exercise, and went to Mutual with other clean-minded youths you grew up strong and happy. Across the table my sister Veronica ate everything on her plate; her shoulders were strong and brown and she was as placid as a young heifer. What was the matter with me? A voice that seemed to come out of the walls, from under the table, from inside my chest, ordered me to go forth; I was cast out, unworthy of Zion. I was probably a little crazy; I really heard the voices and they were no metaphor. I knew that my heart was evil, wicked, rebellious.

There was no one who could help me, and no one I could explain it to. What would I tell them? That I read too much, that when I tried to go to sleep, I heard the surf in my ears beating on the beaches of Java? My complexion suffered from too much brooding indoors, and I think my father attributed it to self-abuse. As bishop of his ward, he was aware of adolescent vice. To my mother it was simply a problem in alimentation. "The poor thing can't live on air," I would overhear her saying plaintively to my father. "Last night he left half his broccoli."

There was a night when, at eleven o'clock after I should have been asleep, I was reading *The Secret Sharer* under the covers. The beam of the flashlight turned yellow, then a brownish orange, and then there was only a tiny red glow in the center of the lens. I suffered from a lack of broccoli and the flashlight needed new batteries. I came out from under the covers and turned on the bedside lamp and went on reading. A half an hour later my father saw the bar of light under the door, and when I heard his footsteps coming down the hall, I knew it was too late to turn out the lamp. Instead I did a queer thing, out of an impulse I didn't understand then and have never really understood since: I stuffed the Conrad under the covers and pulled from the nightstand one of the girlie magazines from Mr. Feigel's drugstore. Perhaps it was because there was something secret and personal about my relation to Conrad that I wanted nobody to see; I preferred to be caught in a common vice rather than one that was unheard-of and incomprehensible even to me. At any rate, when my father took the magazine out of my hand, he found it open to a picture of a girl with breasts like ice cream cones, wearing a cowboy hat and a dazzling smile and pretending unconvincingly to lasso a calf. He was more baffled than indignant. "Where have we failed?" he asked me earnestly as if he really wanted to know the answer. "Where in the home we have provided for you did you get the notion of polluting your mind with such trash? Was it in Church that you got such ideas? Was it in Mutual? Is this what your teachers in school give you to read?" I didn't answer. All I could think about was that I would never again be allowed to shut my bedroom door. I might have whispered hoarsely "Feigel's drugstore". If I kept silent it was not out of loyalty to that lonely little Jewish merchant who sat all day long behind his counter for a few nickels and dimes but simply out of a vast emptiness, an inability to say anything that would communicate the way I felt or explain why I behaved as I did.

My father stood by my bed for some time with his eyeglasses glinting, and then he closed *Nifty Pics* and looked at the cover. When he saw the price, he finally managed to work himself up to a convincing anger. "And this cost thirty-five cents!" he said, his voice shaking. It was the middle of the Depression and he was really shocked.

For an hour I lay in the darkness abandoning myself to the day-dreams that most seventeen-year-olds indulge in under these circumstances: a rope thrown over a rafter, a ghastly form swinging at dawn, my parents' remorse, etc. But I only succeeded in terrifying myself thoroughly, and instead of hanging myself in the garage with my sister's jump-rope I ran away from Spanish Creek that night and never came back. I waited until everybody else was asleep and then I groped in the kitchen and found the grocery money in the jar in the cupboard, a little over thirty dollars in bills and small change. I went by the library and dropped the copy of *The Secret Sharer and Other Stories* in the night box (the statue of Andrew Carnegie contemplated me stonily in the moonlight) and then I caught the Greyhound bus that stopped at the cafe on the highway at one-thirty in the morning. I thought how many times I had heard that bus as I lay awake reading Conrad in bed: the bleating of brakes, a tired hiss of air, voices, then the door slamming and the rising growl of the exhaust in the night air as it pulled away down the highway again—now I was the outcast, the Secret Sharer, the traveler setting out into the heart of darkness! I wasn't sleepy and I sat in the back of the bus, as wakeful and solemn as an owl. It was not odd that I ran away from home or even that I had briefly considered committing some form of suicide; I suppose everybody does at seventeen. The odd thing was that when I set foot on that bus I still believed in God (I still do, but I mean the old angry God of Moses and of my father who was bishop of his ward) and I believed that by my act I was damning myself, utterly and eternally. And yet I had to go; my demon gripped me. It was not that I had been caught by my father reading a magazine which as a matter of fact I hadn't been reading. I understood even then that this was only an excuse. What then? I didn't know. I bought a ticket and got on the bus. I was calm and almost happy.

At Salt Lake City at three o'clock in the morning I had to change buses, and in the depot, I sealed my fate completely by buying two packs of cigarettes. Having set one foot in Hell I knew there was no reason not to go on. I had heard it explained often enough: after cigarettes came apostasy, blasphemy, fornication, murder, and finally the electric chair. I opened the first pack and lit one with hands that trembled, burning half the end off it in my ignorance of how the thing was done. A crisp sensual aroma, with a tang as of houris and half-naked odalisques, rose into my mouth. Sitting there in the bus I experimented cautiously, sending the smoke in twin plumes from my nose. Nobody paid any attention to me. As the bus boomed through Grantsville, Utah, I crushed out the first cigarette and lit another one.

On the trip to Oakland, which took a little less than twenty-four hours, I smoked all forty of them, one by one. By the time we crossed the Sierras my mouth tasted yellow and there were spots before my eyes, but I went on, dizzy and half sick but feeling a magnificent Byronic contempt for the abyss that yawned under my feet. Lonely and cold, half nauseated by the cigarettes and the stench of perspiration in the bus, I was oddly happy. At last, somewhere in the Sacramento Valley, I went to sleep. When I woke up the bus had stopped. We were standing in a depot and all the other seats were empty.

"Okay, stovepipe, end of the line," the driver told me.

It was after midnight. I walked out of the depot into Oakland. Everything was alien and unreal. Even the air was different; the city smelled of stagnant water and fog. I walked for perhaps an hour through the streets, staring through red neon signs into beer joints and waterfront cafes. My eyes burned with sleeplessness. Old men who smelled of whiskey lurched around me as though I were invisible. Stifled laughter, cheap music, the smell of fried food came at me out of doorways. I hadn't eaten for almost thirty hours, but I wasn't hungry. I didn't know what I wanted. I was sleepy but I didn't want to go to bed. I went on walking.

Finally, I left the lights behind and I was somewhere near the waterfront. I couldn't see the bay but I sensed that it was near from the smell of salt and rotten weeds. I was on a street lined with vacant lots, decayed wooden buildings, empty shops with broken windows. At the end of the street there were docks, and over the roofs the slanted funnel of a ship dimly outlined in the floodlights. I walked toward a ruby clot of neon signs, and there, where the hungry cats coiled along the gutters, I found a Mexican girl, fat and gaudy, standing in the light from an all-night cafe. From a block away she was only an indistinct plump figure in a purple dress, silhouetted in the pink light from the window. Her skirt was too short and she stood on tiny spike heels that seemed too frail to support her weight. Three sailors from the naval air station were coming up the street toward her, and now they were almost abreast of her. In their tight-fitting summer whites they were exactly alike, like a musical comedy team, except that they all wore their hats at different angles. They stared around at the Mexican girl as they passed, then they made a small circle on the sidewalk and came back toward her. I could hear their voices coming thinly up the deserted street.

"Lissen honey, I'm not kidding, your type appeals to me."

"Okay buddy, you're second in line, right after Long John. I seen her first."

"You saw her?"

"I seen her."

She went on looking down the street as though they weren't there.

"Oh, go peddle your papers," she told them after a while in a bored voice.

There was a sotto voce comment I couldn't catch, then a burst of laughter.

"You think you're funny but you're not very funny," said the fat girl.

"Whaddya standin' around waitin' for then, the Prince of Wales?"

"Come on, I told you, there's nothing doing here."

"Wait now, lissen—"

"You heard her, no sailors or dogs."

"She didn't say nothin' about dogs."

"Arf, arf," one of them began yelping hopefully, bounding around the street on stiff legs.

The fat girl sighed and looked scornfully the other way, down the street.

"Come on, I tell you we're wastin' our time."

The other two pulled the dog-impersonator away and they came up the street toward me, casting back several mocking fluty farewells. They passed by me so close I could hear the starched rustle of their whites and smell the acrid scent of male sweat and alcohol. The fat girl turned around, arranged a lock of hair in the reflection from the cafe window, made a grimace into the glass to press out her lipstick, and then turned back on her tiny heels toward the street again. The sailors were a half a block away. One of them flung a falsetto birdlike greeting at a band of girls on the other side of the street and was rewarded by a stifled peal of laughter. Then they were gone. I went slowly down the sidewalk and looked into the cafe as though I were uncertain whether to enter. I was alone on the street with the fat girl. She glanced at me and then shrugged, a tacit comment on the scene that had just taken place.

"Sailors!" she said contemptuously.

Her manner was amiable, placid, but indifferent. After the first glance she hardly bothered to look at me. Her plump feet overflowed out of the tiny spike-heeled shoes, and her face was made up clumsily like a picture drawn by a child: round cupid-bow mouth, mascara lashes, mauve eyelids as bright as humming-bird wings. I saw now that she was probably not much older than I was.

"They're just looking for a little fun," I suggested, groping for something to say.

She accepted both my presence and the remark. "They've got more jokes than money," she commented without rancor. "Sailors, the town is full of them. Far as I'm concerned, they're trash."

"I guess they're a nuisance," I conceded, feeling that the subject was rapidly becoming exhausted.

"They've got more jokes than money," she said. This epigram seemed to please her, since she repeated it for the second time.

She raised her hand mechanically to lift the hair at the back of her head, yawned, and let it fall.

"How about you? Do you know any jokes?"

I couldn't think of anything else to say, and finally she burst out laughing. "Well then, maybe you've got some money."

Her room was large and musty, with an odor of damp wood and a faint and not unpleasant scent of cheap perfume. The two windows were hung with imitation-velvet drapes. There was a sagging bed, a dresser, and a table with a faded chintz flounce tacked around it like a skirt. The table was littered with various objects: a flaxen-haired doll, piles of underclothing, a portable phonograph. On the dresser was a miniature shrine with a gimcrack plaster saint who held up his forefinger rather stiffly, as though he were pointing at something on the ceiling. A yellow palm branch was tacked over the bed.

She moved around the room mechanically, patting a satin pillow, throwing a stray blouse out of sight behind the furniture, switching on a lamp by the bed. Then, yawning, she sat down on the bed and lazily peeled off her stockings, shaking each one and 'hanging it carefully over the back of the chair.

"You didn't even tell me your name," she complained perfunctorily as though she were reciting a part.

"Larry."

"Larry what?"

"Backus."

At this she made a small stifled titter, a kind of hiccup of amusement.

"Okay," I countered half-annoyed, "what's your name?"

"Connie."

"Connie what?" It was an insane litany, but at least it was better than talking about the sailors.

"People like me don't have last names," she said vaguely. After a while she asked me, "How old are you, anyhow?"

"Twenty."

This produced a small skeptical shrug; her lips stretched a little and she raised one eyebrow.

"I bet you don't even like me after I asked you up to my room," she remarked as though she was thinking about something else.

"I like you fine," I said loyally.

I felt more at ease now; these efforts to entertain me, perfunctory as they were, made me realize the purely economic nature of what was happening. Earlier, in the street, she had seemed like a figure of mysterious evil, a kind of Stygian sorceress, painted and enigmatic. Now I saw that she simply wanted to provide me with a service for a price, and that what I had taken for contempt was perhaps only uneasiness over whether what she had to offer would be worth the money. For the first time I began to see her as she really was: an inexpertly painted fat girl, not very pretty, that nobody in her hometown had wanted to marry.

"My feet hurt," she complained, rubbing the line across her soft arch. "Those shoes, I told them they were too small." She stood up stolidly with her bare feet apart and began pulling off the rest of her clothes. The purple dress went over her head, large expanses of peach-colored underwear appeared, then flesh: pale, convex, and pendulant. Ludicrously she left her brassiere on. I stared with fascination at these details that looked more like medical illustrations than like the pictures in Mr. Feigel's magazines. The gaudy mask of her face, with its painted eyes and cupid-bow mouth, seemed incongruous joined to the massive pale innocence of this body.

Moving bearlike on her fat feet, she went to the portable phonograph and twisted the crank, picking up a record and examining the label. "Maybe we could play some music," she suggested hopefully.

I shook my head.

"Would you like a drink?"

I nodded.

She turned her back and bent over to open the bottom drawer of the dresser, while I stared at two pale hills with a shadowy cleft between them that widened as she bent. When she turned around again she was carrying two not very clean tumblers, one half full of an amber fluid and the other containing only a few drops. The half-full glass she handed to me.

I took the glass and drained it in two strangling swallows, while she sipped hers slowly. Then I set the glass down. Somnambulistically, as though my fingers were little machines that moved without my really paying attention to them, I undid buttons and my shirt came off.

She had pulled back the covers and slipped half into bed. Now she undid the brassiere, and I saw why she had not taken it off before. Two pink masses sprang out and rolled heavily to the sides: shapeless, pendulant, so huge that at first I took them for some sort of a deformation, with two brown bumps in the middle that quivered for a moment and then came to rest. Clearly it would have been impossible for her to stand up with these objects unconfined. She smiled at me a little uncertainly, the round cupid-bow curving upward.

I felt no sense that anything important was taking place. The first irrevocable step had been taken when I stole the money from the grocery jar, and after that it had all followed inexorably. I stood up and turned out the light. Then, with my eyes closed, I sank into that vast expanse of flesh that smelled of cheap silk and dime-store perfume. Connie performed her duties with the usual perfunctory mechanicalness of the underpaid. Then, unexpectedly, there was a spasm and a series of staccato wrenches. For the first time I felt some emotion; I thought something was broken inside me, that the blood was gushing out and I was dying. But this terror lasted only a second. My heart pounded for a while and then slowed, and there was calm dominated by the odor of perspiration. I extricated myself like an accident victim from the wreckage.

She was saying something, and I understood that she was asking me if I wanted to stay with her all night. I shook my head mutely.

She looked at me as though for the first time. "I'll bet you're not even twenty," she said with a childish spite, as though to get back at me for my silence and my refusal to stay. But the tone was not convincing; it was enough for me to glance at the drooping pink bags for the corners of her mouth to drop. Turning away, she slipped out of bed with her back to me and reached for her clothes.

She pulled a cheap nightgown over her head and shook it down over her soft enormous hips. It was an elephantine gesture, vulgar and yet reassuringly domestic, and with it the last vestige of evil and mystery melted away from her. She didn't meet my glance and I saw that I had won. In spite of my innocence and clumsiness, in spite of the unconvincing lie about my age, it was she who had prostituted herself and not me. After that neither of us spoke. I dressed quickly and left, leaving in her damp plump hand five dollars of the money my mother had put aside in the jar for corn flakes, sugar, broccoli, but not for coffee, which was forbidden by the Word of Wisdom.

Below in the street it was almost daylight. A fog had begun to gather, drifting over the yellow pools in the gutters. I began walking down the short block to the waterfront. From somewhere out in the bay came the hoarse bass of a ship's whistle, echoing off the hills behind the city. Then silence: I heard my own footsteps on the gritty pavement, the scratching of a paper blown along the street. A cat the color of fog crossed my path, then crouched and watched me as I passed.

I had no place to go and I was sleepy now. I had a vague idea of finding an empty store or a warehouse to sleep in. As far as I could see in the thin fog the streets were deserted. It seemed to me strange that all the millions of people in the city around me had a place to sleep, that for each one of them there was a room and a bed, a place where he belonged. I had always accepted this as natural, and yet now it seemed to me that to have a bed, a room that belonged to you, was a kind of miracle, an accident of the most improbably good fortune. How could it be that I too had once had a place to go, a room where I could shut the door and be alone with the things that were mine, books, clothes, the faded souvenirs and trophies of my childhood? And then, with an unexpected clarity, I saw the room seven hundred miles away where I had slept for the last time, the bed empty now, the spread folded carefully over the pillow, the shoes lined in a neat row under the dresser. In the room across the hall my mother and father lay stiffly side by side in the big bed, their arms crossed on their breasts. The clock ticked, my sister breathed gently with her face buried in the pillow, as the dawn came up, the desert wind rustled in the poplars outside the window. There was a tightness in my throat: what was this stupidity? My face was wet with tears. Angrily I rubbed my eyes and shook away the hot drops from my hand. Then I took a breath and felt the cool fog in my throat, and after a while I was calm again.

What was I, a child? First I wept tears, then I was angry with myself, and then I saw everything coldly and dispassionately.

What had happened? The victory had been too easy. I had the sensation of a prisoner who rises up in a sudden desperation and lunges at his chains and finds they are only paper; they fall away and he is free. In the room I had just left fat Connie was already sleeping, probably, with the same placid innocence as my sister. Was this all? Was this the unspeakable sin without forgiveness they had thundered fire and damnation about? Standing in that Oakland street in the fog I made a remarkable discovery: the people I had grown up among had not known very much about sin and so they had overrated it. And then the idea struck me that perhaps Hell was overrated too; it was hard to imagine anyone being punished for what I had just done. And Heaven? Suppose you did as they said, lived virtuously, paid your tithing, went to church every Sunday, and later the ecstasy they promised you turned out to be like going with the Mexican girl: insipid, sweaty, a little boring?

I felt an odd sensation of vertigo. There seemed to be too much empty space around me, my limbs were light and unreal from lack of sleep, the slightest noise I made seemed to be magnified until it filled the street and echoed from the buildings. I went on walking toward the docks. On the waterfront all the warehouses were locked; there was nothing but a wall of corrugated-iron fronts. A half a block farther on, the warehouses ended, and a big high-sided barge was tied to a dock with a dredge rig on it. The dredge had an old steam plant at one end, and at the other end a bucket-conveyer sticking up at an odd angle into the sky. A makeshift gangplank led out onto the barge from the dock. I broke into a run, scrambled across the plank and onto the rusty steel deck. When I got to the other side of the barge there was nothing beyond but the bay. Out on the water I heard the cry of gulls, the hoarse sound of whistles. Something was building up inside me as though some substance under terrific pressure was leaking into my chest. "Hey!" I shouted.

I felt silence all around me, the terrific vastness of space. An urge came to me to inflict violence on something. In a rage of rebellion against everything, my own emptiness, the indifference of the fog, I began picking up everything I could lay my hands on and throwing it: bolts, tin cans, broken boards. I felt that the silence of the fog was a physical enemy and I wanted to fling things into it, to inflict pain on it for its indifference. Paint pots, a rusted wrench, scraps of lumber rose up and vanished soundlessly in the gray air. The fog absorbed it all. By this time, I was panting and I began scrabbling around on the littered deck for something else to throw. I kicked a winch but it was intractable, solid cast-iron.

"You! You!" I shouted. "Pay attention, God damn it, now listen to me!"

Probably I was still a little drunk from the whiskey. I threw a crowbar, a heavy one; it soared end-over-end and vanished softly and invisibly like a bird.

"Listen! This is serious!" I yelled.

It wasn't that there was nothing there. It was that the silence was there, a physical presence, and wouldn't answer. I wouldn't have minded if there had been no God, then the universe would be empty and all things would be possible. But that He should exist—that He should hover up there looking at me like the fog and be indifferent—was intolerable. In a paroxysm of rage, I scrambled up the long beam of the bucket-conveyer. It was too long to lower on deck and they had left it hanging out over the dock, festooned with cables. The beam swayed and the cables rattled. Then I let go and stood up, tottering and flailing for balance. I was walking high up in the air, my hands outstretched like an acrobat.

"Hey! Hey!" I went on yelling, my voice cracking. "I'm defying you, goddam it, make me fall!"

I was rather hoping He would. If He had it would have been a lesson to me, and after that I would have known where He and I stood. But five seconds went by and I decided that He just didn't give a damn.

"You! You! Listen now!"

At that moment, I lost my balance and fell twenty feet onto the concrete dock. For a while I groped in the air, my arms outstretched. Then I turned sideways and smacked. Everything was knocked out of me, childhood, tears, fears, and the last of Spanish Creek. Physically I didn't break anything at all. It was just as I thought, He couldn't do it, or if He could He wasn't interested.

All this happened on Pier 18 in the inner harbor, Port of Oakland, exactly four months after my seventeenth birthday. I did wrench my wrist a little, and the next day I bought some Sloan's Liniment to rub on it. My yelling when I was up in the air had woken up the watchman, and he came out of his little hut and chased me off the dock.

"Listen, young fella, you can fall off one of them dredges and hurt yourself," he told me.

Chapter 2

.-- .... --- .- -- .. .-- .... --- .- -- .. .-- .... --- .- -- .. .-- .... --- .- -- ..

I slept all morning in an abandoned candy store, with a cracked front window and a busted screen door at the rear through which I crawled in and out. Everything was dusty, the odor of stale chocolate lingered in the corners; I was sleeping the last time with my childhood. About noon I woke up and began wandering around the waterfront. The place where I had fallen off the dredge was only a couple of blocks from the ferry landing, and that afternoon I got a job washing coffee cups in the lunchroom of the Oakland—San Francisco ferry. It only paid sixty dollars a month, but I could eat all the doughnuts I wanted, and whenever the counterman left to go to the washroom, I drank the coffee cream straight out of the dispensers. That was my first ship, the ferry with two front ends that couldn't make up its mind which way it was going. I didn't know either, and for eight months the ferry and I went back and forth.

The day after my eighteenth birthday I took out my seaman's papers and shipped out as a wiper on the Lucknow Line. I sailed with this same company for five years, as wiper and oiler and later as third engineer. It was on the old *Emil Lucknow*, my first deepwater ship, that I met Victor Gamoff. In those days he was sailing as second mate, a small wiry Russian with a red face and narrow shoulders, his ack eyes set in the deepest crow's-feet I had ever seen. He was probably only in his late fifties then but he always seemed to me like an old man; he had an old man's dry odor, an old man's quick birdlike way of moving his head, a habit of sniffing to himself when he was standing watch alone on the bridge. His short iron-gray hair was beginning to get thin, and the scalp underneath was seared and mottled by the sun. He had been sailing in the tropics for twenty years but his skin never tanned; instead, it burned and peeled off and then burned again. He never paid any attention to this or any other physical discomfort. He never wore a hat, and all the years I knew him he always dressed the same way: blue serge pants, a black turtleneck sweater, and a pair of soiled tennis shoes. In the winter he would add a Navy officer's greatcoat two sizes too large for him, fastened in the front with a single gold button. Sometimes on the beach the police would take him for a vagrant; Victor would say nothing for a while and then he would foxily pull out his seaman's papers.

Victor was always talking and yet somehow he gave the impression of being reticent. He was devious about his past and told a number of contradictory stories: that he had been a cadet in the Czarist navy and escaped from Kronstadt on a schoolship at the time of the October Revolution, shipped out as a cabin boy on the P & O, fought in the Civil War with Budenny's cavalry, helped to shell the Winter Palace from the cruiser *Aurora*. He also had a story about living in Paris with Clemenceau's old mistress, and another one about sailing around the Hom on the grain barks from Australia. I never knew which of these stories to believe and in those days I more or less believed them all. Perhaps they were all true, because it was obvious he had been around for a long time; he spoke four languages and he seemed to know all the back alleys and cheap hotels in any port where the ship would happen to call. Victor took a liking to me from the first, treated me like a son and told me who to watch out for on the ship and who I could trust, and the first time I went ashore with him he got me drunk and robbed me of sixty-five dollars.

We had just come back from Australia and Mexico and the ship was tied up in Alameda, at the Bethlehem yards. The engine room was shut down and I had nothing to do, but I was supposed to be on watch from eight till midnight. About eleven o'clock he came in the crew's messroom where I was sitting drinking coffee. I knew who he was by this time, but I had never spoken to him. He sniffed at me once or twice and then he said, "Come on, kid, we're going on the beach."

"I can't, I'm on watch."

"Agh, I'll square it with the engineer. Come on now. What are you watching anyhow, the coffee pot?"

I don't think he even knew who I was; he just didn't like to go ashore alone. I was wearing a blue work shirt and a pair of dirty khaki pants, and he wouldn't let me change clothes. He dragged me after him through the shipyard to the Webster Street bus. As long as I knew him, he would never spend any money on taxis; he would walk or go in buses, or if necessary, he would hire a car, but he refused to ride in taxis because he didn't like to listen to the meter clicking.

"Na listen, a man you can argue with, but that machine it's got you by the short hair." Victor disliked anything involuntary, even sneezing, because he liked to be the one who made things happen and not the one things happened to. For this reason he was a good ship's officer; he knew everything that was going on in his watch and it was done the way he wanted it, not the way somebody else thought it ought to be done.

That first night it seemed to me that Victor had a funny way of amusing himself on the beach. We took a bus into Oakland and then we started walking. Victor went by all the back alleys and after the first half hour I was helplessly lost. Finally we ended in a kind of tavern on the east side of town near San Leandro Bay. Victor went into the washroom first and stayed a long time, and then he came out and had a mysterious conference with somebody in the back room. While all this was going on I sat out in front with a beer which I bought with my own money. After this business was over, I thought Victor would sit down and have a drink, but instead he came out of the back room looking elaborately inscrutable and beckoned me to follow him. We left the tavern and started walking again. This time we went downtown and took a bus to a Chinese restaurant out on San Pablo Avenue, halfway to Berkeley. He told me to wait in the bar and then he disappeared again. By this time I felt a need to visit the men's room myself. The urinal was occupied, so I opened a stall and found Victor with his coat unbuttoned and the front of the turtleneck sweater pulled up. I saw a strip of adhesive tape across the lean belly, and above it the ribs outlined in the hard flesh. "Go on, lad, get out," he told me.

"What are you doing?"

"I'm looking for fleas. Go on now, beat it."

I'm getting tired of this. I'm going back to the ship."

"Agh, now wait. You kids are all alike, you've got no patience." He disappeared into the back room again as he had in the other place. I didn't know what was going on but it seemed that a lot of money was changing hands. I thought perhaps Victor was paying his bills from the last trip, or for some reason these places owed him money. I sat in the bar drinking beer for almost an hour, with nothing to look at but a calendar distributed by a Chinese undertaker in Hongkong. The place was deserted. Finally he came out with his usual foxy look and we went off to catch another bus. When we got back to the waterfront it was two o'clock in the morning, and Victor took me to a house he knew off Middle Harbor Road near the railroad yards. There he went into the washroom again and came out pulling pieces of adhesive tape off a ten-dollar bill. With this he bought a bottle of rye which we drank out of tumblers, sitting on a rump-sprung plush sofa in the parlor. It was a slow night and the girls were sitting around in kimonos, bored. They knew Victor and they knew he wouldn't spend any money except for the six dollars he had paid for the whiskey. One girl who was evidently new plumped herself down and began patting his cheek, but he told her to go about her business. "An old man like me, it isn't good for the heart," he muttered to the other arm of the sofa.

Later, after I had gone ashore with Victor in a lot of different ports, I began to understand the private way he had worked out of making love. He would sit around all night drinking whiskey and looking at the girls with his money taped to his chest, and then he would go back to the ship and take care of the matter in his own way, behind the locked door of his cabin. It wasn't that he was stingy; it was his emotions he was wary of giving away and not his money. The idea of paying to have this taken care of by somebody else contradicted his whole private philosophy. It was a situation in which the girls remained professional while you got excited. He knew he was highly sexed and basically emotional, and he was afraid of revealing something private about himself in a moment of excitement to these girls who were cynically interested only in his money. Victor preferred to arrange things so that other people lost their heads while he remained calm.

That night, before I understood all this, I thought perhaps that he was impotent or just that he was an old man and afraid of his heart, as he said. I didn't spend very much time puzzling out other people's psychologies anyhow and it didn't make any difference to me. I sat around for an hour or so drinking his whiskey, and then I got bored and decided to *go* upstairs with a girl named Abby, who was short-legged and strong as a bull and looked ready for anything. Everything about her was hard, mechanical, and business-like; it was like going to bed with a tractor. There was a half a bottle of whiskey

standing on her dresser and afterwards I helped myself to a drink.
I imagined the bottle was a courtesy she provided for customers,
but when she added up the bill she wanted me to pay extra for the
whiskey. "Five dollars short time, a dollar for the drink, makes six
dollars," she told me, counting it up stolidly on her square fingers.

We had an argument about it but she was as hard as nails.
My voice began to rise as I explained to her how unlikely it was
that I would pay this exorbitant price for two ounces of drugstore
whiskey. Finally I was making a disturbance. She had the build
of a female wrestler and she could have thrown me bodily out of
the room if she wanted, but she only sat on the bed with her arms
crossed and said nothing. The noise I was making was disturbing
the other guests and finally they sent for Victor. As soon as they
explained it to him he told me, "Pay the girl, kid."

"Like hell."

"You drank the drink, didn't you?"

"Yeah, what you use you pay for," agreed Abby in her toneless
voice. "Otherwise go to the Midnight Mission."

"A dollar for a drink? I'll give you a fat ear before I give you
that."

Victor said it was not yet established who would give who a
fat ear. They had a strong boy out in the kitchen who had had a
lot of practice. "Pay the bill, kid. How much do you want from
this girl? A dollar's worth? Ten dollars? She's going to give you
exactly what you pay for." He looked at her as though asking her
to confirm what he said.

"Eh?"

Abby shrugged, sitting on the bed in a sleazy wrapper that
had fallen open in front.

I told him, "What she gave me wasn't worth a lead nickel."

"Make up your mind, kid. It's the way she says. You can go to the
Midnight Mission and sing hymns for soup, or if you want to pay
your money you can play with the girls. Give her the money, kid."

42

When I took out my billfold he snatched it from me, found a twenty-dollar bill, and gave it to Abby. "Here, go get the kid a bottle of his own if he wants to drink. The bonded rye, not this stuff you've got in your room, it's good for cleaning paint brushes maybe."

Abby padded away to the kitchen and got a bottle of rye. Victor sent her back for some glasses and ice and she obediently did as he said, coming back carrying the three glasses with her fingers inside them. I didn't know what to do, break something, get up and hit Victor, or just say nothing and go away. Instead the minutes passed and I sat there with them and drank. The three of us finished the bottle, there in the sour-smelling room with the unmade bed and the bare bulb hanging from the ceiling. Abby was on the bed with one leg folded under her bare haunch, I sat on a chair, and Victor on a kind of pouffe or footstool with busted springs. The covers were thrown back and in the middle of the bed there was a damp spot the size of a saucer. Victor drank very little; I don't think he filled his glass up after the first round. Sometime later I had a vague memory of moving to the floor, which was softer than the chair and didn't share its peculiar tendency to tilt slowly to one side as though the legs were sinking in sand. But after a while the floor began tilting too. Gently, almost imperceptibly, the whole room turned until I felt the carpet rise and touch my ear. I could smell the dust of the floor, and from somewhere inside my head there was a soft and not unpleasant buzzing sound, like the wings of moths.

"Agh, he's only a kid."

The walls and the floor went on revolving slowly. Hands fumbled and searched in my pockets; I was lifted from the floor and put onto something soft. There I lay with my eyes closed listening to the soft buzzing, while voices that had nothing to do with me talked a long way off.

When I woke up, it was dark and I was alone in the room. I was lying face down on the bed with one leg dangling onto the floor, while rhythmic waves of nausea formed in my stomach and rose toward my throat. I got up and groped my way to the bathroom with my eyes half shut, feeling my way along the wall. I found the right door, but barely in time. After I had been sick, I felt better. I was still weak and my stomach felt fluttery but my head was clear.

I looked at my watch and saw it was after five o'clock. I felt I needed a smoke and went back in the bedroom to look for my cigarettes, but I couldn't find them. Downstairs in the parlor the lights were still burning, but the room was empty except for a girl lying asleep on the sofa with her mouth open. She was naked except for a soiled dime-store kimono; it had fallen open and one breast hung out like a spoiled orange. I found a pack of cigarettes in the corner of an overstuffed chair and lit one, wondering if I was going to be sick again. They were women's cigarettes, weak, with a sweetish taste. I sat down and smoked, trying to swallow my nausea.

The girl on the sofa was lying in an odd posture. Her head had fallen to one side, and with her mouth open she looked like a corpse. I went up closer and looked at her. Where the kimono had fallen open I could see the yellow breast rising and falling; there was a bruise on it, a splotch of blue-black streaked with green. One leg hung over the edge of the sofa, the slipper half off and dangling from the toe. I stood looking at her for a minute and then I turned away.

The room smelled of cheap liquor, fried onions, and perfume. I felt I had to get out or I would be sick again. But I hadn't paid any attention to the plan of the house when I came in, and now I couldn't find the door. In a panic, the nausea rising in me again, I felt my way down the hall, found a doorknob, and got outside into the street barely in time.

In the cold air I felt better. It was winter and still dark; the air was chill. A light rain had fallen and the streets were wet. I began walking down the road looking for a taxi. I had no idea what part of town I was in except that it was somewhere near the waterfront. I turned onto another street that went over the railroad tracks on a bridge and came out on the other side in a shabby district of warehouses. There were no streetlights and it was so dark I could hardly see the buildings on either side. It didn't look like a very good place to find a taxi, but it did look like a good place to get rolled. When I thought of that I reached back mechanically to check for my billfold, but the pocket was empty.

My first impulse was to go back to the house and look for it. But then I realized the door was locked and everybody asleep, and even if anybody came to the door, I would look a little naive explaining to one of the girls or to the strong boy in the kitchen that I wanted my billfold back. Besides, it was not very likely that the billfold was in the house. I began to remember dimly the sensation of hands going through my pockets, unhurriedly and systematically, the way you check the pockets of a suit before you send it to the cleaners, and I knew now whose hands they were. There was still some change in my right-hand pocket: a quarter, a dime, and three pennies. In a sudden anger I threw the coins across the street and heard them jangle on the pavement in the darkness.

I started walking again. I didn't know which direction I was going but I felt I had to walk, I had somehow to expend my physical energy, or I would break out in an uncontrollable anger with nothing to be angry at. At the same time I wanted to be angry, but I wanted to save the anger for later. I wandered around in the dark streets for perhaps a half an hour, deliberately letting the pressure build up in me because I had an idea that until I passed the cracking point and did something violent, broke something or hit somebody, *they*, the others, would not accept me and would go on treating me as a child. This was a primitive idea but no one had ever offered me any better ideas. I even felt a kind of exultation now that the solution to everything was so simple. A light rain was beginning to fall again and I felt the chill through my thin shirt. Then in a long street lined with a corrugated-iron fence, I heard a noise behind me, the sound of tires on the wet pavement. I turned, and a car appeared out of the darkness and pulled in beside me with its headlights switched off. A red light came on and glared at me blindingly.

The door opened and somebody got out on the right side. When he came out into the red light I saw it was a young cop in a rubber poncho carrying a flashlight.

"Where're you going, fella?" he asked easily.

"Back to my ship."

He was holding the flashlight on me and I couldn't see him very well. "Got your shipping papers?"

I reached for them mechanically, but they had been in the billfold. "No," I said flatly, almost belligerently.

"Haven't you got a landing card or something?"

Finally in my shirt pocket I found the slip of paper the guard had given me at the gangway. I handed it over and he looked at it in the light from the flashlight.

"What ship are you on?"

"*Emil Lucknow*."

He turned questioningly toward the car. From inside a scratchy voice said, "She's over in Alameda, at the Bethlehem."

The younger cop who was talking to me was impersonal and detached but there was no unfriendliness in his voice. "You're going the wrong way, fella. It's kind of late to be walking around. Get in, we'll give you a lift."

He handed me back my landing slip and I got in the back seat of the car. There was a wire screen between the front seat and the back, and the door handles were taken off so you couldn't open the doors from the inside. The other cop put the car in gear and drove off without a word. In the light from the instrument panel I could see that the one who had talked to me was not much older than I was, with a clean pink face and white, almost albino hair. His poncho and the plastic cover on his cap were beaded with raindrops, and there were fine drops like dew in the white hair on the back of his neck. The other one, the driver, was an old waterfront cop with a creased brown neck like a buffalo. He didn't turn around and I never saw his face. Inside the car, it was warm and comfortable and there was a smell of cigarette smoke. The blond cop had laid a cigarette in the ashtray when they stopped, and now he picked it up and began smoking again. I sat quietly in the darkness, my hands in my pockets with the fingers clenched in a ball. When the car stopped, I had been ready to mix it up with them if they gave me any trouble. I would just as soon get hurt as not and I was ready to be just as tough as they wanted, but they hadn't wanted to give me any trouble and I saw now they were just earning their living, like the girls back in the house sitting around in kimonos and getting bruised by drunks. I was just a piece of routine to them, one of the fifty or sixty things they had taken care of that night. They drove me down Broadway and through the tunnel under the estuary, neither of them speaking. Once there was a scratching noise on the radio and the dispatcher said something I couldn't catch, and the cop with the creased neck picked up the mike and said laconically, "Sixty-one goin' to Alameda."

We pulled up at the gate of the shipyard. The younger cop got out and opened the rear door. I bumped into the door as I got out, and he took my elbow to help me.

"How do you feel, fella? Okay?"

I nodded. My head was perfectly clear and I felt fine except that my legs were weak.

"Get your hands off me." I didn't feel like talking but I didn't want him to touch me. I felt I was balancing on the keen edge of violence and that if something gave me a little push, I would swing at him. I didn't want to do this because I didn't want to spill my anger; instead I carried it very carefully, the way you carry a glass of water when it is full to the brim and even over the brim, until you get it to the place where you want to drink it.

Still holding me by the elbow, he turned me toward the gate where the night watchman was sitting in his booth. "There you go, fella, straight ahead. You see the gate?"

I shook my elbow loose. "I can see it. Leave me alone, for Christ's sake."

"Okay, fella, you're fine. You get some sleep."

The car turned around with a squeak of tires on the wet pavement and the taillights dwindled away in the darkness. The street was deserted. It had stopped raining now and the sky was beginning to turn a dirty gray in the east. I went to the gate and showed my landing card to the watchman, and then I walked through the shipyard under the blue floodlights that gave everything an unreal translucent quality. My sense of reality was a little distorted anyhow and the machinery and heaps of steel plates seemed to me like a landscape on the moon. They had moved the ship during the night and it took me a little while to find it. I went up the gangway and straight to Victor's cabin and opened the door. He was asleep; I could hear him breathing. I switched on the cabin light. "Give me my money," I told him.

He opened his eyes and sat up without surprise under the blankets, squeezing his forehead. Then he coughed and looked at me. "You missing your money? I guess the girls got it."

"The girls didn't get it. They know if they started rolling the customers the police would close the place up in a minute."

He looked at the clock, sighed, and swung his feet over the edge of the berth, blinking against the light. He was in his underwear and his thin shanks were bare. He pulled up a foot and massaged it in his hands, and I saw that the balls of his feet were curiously white, like the hands of a girl. He looked for a handkerchief, couldn't find one, and sniffed loudly instead.

"Agh, you kids. You think nothing of a man's sleep."

I didn't say anything.

Without looking at me he got up and began fumbling around the cabin, picking things up and setting them down. Once he turned to me and made a helpless gesture as though he couldn't find what he was looking for, raising his arms and letting them fall with a clap to his sides. I watched him without expression. Finally, when he saw I was going to stay until I got what I wanted, he gave up and took the billfold out from under the mattress where he had hidden it.

There had been almost a hundred dollars in it when I went ashore, the wages from my first voyage; I had spent a dollar or two for beet and Victor had given Abby a twenty, but now there was about sixteen dollars left.

"Where's the rest of it?"

He moved around the cabin, snuffing and grumbling. Somehow he managed to give the impression that he was the one who had the grievance, because I had come in and turned the light on when he was asleep. "Agh, what do you mean, the rest of it? You're lucky you have anything left. The girls took it, I took it, what's the difference? Where were you when it floated off? You were kissing the rug, as cold as a mackerel. I thought it might get lost so I took care of it for you. Your money, eh? You talk about that money like it had your name on it."

He rubbed his finger violently under his nose and sniffed. "Let me tell you something, kid. Nothing's yours that anybody can take away from you. Remember that and it'll save you a lot of trouble. I had a commission in the Russian navy once." (He had promoted himself from a cadet.) "Where is it now? I was lucky I got out alive. Instead I joined the Reds and went on the *Aurora*. And you know why? Because I'm a realist."

"You're a God damn thief."

It was impossible to insult him. "You listen to me now, kid," he went on calmly, groping in the coat hanging beside him for

49

a cigarette. "You haven't got a right to anything, even the air you breathe." He lit the cigarette and began telling a long rambling story. "One time in Odessa I saw a fellow strangle on a piece of sausage. I was at the next table, as near as I am to you, and he was with his friends eating sausage and drinking wine. They were a bunch of Greeks and they were having a party. One minute he was sitting there laughing and talking to his friends, and the next minute he was dead with his face the color of liver. That's what the world can do to you any time it wants. And you talk about your money. Agh, why don't you go back to the convent? I took your money to teach you a lesson. Next time you'll know better than to pass out in whorehouses."

I got up without a word and took a terrific swing at him, and with surprising agility he ducked and caught my wrist in his vise-like fingers, bending it suddenly until I thought my arm would break.

"Agh, what are you now, a hero? Hit an old man." He must have been close to sixty but as hard as a wrestler; he seemed to be made out of steel wire and vinegar. He struggled for a long time while his small black eyes watched me, the cords in my neck breaking with exertion. I wanted to kill him and I would have if I could; afterward I probably would have said it was because of the money, but actually it was for reasons that were deeper and more obscure and that I only half understood myself, because the things he said were true and I didn't want to admit it. But I didn't kill him, because he was the stronger. Finally he twisted me down onto the floor of the cabin, an unbearable pain shot through the bone of my arm, and I gasped. He let go and turned away scornfully. "Agh, before you hit an old man you'd better go learn how. Anyhow it's not my fault."

He meant everything, the money, my rage, the agony of the sausage-eater in Odessa. Doubled up with pain on the floor of the cabin I saw he was right, and I had been wrestling with the wrong person. It was a part of myself that was my enemy; I still had a childish illusion that the flesh on my own bones was somehow unique and precious to the universe, in some obscure corner of my mind I wanted the others to love me and make exceptions for me simply because I felt heat and cold, pain and loneliness as they did. Now this was gone once and for all, and I understood there were no exceptions and no one was invulnerable, we all had to share the same conditions and in the end this was simply mortality, the mortality of things as well as ourselves. After that I didn't expect anybody to love me and I understood why Victor kept his money taped to his chest. I got up off the floor impassively and went away without a word. Victor didn't give me back my money, and neither of us ever mentioned the subject again.

I started going to sea in the worst years of the Depression; it was a time when a lot of people who had been sailing all their lives went on the beach or ended up on relief, but I always had a berth and I never had to sing hymns for soup at the Midnight Mission. I learned very quickly how to stay out of trouble and get what I wanted, and it was Victor who showed me, my father and enemy who stole from me and gave me good advice. He taught me a lot of valuable things that were not taught in the high school in Spanish Creek: how to detect wood alcohol by the smell, how to say whorehouse, gonorrhea, and go violate your mother in Spanish, how to kill crab lice with kerosene. He spoke four languages well enough to deal with bus drivers, madams, and harbor police, and he knew the geography of the whole world by heart, or at least that part of the world that lay within a half mile of the waterfront. His philosophy was summed up in a few simple beliefs: that the world was out to get you and that it was better to be a live jackal than a dead lion. He knew he didn't have to love his neighbor because his neighbor would take care of that. The only thing I ever found out for sure about his politics was that he was antisemitic. His explanation of the October Revolution was that the Yids were taking over the world beginning with Russia, but he didn't waste any love on capitalism either and believed the Wall Street Jews were in league with the Bolsheviks. The whole world was on one side and Victor was on the other, but they couldn't get him because he was inside his head outthinking the whole bunch of them, and nobody knew what was going on in there. His scalp had a ridge running up through the center of it, and on the back a flat spot the size of a saucer as though it had been pressed with a hot iron. Once he pulled apart the stiff hair over his temple and showed me the scar where Clemenceau's former mistress had hit him with a cheese-grater when he told her he was going to leave her. She was older than he was, and her emotions were unstable because of the menopause. "After that I learned a lesson, don't tell them, just leave them." He was never sick and his senses were abnormally acute; he was as strong and alert as a fox. His ears over-secreted wax and periodically he would clean them with a match. His only other fleshly frailty was a chronic stricture due to gonorrhea; sometimes he would disappear in the toilet for a half an hour and I would go in and find him clutching himself with a clawlike hand and gritting through his teeth: "Come on, you beast, all I want you to do is make some water."

Victor and I sailed together on the *Emil* and on the other Lucknow ships, the *Julie Lucknow* and the *Orion*, and usually we would go ashore together when one of us wasn't on watch. After I had been going to sea for a couple of years I almost forgot I had ever done anything else. I didn't fall off any more dredges and nobody stole my money now; I had learned how to take care of myself. I had found out that everything I was taught up to the age of seventeen was false, so I decided that nothing was true, or at least it wasn't worth arguing whether anything was true or not. It seemed to me that Victor had found the only way of dealing with a life which was in the end only a dirty game of hide-and-seek with the undertaker. You could spend thirty years wrapping up your throat and taking pills for your liver and then fall through an open hatchway and your neck, or strangle on a piece of sausage. The only thing as to make yourself as invulnerable as possible: for seventy years, but in the end it would be all the same. At least Victor wasn't going to fall through any hatches if he could help it. At sea he stood his watches, and ashore he sat around chain-smoking and watching the girls without buying anything. He had never read Zeno or Marcus Aurelius but he was an authentic stoic.

I wanted to be a stoic too, and I spent several years watching to see how Victor did it. After a while I began to see that most people who went to sea all their lives were the same. Going to sea was a little like being in prison or in a monastery. You had a place to sleep and work to do and everything was settled for you. There was none of the confusion of the free world where you had to think, choose, negotiate, struggle, relate to other people. In that other world on the beach you were always confronted with questions and decisions. Did you want peas and carrots for dinner, and should you wear a blue necktie or a striped one? "I love you, do you love me?" they were always asking you. "If I give you this, what will you give me? How could you do this to me? Don't you love your mother? Aren't you human?" They drove you crazy with their questions, and in the end everybody wanted you to give a part of yourself until there was nothing left. At sea nobody loved anybody and there was no bargaining. You ate what was put in front of you and nobody asked you any questions. You didn't have to negotiate or apologize, and nobody asked you whether you believed in God and weren't sorry for what you had done. You stood your two watches a day, ate your three meals, and people left you alone. The watches were all exactly alike, every day you oiled the same machinery and watched the same gauges for exactly the same number of minutes, and when you went ashore the ports were all the same too: Melbourne, Guayaquil, Santiago, Vancouver, Suva, the same joints that smelled of beer and damp wood, the same girls, the same sweaty wrestle in the room with the douche-bag hanging over the basin and the gaudy oleograph of Our Lady who always understands and gives you another chance, the same muddy street leading along a blank fence back to the ship at dawn. Even the prices were the same in Papeete or Tacoma: five dollars short time, ten dollars all night. I began to realize that nothing of very great value could be obtained from a coin-operated vending machine: the so-called act of love had become a purely hygienic function, like sneezing into a handkerchief. But I didn't really mind because it was part of a compromise I had made with the world of things, a kind of truce by which I was given food and a place to sleep and receptacles to empty my desire into and in return I accepted boredom, a state of mind halfway between happiness and suicide. This was the way everyone around me lived, and I accepted it as natural. In those five years of my life, I sailed all over the world and went ashore in twenty different countries, and I never saw any more of it than the first half-mile back of the waterfront.

In those years toward the end of the Depression there was a lot of bitterness and labor trouble; there were strikes and people got hurt. I had a union card and I had heard Harry Bridges talk in the Oakland labor hall, but I wasn't very interested in politics. To be interested in politics you had to believe in an idea—if not in a cause or a party at least in the idea of injustice—and this would mean surrendering a part of yourself to something abstract. I didn't believe in justice or injustice anymore and I wasn't interested in abstractions. In San Pedro during the maritime strike in 1939 I watched a lanky pink-faced man with white hair being arrested for reading the Declaration of Independence from a soapbox. They led him away holding up the book and smiling to the crowd, as though it was a private joke he was playing on the police. Somebody said he was a writer. After they had taken him away the crowd began to get ugly; somebody began singing the *Internationale* and rocks sailed through the air. A cop told me to move on, I stood on my rights as a decent left-wing American citizen, and the cop busted my nose with his nightstick. Evidently they hit you whether you were interested in politics or not. After that I still had no politics, but I decided I was a cop-hater. The inside of my nose was fouled up for life: deflected septum with cartilaginous occlusion. Victor pulled out the splinters of bone for me with a pair of tweezers. He didn't particularly care for cops either but he was just as contemptuous of revolutions. "The little guys get their heads broken for nothing and after it's over the same ones creep back in. What do you think? Harry Bridges is paid by Wall Street, they own the unions, everything." Victor had his own political party and it only had one member.

There was always a lot of free time at sea, the watches were eight hours and you couldn't sleep for more than nine or ten, and various people passed the time in various ways. Some of them would play poker in the messroom, some would loaf around in bunches telling stupid stories, and some would sit out on deck in the sun squeezing each other's blackheads. I spent my time off watch reading books.

This was about as queer as you could get, but I didn't care what anybody else thought about me and after a while I began to get a reputation as a bookworm or some kind of a screwy Merlin. When they were in groups they would sneer at me, but then they would come alone one by one to ask me whether it was true that Roosevelt was an epileptic and whether you ought to eat green peppers when you had gonorrhea and whether Chinese women really had genitals that ran the other way. They weren't interested in what was really in the books, and if they had asked me I wouldn't have told them. The books were a private part of me that I carried inside and guarded and didn't talk to anybody about; as long as I had the books I could convince myself I was different from the others and my life wasn't quite as stupid and pointless. It wasn't that I thought I was improving myself, it was just that I was doing something they didn't understand and this was enough to make me feel different from them, which was what I wanted. During those five years I read on the average two or three books a week, but I had never been educated properly or shown how to read books and I would get things all mixed up and twisted in my head. I never could get it straight that there were two Samuel Butlers and what the difference was between Malraux, Maurois, and Mauriac. I didn't read Conrad anymore because I had decided he was a sentimentalist. In San Francisco or Melbourne I would buy a box of books and when we got out to sea I would take them out one by one and read the first ten pages. If it didn't interest me I would throw it overboard or give it to Sailors' Relief. In this way I discovered Malthus, Ricardo, Gibbon, Veblen, Spencer, Bakunin, Kierkegaard, Vico, Mencken, Fourier. I didn't like Hegel or Kant or any author who got involved in abstractions, and any kind of speculation or general theorizing made me impatient; I wanted the books that had the answers. I read everything, biography and fiction, but it was the same with the novelists; I threw away books by tea-party fairies like Proust and read the naturalists, Zola, Crane, Dreiser, Celine, Steinbeck, Dos Passos. Somewhere on the bottom of the Pacific is a copy of *The Forsyte Saga* I heaved overboard one afternoon. I very quickly saw what was wrong with it; Galsworthy was a gentleman, and no gentleman would ever write a good book.

Meanwhile I stood my watches. I didn't particularly care for machinery but I understood it and I had an instinct for how to take care of it. I found out I was as intelligent as other people and I could learn quickly when I made the effort. It wasn't easy trying to learn something about marine engineering in those Depression years because everybody was afraid for his job and they wouldn't tell you anything. When you were on watch instead of explaining to you how the machinery worked they would let you go ahead and do something wrong and then gloat over the mistake. Every time you pulled some stupid blunder, stripped a metric bolt trying to screw an English nut on it or pumped salt water into a fuel tank, it was a little less likely you would get your license and this made their own berths a little safer. I only made each mistake once, and some of them I figured out for myself and didn't make at all. After I had been going to sea for a couple of years I began studying textbooks, but here again there were some books I didn't have the patience for. I wasn't interested in thermodynamic principles or theoretical physics; I wanted the books with the answers, the ones they asked you in the examinations for licensed engineers. All this I read to the last dot, and when I was done I knew it better than the people who had written it. I sat for my ticket after I had been going to sea for three years, and I got my first berth as third engineer in 1938, when a lot of people who had chief's papers were sailing as oilers. In an Army- Navy store on Market Street I bought a cap with a propeller embroidered on the front in gold braid, between two acanthus leaves. I was twenty-one years old.

Chapter 3

.-- .... --- .- -- ..   .- -- .... --- .- -- ..   .- -- .... --- .- -- ..   .- -- .... --- .- -- ..

In those days Victor used to smoke skinny yellow cigarettes that for a long time I thought were Russian, but later I found out they were Mexican reefers he would buy wholesale in Mazatlan or La Paz and take ashore with him when we got back to the States. I never did find out how he got them aboard, but I knew he would go ashore in San Francisco or Oakland taped up like a mummy with small flat packages fastened under his sweater. Under his ribs his abdomen was lean and concave like a cat and there was plenty of room to tape the packages, which were flat and curved to fit his body. Anyhow in the winter he wore his Navy overcoat, which was big enough to carry a parrot cage under it if he had wanted.

The whole business was more complicated than it seemed, or at least Victor made it terribly complicated. He never kept the packages in his cabin and instead he had caches of them tucked away all over the world: in rented rooms in Melbourne, cafes in Suva, bank deposit boxes in San Francisco and Long Beach. He had a lot of mysterious connections and was always going off to meet somebody in a chop suey place on Grant Street or taking a walk around Lake Merritt in the fog. The amount of wile and ingenuity he expended was all out of proportion to the results. But he took it all perfectly seriously and his precautions were so intricate that he never got in trouble; he had a keen intuition for whom to trust and whom to steer clear of. Sometimes he would spend half the day taping packages to his ribs, go out to the gangway and take one look at the customs guard, and come back to his cabin and unwrap the packages again: "I know that guy, he's got a hoodoo eye." Later that night the second cook would get caught taking heroin ashore in a clumsily-made suitcase with false sides.

What Victor spent his money for I don't know. All the time I knew him he wore the same clothes; when the blue serge pants wore out he bought another pair on Market Street for seven dollars. He didn't care about food and never seemed to notice what he was eating. His only luxury was an occasional bottle of bonded rye, and usually I would drink most of that. ("Forget your pocketbook? Sure, go ahead, graft off an old man.") It was hard to see what he was getting for all his time and trouble. In the end I think he did it simply because he enjoyed surrounding his life with an aura of mystery: the lonely walks around the lake, the appointments in code in a little notebook, the packages left as if by accident among the chow mein dishes. After I had gone around with Victor for a while I began to understand why Russians made such fine revolutionists: they were natural-born conspirators.

Once in a while Victor would make me a present of three or four of the Mexican reefers, and I would put them in my pack along with the Lucky Strikes. At first they made me sick, but later I began to find the sensation interesting, if not exactly pleasant. Now came a new way of going ashore with Victor; and probably this was what he had been cultivating me for all along, to try me out and see if I would do as a kind of sorcerer's apprentice in his conspiratorial world of appointments, packages, and mysterious meetings. Usually we would go someplace to deliver a package first, and then we would sit the rest of the night smoking in some Chinese cafe or in a Russian place he knew in North Beach while he explained to me over again how the world was out to get me. The Russian place was called the Yasnaya Polyana, and it was a kind of a tea-room-restaurant and gathering place for Czarist emigres. It was inconspicuous from the street and probably a lot of people who thought they knew North Beach well had never noticed it. On the outside it was only one window and a door wide, with lace curtains on the glass and the name gilded on the door in Russian characters. Inside it was long and narrow like a Pullman car; from the bottom of the room it was like looking out at the street through a tunnel. Through the brownish lace curtains you could dimly see taxis passing and the silhouettes of pedestrians on the sidewalk. Whenever the street door was opened a bell jangled, or rather made a dead clunk: a screw had fallen out and nobody bothered to replace it.

In this place Victor and I used to sit by the hour, smoking and talking or just staring at the wall. After a while his mock-angry manner seemed to leave him and he became almost amiable; the smoke coiling around his head and the lines in his face made him seem wizened, placid, and oriental. He would sit with both hands tucked into his armpits, take out one hand to pick up the yellow cigarette and suck at it briefly, and set it down again. Because of the smoke he kept one eye narrowed and a pattern of wrinkles screwed into his forehead, and when he talked he seemed to address his remarks to the wall instead of to me. I would say very little, looking out through the brown lace curtains and drawing the sweet, slightly sickening smoke into my lungs. The space around me would balloon until the room was as big as a basketball court, the walls a hundred yards away; time slowed until each moment seemed to hang in the air indefinitely, lucid and metallic, before it moved precisely on to the next one. I felt a keenness of perception so great it seemed I could hear the grains of dust falling on the floor and see the individual particles of smoke, and yet at the same time an indifference, a serenity. I began to see why Victor drank so little and instead preferred smoking weed. Alcohol was for people who basically wished to be dead but lacked the courage to kill themselves. It was a kind of little suicide; it annihilated you for eight hours during which you had the sweet peace of a corpse and then it gave you another chance, your head thudding and your mouth tasting like a parrot cage to remind you that you had been somewhere. With the reefers it was the opposite: the world around you got drunk while you stayed awake, foxy and alert. The things around you, tables, chairs, voices, other voices, softened and blurred into an even grayness and after a while only the perception was left, sharpened as fine as a razor. You were poised up there beyond emotion and beyond desire; there was nothing to desire, since there was only grayness and things didn't exist anymore. The awareness was suspended somewhere beyond the frailty of the flesh, beyond pity for itself or any feeling for others: immortal.

Now I saw what had been the matter before: it was the *things* that had been my enemy, the whole world of matter and dimension. I had found out what I was, a nihilist, and I had achieved the dream of all nihilists, that of annihilating the universe. Victor had got there before me. He had worked it all out inside his small narrow head and he had beaten them all: the customs police, the whores, the Drunken Craftsman who had slapped together the universe and invented the seven sins. It was a botched job and Victor wouldn't have anything to do with it. Food, sex, all the other biological inevitabilities, were traps the universe had set up for people who weren't foxy enough to avoid them. He was tolerantly sarcastic about my spending my money on girls. "Sure, I know, you kids are all alike," he would tell me, sucking at the yellow cigarette. "All you think about is the bearded clam. One sniff of pussy and your head comes unscrewed."

"I can take it or leave it."

"I'd like to see you leave it. Your brains are all in your pants."

It was this thinking below the belt, he maintained, that caused people to get married. But agh, what happened? As soon as she got her hooks into you, your wife stopped fixing herself up, she got fat and didn't comb her hair, and you ended up with bills, kids, worries, runny noses, and hairpins in bed. "Don't tell me, I've seen these guys on the beach, beaten down with kids all over the place, the wife yelling at them to go out and get some money. And what for? You take away the moonshine and what's a woman? A receptacle."

Love, literature, Paolo and Francesca, Romeo and Juliet, it all went down the drain with Victor's turd-shaped epigrams. When the stub got too short to hold he would stick a pin in it and suck out the last of the smoke, crushing it between his fingers afterwards and putting the crumbs carefully in his pocket. "They talk about habits," he would say, getting out another yellow stick and lighting it, "listen, you get hooked on a woman and you're through."

I didn't trust Victor and I only believed about half of what he said, but he had found out something I wanted to know, how to get what you wanted without having to give anything to anybody else, and it was all right about not trusting him because he didn't trust anybody either. I never went ashore with anybody else now, and I sat listening to him in the Yasnaya Polyana in a hundred white nights at all merge together in my memory. I knew that Victor was only using me in the way he used other people, but I let him do it because I thought it didn't matter as long as I knew what he was doing, and the important thing was that everyone should know exactly what he was getting. Gradually he led me into his hashish-world of Chinese restaurants and walks around the lake, and after a while I found I was running errands for him. Once I remember taking the Key System from Alameda all the way in to

San Francisco, carrying a brown paper bag with two cans of sardines and a package of cornflakes, which I delivered to an Italian with a harelip in a deafening Howard Street joint with a jukebox. It was the cornflakes box Victor had tampered with. I didn't know what the sardines were for; perhaps the Italian just liked sardines, or perhaps cornflakes and sardines were Victor's idea of what would be found in a typical American shopping bag. In the back room on Howard Street the Italian sucked his teeth suspiciously and finally counted out for me a hundred dollars in tens. When I got back to the ship I turned the money over to Victor and he gave me one of the tens, or rather dropped it absent-mindedly on the berth beside me.

"I take all the risk and I get ten percent?"

"What do you mean all the risk? I take plenty of risk."

"Sure, you might cut yourself with the razor blade I saw you opening the cornflakes box with."

"I've got wholesale costs, other things," Victor muttered to the wall.

"How do I know? Show me the figures."

"Agh, you're a jolly boy," he said vaguely. "If you don't like it, go in business for yourself."

I remembered the night he had taken my billfold with the sixty-five dollars in it, and I wondered what he would have done if I had kept all the money. In a way it might have given him satisfaction. Anything that tended to prove his theory that the world was out to get you secretly pleased him, even when he was on the short end. If I had stolen his money he would have threatened, blustered, tried to steal it back, pulled every trick he could think of, but in the end he would have concluded philosophically, "What do you expect? From a grifter like you." It wasn't that he disliked me; I don't know whether he ever liked or disliked anybody, and probably this was the kind of a question that didn't have any meaning when applied to Victor. The point wasn't to like or dislike people, but to understand them and be able to predict how they were going to act, so you could deal with them with only a minimal chance of getting shot or made a fool of or betrayed to the police. He created his own world and then set up the rules, and the funny thing was that other people obeyed the rules, or acted as if they did. I, for example, acted exactly as Victor expected me to ("You kids think of nothing but yourselves, your brains are all in your pants"). Like all stoics he liked a predictable world, one in which the atoms never swerved in their orbits. It may have been for this that he liked to go ashore with me or at least tolerated me, because he could always see what I was going to do next. Or it may have been just that he liked to talk once in a while and needed an audience for his theories about habits, the bearded clam, and the world being out to get you. In his way he was quite a philosopher. Once I told him he should read Schopenhauer and he said, "I don't read Yiddish."

Victor claimed he had connections in the Lucknow office, and for all I know he had. He knew everything that was going on in the Line, which jobs were vacant and who was likely to get them. In the summer of 1940 the company launched a new ship, the *Crown Lucknow*, and Victor and I both got berths. It was a good ship, the best I ever had. The engineers' quarters were midships with the deck officers instead of back aft over the propeller shaft, and I had a private cabin with running water and a tiled shower. I fixed up a bookcase and had my Ricardo, Spencer, Veblen, Sade, Dostoyevsky there along with the cram books and engineering manuals I had studied for my ticket. I didn't go ashore as much now. Once in a while I would go with Victor to the Yasnaya Polyana or to the house in Oakland, but more often when we were in port I would stay on board and read. There was one last time that fall when we went ashore together. The ship was tied up on the Embarcadero, and a little before midnight Victor came in my cabin and found me in bed in my underwear reading Bakunin. "Come on," he told me, pitching my pants and shirt at me, "we're going on the beach."

"I'm reading."

"I'll show you something about the vegetable business." He took the book, looked at it, and threw it back to me. "Agh, that Bolshevik. Get out of bed, now. Are you going with me, or do you want to stay here all night and play your piccolo?"

Reluctantly I got out of bed; I couldn't find a bookmark and so put the book face down on the desk so I could find the place when I got back. Victor wandered restlessly around the cabin fiddling with things while I got dressed. It was a mild autumn night and I simply pulled on the khaki pants and blue work shirt I had been wearing all day. I dampened a comb and pulled it through my hair, and then I found my cap and stuck it on at the usual angle over my left ear. The cap was the only material possession I took pride in. The braid was tarnished and spotted with oil and I had taken out the stiffener so the top hung limply over the sides, and sometimes on the long night watches I would put in another couple of spots with the oil can. It had got to the point where I was satisfied with it now; it looked as though somebody had been going to sea in it for at least fifty years.

"Agh, that cap," said Victor. "You want to look like an admiral, eh? You've got a lot to learn."

He pulled it off my head and sent it sailing across the cabin, and we went ashore. He was hatless as usual, his pink skull glinting under the stiff gray hair, and he was carrying a cheap canvas kit-bag, the kind sold in drugstores. At the gangway the customs man looked in the bag and grunted; it contained a razor, an unopened tube of shaving cream, and some underwear. We went up the Embarcadero to Market Street and then turned on Beale toward the East Bay Terminal. In the station he went to the waiting room, took a key out of his pocket, and unlocked one of the pay lockers.

Here he rapidly stowed away the underwear and shaving gear and transferred the packages in the locker to the kit-bag.

"Got a quarter?" he asked me without turning around.

I gave him the coin, and he dropped it in the slot and locked the door again. I knew he would never go back to the locker to claim the underwear, but it was typical of him to lock it before he left, and with my quarter. Later he would throw the key in the bay and the underwear would end up in the Department of Unclaimed Packages. Some bureaucrat would puzzle over it and the locker company would have to make a new key. It was a little sand poured in the gears of Capitalism.

We came out of the station and crossed Market again, and Victor began working his way uptown through the cross streets. For ten or fifteen minutes I followed him through a part of the city I didn't know very well. It was some kind of a commercial and wholesale district and at this hour after midnight everything was dark; occasionally we would cross the yellow circle of a streetlamp. We walked through five or six narrow streets without meeting anybody or even seeing a light in a window. Then unexpectedly we turned a corner and came out in the middle of the vegetable market. Here at this time of night everything was at the height of its activity; the lights were all on and the street was full of movement and noise.

Trucks were pulling up and unloading, crates of lettuce were stacked the pavement, the cafes were full of truckdrivers and produce brokers. There were no sidewalks and we had to work our way down the street through the moving trucks. I followed Victor's blue overcoat and pink scalp around a pile of tomato crates, and we turned the corner onto a side street. Here we went into a kind of Italian place with a bar in front and tables for eating in the rear. Victor set the kit-bag down on the bar and ordered two beers. I was thirsty and I drank mine in two swallows, but he barely sipped his. When he saw I was finished he ordered me another one. I didn't really feel like drinking.

"What are we waiting for?"

"Big red-haired fellow with a longshoreman's badge."

We were a long way from the Embarcadero and there weren't any longshoremen in sight. The place was full of truckdrivers and vegetable men drinking coffee with their hats on. In the rear a tableful of Italians, eight or ten of them, were eating spaghetti and drinking wine. The Italians were dressed up in suits and ties, and all the truckdrivers had city cartage badges on their caps. I saw them looking at Victor in his turtleneck sweater and Navy overcoat, and I began to wonder whether he knew as much about being inconspicuous as he thought.

"This beer is terrible," Victor muttered to himself. "It's a byproduct of horse urine. These all-night places, I guess they don't have a hard liquor license." I knew this was his way of apologizing for not buying me rye; he wanted to buy me something so I wouldn't run away and he was afraid two twenty-cent beers wouldn't do it.

I wasn't much interested in small talk and would just as soon have been back in my cabin reading Bakunin. "What time is this alleged red-haired guy supposed to show up?"

"Agh, you kids are all alike. You've got no patience. Go on back to the ship if you're getting itchy."

"I'm not getting itchy."

Finally it was two-thirty. The Italians got up to leave and came out to pay their bill. They were full of wine and slapping each other's back and they made a lot of noise as they passed through the bar. After they left it was quieter. Most of the truck drivers were leaving now too and the place was almost empty.

There were still vegetable brokers in the booths drinking coffee. Two new customers had come in, wearing double-breasted suits and neckties. They took a booth in the rear and sat smoking. After a while the waiter brought them a bottle of Chianti and opened it; they filled their glasses but neither of them drank.

The barman lifted our glasses and passed a beery rag under them. My glass was empty again but Victor's was still half full.

"Pair of draughts again?"

Victor shook his head. I knew he didn't like to drink beer because he had a weak bladder and he still suffered from the stricture. He muttered something to me or perhaps to the barman, and after a while he got up stiffly and wandered off toward the back, leaving the kit-bag sitting on the bar. The barman took the empty glass, plunged it into the soapy water, and began washing it. I slid Victor's beer over in front of me, not particularly because I wanted to drink it but so the barman wouldn't take it away.

I was alone now at the bar. In the mirror I saw the two customers in double-breasted suits get up and begin walking slowly to the front. At first I thought they were coming to pay their bill, but when they reached my end of the bar they stopped; I could see them in the mirror standing behind me. One was thin, with a face crepe-like from the scars of adolescent acne, and the other was heavily built with a short pink neck. They were standing directly behind me and I could have touched them with a motion of my shoulder, but neither of them had spoken yet. The heavy man reached for the kitbag and looked briefly into it, and the other one flashed the card in his billfold and took me by the elbow. The barman hardly looked up.

I started to stand up, but the thin one motioned for me to stay where I was. The big man disappeared into the rear of the restaurant. After a moment he came back and shook his head.

"Where's your friend?" the crepe-faced one asked me.

"I haven't got any friend."

"The one you came in with, in the overcoat."

"I was with nobody, I came by myself."

"Okay, have it your way."

Neither of them had anything else to say, and we left. Their car was parked a little way up the street, an anonymous black sedan without a red light and with civilian plates. I got in the back and the crepe-faced man sat beside me, and the other one drove. They didn't ask me any more questions, and I just sat watching the lights go by. I remembered that other time I had been in a police car, how I had wanted to swing at the two cops but how the young one, the boyish ink-faced cop in the poncho, had called me fella and told me to get some sleep. I had been full of bitterness that night, at nothing, at my own innocence, but I had come a long way, now I was beyond innocence and beyond bitterness and I felt nothing, as though something inside me was anesthetized. I looked out the window at the occasional pedestrians on Market Street, at the empty streetcars going by full of lights, as though they were on another planet that had nothing to do with me. The two plainclothesmen said nothing all the way uptown. The crepe-faced one lit a cigarette but he didn't offer me one, and he didn't call me fella and tell me everything was going to be all right. I didn't expect anything from them and I didn't ask for anything. I felt no more resentment against them than I felt against Victor for going out the toilet window and leaving me out in front with the kit-bag; it was natural for him to act the way he did, like a jackal when its companion is trapped by hunters, trotting off and looking back furtively once over his shoulder, pretending not to notice. I knew I could relax and watch the lights go by because the two plainclothesmen had nothing against me; they were earning a living and they left morality to the clergymen and the YMCA. There was even a kind of a calm in the car, an understanding as though we all had our roles and all three of us knew how we were supposed to act.

They drove me not to the precinct but to the central station, uptown in the civic center. The car went down a concrete ramp into the basement of a building I didn't recognize. I got out of the car and stood blinking in the middle of a brightly-lit garage. The crepe-faced man put his fingers in my belt and we walked across the concrete door and into a corridor.

The big man was carrying Victor's bag. At the end of the corridor we went up in an elevator, got out on the mam floor, and walked down another marble corridor to the night room where the sergeant was on duty. When he saw us coming he put aside the magazine he was reading. The big man opened the bag and tossed out the packages in a fan-shaped row, tearing open the last one to show what it was. "Possession of marijuana," he said briefly. That was the first time he had spoken.

The other one still held me by the belt. The sergeant got out a form and began filling it in; the big man gave him the address and the details. "You want to tell us who the other one was?" the sergeant asked me.

"I was by myself."

He hardly paid attention to the answer; the question had been purely mechanical. Stamping the papers with a date stamp, he took out the carbon and handed the copy to the big man. As we left the sergeant went back to his magazine; it was a hunting and fishing magazine and there was a picture on the cover of a man in a red hat, contentedly puffing his pipe and lifting a trout into a landing net. In a hygienically clean room in the records section I was photographed, my fingers were pressed onto an inkpad, and one by one my fingerprints were rolled over the ten printed squares of the form. I felt, not that the ink from my fingers was going into the paper, but that something from the paper was sinking into me, fixing and making permanent the identity I had so far refused to recognize. All my documents were there laid out on the table: the union card, the Coast Guard ID, even the student card from the high school in Utah I had carried around for five years and never thrown away. The police had it all down, my picture was taken and my prints were on the paper, and I thought: I am this person from now on, I am condemned to be myself. I had thought my name, my flesh, the things I had done had nothing to do with me, that whatever happened to the outside of me there was something inside, a core of ego that remained inviolate and guarded its privacy the way the eyelid guards the eye. Now I understood that a man is simply the sum of his acts, that nothing is irretrievable and everything is permanent. The way I had lived and the things I had done had fixed upon me and sunk in the flesh, *become* me. Photographed and fingerprinted, I was at last identified and knew who I was: loner, vagabond, patron of whorehouses and sometime marine engineer, petty criminal. The resentment I felt inside was not hatred for being imprisoned or for Victor who had betrayed me but something deeper: a rebellion against the very way of things that condemned men to be imprisoned inside their own identities. "We know you," the judge remarked without looking up from his papers shortly before he sentenced me. "A very common type." I thought of the book I had left lying face down in my cabin on the ship, open where I had stopped reading in the middle of the page, and I remembered how I had thought I was different from the others because I read books. It didn't make very much difference now and the judge was right.

I spent twenty-two months in San Quentin. I was not what is called a model prisoner; if I had been I might have got out in a little more than a year, but although I didn't yell and bang my bars neither did I cooperate, very much, with the people who were trying to reform me. (I assume that was what they were trying to do.) When they found out I was a licensed engineer they offered to let me run the prison steam plant, but I preferred sewing burlap sacks. I made no friends in the twenty-two months and I didn't take out any books from the prison library, not even Bakunin, assuming he was there. I had probably expected to impress the prison officials with my magnificent indifference, but like the judge they recognized me as a very common type. No one mistreated me, and if you don't object to being processed, handled, and passed from cage to cage like an animal in a zoo, prison can be almost a pleasant place. You don't have to make any pretenses or feel emotion, and you know what to count on. There are no surprises and no decisions, and nothing from the outside can touch you. The war began while I was in prison and it was nothing to me, less than a typhoid epidemic in China. If they knew what prisons were like a lot of people would want to get in.

Chapter 4

When I came out in the summer of 1942, it was Victor who got me a berth. He had sat for his master's license while I was away and now he was sailing as chief mate for a line called Cape American. He had left the *Lucknow* after fifteen years because they wouldn't give him better than second mate even now that he had a master's ticket. Evidently he didn't have as many connections in the office as he thought. I think the truth was that the *Lucknow* had begun to carry passengers now on its newer cargo ships and was going in for a lot of deck chairs and polished brass, and Victor in his turtleneck sweater and tennis shoes wasn't quite elegant enough for them. Victor didn't waste any time arguing with them, because there were plenty of berths now anyhow. The war boom was on and a lot of new lines were springing up to get the Army contracts. The Kaiser yards were launching five or six Liberty ships a week, and even old ships that were ready to be scrapped were patched up and sent out on the Pacific run. Cape American had started out in 1941 with two ships and now they had four or five.

They sailed them under Panamanian registry because the taxes were lower and there weren't so many regulations and safety rules, and they didn't inquire what you had been doing lately or whether you had a union card, which was fortunate, since mine had run out. I didn't feel the organized labor movement would miss me very much.

All this Victor explained in a letter he sent to me while I was still in San Quentin. It was the only letter I ever got from Victor and probably the only one he had ever written. "It is not much of a ship but the way things are going these days it is a chance to get a command About time too since yours truly has been sailing since all those other vags were learning to blow their nose. The Old Man on this ship is some kind of a dago, he has got a stomach-ache and is looking a little peaked and I don't think he will last for long." And then he concluded "Yours as always" and forgot to sign his name.

Along with the letter they gave me a package Victor had sent, wrapped in brown paper and tied with a piece of marlin. Inside I found my old cap with the faded gold braid, a couple of work shirts, some underwear, and a pair of shoes I had forgotten I owned. The shoes were moldy and I threw them away, the rest of the stuff I wrapped back up in the brown paper. I left prison wearing the same clothes I had worn two years before and carrying the bundle under my arm. On the bus going into San Francisco I opened the bundle again and took out the cap. It smelled a little musty from being wrapped up so long, but when I tried it on my head it slipped into place as though I had been wearing it the day before. The bus was going over the Golden Gate bridge and down below I could see a ship coming in through the channel along the Presidio, a tanker looking very small and leaving a track of foam behind it like a white arrow across the bay. There was something that looked different about it and then I saw that everything was painted gray, the hull, the superstructure, even the rigging and the lifeboats. Then I remembered that the war was on and everything would be different; I had thought I could start in again from where I left off, but now I saw the ships weren't the same anymore and I knew I wouldn't be the same either. It was the second time I had come to this city on a us; that other time it had been night and I couldn't see the ships, only hear them, and I had been half sick from the two packs of cigarettes I had smoked. I patted my pockets, but I didn't even have a cigarette now. That time I had started from zero, now it was minus one.

From the bus depot I went uptown to pick up the papers that were waiting for me in the Federal Building, and then I took a streetcar down Market to the Embarcadero. At the ferry building I got off and began walking, still carrying my paper bundle. It was all different; the waterfront was jammed with traffic, there were lines of new jeeps and trucks parked along the railroad tracks waiting to be loaded, sentries with helmets and rifles were standing at the gates to all the piers.

I was perspiring; I wasn't used to the exercise and it was a hot sticky day. The pier I was looking for was a long way up the Embarcadero and I had to walk for perhaps a mile. When I finally found it I had to show my papers to the sentry. When you got close to him you could see he was a National Guard soldier, white-skinned and soft, an insurance clerk in uniform. "Go right on your ship and don't fool around looking at anything else," he told me. He looked as though he didn't know how to hold his rifle and I thought it would be lucky if he didn't shoot somebody out of sheer jitters.

I walked through the warehouse full of stacked Army crates and jeeps and out onto the dock in the sunlight. In the first berth there was a small Socony tanker with a hole in the side large enough to drive a truck through. I went to the edge of the dock to look at it. The whole ship looked oddly bent and the windows in the pilot house were shattered, and the deck over the hole had bulged up like a mushroom but it hadn't broken. The oily harbor water was surging in and out of the hole with a sucking noise. There were Navy officers all over the deck, and another one of the insurance-clerk sentries at the gangway. I went up and asked him where the tanker had picked up the hole.

"What're you looking for?"

"*Chileno Cape.*"

"Down the dock," he told me, motioning with his head without taking his hand off the rifle sling. He had his helmet down over his eyes and his rifle slung upside down as though he had just got off Bataan with MacArthur. Probably he had been seeing too many war movies. As I left a Navy officer went up the gangway and the sentry came to attention violently, with a chorus of clinks and jangles from his gear as though somebody had dropped a cupboard full of saucepans. It was the first time for two years I had seen anybody taking anything seriously.

Astern of the tanker I found the *Chileno Cape*, an old-fashioned well-deck freighter with a wooden superstructure painted a tarry gray. There were streaks of rust under the scuppers and a dirty Panamanian flag hung over the stern. I saw there were fuel lines draped over the side, so at least she was oil-fired and I wouldn't spend the next six months up to my neck in coal dust.

At the gangplank there was another Metro-Goldwyn-Mayer sentry and a customs man, and I had to show my papers again. I began to see the Japanese would be landing in Santa Monica while we were all showing each other our papers. I thought I recognized the customs man, and I asked him where I could find the chief engineer. "I don't know if these spic ships even got one," he said.

There didn't seem to be anybody around out on deck, spies or anybody else. I wandered around the ship trying to find someone to tell me where my cabin was. There was soot all over everything, rusted tackle lying around, scraps of lumber all over the decks. A gang of longshoremen was loading Army trucks into one of the forward holds, but nobody else seemed to be working. A cook in his undershirt came out of the galley and stared at me, scratched his armpits, and spat over the side. He didn't have anything to say to me and I didn't feel I had anything to say to him. I decided to go back aft where I knew the engineers' quarters would be and find the cabin for myself. The after well deck was loaded with aviation gasoline in steel drums, standing on end and lashed down with wire cables. There were no smoking signs everywhere, and sitting on one of the drums with his foot propped up was a man smoking a cigarette. He was naked except for a pair of dirty khaki pants and sandals and his chest was absolutely hairless, as though it had been shaved. He examined me for a while with a silent stare, pulling at the cigarette.

"Looking for something?"

"The chief, I guess."

"Who are you?"

"Backus. Third engineer."

"The chief's ashore."

This seemed to be all he had to say. He took the cigarette out of his mouth and ran his tongue over his lip, still staring at me. His teeth were yellow and broken.

'Where's your gear?" he asked after a while, looking at my paper bundle.

"That's all I've got."

Your cabin's aft," he told me finally. "The only empty one." As I went away he lazily threw away the cigarette and sat watching me.. "I'm the second," I heard him say behind me. "I'm on watch, you relieve me at noon."

The cabin was small, with a single porthole which somebody had blacked out by carelessly slapping gray paint over it. There was no other ventilation and an odor of fuel oil hung in the air. The mattress on the bunk was folded back, and there was no pillow and no bedding.

I looked at the porthole to see if I couldn't open it and get some air in the cabin, but it had been welded shut. When I turned on the faucet in the washbowl a trickle of rusty water came out. I threw my bundle of shirts and underwear on the berth and went out, leaving the door open. There didn't seem to be any key to the door, but I didn't have anything to steal.

I found Victor in his cabin up forward under the bridge. The cabin was bigger than mine and had two portholes, but they were welded shut too. Victor was still wearing the same serge pants and turtleneck sweater, war or no war. I don't know what else I expected, perhaps to see him in a tin helmet with a slung rifle. We didn't have very much to say to each other. Neither one of us was addicted to small talk and there didn't seem to be much point in discussing the night in the Italian place or what had happened since. I sat around for a while looking at everything, and finally I said, "Thanks for pulling me the berth."

He was bent over trying to find some papers in the bottom drawer, and with his back turned he said, "I told them you'd been on the beach running a power plant up in Marin County. All you've got to do is keep your mouth shut."

"As a matter of fact they did want me to run the steam plant, but I turned them down."

He didn't seem to be interested in discussing my two years on the beach. Instead, as in the old days, he began filling me in on the crew, who I could trust and who I was supposed to watch out for. On this ship it seemed *I* was supposed to watch out for everybody but Victor.

"Did you talk to anybody yet?"

"The second engineer. He was out on deck."

"Agh, that Kouralis. He's a fairy, leave him alone."

"I could see that for myself."

"He always sails with the same kid, an oiler named Riga,

they're a couple of Greeks. These people, I don't know where they get them, they come crawling out of the woodwork. The cooks are no better and the deck gang is a bunch of vags they found in some Sailors Mission. The Old Man's sick, there's something wrong with his stomach. He never comes out of his cabin and he spends all day taking pills." He found a cargo plan he was looking for, stuck it up on the desk, and went on searching. "Stay out of the way of the chief steward, he's one of these operators, has his hatchet men in the galley and he gets a cut on everything that goes on. Kammerath, a Dutchman. I knew him out on the islands, he's been sailing for years."

It seemed the briefing was over. Victor went on looking through the drawer and didn't say anything for a while.

"What happened to the Socony tanker up ahead?"

He turned around for the first time, sat in the chair and lit a cigarette, and began talking while he was still shaking out the match.

"Agh, they picked that up on the Honolulu run," he said scornfully, as though getting torpedoed was a stupid trick that only happened to amateurs. "A lot of things have changed since you were sailing, kid. You notice the welded portholes? No lights on deck now, and you can't throw trash overboard in the daytime. It leaves a track in the water and they can come up behind you. The *Emil* is a month overdue from Sydney. Bettieman, the nigger cook, the old chief, all those guys were still on her." He wasn't quite so optimistic as he had been in the letter. It was a new side of Victor. I had never heard him complain about anything before, but now he was talking about the war as though it was a personal affront. "In the Atlantic it's even worse, they're sinking them right off the Carolinas in sight of the coast. They and their lousy war, you spend thirty years going to sea and then you end up making a hole in the water." It was not clear who he meant by "they": the Pentagon, the Nazis and Japanese, or possibly the mysterious Jewish gray eminences of Wall Street. It didn't make any difference to me and I wasn't in the mood for Victor's labyrinthine antisemitism.

"Listen, Victor, I'm broke. I need cigarettes, shoes, some work clothes. I've got nothing."

He looked at me, his red face expressionless. "I thought they gave you something when you got out, some pocket money."

"I spent it on the bus, other things."

"Agh," I could hear him wheezing to himself. He got up and began wandering around the cabin, fumbling through the pockets of clothes. Several times he threw up his hands, as if to indicate that he couldn't find what he was looking for, exactly as he had that night years before when he had stolen my billfold. I waited. Finally, when he saw I wasn't going to leave, he unlocked the drawer under his berth and took out his wallet and gave me fifty dollars. "You kids, you never think of anybody but yourselves. I've got expenses, medicine, I spend a lot of money on doctors."

"What's wrong with you?"

"Arthritis, they call it, but what do they know? Agh, the fatheads."

He went on grumbling to himself as he put the wallet away. It was the first time I had ever heard him talk about his health or admit to any physical frailty. I put the fifty dollars in my pocket; it wasn't very much for the two years he had taken out of my life but it was more than he had ever given me before.

The next day the shipping commissioner came on board with an agent from the line and we spent the morning signing articles. When I came into the messroom around nine o'clock there were already eight or ten people waiting, and Kammerath, the steward, was sitting in an armchair smoking while the commissioner made out his papers. He was a massive pale man with a milky face, and his corpulence somehow had a synthetic look, as though he were made out of some chemical substance that had nothing to do with ordinary flesh. On the other side of the table the shipping commissioner and the man from Cape American passed the papers back and forth and talked in an undertone, but Kammerath just sat there with his flesh squeezing into every crevice of the chair and ignored everything that went on around him. His two followers, the first cook and the radio operator, stood behind the chair, and once in a while one of them would bend over to speak to him, but Kammerath never bothered to answer. When the commissioner asked him for his next of kin he merely stared back at him with his slightly contemptuous indifference and said, "None."

The commissioner was a somewhat overworked bureaucrat with a coat and a tie which he wore in spite of the heat in the messroom, and his rimless glasses were already beginning to leave a red spot of the bridge of his nose. "You're entitled to war risk insurance, a paid five-thousand-dollar policy, but you've got to name someone as beneficiary," he explained patiently.

Kammerath didn't bother to answer. The first cook did all his talking for him. He was a Brooklyner named Cheeney, a small nervous man with a wrinkled forehead and little protruding ears set at right angles to his head. "He knows that," he told the commissioner. "He's been sailing for thirty years."

"Who's signing articles, you or him? I've got to have a next of kin to put on this form."

"He already made all those papers when he signed for the last trip," broke in the radio operator. "This is his second voyage."

"I don't care about that. I'm signing him for this voyage."

Cheeney bent over and said something to Kammerath, but the big pale man shook his head. Finally he raised the cigarette slowly and put it back into his mouth. "Make it out to the Red Cross," he told the commissioner.

The commissioner muttered something under his breath and wrote down "American Red Cross" on the form. When Kammerath had signed he got up and moved off like a pale cloud toward his cabin, and the first cook and the radio operator followed him. Somebody said he had been taken first because he had heart trouble and couldn't stand waiting in line. The rest of us went on signing articles, but we didn't sit in the armchair and we didn't smoke. The next one in line was the chief engineer, a crusty old Scotchman with a whiskey complexion. He left his insurance to the San Francisco local of the union, and the first engineer wrote his out to Sailor's Relief. When the commissioner came to Victor and me he lost his patience. Neither of us had anybody to leave the insurance to either, so we had made it out to each other.

He flung his pencil down. "What are you, all crazy today? Now listen, you two, be sensible. This way if anything happens to the ship—" the cautious insurance-man's euphemism—"if anything happens to the ship neither of you would collect. Haven't you got anybody on dry land to leave it to?"

Victor thought for a while, and then he said he wasn't particularly interested in what happened after he drowned.

The commissioner turned to me, his eyeglasses glinting. "And you?"

"Well, if I can't give it to Victor suppose I make it out to you?" I suggested. "You're on dry land."

He gave up, with an exasperated wave of his hand, and Victor and became each other's next of kin. I think at the bottom the reason we resented the insurance was that we didn't like the idea of anybody else making a profit out of our misfortune.

That afternoon I went ashore and bought some clothes and some other things I needed with Victor's money. The tugs came alongside about four o'clock, and by six we were out through the Golden Gate. When I came out on deck after supper the sun was setting; the land astern was only a smudge on the horizon and you could see the Farallons off the starboard bow. I was supposed to go on watch at midnight and I decided to go to my cabin and try to get some sleep for an hour or two. It was dark in the cabin and the air was thick and fetid, with the odor of fuel oil that hung over everything in the ship. I couldn't sleep and for a long time I lay with my eyes open in the darkness, listening to the rhythm of the propeller and the hiss of the long Pacific swells rising under the hull. I knew it was not a very good ship but it didn't matter very much; at least I had a place to sleep and nobody could bother me here, it was where I belonged. The sounds and odors, smell of fuel oil and the clatter of dishes from the galley, were familiar and reassuring and it was as though the two years hadn't happened or as though I had spent them asleep. I thought how strange it was that this cabin where countless anonymous engineers had slept, identical to all the other anonymous cabins in all the other ships, was my place, the only place on earth where I was not an outsider and an exile. It didn't matter very much and the important thing was that there would be food and sleep, and twice a day for four hours there would be work to do. The ship began to roll a little, I could feel the seas coming up under the hull with a harder lurch, and I knew we had cleared the Farallons and were turning to the south. Finally I managed to sleep a little, about a half an hour.

When I was called at midnight I went below and relieved Kouralis. The engine room was like all the others, only a little more decrepit and badly cared for. The machinery was old and had only been patched up instead of overhauled; there were steam leaks in all the joints and nobody had bothered to tighten them. Everything was slippery with grease, a rancid slime that came off continually on your hands and clothes. My wiper was a Mexican boy who was only seventeen or eighteen; he didn't seem to understand very much English and apparently he knew nothing about machinery. When I told him to start tightening some joints he just grinned at me, and finally I had to show him how to do it myself. The fireman was a small pudgy man named Squires who seemed to be some kind of a religious crank; he brought a Bible with him on watch and sat in the boiler room on a chair reading it instead of paying attention to his job. I saw the only one in the watch I could count on was Welsh, the oiler. He was a hard-bitten old bird who had been sailing in the Pacific all his life; he was taciturn and dirty and I knew he would be lazy and dodge all the work he could, but in the end he knew machinery and was not going to let it run out of oil while he was watching it.

"You seen that feed pump?" he asked me.

"What's wrong with it?"

Instead of answering he made a snort of contempt and spat on the throttle platform under his feet. I looked at the pump and saw we were going to have trouble with it, but there was nothing we could do until it actually broke down. The old reciprocating main engine flogged away, somehow the shaft went on turning, and I stood my watch for four hours. About three-thirty I went forward to the boiler room to check up on Squires. This time he wasn't reading the Bible, but he was sitting on the busted wooden chair paying no attention to a smoky burner that needed changing.

"How long have you been going to sea?" I asked him.

"My wife thrown me out three years ago. Since then I been wandering around, no place to lay my head. You know, mister, these are the last days, and then after that comes the time of Judgment."

"How about changing that burner?"

"It smokes a little. It don't matter anyhow in the last days."

The officers' messroom on the *Chileno Cape* was forward under the bridge and the galley was aft. The messboys had to carry everything across the deck, through the deckload of gasoline drums, and by the time the food got there it was usually cold. Luckily very few people on this ship were gourmets. The next morning when I went in to breakfast I saw the captain for the first time. Nobody introduced me to him, and I don't think I spoke to him more than once or twice all the time I was on that ship. He was a Guatemalan named Firmín, and as Victor had said his stomach was bad. He ate very little, for breakfast only some toast soaked in canned milk. He sat by himself with a bottle of brown pills on the table in front of him, and he was always studying some kind of a paper while he ate, a radiogram or a bill of lading, pondering over it as though it were his death sentence written in an unknown language. You could see he was not used to papers and they gave him a stomach-ache, and this was why he had to take the pills out of the brown bottle. Except for meals he almost never came out of his cabin. I never heard him give an order and the crew paid no attention to him. They went ahead and did their jobs, some well, some badly, but in any case without talking. Once in a while Firmín would come up on the bridge, start puzzled into the compass like an Indian looking at a gramophone, and brood for a while over the chart laid out on the chart table. Evidently he couldn't make anything of it, because after ten minutes he would go silently back to his cabin. As far as I could tell he was harmless, but he could have died of whatever it was that ailed him or fallen overboard and nobody would have known the difference. He was not a great leader of men.

There were three tables in the officers' messroom: one for the captain with his milktoast and pills, one for the deck officers, and one for the engineers. That first morning I sat down across from Kouralis and started eating my scrambled eggs made out of egg powder. I noticed him staring at my hair which still had a San Quentin haircut: high on the sides and straight across the back of the neck. He had a way of looking at you with a kind of contemplative insolence while he ran his tongue over his lower lip, as though you had egg on your face or had left something unbuttoned. I didn't pay any attention to him and went on eating my breakfast. Finally he said, "You been in the Navy?"

"I've been in a lot of places."

"I thought maybe you'd been doing a stretch," he said, making a kind of a grin on one side of his mouth.

"Yeah, I shot McKinley."

"All right, kiss my ass," he said indifferently. After that he left me alone. He still stared the same way when he passed me on deck or when I relieved him in the engine room, but I don't think he ever spoke to me again. The only ones I ever talked to on that ship were Welsh in the engine room and Victor. Victor had the four-to-eight and was on watch when I had breakfast, but usually I had dinner and supper with him. After that first morning I moved over to the deck officers' table so I wouldn't have to look at Kouralis while I ate. The food on the *Chileno Cape* was the worst I had even seen. We ate goulash in a greasy yellow sauce, leathery steaks, canned peaches covered with a fuzz of green mold. We didn't have a baker and Kammerath had bought a lot of bread in San Francisco and put it in cold storage. When we were a week out the refrigerating system broke down; we fixed it and it broke down again. By this time the bread had begun to crawl and some people wouldn't touch it, but I didn't think it was any worse than the goulash. I always socked mine with my fork before I ate it, and little black specks would crawl out and run across the tablecloth. Nobody complained; some people ate the bread and some didn't. If you didn't want to eat it you didn't have to. I stood my watches, slept all morning, and ate the yellow goulash without a word, and nobody else said anything either. If the food was bad, well let it get worse. There never such a taciturn bunch since men started going to sea. We sit there every night eating supper and nobody would talk to anybody. Firmín, that melancholy Aztec, would sit at the table by himself with his brown bottle, chewing methodically and silently. Usually about halfway through the meal the old red-faced chief engineer would come in and sit at his table, and they would eat without talking. Sometimes Firmín would mutter, "Hullo, chief," but the old Scotsman would never answer him. He had been going to sea for a long time and he wasn't having any of the goulash; for supper he had some tack crackers with canned sardines.

Usually after supper Victor and I would go out and sat on the hatch and smoke for a while before I went in to sleep. It was quiet there, in the lee of the deckhouse out of the wind, and we sat smoking with the cigarettes cupped inside our hands because you weren't supposed to show any lights on deck. Victor and I were like two strange cats; we didn't trust each other but we were willing to be there together, and it was as though for the time being we had reached a sort of a truce. He even seemed to have a kind of respect for me now and after a while I understood why. I knew him well enough to guess what was going on in his head, but he couldn't tell what I was thinking. He was waiting for me to say something about that night in the Italian place, but I never did. I was different now in a way he couldn't understand and I didn't really understand it myself, but it was as though in prison the muscles of my face had rearranged themselves. I was inside the face but I had nothing to do with it; it had become a thing I could lift and wove if I felt like it. Even my eyes were beginning to feel the way Victor's looked: alert, opaque—I could see out but nobody could see in. The oilers and wipers couldn't figure me out either, but in the meantime they were careful not to give me any trouble. "That guy, he don't give a damn for anybody," they would say about me. This was about as much praise as you could get from anybody on the *Chileno Cape*. I wasn't very interested in what they thought about me. I stood on two watches a day and ate my three meals, and if Victor wanted to talk I listened to him. Every evening we sat out on the hatch he talked in his choppy contemptuous fragments, looking not at me but out at the horizon, and I answered in monosyllables. I supposed the others, the ones who saw us from the outside, had the idea that we were friends.

In any case Victor at sea was a different kind of an animal from Victor on the beach. He smoked Old Golds, he didn't steal my money from me, and he didn't drink. He wouldn't have anything to do with the others on the ship. Half of them were incompetent, and most of the rest of them were drunks. Even the old chief went around smelling like whiskey and slept half the day. If Firmín noticed he never said anything. When the ship was two or three days out of San Francisco somebody started a floating poker game up forward in the paint locker. The same gang was always there: Kouralis and his boy Riga, the bosun, two or three Jamaicans out of the deck gang, the oiler Welsh from my watch. They got a washtub and filled it full of canned fruit and poured a gallon of tequila in on top of it and they would sit around all day eating it with spoons while they slapped down the greasy cards. Whenever somebody left to go on watch somebody else would come and take his hand. After the fruit salad was gone they would start dipping out the sauce with coffee mugs. I don't know why they bothered with the fruit anyhow except that Welsh said after you left it for a while the alcohol fermented the fruit juice; I don't think any of them knew very much about chemistry. A lot of money changed hands in this game and it seemed that Kouralis and his followers, Riga and the others, won most of it.

Victor had nothing but contempt for this bunch. "Agh, you think these guys are sailors. They're nothing but a bunch of vags. I was under sail in the grain barks from Melbourne, around the Horn in the winter. That was going to sea, you made it or they shoveled you over the side." Victor was no moralist, he didn't care if you drank wood alcohol or Sterno, mainlined with heroin or cut up little children, but he had a contempt for anybody who would go to sea all his life and not care enough about it to do the job right. One of the few he respected was the old chief; he was a drunk but he was a good engineer, and he never got so drunk he didn't know how much fuel he had left in number three tank. I don't know whether Victor was a good chief mate or not but he was a professional. He could tell by looking at the stars, sitting there on the hatch in the dark, whether the helmsman was on course or not, "That ape is five degrees off," he would mutter to himself, squinting through the rigging at the constellations. A little later you would hear the watch officer up on the bridge barking at the helmsman, and the ship would turn slowly and settle back on the course, leaving a ragged bend in the wake behind.

The helmsman never got off course when Victor was on watch. He spent the four hours pacing constantly back and forth on the bridge, scratching his ribs through the old Navy sweater and staring out at the horizon. Whenever he passed the compass he glanced at it. He was on the wrong side of it but he could read it upside down. "One ninety-two, you farmer," he would snarl if the card was beginning to drift a degree or two. At the other end of the groove he wore in the deck, out on the wing of the bridge, he would lift the big binoculars that always seemed too heavy for his skinny body and scan the horizon briefly before he went back in the wheelhouse. The binoculars were an unwieldy old-fashioned model, made by Zeiss for the German navy in the First World War, and they were one of the few possessions that Victor had carried around with him from ship to ship in the years he had been going to sea. He would only look out through them for a few seconds but he never missed anything. Half-sunken crates, dead fish, the smoke of passing ships, he saw it all, and before he went off watch he would write it down in the log: "0715 passed school of porpoises. 0735 kapok life jacket abeam starboard 1 mile." One time off the Marquesas where a ship had been torpedoed the week before he saw something ahead that looked like a periscope from five miles away. All the bells started ringing and everybody ran around shutting watertight doors. Firmín came up on the bridge and stared out gloomily through his binoculars, saying he couldn't see anything. "I dunno, Mister Gamoff, maybe you shouldn't get everybody all upset until you're sure. You know, I was asleep." Victor didn't say anything, and just kept raising the binoculars now and then to see if it was still there. Finally we ran it down: it was a corpse, face under, one ballooned leg floating, a black arm stuck straight up in the air like a mast. Victor changed the course a little and it drifted by ten yards away on the port side. As the wake struck it it rolled, reappeared once more in the foam astern, and sank.

In the South Latitudes there was no wind, the sea was hot and viscous, the steel plates baked. Kammerath sat in his cabin now and seldom came out. The rest of the crew spent most of their time making up legends about him. For example a rumor went around the ship never slept, that he had had an operation for trachoma or something and they had cut off his eyelids. There was nothing to this; if you watched him carefully you could see his eyelids flicker once in a while, invisibly fast, like the shutter of a fast camera. You couldn't tell this to the rest of them because they preferred to think of Kammerath as omniscient, as some kind of a Baal or a voodoo god. "He doesn't look like he's watching, the sonabitch, but he sees everything that goes on," Welsh told me. I hadn't heard of a Jonah since the days when I read *The Nigger of the Narcissus* and I didn't know anybody believed in them anymore. On this ship they blamed Kammerath for everything that went wrong, from the bad weather to the food. They claimed he sucked the juice from the meat, fattened on the nourishment while they got the pulp, kept the fresh coffee for himself and gave them coffee made out of used grounds and old socks. Instead of complaining about the food as they did on most ships they complained about the steward on account of the food: "That fat crook, look what he gives us to eat." In this way Kammerath was useful to them; he gave them something to blame for the whole pointless lousiness of their lives. If they were on a tenth-rate ship and did their jobs sloppily it was because that fat slug sat in his cabin and put a jinx on everything.

If Kammerath was aware of all this he gave no sign. He stayed in his cabin most of the day, smoking and malting entries with a fountain pen in a big ledger. Instead of coming to the messroom he would have Cheeney bring his meals to the cabin on a tray. After he had served the steward's dinner Cheeney would come out on the hatch and sit there in his white undershirt and his flour-colored cook's face, waiting for somebody to talk to him. Because he was Kammerath's toady nobody else on the ship would have anything to do with him, and this made him nervous, but he had to go on as he was because he sensed that in some way Kammerath was a source of power, and he felt insecure and this gave him the only identity he had. It was as though Kammerath exuded a kind of mysterious fluid that hung in the air around him, and his followers sucked in this fluid and were nourished by it, and it was from absorbing this stuff whatever it was that Cheeney himself had become so pale and milky, the same color as Kammerath himself. But he knew the others outside the galley despised him for it and that made him uneasy, and this was why he came out and sat on the hatch after supper, to try to talk to the others and make friends so he would still have connections on both sides. Welsh knew it made him nervous so he would always needle him about it, trying to get him to talk about Kammerath.

"Why don't he ever come out? What does he do in there all day?" he would ask him.

"I don't know. How would I know?"

"You're his friend, ain't you?"

"Me?" Cheeney would say, alarmed. "I'm not his friend."

"You'd be his friend if he had a friend. What do you talk about in there when he's eating dinner?"

With a small tremor working his cheek Cheeney would report what Kammerath had said. "He was telling me about during Prohibition he was a rum-runner. They used to run it across the Detroit River in speedboats. He had six guys working for him, and they would peddle the moonshine some other guy made up in Canada in a garage. In those days he made around a hundred thousand a year."

"That wasn't the last gut he ever rotted. What else does he say?"

"That's all. That's about all he said."

"What did he say yesterday?"

The stories got more and more fantastic, and probably after a while Cheeney was making them up so he wouldn't lose his audience. "Yesterday he was telling me about when he was on a ship running down from Macao to Hongkong, carrying Chinamen. He was a cook then himself. They used to steam up a barrel of rice for the Chinamen and throw in a gallon of fish-eyes. They lapped it up, according to

"Wish we had some of it now."

Another time," Cheeney would go on, with a sidelong glance as though he expected to see Kammerath floating up behind him and listening, he went on the beach once for five years in Malaya. He had a chippy to go to bed with and clean up the house and everything. He had it high to hear him tell it."

"He should of stayed there," grunted Welsh.

"He can't take the heat so well. It's bad for his heart."

"If he's got a heart, I'm a Chinaman, and I'll eat fish-eyes to prove it."

"I'm just telling you what he said," Cheeney would say, getting more and more nervous.

Welsh was a kind of universal cynic, but he knew everything that was going on on the ship. When he wasn't loafing out on the hatch he would sit in on the paint-locker tequila parties, and he used to tell me what went on up there. It seemed that about two weeks out of San Francisco there was a showdown between the paint-locker crowd and the messboys in the galley. It started when Kammerath refused to let them have any more canned fruit out of the stores. For a couple of days they drank the tequila straight out of coffee mugs, but when they brought the cups to the galley to be washed the messboys confiscated them and wouldn't give them back. "Mister Kammerath, he says no cups to be taken out of the messroom," Cheeney told Kouralis. There was an argument, and Kouralis came back with two or three of his shock troops, Riga and a couple of firemen. They pushed into the galley and walked off with the mugs, leaving Cheeney standing there with the corners of his mouth working.

After that it almost broke out in open war. Emissaries went from Kammerath to the chief engineer and back again, and some people even said that Firmín was consulted, although this seemed unlikely. That night the matter was settled. Kouralis and the firemen had to bring the cups back; Cheeney told them it was against the rules to take crockery out of the galley, but Mister Kammerath would sell them the cups if they wanted to pay fifty cents apiece for them. He didn't explain whether the money would be passed along to the stockholders of the line, who were the legal owners of the cups. Kammerath had never moved from his chair in his cabin,

"That sonabitch," Welsh commented that night in my watch, "he don't care about the cups. He just don't like to have anything going on aboard that he don't have a finger in."

The story down in the engine room was that Kouralis was plotting some kind of dark revenge and had said Kammerath had better be careful walking around on deck at night. But Kammerath never came out on deck at night, and only very rarely in the daytime. He went on sitting all day in his cabin, making entries in the ledger and smoking until the fingers of his left hand were stained yellow with tobacco. Three times a day, morning, noon, and night, Cheeney brought him his meals on a tray, provided with the same linen and silver service as the officers' mess. If you happened to be going down the passageway you could look in through the half-open door and see Kammerath sitting in front of the white tablecloth, drinking his coffee out of a china teacup. Sometimes after dinner, when it was a little cooler, he would come out on deck and move ponderously toward the rail and stand there for a while looking out at the sea. In the daylight you could

see that his face was not really white but faintly yellow, with a
greenish shadow along the jowls where an ordinary man's face is
blue-black. He would' stand there by the corner of the deckhouse
watching the horizon for a while, and then when his cigarette was
finished he would drop it in the sea and go back into his cabin.

Chapter 5

.-- .... --- .- -- ..   .-- .... --- .- -- ..   .-- .... --- .- -- ..   .-- .... --- .- -- ..

On the second of September we made our landfall off Moreton Bay, and that afternoon we went up the river to Brisbane. The river was full of ships waiting for their turn at the piers, and nobody on the beach seemed to know where we were going to dock. We anchored in the stream for a couple of hours while the pilot went ashore and argued with somebody. Then a little after dark the pilot came back with an American Army captain and the tugs took us downstream to dock in Hamilton Reach. As soon as the gangplank was over a gang of stevedores came on board and began unloading the cargo. The stevedores were Americans, from an Army dock battalion. They had the hatch covers off in five minutes and they seemed to know what they were doing. I started to tell one of them to crack the valve first and let the water out of the winch so he wouldn't break it, but he said, "Don't tell me, buddy, I was on the waterfront before you were born." There was nothing to do on board, and Victor and I went ashore.

It was a twenty-minute tram ride from Hamilton into Brisbane. I had been in Brisbane a dozen times before but I hardly recognized it. Everything was blacked out after dark, and all the stores had sandbags stacked in front of the windows. The streets were swarming with American and Australian troops and there were no male civilians to be seen. Everybody in Australia had been expecting the Japanese to land in the Northern Territory for three months, and the country was mobilized to the teeth. When the merchant crews went ashore in civilian clothes middle-aged females would come up and pin white feathers on their chests to identify them as slackers. These women traveled around in swarms armed with hatpins; they seemed to have an unlimited supply of feathers and nothing better to do with their time. I got my white feather that first night on the tram, and I wore it all the time I was in Australia. When I changed clothes, I would take it off and pin it on the clean shirt. The patriotic females would look indignant every time they saw me, but at least this way they left me alone.

That first night Victor and I went straight to a place he knew in Red Hill, run by a Polish woman named Mrs. Lubin who wore flowery prints and looked like a perambulating garden. Mrs. Lubin had a girl in her house named Clara, who was stupid as a salmon and had a loose tooth she liked to wiggle between her thumb and forefinger. She used to wiggle it even when we were in bed; it interested her more than I did and sometimes she seemed to forget I was there. At first this bothered me, but after a while I decided I liked it better that way. You didn't have to talk to Clara and she had found something to keep her amused while she worked. She was very clean and knew how to make her own bed, and she never drank. "I don't know why people like it, it makes me woozy," she confessed to me once.

Victor spent most of his time in this place talking to Mrs. Lubin, who sold him bogus scotch made in Hongkong for which she charged eight dollars a bottle. While I was upstairs she and Victor would sit in the kitchen talking Russian together, at least I supposed it was Russian, although for all I knew Victor might have known Polish along with his other accomplishments. Mrs. Lubin was an honest woman; she would write his name on the bottle of Chinese scotch and when he left she would paste a paper seal over the cork so no one would touch it until he came back. Victor spent more money in the place than I did because Clara, tooth and all, was very reasonable: two dollars short time, five dollars all night. Mrs. Lubin accepted only dollars because she had a hobby of saving American money; I think she was convinced Australia would be occupied by the Japanese and she wanted nothing to do with pounds. She left patriotism to the women with the white feathers, but she was very honest, and she was the only woman I ever saw Victor talk to for more than five minutes, which was a distinction in itself. Once I asked him what they were talking about, and he said, "Agh, we were telling each other a lot of lies. I told her I was on the *Aurora*, she said she knew Paderewski. I never knew a Pole that wasn't a liar." Except for going to Mrs. Lubin's I didn't know what to do with myself while the ship was in Brisbane. In the daytime it was too hot to walk around in the streets, and usually I stayed on board until after dark. One afternoon I went to a movie by myself. As it happened it was Walt Disney's *Bambi*, but it was the only movie showing that afternoon and the theater was full of Australian soldiers. I remember that at one point this fawn who was the main character was tripping through the forest looking pathetic and calling out, "Mother! Mother!" Its mother didn't seem to be around and finally a voice in the back said in disgust, "She's owt with some bloody Yank." Somehow I couldn't associate myself with Bambi's problems and I got up and left the theater. In a bookstore in Albert Street I bought a volume of Saroyan's stories and took it back to the ship, but the stories didn't seem to be any more real than Bambi, or perhaps there was something wrong with me. The first story was about a poet sitting up in a garret all day polishing a penny until finally he died of starvation. I tried for a couple of hours to read this and then I threw it overboard. After that I lay in my berth in the hot cabin, smoking and thinking of nothing, waiting for it to get dark so I could go to Mrs. Lubin's.

It took the Army stevedores four or five days to get the trucks out of the hold. Meanwhile a lot of stores were coming aboard, flour in sacks and cases of canned goods, as though we were going to make a long run somewhere. One afternoon a load of meat was delivered to the dock in a truck. Nobody in the crew believed it would be any better than the meat Kammerath had bought in San Francisco, and they were right; the Australian beef was worse than the other. It sat on the dock for two hours in the hot sun and the deck gang refused to carry it on board. The bosun wanted Kammerath to come down on the dock and look at it.

"He says to carry it down in the cold room," Cheeney told him. "He can't come out in the sun. It's bad for his heart."

"Tell him he better come out and look at it before it walks away."

Cheeney went back to Kammerath with the message, and the negotiations went on for about an hour. Finally there was a coin promise. The bosun and a sailor carried a side of beef, the worst one they could find, up the gangway onto the ship and set it down on deck. After a half an hour Kammerath emerged from his cabin floated out in the sunlight to look at it.

"What the hell are you complaining about?" he told them. "The meat's all right. That's only on the surface. You handle your job and I'll take care of mine."

He brushed the maggots off with a slow sweep of his hand, and then he turned ponderously and walked away. Nobody said anything. The deck gang wouldn't touch the meat, and after a while the messboys came out of the galley and began carrying it down to the cold room.

From then on the messboys carried aboard all the provisions. We were supposed to have loaded stores for six months in San Francisco but Kammerath continually bought more: meat, dried milk, ice-cream powder, flour in hundred-pound bags, coffee by the case. Some fresh bread came aboard which by some miracle didn't have weevils in it. In the mornings in Brisbane there was a continual coming and going of ship-chandlers and grocers' agents in Kammerath's cabin. They were the only happy men I ever saw on board the *Chileno Cape*. They all dressed alike, in blue serge suits with pants too wide at the bottom, and they had round, red, prosperous Australian faces. After they left, if you happened to be passing by the cabin, through the half-open door you could see Kammerath putting things away in his billfold.

After Brisbane nobody knew where the ship was going. There were all kinds of rumors and you could take your choice. Some people said we were going north into the war zone, to New Guinea or Port Darwin, but somebody else pointed out that if this was the case they wouldn't have unloaded the Army cargo in Brisbane. There were other theories that we were going to Melbourne for wheat, that we were sailing empty to Chile for nitrate, that we would stay in Australia for six months on the coastal run. Nobody had any facts, and they couldn't decide what they wanted anyhow. Some of them wanted to load the Australian grain and go right back to the States, and others wanted to run back and forth to Noumea and Port Moresby for a while and collect the port bonuses. You got two hundred and fifty dollars for every port the ship called at in the war zone, and somebody figured out that if you ran steadily between Townsville and Port Moresby you could clear a thousand dollars a week above your wages. But somebody pointed out this didn't allow any time for loading or unloading. All the theoreticians has their pencils out.

For three or four days nobody talked about anything but port bonuses. Firmín stayed in his cabin all day, listening to the news on the radio and looking worried. It was about a month after the Marines had landed on Guadalcanal; I don't know whether they got a port bonus or not but according to the radio they were having a rough time on the beach, and the prediction was that if we lost the Solomons the Japanese would be in Australia next. Here too everybody had his theory. Some said they would land around Port Darwin and others that they would bypass Australia and invade New Zealand. Victor's theory was that it didn't matter very much; the Japanese would probably let Mrs. Lubin alone, and as for the women with the white feathers what would happen to them was just what they needed. "That's what they all need. Lady social workers, patriots, Edith Cavells." It was true the girls at Mrs. Lubin's weren't very patriotic. I asked Clara once what she thought about the war and she said vaguely, "I don't know, it's more fun now. Americans, and there's spam, I got some stockings." She thought for a while as though she was working out some more profound political comment, and then she said, "They say that 'Itler doesn't care for girls."

Victor of course maintained that the war was just another shell game concocted by the Wall Street bankers. "What do you think? Agh, it's all rigged—the Krupps, DuPonts, Rothschilds, the big cartels." We would sit in Mrs. Lubin's drinking Chinese scotch while he explained it to me. After the Russian Revolution, it seemed, the Rothschilds had picked out Hitler and financed him secretly because he was against the Jews. They knew that sooner or later he would start a war against Russia and lose, and this would make the Yids look good.

"How do you mean, look good?"

"What do you think? Hitler pushes them around a little and everybody feels sorry for them. Wall Street lent him the money to build the concentration camps. Agh, they're all in it together, the English, Mussolini, the Japs. You ever heard of the Hairy Ainus? They live up in Japan in the northern islands, around Hokkaido.

Sure, you're a bright boy and you read books, you know it all. What you probably don't know is that they're pure Semitic, descended from one of the lost tribes of Israel. Listen, I'm telling you that the whole Jap royal family is descended from those Ainus."

In later years I came to think that this was the most remarkable of Victor's accomplishments, his malting the Emperor Hirohito into a Jew. He also claimed that the cable between Wall Street and Tokyo had never been cut after the war started, and there was a continual stream of messages going back and forth twenty-four hours a day.

"You know what they make smokeless powder out of?" he told me "Nitrocellulose. Sure, you know it all, but what you don't know is that the Japs are malting it out of old movie films that Sam Goldwyn sent them, right up to Pearl Harbor Day."

Finally one morning Firmín went ashore to some office and came back with orders to sail for Sydney and load general cargo for the States. The news went around the ship a little after lunch but there was some delay in the sailing; it seemed that Kouralis and a couple of AB's were still ashore and nobody knew where they were. Around three o'clock they found the sailors, but the chief said he wouldn't sail without a second engineer. A pair of Australian detectives came on board with an Army intelligence man to talk to Firmín. The door shut, then they opened the door again and sent for the old chief, and they had a conference in the cabin that lasted for a half an hour. When the chief came out he sent for me and told me Kouralis was on the beach in the hospital and was going to be left behind. He wanted me to stand watch-and-watch with the first engineer for the rest of the voyage, six on and six off. It wasn't a union ship and he was within his legal rights; he didn't have to hire another engineer until we reached our port of discharge. I told him in that case he better count on sailing without me too. I was a licensed engineer and I worked eight hours a day. He told me I had signed articles and if I refused duty it might mean trouble. That was all right with me; I would go to jail or to the hospital with Kouralis, but I wouldn't stand six-hour watches.

"You wait, sonny boy, I'll have your ticket when we get back to the States."

"You can have it right now if you want it."

Then he appealed to my patriotism. "We've all got to contribute. There's a war on," he said in an unconvincing voice.

"You contribute."

At the end, this is what happened; the chief had to stand Kouralis' watch himself. He went around looking black about it for a while, but Firmín consoled him by putting him on the payroll twice, once as chief and once as second engineer. The oilers and wipers used to argue about whether he could collect two port bonuses or not.

When we finally sailed it was after eight, and we went down the river in the dark. It was too hot to sleep and I sat out on the hatch while Welsh filled in on what had happened to Kouralis. It seemed that ever since the battle of the coffee cups he had been making dark threats and predicting some accident was going to happen to Kammerath. He had the engine room gang on his side, and he probably thought that if it came to a showdown they could handle the messboys. Then in Brisbane there was a new development: Kouralis was seen going ashore with one of the messboys, a Filipino named Malahay. "You seen him, the kid with the black eyes and all the oil in his hair, quiet like a cat." They went around to all the pubs and sometimes they stayed out all night. For a few days Kouralis' sweetheart Riga went around looking broody and dangerous; I had noticed this but I didn't know what was wrong with him. Everybody thought that Kouralis had just found a particularly devious way of getting even with Kammerath, or that he was trying to provoke Kammerath into taking some action as he had with the coffee cups. Kammerath showed no sign that he noticed what was going on. No one knew what Malahay thought. "Anyhow them Igorotes, I guess they don't care who buggers them," Welsh concluded philosophically.

This went on for four or five days. Then the night before the ship sailed Malahay lured Kouralis up a dark alley behind the railroad where the other messboys were waiting. "They took him out in the lots and worked him over with the vegetable knives," said Welsh. "I don't know what they done to him, but I don't think he's going to be so fond of the boys anymore." He spat on the deck and placidly spread it around with his foot. "Before you cross that Kammerath you want to pay up your insurance."

I went on watch at midnight. At the mouth of the river we dropped the pilot and started down the channel around Moreton Island, but a half an hour later the bridge rang down stop engines again. The boilers were all fired off for sea and the steam pressure began to rise. After ten minutes I called the bridge and asked them if we were going to be stopped for long. They said they didn't know; the signal station on Moreton Island was sending us a message. Finally the word spread that we had orders to turn around and *go* back to Brisbane. Nobody knew what it was about. It took Firmín almost an hour to turn the ship around in the narrow channel without a pilot, but finally he got it headed the right way and back up the river. Somebody started a rumor that the reason we had turned around was a Japanese invasion force was headed for Sydney. When the first engineer relieved me at four o'clock he said the story was we were going to load the same trucks again and take them to New Guinea.

"I'll buy that, it sounds like the Army," Welsh grunted.

"Why?"

"Because there ain't roads in New Guinea."

"At seven o'clock in the morning we docked again at the same pier in Hamilton. This time there was no going ashore. The Army put guards at the gangway, and some types in civilian clothes and military haircuts came aboard to talk to Firmín. The ship was reloaded in twenty-four hours, working around the clock under floodlights in spite of the blackout. They put four thousand tons of artillery shells and anti-aircraft ammunition in the holds, and the types in Army haircuts told us to drain part of our culinary water and load fuel oil in the tanks. Evidently they needed a lot of fuel oil wherever it was we were going, and nobody seemed to care whether we were thirsty or not. The only one who left the ship during the twenty- four hours was Cheeney, who went ashore in the afternoon and came back in a taxi with a crate of live chickens. None of these chickens ever showed up in the messroom, although Cheeney was seen in the galley once chewing on a wing. "Father Kammerath will be telling us soon whether we can have the feet," growled the old chief.

The morning of the second day we sailed again, this time with an Australian naval lieutenant aboard instead of a civilian pilot. The lieutenant came on board in white shorts, a white shirt with epaulets, and a spotless white peak cap. I don't know what he thought of the dirty dungarees the rest of us wore in the messroom. Probably he had a rather low opinion of the ship in general, but he never expressed himself on the subject. He didn't even permit himself to comment on the food. Whenever anybody said anything to him he would agree in a clipped British accent: "Quite so. I dessay."

Probably the lieutenant and Firmín knew where we were going, but if they did they didn't confide in anybody else. About noon we passed Moreton Island again and settled on a course to the northeast. A little after I went on to watch Firmín called the engine room and told us to make fourteen knots. The ship had never made more than twelve, and I didn't think the old machinery would stand it. The steam lines began springing leaks and we spent the watch wrapping them in white lead and rags. Under the vibration the hull began to leak; there was more rust than steel in the old plates and the strain was loosening the scams. I didn't particularly care one way or the other; I thought perhaps the ship would shake itself apart and this would prove to Firmín it couldn't make fourteen knots. By the end of the watch I could hear the water gurgling back and forth in the bilge under the floor plates.

Then the feed-water pump broke down, as I had been expecting it would for a month. We shifted to the auxiliary pump and tore it down. I was supposed to go off watch at four but I had to stay below and work on it with Welsh and the first engineer. We could only make twelve knots on the auxiliary pump, and the Australian lieutenant kept calling down from the bridge to ask how we were doing. "Tell him we ain't doing nothing if we have to keep talking Australian to him on the phone," said Welsh. All that afternoon and most of the night I worked on that pump until I knew every bolt and nut in it by heart. About ten o'clock we put it together again, and the first engineer set up too hard on a bolt and cracked the casing. We had to take it apart again and weld it. I was covered with sweat and my nerves were ragged; that collection of gears and shafts and bolts spread out over the engine-room floor had begun to stand in my mind for the stupid intractability of all physical things, the whole world of shoddy objects that broke in your hand and smelled of fuel oil and grease. I couldn't convince myself that the pump had any importance or that it really mattered whether the ship got to where it was going or just sat there in the middle of the Coral Sea until it rusted and sank. At two o'clock in the morning we finally got the pump back in the line and began making fourteen knots. Immediately the vibration began again, and Welsh came forward with his oil can and told me the shaft alley was full of water.

I called the bridge and told them the ship was leaking and I would have to take some steam out of the line to pump it out. There was a long discussion while I waited on the phone. The third mate was explaining it and in the background I could hear the clipped British voice saying, "I dessay but we cahn't help that." Finally Firmín himself came on the phone and asked me what was the matter.

"The shaft alley's full of water. It's coming in through the packing or through the hull seams. I've got to take some steam out of the line to pump it out."

"Well, let it leak," said the discouraged voice over the phone. "The lieutenant here says we got to make fourteen knots."

On the floor plates under the main engine Welsh and the Mexican wiper were wading up to their knees in greasy water to oil the machinery. I had been in the engine room for sixteen hours without any rest. I started up the bilge pump anyhow and bailed out the shaft alley so the oilers could work. After that we made thirteen point nine knots, but nobody seemed to notice.

In the night we passed Noumea and went to the north. I got five hours' sleep, and then a little after nine they called me and told me I was wanted on the bridge, right away. The gray lump of New Caledonia was on the horizon behind us and I heard the roar of engines; a plane was circling around the ship a half mile or so away. It was Victor's watch and the lieutenant and Firmín were both on the bridge. It seemed the plane was trying to send us a message and the Aldis lamp wouldn't work because a fuse was blown in the wheelhouse. Still half-asleep, I stuck in a new fuse and ran the extension cord out to the wing of the bridge. While I was working the plane made a low pass over the ship and then bent away to the south with one wing down. It was a Catalina flying boat with red-white-and-blue Australian emblem on the side, and it passed so low you could see the pilot looking at us with big rubber earphones clamped on his head. Finally they got the Aldis lamp working, and on the plane a light started blinking out of the glass gun-blister. The code was coming to fast for anybody but he lieutenant to read, and he had to take the message himself. The plane went round and round like a circus horse while he called out the words for a sailor to write down: "*Cape... cahncel...immeejityly... priority...*"

When they got it all down they read it to Firmín. "Previous orders *Chileno Cape* canceled proceed immediately Noumea priority reassignment ComSoPac[1]."

"They ought to make up their minds," said Firmín discouragedly.

"I dessay there's some reason."

"Yeah, they always got a reason, but they keep changin' their reason."

"I don't doubt the logistic situation is quite fluid."

"They got the fluid inside their heads, is where they got it."

"My dear fellow, I didn't invent this war," the lieutenant told him a little stiffly. "Frankly there are several other places I would rather be. But my orders are to take this ship to its destination, and I dessay the people who are running the war have not lost their wits entirely."

While they were arguing about it, Victor has already laid out the new course on the chart. "Come right to two sixty," he told the helmsman without looking up from the chart table.

"Two six oh," repeated the helmsman a little startled. He spun the wheel with both hands, the wake behind curved into a ragged U and snaked back and forth for a while until finally it settled into a straight line. "Two sixty, you sheepherder," Victor glared at him. "Where are you going, the South Pole?"

"If we're just gonna run back and forth across the ocean we might as well go twelve knots," complained Firmín. "It makes the ship leak, goin' so fast."

"Fourteen knots, old fellow," said the lieutenant between his teeth. "Fourteen knots. And you," he told me, "if you've finished your business here, off the bridge, if you please."

---

1   Acronym: Commander, South Pacific.

In Noumea we sat in the harbor and nobody knew what we were going to do. All you could see of the town was a pier, a lot of tin roofs, and the steeple of the French cathedral. It was four o'clock in the afternoon and dead calm; at anchor the ship was unbearably hot and it was five hours before it would get any cooler. There was a steamy moulding smell to the air like the smell of a poorly ventilated laundry. On the pier a mile away there was a warehouse with a tin roof and a flagpole, and on the flagpole a little French flag hung limply in the heat.

The Australian lieutenant spent the afternoon climbing up and down the bridge to send messages ashore with the Aldis lamp. The signal station was down the beach in the middle of the jungle, a mile or two from town. The lieutenant, covered with perspiration, would bang away with the Aldis lamp for a long time, and finally a sleepy yellow pinpoint in the jungle would start blinking back. After he sent the message the yellow light went out. There was never any answer.

In between signals the lieutenant would go down into the holds with a thermometer to see whether it was getting too hot for the cargo. He didn't say whether it was, but about five o'clock the bosun got a gang and went around rigging canvas ventilators to deflect the wind into the holds. Probably this was not very effective, since there wasn't any wind. A rumor went around the ship that cordite exploded at a hundred and twenty degrees. It seemed at least that hot on deck; there was no telling what it was in the hold.

Nobody had any appetite because of the heat, and nobody ate very much supper. That night there was an air raid, which it seemed to be a regular evening feature in Noumea. It began around eleven o'clock. For a half an hour you could hear the sound of sirens from across the water, and then there were flashes in the sky on the other side of town and some muffled thuds, like heavy weights falling onto the ground. The thumps and flashes went on for some time. Now and then the sound seemed to come closer, but the flashes were still across the hill on the other side of town. If they were trying for the harbor their aim was bad. An Australian corvette got under way and went charging around in the dark with its lights out but it had nothing to shoot at. It was the second night I hadn't slept more than four or five hours but I sat out on deck watch the raid until it was time to go on watch at midnight. It was too hot to sleep anyhow, and the crew sat out on the hatches watching the distant flashes against the hills and listening to the rumble. No one said anything, but in the darkness you could see the whites of their eyes and you knew they were thinking of the four thousand tons of ammunition they were sitting on.

A little before midnight I went into the messroom for a cup of coffee and found Victor sitting there smoking. He hadn't even gone out on deck to look at the raid. You could still hear the bumps and thumps on the hill. I borrowed a cigarette from him.

"Are they talking port bonuses out there now?"

"They aren't talking anything."

"Agh, that bunch of vags. They thought they were getting the bonus for nothing," he muttered contemptuously into his coffee mug. "Let me tell you, kid, nobody gives you anything for nothing." He didn't seem to want to talk and I went on watch.

The next day it was even hotter, or at least it seemed hotter, but perhaps it was only because it was getting on our nerves. Firmín stayed in his cabin listening gloomily to the radio, and the Australian lieutenant spent the morning checking the temperature in the holds. In between inspections he would climb up to the bridge again to blink away at the jungle with his Aldis lamp. Finally about eleven o'clock a launch came crawling out from across the water from town, and an American naval commander came on board to talk to Firmín in his cabin. The commander was in unpressed khakis with his shirt open at the neck and he was wearing a khaki baseball cap; evidently they played softball over there on the beach. Five minutes after he left, word went around that we were sailing for Tulagi in the Solomons.

Out on deck under the awning somebody got out a map, an old National Geographic chart of the South Pacific that the engineers had been passing around from hand to hand until it was covered with grease. There was Tulagi, right across the sound from Guadalcanal. It was the place the announcer on the radio called Iron Bottom Bay, where the Japanese navy had been coming down every night to shell the beach. Half the gang out on deck said it was a mistake, and the other half thought they were probably sending us there because it was an old ship and not worth a damn anyhow. The sea lawyers all started trying to prove they had no right to send a merchant ship there and that we hadn't signed articles to go in the combat zone. This point hadn't come up when they were talking bonuses, three or four days before. Theories bloomed like flowers in the spring. The third mate said they had originally planned to send us to Espiritu Santo and transship the cargo to Guadalcanal in barges, but they needed the ammunition right away and had decided they didn't have time for the barges. I don't know where he found out this piece of intelligence; perhaps from the Navy commander, or perhaps from one of the messboys. There was a rumor that Guadalcanal was going to be evacuated anyhow; somebody had heard on the radio that the Marines were going to pull out and make a stand on New Guinea, but this may have been a Japanese broadcast. Most of the people on the *Chileno Cape* didn't care whether the Marines made their stand in Dixieland or on top of Mount Everest. They had lost their interest in the war now and were willing to give the port bonuses to anybody who wanted them. "Next trip I'm shipping out on the Great Lakes," said Welsh, snuffling his nose with the back of his hand. "Ore boats. They pay scale."

In the officers' mess everybody sat around listlessly drinking lukewarm tea. The engine room was ready to sail, boilers lit off and steam to the throttle. Victor had already left to go up forward and heave the anchor short when Cheeney came in to the messroom to talk to the captain. Cheeney whispered, while Firmín looked at him with the wrinkles screwed into his brow. Finally he got up and went away with Cheeney, still carrying his napkin and chewing slowly. In five minutes he came back and called the Australian lieutenant out into the passageway. In the messroom it was too hot to talk and you could hear them through the open door.

"Listen Lieutenant, my steward here is sick. I don't know what to do."

"Well, we've got to sail in a half an hour."

"I dunno, he looks pretty sick. He looks to me like he ought to be in the hospital."

"Ah, see here now. What's wrong with the fellow?"

"I dunno, I'm not a doctor, but it looks to me like he had some kind of a stroke. I wonder if mebbe we ought to wait and see how he's going to be, before we sail."

"Out of the question. Out of the question."

After a lot of discussion it was decided to send for a doctor from ashore. It was an hour before he came out, and the lieutenant kept pacing back and forth looking at his watch. When the doctor finally came alongside in a launch he was afraid to climb the pilot ladder to the deck. He was a frail little old Frenchman in a white linen suit, and he could only use one hand because he was carrying his bag in the other. He climbed the ladder one rung at a time with his knees shaking. When he managed to get over the rail they took him to Kammerath's cabin. In about ten minutes he came out, and there was a long argument involving the doctor, Firmín, and the Australian lieutenant. The doctor knew very little English, and he kept saying, "*Alors je m'en fiche, je m'en fiche.*" Finally Victor called the bosun and told him to break out the cargo gear and rig a boom over the side; they were going to put Kammerath in the doctor's boat and send him ashore.

The deck gang laid out a cargo net on deck under the boom, and then they went in to get Kammerath with a wire Stokes litter. There was a bumping and stumbling in the passageway, and four sailors came out carrying Kammerath in the litter wrapped in blankets. His face was the color of sour milk, and there was a branchlike pattern of purple across the cheek. One side of the face was drawn down and on that side the eye was shut; the other eye stared straight up, unblinking. The sailors set the litter down in the middle of the cargo net, and then they gathered up the four corners of the net and hooked it onto the cargo gear. Now the litter was inside a kind of cage made out of the net, and inside the litter was Kammerath. At this point there was a curious reaction on the face. The milky cheek trembled and twisted with effort, the mouth opened and a little saliva appeared at the corner, and finally an extraordinary croak came out.

Somebody sent for Cheeney. He bent down and Kammerath made the croaking noise again. After he had listened several times Cheeney managed to understand what it was that Kammerath was saying. He went away to the cabin, and in a little while he came out carrying a billfold. Although he tried to hold it concealed in his hand you could see it was stuffed with Australian and American currency, so full it wouldn't shut. Cheeney tucked the billfold away among the blankets; both eyes in the sour-milk face were shut now. The bosun got on the cargo winch and began carefully tapping the throttle. Slowly Kammerath was hoisted up; the litter curved outward over the rail and began to descend, even more slowly, toward the water. When it settled into the launch the Kanaka boatman unhooked the net, and the doctor climbed trembling down the ladder again. The launch went off, the little doctor sitting in his white linen suit holding Kammerath's wrist. On the pier a mile away you could see an ambulance parked in the shade of the warehouse.

By sundown New Caledonia was only a blue smudge on the

horizon. The darkness came down suddenly without any twilight, and across the absolutely black sea the ship went on to the north-west. It' was a humid and stifling night and the clouds hid the stars. From the bridge you could hear the Australian lieutenant yelling, his voice beginning to crack a little. "*Shut out that bloody light* or I'll shoot it out!"

Chapter 6

.-- .... --- .- -- .. .-- .... --- .- -- .. .-- .... --- .- -- .. .-- .... --- .- -- ..

Those two nights on the run to Tulagi: black sea, cloudy sky, heat that hung over the ship like an oily blanket. It was impossible to sleep in the cabins and I got a canvas cot and set it up on the fantail, at the very stem of the ship where the deck was cluttered with bollards and winches. The cot shook there with the bumping and grinding of the propeller shaft but at least there was a breath of air once in a while. The rest of the crew was sleeping out on deck on mattresses thrown around on the hatches. That first night when I came off watch I got an hour or two of sleep this way, and woke up with a taste of fuel oil in my mouth. It was dawn and there was a fitful breeze from astern; the smoke from the funnel rose straight up and hung over the ship. All that day we ran north under a smudgy private cloud that rained fine particles of soot. Sometimes the cloud would drift ahead a little and wait for us, then the ship would catch up and nose into it again. The odor of fuel oil and soot hung over everything: in the food, in the tepid drinking water, in the bedding.

The Australian lieutenant never left the bridge now. He hadn't shaved for two or three days but his white shirt and shorts were still immaculate. The second day the overcast broke a little and twice we saw planes: an Australian seaplane that circled around us four or five miles away and in the afternoon, flying very high, a formation of bombers from Espiritu Santo going north to Rabaul through the broken clouds. It struck me for the first time how conspicuous the ship must be from the air, gray against the bright green sea and leaving a dirty track of foam behind it for miles.

At sundown it was overcast again and we went on to the north through small rainsqualls. The Solomons were only a hundred miles ahead. At ten o'clock that night a destroyer was supposed to meet us off San Cristobal and take us through the islands to Tulagi. The Australian lieutenant went around the ship dogging down doors where lights were showing and putting out people's cigarettes. Around nine o'clock I was lying on my cot on the fantail and they sent for me to come to the bridge again. This time all the fuses were blown and there was no light for the compass or the chart table. A sailor was holding a flashlight on the compass so the helmsman could see, and the lieutenant had another flashlight to look at the chart. He glanced up at me and said, "Oh, there you are. There's no light," and immediately looked back at the chart.

"The mates are supposed to take care of the electricity on deck." "The mates don't know bloody beans about it. I'm not in the mood for a trade union dispute. Now get to work and fix it."

"All right, Nelly, don't get emotional."

I got a flashlight and started checking outlets. When I took off the first cover plate I saw that the wiring was completely rotten. The insulation was hanging down in tatters and through the hole I could see bare copper wire running inside the bulkhead. I worked for an hour winding friction tape around the wiring as far as I could reach with my fingers. Then I would bend each wire and adjust it carefully so the bare copper wouldn't touch steel.

Finally I got the light on in the compass again. By this time the lieutenant was out on the wing of the bridge with his binoculars, trying to find the destroyer in the darkness ahead. The third mate had nothing to do when the lieutenant was on the bridge and he was pulling a hangnail off his finger. Down in the boiler room the fireman chose this moment to change burners, and there was a shower of sparks from the funnel. The lieutenant yelled for somebody to call the engineers and tell them to watch their bloody fires. "Boiler room, yer makin' sparks!" bawled the relief helmsman into the phone. And then in a disgusted voice, "Gawd, that Limey is worse'n Kammerath, at least he slep once in a while."

At ten o'clock I was still fooling with the wiring and there was no sign of the destroyer. Evidently they had something more important to do than play nursemaid to a merchant ship. The lieutenant rang down stop engines, and the ship lost way and drifted while he and Firmín argued about what to do.

"I dunno, I think the best thing to do is anchor and wait for morning. In this dark you can't see what you're doing."

"And how in blazes are you going to anchor, may I ask, on a lee shore and no bloody bottom?"

They went on like this for ten minutes until the ship was dead in the water. She wouldn't answer her helm and her head was drifting around to the south. It was impossible to stay there and there was nothing to do but go on.

"Half ahead," said the lieutenant, ignoring Firmín.

In the darkness someone swung the handle of the telegraph, and the ship stirred, began to move, and wallowed on to the north-west through the islands. Indistinct black lumps of land slipped by to port. At midnight I gave up on the wiring and went below to go on watch. The air in the engine room was unbreathable, so hot it irritated your eyes and mouth. We stripped to our under-wear and ate salt tablets, drinking water and watching it ooze out white and salty onto our skins. Welsh was working in the shorts he hadn't changed for two weeks, a yellow streak of urine down the front, and the Mexican wiper was stark naked with his lean brown flanks wet with sweat. I could hear the water underneath surging back and forth in the bilge, and I told Welsh to get the pump going. Then I stood dully watching the gauges and waiting for the four hours to be over. Outside in the water the propeller blades boomed monotonously: pough, pough, pough until the sound seemed to be inside my head; by my ear the revolution counter clicked like an insect. The steel plates under my feet radiated an acrid and oily heat. At last I lost track of the time. When my relief came I grunted something unintelligible to him and left without bothering to put on my clothes.

Out on deck it was absolutely dark. The ship was rolling evenly and almost imperceptibly in a slight swell. The foam slipping by under the rail was faintly phosphorescent against the water, and astern the milky gleam of the wake tapered away and dissolved in the dark. A kind of luminescence seemed to hang over the whole ship, outlining the black shapes of the bridge, the funnel, the curve of the bow. I groped my way back aft to my cot and lay down. My shorts were soaking wet and in sudden disgust I took them off and threw them over the rail. Then I stretched out again on the bare canvas. It was the third night I hadn't slept more than an hour or two and my eyes were swollen and heavy, but I couldn't go to sleep and instead I lay thinking. I thought what a rotten ship it was and how I could never sail on a good ship again because of my record, and I knew I would spend my life standing watches in an engine room full of shoddy machinery, eating bad food, trying to sleep on a hard mattress that smelled of fuel oil and sweat. Four on and eight off: your life slipped away from you and after you were gone it would be the same as if you never had been. It would go on this way and I didn't know how to change it. To change you have to have a new point to start from, and I didn't know how to find this or what it would be. The war would go on, I would be killed in it or go on living but it wouldn't make any difference. I wondered if the others felt it too, the pointlessness of everything and the impossibility of changing the way you were, or whether they had somehow managed to come to terms with it in their own way. Kammerath, Kouralis, Welsh, Cheeney: we all lived together and were each other's enemies in this private hell we had made. I thought of Kammerath with his milky face clutching his billfold as he sank through the air in a litter, of Kouralis left to bleed in an alley. It was stupid to lie awake thinking of these things but Kammerath's large pale moist face would not go away, it hung in my thoughts as though it had something to say to me, something about the human heart perhaps, in a voice that smelled of sour milk and money. He was the one who had it made, the one the others hated because they envied him and wanted to be as he was, but in the end the fat he had sucked from us had crushed his heart and now he lay at the bottom of a muddy hole or in a hospital bed in Noumea with an oxygen mask over his face. I knew that the people I had chosen to spend my life among would watch me die as callously as they had watched Kammerath lowered into the launch: without sympathy, without curiosity, simply indifferent. But where had I chosen, how could I have made things happen any other way? I didn't know, and in the end I forced myself to stop thinking about it. But when I finally went to sleep it was hearing the poplars rattling at dawn outside my bedroom window and the familiar creaking of the old house in the wind and knowing I was not there, forever, and that my bed was empty.

When I woke up it was to find myself lying on the steel deck beside the cot where it had fallen over sideways. It was still dark and there were confused sounds I couldn't identify, thumps and hissings. I was lying with my arm bent under me and a violent pain in my elbow, and at first all I felt was a muddled anger at whatever it was that had awakened me and banged against my arm. For a few seconds my main impulse was to forget about the whole thing and go back to sleep again as quickly as possible; I pictured myself setting the cot upright and climbing gingerly back onto it in order not to disturb that last morsel of sleep I still clung to inside. But then I began to realize that this was impossible because there was something terribly wrong with the ship. It was acting exactly like a trash can into which a kid has dropped a lighted string of firecrackers; not very good firecrackers, the fuse was damp and they exploded only sporadically and half-heartedly. Every now and then there was a small muffled bang, and with each pop the ship seemed to stagger a little in the water and clanged like a garbage can. Forward there was something strange about the silhouette of the deckhouse against the night sky, and I finally grasped what it was: the funnel had collapsed and was lying across the bridge like a broken arm. I remember thinking that it was going to be impossible to get a draft in the boiler room with the funnel fallen down. Then lower under the deckhouse I saw something brighten and spread, the first orange tongue of flame.

I got up and groped my way forward through the dark, holding my elbow in my hand. There was an odd silence; the only sound was a metallic belch now and then from inside the ship. I passed a sailor carrying a radio in one hand and a cheap suitcase in the other, and somebody else in white pants, perhaps a cook, with what looked like a portable phonograph. The old chief went by clad only in an undershirt, his genitals dangling ludicrously. In the pink light forward by the deckhouse I saw Victor untangling a fire hose. He had hold of one end of the hose and the bosun had the other, and they were patiently pulling the kinks out of it. I went down the ladder to the well deck, pushing past two or three people who were bumping confusedly up, and as I reached the bottom of the ladder there was a deeper explosion from inside the ship, a dull gassy oof! like a man struck in the stomach.

Victor dropped his end of the hose and vanished from the pink light. A moment later he materialized out of the darkness and seized my arm. "It's you. There's no water on deck, get below and see what's wrong with the pumps."

He disappeared into the darkness.

"Victor!" I yelled after him. "What are you talking about, the boiler room's flooded, there's no steam!" He was gone. For a second I hesitated. Somebody else bumped into me; it was a messboy with a cardboard carton, evidently full of canned goods, which he was trying to cram into a lifeboat. It seemed to me that everybody around me had lost their senses, Victor included. Half of them seemed to think they were going on a picnic, and the others were dribbling little streams of water on a ship that was going to blow up any second.

There was another dull lurch from inside the ship. "Victor!" I yelled into the darkness. "It's no good! She's going, can't you see?"

There was no answer. From up forward I heard a falsetto voice, not Victor's, squealing, "I got the goddam thing turned on."

I turned and began running back toward the stem. This time I passed Squires sitting on the well-deck ladder holding his head in his hands. When I squeezed past him he looked up at me without recognition, and then went back to staring at the flames. He seemed to have lost his wits. The after deck was almost deserted. When I reached the fantail I stumbled over my overturned cot and groped past it until I felt the round bar of the rail under my hand. I climbed up on it and balanced for an instant with the bar pressing against my naked feet, and then I pushed outward and fell into the darkness. The fall through the air seemed to last for an extraordinary time, then the back of my neck hit the water with an unexpected violence. The water was neither hot nor cold but incredibly solid; it struck me a crushing blow under the ear and for a while it stunned me. I went deeper than I expected and stayed down for a long time. While I was still groping toward the surface there was an enormous bump and a painful stab of pressure in my ears: it was as though from all sides an enormous blow had been applied with some plastic substance, hard and unyielding but exactly fitting the contours of my body, even to the openings of the ears and nostrils. The shock staggered me and my sense of up and down vanished; I had no idea which way it was to the surface. My body turned slowly under water while something rang in my head, a metallic buzz.

At last I broke through to the surface and swallowed enormous gulps of air. It was absolutely quiet; the long swell lifted slowly under me and settled again, a few stars were visible through the broken clouds. There was no sign of the ship. My ears still rang with the crushing blow I had felt under water; it seemed impossible that such an explosion could leave nothing behind it, no debris, not even a flicker of light on the sea.

There was no sound but the washing of the water around my body and the faint buzzing in my ears. I reached out and paddled with my arms a little, but immediately I went under and swallowed salt water. After that I floated and saved my strength; there was not much point in swimming because I didn't know which direction to swim anyhow, and if I had known it would probably be too far. The water that had been so hard when I struck it now seemed light, ethereal, fragile; it seemed impossible that such a thin fluid could support a solid body for long. The sea was invisible, the few stars overhead were indifferent in the black sky, there was nothing. I had the odd sensation that the nothingness began at the surface of my skin and went on forever, in every direction, to infinity. Well, I finally had what I wanted, I was alone! As I floated the water rippled gently a half inch from my mouth. Whenever I tried to swim it rose over my face.

For what seemed like a long time I floated like this, moving my hands weakly to keep my face above water. Perhaps it was only a half an hour. Then it began to get light, and on both sides I began to make out dim outlines on the horizon, low clouds or islands, I couldn't tell which. Nearer on the water I saw darker lumps which at first I took for debris from the ship. Then as daylight came I saw they were floating clumps of vegetation washed down the rivers by the monsoon, pieces of trees and bushes clotted with dead leaves. They were scattered over the water as far as I could see, some only as large as a man's hand, others the size of small haystacks. I began working toward one of the larger clumps, but it was farther away than it looked. Whenever I stopped to rest for a moment my feet would sink under me, and it was only with a tiring effort that I could bring them back to the surface again. For a long time I swam this way, groping in the water clumsily and kicking with my feet, while the clump of vegetation seemed to stay as far away as ever. At last I came up to it and sank my fingers in the mass of twigs and vines. I had expected it to be fragile but it was unexpectedly solid, smelling of mud and sodden leaves. Hanging on gingerly, I floated and rested until my breath slowed.

For the first time I realized how tired I was. I had lost my whole grasp of time; I had swum or drifted for what seemed like several hours, and yet I had come off watch at four and now it was barely daylight. A crazy idea struck me that I had been in the water for twenty-four hours but I had been delirious or asleep or something and forgotten it. I realized that I was losing my grip on reality and no longer thinking logically. Everything seemed strange, and above all the silence. The sea that had seemed so flat from the deck of the ship was undulating, crossed with long low swells that lifted me slowly and settled away again as they passed. As the light came up I could make out a long line of shore to the south, an uneven dull green with a white fringe of surf at the bottom. In the opposite direction there was another grayish-green island, but farther away. The light wind was coming from the east and the clump of vegetation was drifting with it slowly, carrying me to the west where it was still dark and I could see nothing.

Then I realized that for some time I had been listening to something, the sound not of surf but of water washing gently on rocks. There was a gurgle as it came in, a moment of silence, then a retreating hiss as it drained away. It seemed to be coming from ahead and to the right, where I could make out a faintly darker loom on the surface of the water. When I stared hard I saw nothing; it was only when I looked slightly away that I sensed something was there. It was mainly the sound that convinced me it was real and not something I had imagined. Whatever it was, it was too far to the right and probably the current would carry me past it. As the sun came up I could make it out more clearly: a line of black rock in the sea with a little jungle growing out of it, perhaps a half a mile away.

As I watched it I became aware that it was changing direction and imperceptibly moving around to my right. If I went on drifting I would pass it probably a quarter of a mile away. Dimly I realized that I was going to have to make a decision: whether to abandon the temporary security of my clump of rotten leaves, or hang on and continue drifting. If I let go I would have to swim a quarter of a mile across the current, and I didn't think I could make it. I lacked the will to swim ten yards, let alone that immense distance to the line of black rocks. And yet if I hung on, probably, I would drift past it out to sea. I couldn't decide. My fingers were locked into the branches and in my exhaustion and apathy, in the familiar smell of mud and leaves, I was almost comfortable. I didn't want to let go. A kind of resentment rose in me against that scrubby black rock that had come drifting by and forced me to think.

It was more than a rock; I could see now that there were good-sized trees on it, and here and there a tiny beach of black sand. It moved so slowly that the eye hardly noticed the motion, but in a few minutes it would be past and I would never reach it against the current. With a convulsive wrench I pulled my hands out of the tangle of branches and fell backwards into the water.

Immediately my face and mouth went under; I flailed my way back to the surface. When I came up I had lost my bearings and the islet was nowhere in sight. In a momentary panic I looked around for the clump of vegetation; if I had found it I would probably have swum back to it and hung on for good. In the last instant before I lost my head I saw the islet again, around to one side where I hadn't expected it. Methodically, my hands working like weak fins, I began working my way toward it. Now and then I stopped to rest, floating with only my eyes and nose above the surface, In a surprisingly short time I felt the bottom under my feet, sharp coral covered with seaweed. I stood up waist-deep with the water streaming off me and lurched across the reef, but beyond it was another pool of deep water. I had thought I was at the end of my strength, but now it seemed I had to make another effort. I fell forward into the water and somehow floundered on, with convulsive motions of my hands and feet. At last my knees struck sand. I put down my hands and crawled on all fours up a coarse beach littered with stones. My head hung down and mechanically I watched the smooth water-polished stones going by under me, six inches from my eyes. My crawling was awkward and ungainly and several times I almost fell, but I positively did not want to lie naked on the open beach with the sky watching me. I went on lurching across the sand until I reached the green line of vegetation beyond, and there I fell on my side and went to sleep, the rotten smell of leaves and comfortable shadows enveloping me.

Chapter 7

.-- .... --- .- -- .. .-- .... --- .- -- .. .-- .... --- .- -- .. .-- .... --- .- -- ..

When I woke up it was because the hot sun shining through the leaves had fallen across my face. My cheek was hot and my left side and arm were irritated from lying on the rough sand. I sat up reluctantly, brushed the sand off myself, and chased away a small cloud of fleas that drummed a few inches in front of my face. I saw the black beach scattered with round grayish- white stones, and like a memory of something that had happened a long time ago I remember crawling across it on my hands and knees. The sand was coarsely crushed black lava, sharp and uncomfortable to the flesh. The rocks of the island where they stuck out of the vegetation were the same grayish black, crumbled and streaked with bird droppings.

At the edge of the water the beach was littered with debris: vegetable scraps, a scum of oil mixed with salt foam, here and there a box or a piece of a broken crate. I squatted down and washed off the sand in the sea. The water was cool and felt good, but the salt irritated the places that had been rubbed raw by the sand. It seemed to be around noon now and the sun was high in the sky. Across the water I could see a larger island, a long lump on the horizon perhaps ten miles away with a thread of smoke rising out of one end. Except for the smoke there was no sign of life on it. At one place I thought I could make out a black spot against the jungle, and after I looked at it for a long time I decided it was the hulk of a burnt-out ship- Farther to the west there was another island in the sea, a low volcanic cone with a fringe of green around the bottom of it. The sky v/as clear now, with only a few scraps of gray cloud that slowly dissolved in the sun.

Out in the open the heat was making me dizzy. I went back and sat in the shade of the thicket where I had slept. The hot sun had dulled my will and I sat apathetically, reluctant to move but not really tired. Over my head was a low arching tree with fan-like leaves which was perhaps a pandanus, although I had never taken a very great interest in botany. The tree hung down almost to the ground and if you crawled far enough back it was like a cave, cool and smelling of decayed vegetation. Now I made a new discovery: the black sand was full of fleas. There was decomposed vegetable matter buried in it and it smelled rotten, and when I kicked it with my bare heel a small cloud of fleas would arise and hover over the hole. The salt had dried on my skin and made it itch; my eyelids burned a little. I realized I would have to go look for water.

After I had explored a little I saw that leaving the small strip of beach where I had landed was impractical, at least without shoes. The jungle behind the beach was an impenetrable mass of sharp twigs, with gnarled roots underfoot and various kinds of nettles. At each end of the short beach there was an outjutting of volcanic rock. I tried climbing up one of these miniature cliffs to see what was on the other side, but my feet were softened by the water and salt and the rocks were too sharp. I did manage to get high enough to see what was beyond. The islet I was on was small, a half-mile long and only a few hundred yards wide, and it was part of a chain of volcanic rocks connected by shallow reefs. The water was breaking a little on the reef and I saw that theoretically it would be possible to wade over to the next islet, but it was smaller than my own and I couldn't see that it was any better. I didn't care very much. I was curiously tranquil. In the intellectual part of my mind I was aware that fresh water would have to be found, but somehow nothing mattered, as though my brains were made out of wax and sitting in the sun had softened them. My mind was perfectly logical, even lucid, but it was terribly passive. I didn't think about the night before or what had happened to the ship, or try to explain to myself why I had acted the way I did. That part of my mind was numb, and if I happened to come across that kind of thought I just drifted around it for the time being. There had never been any doubt according to old-fashioned heroism I should have gone down to the engine room to start the fire pumps and got blown up with the rest of them, but I wasn't a copy-book hero and nobody else on that ship was either, and it was too much to think about. It was as though that part of my head was stuck full of glue; later perhaps it would melt and I could start thinking about it again, but right now it was too much effort.

All that existed was the present: I was sitting in the sand with some green leaves over my head, and the universe around me seemed to be a series of senseless phenomena succeeding each other without any connection. I observed everything, one detail at a time: the fleas in the sand, the scum of oil on the beach, the fecaloid shape of Guadalcanal across the water with the thread of smoke hanging over it, an inch of raw carrot which I found lying at the edge of the water, probably dropped overboard by the cook on some passing ship. I accepted the carrot as a natural phenomenon like the fleas, and I ate it although it was saturated with fuel oil. It tasted neither good nor bad. I wasn't very hungry anyhow.

It did, however, make me thirsty. I got up unwillingly and a little stiffly and made a second attempt to force my way into the underbrush behind the beach in search of water. I wrestled through it a foot at a time, limping over the sharp twigs and fighting branches that snapped back and hit me in the face. After I had gone perhaps ten yards, which took me a half an hour, I found some putrid-looking green water in a hollow in the ground. I drank two or three double handfuls of it, felt sick, and immediately threw up. This left me weak and I sat down where I was and made an effort to think for the first time. The salt and the fleabites had left my skin raw, and now under it a dull irritability began to spread through the flesh, a kind of smoldering resentment against whatever it was that had forced me to deal with these ignominies, fleas, raw skin, vomiting, thirst. Then I realized what I was angry at and what had become my enemy: the survival instinct. Well, what was so damned important about staying alive anyhow? That was the question that needed answering. It was this stupid instinct that had made me swim around half the night until I was exhausted, and now it had me floundering around like a madman in this sharp underbrush looking for water. And I had never asked the simple question: why? Now that it had occurred to me there was no real imperative that obliged me to stay alive the whole problem became much simpler. I grappled my way back to the pandanus on the beach and lay down again. I felt I was somehow getting even with something, it wasn't quite clear what. The Universe perhaps. I went to sleep tranquilly in spite of the thirst.

When I woke up I began to see it was not as easy to die of thirst as I had thought. My mouth and throat had dried, and every time I swallowed or moved my lips it felt as though the flesh was cracking. My tongue was too large and seemed to lack connection with its muscles; it lay in my mouth like an awkward lump. It was no good, I would have to go look for water. I spent the rest of the afternoon searching, and toward evening I found a pint or so in a crevice in the rocks at the end of the beach. It was rainwater, sheltered from the sun by an overhanging rock, and only a little salty. I drank a little, and as soon as I had climbed back down to the beach I realized I hadn't drunk enough and was still thirsty. I had to climb back up the sharp lava rocks again, and each time I went up I knocked a little more skin off my hands and feet. Coming down the second time I cut my foot badly on the inside of the instep. The blood that welled out was a blackish red, surprisingly thick. It was the first live and vital thing I had seen for some time and I squatted on the beach with my legs turned up and contemplated this odd substance coming out of the bottom of my foot. It didn't hurt particularly but it reminded me that an organism, for instance a human body, had a metabolism and needed food to sustain itself, and you were no more free to ignore this than you were to ignore the problem of water. The survival instinct was better organized than I thought. If you didn't drink water your throat hurt, and then hurt more, and then hurt like the devil, and finally you had to go look for water. It was a kind of an enemy inside that made you live whether you wanted to or not. Probably it was the same with food, and carrot ends really wouldn't do in the long run. I gave up. The life instinct was only the last of a long series of things I had surrendered my free will to.

I slept hungry that night in the black shadows under the pandanus, and the next morning I found something better to eat. In the sea off the end of the rocks, two feet under water, tiny shellfish grew in thick black clusters set on edge like razor blades. Standing up to my knees in water I wrenched off chunks of them, cutting my hands on the sharp edges. Each individual mollusc was about the size of a man's fingernail, and inside was a tiny pinpoint of meat. After several unsuccessful attempts to open them with my fingers (more cuts) I learned to smash them with a rock. In this way, with an hour's work could collect half a handful of fishy black spots of meat. For the two days I spent most of my waking hours prying the nourishment out of minute shards of shell, each piece of meat about the size of something a civilized man would pick out of his teeth. I began to see why the Solomon Islanders had never developed a civilization; they were too busy smashing molluscs. The fleas were attracted by the fishy smell and settled on the meat where I had piled it on a rock. Before I ate it I brushed them off, at least most of them, and if any of them were left that was their lookout. In between I would climb up the sharp lava to visit my water hole. At a handful three times a day there was still enough for a couple of days; by that time perhaps it would rain.

Around the end of that second day I became aware of a terrible mistake. My skin was softened by the night in the water and I had spent two days in the sun stark naked, and I was getting badly sunburned. The skin was already peeling, especially on the buttocks where I was chafed from sitting on the sand, and the new skin that came out underneath was pink and sensitive. I peeled off ribbons of skin and threw them on the sand. Perhaps the fleas would like it. Take that, you bastards! I've eaten you too, on a piece of mollusc meat. In the long run we helped each other, the fleas and I.

Staying out of the sun as much as I could, I pounded shells all day and slept under the pandanus by night. The sand irritated my sunburned skin and I slept fitfully. Sometimes in the middle of the night I would be awakened by the rumble and bump of gunfire, and I would crawl out on the beach and see orange flashes in the jungle across the sound. If the sky was overcast the flashes would be reflected on the clouds, the same orange but paler and more diffuse. The sound would come a few seconds after the flashes, a series of running bumps or thuds filtered by the distance so that they had a curious soft cottony quality. Sometimes you could see tiny intermittent points of light springing out of the jungle and rising up toward the clouds: anti-aircraft tracers. I watched all this as though it were a distant electrical storm or some kind of astronomical phenomenon, an eruption on Saturn. It had nothing to do with me and after a while it wasn't very interesting. I would watch for a while, sitting in the sand with my arms around my knees, and then I would crawl back under the pandanus and go to sleep.

Those first two days the wind went on blowing from the west. It was the seasonal trade and I knew it would go on for months except when there was a storm or a local disturbance. I pondered vaguely over ways of getting off the islet, perhaps finding a tree trunk or another clump of vegetation to float on, but the wind was the wrong way and I would only blow out to sea. Anyhow I would probably drown because I was weaker now and probably I would have to swim farther. All this was a kind of daydream, taking place in some rather remote logical part of my mind and not having much to do with my immediate thoughts, which were concerned with pounding shells and staying out of the sun. I had the intelligence, approximately, of one of the more complex insects. I was capable of putting food in my mouth and of pulling off strips of skin, but if a fully equipped motor launch had stranded on my beach I probably would have been incapable of climbing into it; all my instincts were against it. Under the pandanus was Home; it was shady there and there was protection from nature, which was vast and indifferent and perhaps hostile. The food was terrible and the roof leaked but it was no worse than some of the ships I had sailed on. I had been a loner all my life and I had finally reached the paradise of loners. It was almost pleasant. I left the shade only reluctantly and kept the pandanus always in the corner of my eye as I wrenched off clumps of shell in the shallow water, knowing I could *go* back there and crawl under the shade whenever I wanted. The rest of the world was full of uncertainty, burning sun, water that drowned, and it was better to hold on to what I had and squat there with my knees hunched up under the leaves where it was cool and safe. The insects, the cutting sand, the smell of rotten vegetation were part of it and I wouldn't have wanted it any other way.

All that second day clouds gathered, and toward nightfall it started raining. The first drops came, hitting the hot beach and kicking up little puffs of black sand, and then there was a gathering patter on the leaves which rose steadily to a rush. The water came down solidly. Under the pandanus I was almost dry and I looked out at the storm, the water running down the black sand, the fleas hopping above the splashes. It went on raining until a little after dark. To the west it cleared a little and I could see stars through the gaps in the clouds. After the rain stopped it was quiet and there was a smell of coldness, fresh like electricity. I sat listening to the water dripping from the leaves and feeling with something like pleasure the sand gritting in the irritated skin on my haunches, the subdued itching of the fleas and the sunburn. They were the price I paid to be out here out of the rain, out of the violence and the uncertainty. I knew now I would go on living out of laziness. Moving little, I needed little, and tomorrow there would be plenty of fresh water in the crevice in the rocks.

The next morning before dawn the sound of cottony bumping woke me up, and I thought it was the thunder again. But when I crawled out into the open I saw it was calm; the sky was overcast but quiet. It hadn't rained any more during the night and the sand on the beach was almost dry. On the island across the sound there were occasional flashes, and I saw that what I had taken for thunder was the sound of bombing. The noise was heavier than it had been before, a muffled shaking that seemed almost to come up through the ground. In between the thumping I heard the faint sharp staccato of antiaircraft fire. I had never heard this even before when I had seen the tracers, and I thought perhaps it was because the storm had cleared the air.

After a few minutes the bumping stopped, and then a half an hour later it began again. As the sky grayed, the outline of the big mountainous island appeared unusually clear across the sound, and against the jungle I could see a column of ships moving down the coast to the left. A few minutes later they turned abruptly and swung away from the island, and on each ship little flashing pinpoints of light began to appear. It was daylight now and in the clear air after the storm I could see them plainly, a row of high-bowed destroyers with two funnels set well forward. Over the ships a pattern of smoky balls began to form in the sky. There were dozens of tiny puffs, then hundreds until they filled the whole sky over the landing beach. The drifting puffs seemed to have nothing to do with the ships below; they sprang into the sky in silence, expanding quickly at first and then widening and softening as they blew along with the wind.

It was impossible to see what the ships were firing at. I squatted on my heels in the sand watching, still only half awake. The rain had cooled the air a little but it had left it sticky and tepid; collecting your thoughts in that viscous atmosphere was like wading through molasses. Over the beachhead, ten miles or so across the sound, two or three columns of black smoke had formed, rising up straight until they caught the breeze and then flattening and bending to the west. Now I realized that the smoke-puffs over the destroyers were drifting west too; the wind had changed after the storm. The ships had turned again and were almost invisible against the jungle. Occasionally I would see a pattern of winking flashes against the green, and a few seconds later the puffs of smoke would appear high overhead. When the sound came a long time afterward it seemed to have nothing to do with the flashes or the smoke-puffs, which sprang into the sky in the upmost silence. For perhaps a half an hour longer I watched. I was too stiff to stand up and too lazy to go smash shells; I squatted on my heels watching the distant battle simply because it had wakened me up and now it was too light to go back to sleep.

Then after a while I saw something else moving along the shore of the island across the sound, a black spot that might have been an insect. It was moving too fast for a ship, and now and then I lost it against the pattern of the jungle. A minute later it detached itself from the shore and moved out across the sound, and I saw it was a plane, flying low over the water toward me in a wide curve. As it came on it grew larger and expanded into a round dot with the thin line of the wings on either side. When it was a mile or so away it turned shakily and began banking to the right. It passed by my beach so near I could see the red ball painted on the side and the tatters of metal hanging from the crumpled wing. The engine was trailing a thin thread of smoke and it faltered and ran raggedly, as though the pilot was coaxing the last life out of it with the throttle.

When it disappeared behind the rocks at the end of the beach I got up impulsively and went to the water's edge to follow it. It was going away down the line of reefs that connected the islets, wavering slightly, one wing drooping. It was so low now that it almost seemed to touch the water, but somehow it managed to stay in the air a little longer. Once I saw a flash of spray and I thought it had hit, but incredibly it went on, as though it were held in the air by some kind of continuing miracle. While I watched a crazy thing was happening: my muscles were tensing – upward, my stomach held tight to keep in the air for a few seconds longer this piece of defective machinery that sooner or later would have to smack into the sea. It was a reflex, a visceral reaction – what was this now, I was holding my breath over this Japanese aviator? The logical part of me mocked at this stupid empathy, but my stomach tightened anyhow. The two of us, the pilot and I, strained with our entrails and somehow the plane went on a little father. Then abruptly a geyser of spray rose and it stopped, its tail lurching into the air.

It had come down off the next islet from mine, perhaps a quarter of a mile from the shore. The tail settled slowly back into the water and almost immediately a yellow blob appeared next to it: an inflatable boat. The cockeyed empathy I had felt while the plane was in the air now changed to something else, first unbelief, then a kind of irrational resentment. I watched while the yellow spot detached itself and began moving toward the shore. Who did he think he was, this foreigner, this Japanese? He had come along when I was peacefully sleeping under my pandanus tree, first he had extorted this unwilling sympathy out of me with his tight-rope act, and now he calmly paddled ashore only a half mile away as though he owned the place. The fine perfection of my isolation was shattered. But it wasn't that, it was because he had made me feel emotion for him, for another human being, I who didn't even feel emotion for myself! The yellow dot had reached the shore now, and disappeared into the green edge of the jungle. The plane had sunk.

Up to this point, if I had had no particular desire to rejoin the so-called world of men, it was partly because it was impossible and partly because I had tacitly chosen not to admit that there were other men, or at least that they had anything to do with me. The gunfire and flashes at night were natural phenomena like lightning; I wasn't involved. Now the arrival of the yellow spot on the next islet had changed everything. I could no longer pretend I was alone, and there was a man a half mile away who had a boat. He was there now and I had to relate to him. I didn't want to relate to him, I wanted to go back to sleep. But I couldn't, because with his clever rubber boat he had reminded me there was a social aspect to my predicament. He was alive now instead of drowned because somebody else had made the boat for him, whereas I had had to make do with a bush provided by an impersonal river. But you couldn't get by on bushes indefinitely. Although I didn't like the idea, I had to recognize that until a few days ago I too had lived as a gregarious animal and cooperated with other men for my existence. I had never felt any particular spiritual kinship with the other human beings on the *Chileno Cape*, but at least they had provided me with food and shelter and in return I had kept their machinery running. Now I began to perceive that it was impossible for a man to live for very long without this kind of minimal cooperation. I had to recognize that ten or fifteen miles away there were other human beings who spoke English and wore pants and ate ham and eggs, and eventually I would have to make some effort to establish contact with them; if I didn't I would die. It was an effort which I found terribly boring- but the decision hadn't been made by me. Living was a reflex, as involuntary as thirst. I knew now it was as impossible for me to starve to death as it is for a good swimmer to drown himself. It was in the way of things. And for me to live, I now began to see, it was necessary for someone else to die.

It was this feeling of resentment over the predicament forced on me, more than anything else, that finally made me angry enough to act. I tramped up and down the beach, kicking at the heaps of detritus along the shoreline and looking for a weapon. All I could find was a piece of rusty wire perhaps two feet long, still attached to the fragments of a shattered crate. This was Excalibur, the shining weapon I was going to use to attack the human condition, solitude, the whole cosmic injustice of things? I threw the wire away in disgust and didn't even look to see where it had landed. But I couldn't stop thinking about it. Later I went back and found it again, and took it with me when I went to lie down under the pandanus leaves, wakeful and brooding, to wait for nightfall.

Instead of smashing shells I spent the rest of the day breaking the crate to make handles for the wire, twisting the rusty ends around two scraps of wood that fitted easily in the hands. I tested it by yanking hard: it held. Then I stayed where I was, waiting for twilight when it would be light enough for me to pick my way across the reef and dark enough so I couldn't be seen. A little before sunset I took my piece of wire and went down the beach, trailed by a cloud of fleas, my private version of the Egyptian plague. The sand was dry but the sky was still overcast. The water was the same leaden gray as the sky; the leaves stirred in the light breeze from the east. I climbed over the rocky cliff, scrambled down the other side, and came out onto another beach. This one was only a yard or so wide, a narrow path of sand between the jungle and the water. As I went farther even this disappeared and I was walking up to my knees in the sea, the branches overhead so low that sometimes I had to lift them with my hand.

The end of the islet narrowed and tapered away into a sand spit. Beyond this there was the open stretch of water; with the overcast sky the sea had lost its transparency and the shallow reef was invisible. If you watched carefully you could see a crease of foam or a wrinkle in the water now and then to show where it lay under e surface. As I waded out a long-legged white bird settled on the reef, walked around as if to show me how it was done, and then flew off cawing raucously.

I set out gingerly across the reef, the coral sharp under my feet. The water was deeper than I had thought or else I hadn't found the right place to cross; in places it was over my waist and once I lurched in up to my shoulders. The sun had gone down now, the breeze riffled the water, the mass of jungle ahead was turning dark. Another sand spit led up out of the water on the other side but I decided not to take it; there was no vegetation on it and I would be clearly visible against the twilight sky. Instead I stayed in the water, veering to the left along the shoreline. Here the bottom was a gritty sand and the water was up to my armpits. I was out of the shelter of the reef now and there was more surge from the open sea; it forced me sideways and lifted me off my feet, and once I went under and got a noseful of salt water. I snorted and blew it free and went on.

Staying in water up to my neck, I worked my way down the shoreline to the point where the rubber boat had disappeared into the jungle. The islet was smaller than mine and there were no rocky outcroppings, simply a long sliver of sand with jungle running down the center of it. Now I saw a column of smoke rising out of the trees—he had fire, this oriental Prometheus? I had forgotten I was angry with him, but it was enough for me to look at the smoke, and to remember that he was making me walk up to my neck in water on sharp rocks when I could be lying asleep under the pandanus. I went on working my way down the shoreline until I came to a miniature cove, sheltered on both sides by the undergrowth. Here, dangling Excalibur, I came up out of the water onto the beach.

Crouching to stay below the bushes, I slipped across tire sand and rested for a moment at the edge of the jungle. It was a thick tangle of trees and vines and after a while I began moving through it cautiously, hearing the water dripping from my body onto the leaves. Now that I was closer I saw the islet wasn't as flat as I had thought; it rose to a slight knoll in the middle, a few feet above the sea. When I reached an opening in the jungle I saw the Japanese pilot sitting on this rise in tire middle of a clearing. He was squatting on a rock with his back to me, cooking his dinner over a driftwood fire. It was getting dark now but I could see him clearly in the light from the fire: shaved head, small brown ears, white overalls. He had fish; I could smell it cooking. These miracles—fishhooks! fire! I had forgotten they existed. Never was the disparity between rich and poor greater than between, me and this Japanese aviator, sitting there calmly broiling a fish the size of his hand over an open fire. His boat was drawn up prudently near him on the beach where he could keep his eye on it. I was naked and he had more possessions than he could use all at once. I was the proletarian, he was the capitalist, and my relations to him were reduced to the basic proposition of all revolutions: die, I want what you have. It was the first time in my life I had taken an interest in politics.

He was only fifty yards away, and at the slightest noise he would turn his head. So far the crackling and snapping of the fire occupied his attention and he had noticed nothing. He looked relatively harmless, sitting placidly by the fire prodding his fish with a twig. From the back he looked older than I was, hair thin on top, getting a little thick around the middle. Did he have a fat wife? Play the flute? Go to the movies? Now I noticed he had a revolver in a holster hanging from his overalls, this well-equipped samurai. I was naked and he was armed; my life depended on his inattention. My own existence seemed suddenly fragile, and for the first time I understood that what I was doing had a metaphysical significance. What did it mean, this sudden and violent gesture the muscles of my fingers were already rehearsing? He and I were going to enter into some kind of a relationship, an event was to link us. It would be the most important event that had ever happened to either of us: I would become the obliteration of his existence, and he the means of the continuation of mine. And yet the roles might still be reversed; if he turned his head it would be I who was obliterated with his ingenious little machine made in Osaka, Japan. I comprehended now at last what the war meant. If it had not been for this political abstraction, the war which I had so far refused to acknowledge, he and I might cooperate; he would give me some fish and I would show him how to smash mollusks. But our roles had been determined for us by politicians neither of us had ever seen; I was condemned to be an American and he a Japanese. Noiselessly, clutching my wire, I went forward in a crouch.

He heard nothing. The loop of wire rustled once and sank in a coil over his head. It was then that I saw his face for the first time; when he felt the wire cut his throat he lunged backward, soundlessly but with immense physical strength. But I was behind him and he was off balance with nothing to grip; gradually he sank back until his body lay across my knee, the cords of his neck distended. Then his head fell back and, he looked up, his left hand slipping slowly across my breast until it reached my shoulder. How strangely he died, pressing his hand on my shoulder, as though he wanted to assure me of something, of his sincerity! It was easy for him to be sincere; I was the one who had the difficult thing to do. For a few seconds we stayed locked together, motionless but trembling with effort, staring at each other. He made no sound but his teeth were bared, not in ferocity but instead as though he were making an immense effort to speak. What did he want to tell me, this flute player, this expert on survival? Perhaps he wanted to give me his opinions on metaphysics, or perhaps he merely had a message for his wife. While he watched me I pulled on the wire, the muscles of my arm swelling and aching. He was strong for his age, but he was in an awkward position, bent backwards over my knee. After a long time he was quiet. The Tables of Law – how easily they shattered! They were only papier-mâché after all. He was guilty too, this bald philosopher who came prepared with his revolver; whatever it was that he and I made we made it together. Everybody is guilty so nobody is guilty. And yet sometimes later I used to see him fixed there like a fragment of broken movie film in his speaking look, his fingers pressed on my shoulder, gazing with teeth bared and eyes astonished as though pleading to be heard *you, my copilot, brother, guardian spirit who held me for a moment longer off the water!* Well, it's better not to look in mirrors. How did I get into this? It's hard enough living one life, let alone two. My victim, you are dead, lie down! Nobody seems to know his place anymore.

Chapter 8

.-- .... --- .- -- .. .-- .... --- .- -- .. .-- .... --- .- -- .. .-- .... --- .- -- ..

Well, anyway he had a boat. It was lying there on the beach and now I had to do something with it. It was my alibi: if I didn't want the boat, why had I done what I had done? I became aware I was still holding the piece of wire in my hands and impulsively I threw it away; it sailed end over end and disappeared in the jungle. Then I dragged the boat down the shingled beach, taking care not to tear the rubber bottom on the rocks. When I pushed it out into shallow water and had one leg cocked up to get in I realized I had forgotten the paddle, and I had to beach the boat again and go look for it. It was dark now and it took me a while to find it. I thrashed around in the bushes, and finally my hand fell across it wedged neatly under a rock. I was annoyed with myself for forgetting the paddle and I made a deliberate effort to do things unhurriedly and calmly. This time I pushed the boat out into the water and somewhat ungracefully fell into it, holding the paddle in one hand. I didn't look behind me into the clearing.

The boat was rudimentary, a small oval rubber doughnut not quite as large as a bathtub. I hadn't examined it very well in the dark but I had the impression it was already losing air. When I prodded it with my finger the depression stayed in the rubber for a while and then gradually dimpled out. Under my legs I could feel the water tippling against the thin rubber skin. I started paddling. With each stroke the boat swung in a half circle, and I had to change hands and paddle on the other side to straighten it out. It didn't matter because I wasn't sure where I was going anyhow. The thing was to think about each problem as it came. For the time being I concentrated on learning how to row a round boat with one paddle.

I was beginning to get the trick. I came out from the shelter of the islet and the boat caught the breeze and started drifting down to the west. Later, I knew I would have to start working across the wind, toward the beach where I had seen the ships. This would be the hard part, but for the time being I drifted.

In the open channel the breeze was stronger and there were a few white caps. The sky was still overcast; the sea itself was invisible in the dark and the whitecaps ran along scratching lines of foam into the black surface. Now and then I paddled a few strokes, leaving small clots of phosphorescence in the sea behind me like footprints. Then I would hold the paddle across my knees and rest, making a stroke once in a while to keep the boat headed in the right direction.

Across the sound the usual air raid was beginning; there were flashes on the horizon and once in a while pink tracers rose up toward the cloudbank. I tried to make out the shape of the island against the sky but it was too dark. The clouds were lower now and it was beginning to rain; I heard the intermittent patter of the first drops striking the sea. As each drop fell it left a small pinpoint of phosphorescence that glowed for an instant and then dissolved. The islets behind me were invisible, and I could make out the land I was steering for only by the occasional flickering of orange light. Once for a long time there were no flashes and I rested on my paddle and waited, my eyes fixed on the gloom to the south. Then in absolute silence a line of pink dots came out of the jungle and rose up toward the clouds. It was still a long way off; I hadn't made much progress. There was a half-inch of tepid water in the bottom of the boat now. I couldn't tell whether the boat was leaking or whether it was from the rain. Through the thin rubber I could feel the surge of the sea lifting and settling under my legs.

The next time I stopped to rest I thought I could make out something on the horizon, a jagged uneven line to the south where the land was supposed to be. But the shape, whatever it was, was not the land because it was moving to the left under the clouds. Finally I made out that it was a line of ships in column: three, then four, then five. As I watched, the line began to telescope into itself and merged into a single narrow lump; the column had turned and was coming toward me. The ships made no sound and showed no lights. They were only a set of shapeless spots that moved sideways, blurred together into a single clot, and then gradually grew larger.

They were coming on fast, and it occurred to me that I was directly in their path and they might run over me in the dark without seeing me. I turned the boat and began paddling to the right, rather uncertainly because I wasn't sure which way the ships would pass. They came on rapidly until they were perhaps a mile off, while I splashed clumsily with the paddle. Then the lump separated abruptly into individual ships; the column had turned again. Two, three, four, five: they detached themselves and began moving swiftly to the right. They went by me only a quarter of a mile away, long black shadows like holes in the darkness. They were the same destroyers I had seen that morning across the sound; I recognized the high bulk of the bridge and the two funnels set well forward. For a while after they were gone I could hear the hissing and crushing of their wakes in the darkness.

A few minutes later from downwind there was a series of rapid white flashes and the jagged arpeggio of gunfire. No answer; the ships were firing at nothing, at ghosts. It was raining harder now, and the clouds had lowered until here and there they hung down almost to the water in long black streamers. A few minutes later I heard the gunfire again, this time farther away.

I couldn't see the island anymore because of the clouds and I had lost my bearings, but I was less interested now in getting to the beach than I was in staying out of the way of this vague thing that I sensed forming all around me in the dark. But I couldn't see anything anyhow and there wasn't much point in paddling; my hands were getting raw from the salt water and the boat was deflating. It was developing a crease in the middle like a comic lawn chair about to fold up. I laid the paddle across the boat and rested. An inch of water sloshed in the bottom now against my thighs.

For a half an hour I drifted, listening to the thump and rattle of the distant battle. I could tell the boat was turning as it drifted, because the sound of the gunfire seemed to move around me in a circle. I couldn't tell whether the boat was still losing air. When I lay on my back it seemed fairly rigid, then when I sat up to paddle it would buckle in the middle again. To the west it was still raining and the clouds hung down in inky festoons. It was from this direction now that the sound of gunfire came; I couldn't see the flashes anymore but as I watched I began to make out a kind of pinkish glow in the clouds. It came and went, diffuse: a pink nucleus surrounded by a kind of smokey halo. The whole cloud bank reflected the pink, as thought something was burning and illuminating the clouds from inside. Then the glow faded, and I lost sight of it for a long time.

When it came out of the clouds again it was much nearer; I could see bright spots of flame reflected on the smoke and once in a while something black underneath, the outline of whatever it was that was burning. It was perhaps a mile or so away. The gunfire had stopped now and the only sound was the crisp patter of falling rain. Now and then there was a gurgle of water from the bottom of my boat. I was sleepy and it seemed to me I has been on the water for several hours.

Bleeding pink smoke, the shape came on slowly in the rain. I knew I either had to get out of the way or start paddling toward it, but I couldn't make up my mind which to do, and the longer I thought about it the less reason there seemed to be for doing anything. I was in a curious apathetic state, as though I were half drugged, and I wasn't thinking very clearly. The only thing I felt was a kind of exasperation that this new complication should come along and force me to make more decisions, at a time when it was hard for me to think anyhow and above all I wanted things to be simple and uncomplicated. It seemed vaguely odd to me that the shape should keep burning like that in the rain, and that it should keep coming towards me as though pulled by some invisible force. There was no sign of life on it and it made no sound. It was only a few hundred yards away now, moving toward me so slowly that it broke no ridge of foam before it. There was something uncanny about the burning shadow that came on without a sound, hardly disturbing the surface of the sea, and a queer notion struck me that everyone on board was dead or that they had abandoned it and left it to drift. I knew I should probably start shouting at it or paddle towards it, but it seemed to me that if there was anybody on board they would be just as likely to start firing at me as to throw me a line, and anyhow they had problems of their own without stopping to pick up people who were floating around naked in the dark. All this was not really thinking but just little pieces of logic coming unstuck in the glue in my head. In any case the bow was coming straight at me and only a hundred yards away, and in a minute or two I would have to glue my thought processes together and decide what to do about it. But the bright glow of the fire hypnotized me in the way that you can be hypnotized by staring at a candle flame, and I just sat and watched the burning shape come on.

Then, unexpectedly, there was a flash of light and a deafening crash. At first I was half blinded by the glare and I couldn't understand what it was; I thought the ship had blown up or been struck by lightning. Then I grasped what had happened: somehow, burning and half sunk, the destroyer had crazily fired off its gun into the clouds. After a long time the sound echoed off the land, then silence. I couldn't get it out of my head there was nobody aboard, perhaps it was simply that the flames had reached the guns and set off the charges. But a few seconds later they fired again. It was closer now and the sound was splitting and acute, a blow of physical violence in the eardrums. This time as the echo died away there was an answering crack of gunfire in the distance, and beyond the destroyer a cluster of white columns sprang through the sea and then sank away again. I felt the concussion through the rubber bottom of the boat.

For a moment I was not aware of any danger. The shells began falling more thickly and there were heavy shocks from underwater. The surface of the sea was shattered; I felt a lurch and the boat sagged and settled. Under my fingers the inflated rubber withered, and the water began to rise over my legs. Then for the first time, when I felt the boat softening and settling under me, I was conscious of the sensation of fear, a kind of coppery constriction in my throat and chest. I turned sideways and fell into the water, with a muddled idea of swimming away from the ship. But something held me and I couldn't move my feet; the wet rubber skin of the boat was tangled around my legs. With my face half underwater I fought against that clinging rubber as though it were a physical enemy. I was hardly aware of the falling shells or the noise around me anymore; my whole consciousness was dominated by a panic of this wet slippery animal that held me by the ankles and wanted to drown me. At last I kicked it loose and floated weakly, panting. Then I became aware for the first time that something around me had changed.

There was an odd silence, or rather the quality of the sound had altered. The sea was covered with a layer of sticky oil burning here and there in patches. At first I couldn't find the destroyer, and when I finally caught sight of it I hardly recognized it. In the few seconds I had been struggling with the boat it had been completely shattered: superstructure twisted, mast and funnels collapsed, the whole bulk leaning tiredly to one side. There was a confused din of sounds, and I realized that for some time I had been hearing voices yelling the same word over and over in a kind of chant. "Rage, rage, rage, rage!" It was inexplicable and uncanny. I felt that if I could understand this one word I would finally grasp the meaning of what was happening, that it was the key that would explain the whole senseless chaos of noise, pain, the stench of fuel oil. *Rage, rage*. At what? At death, at God? At the enemy out there in the dark that nobody had seen? But the yelling bore no relation to any reality I knew or could comprehend; it was the chant of maniacs.

"Range! Range!"

And then finally I understood my mistake; the phones were knocked out and the gun crews were shouting for the range to the target so they could go on firing. And yet this seemed to me even stranger and more incomprehensible, than men who were being burned should cling so doggedly to their technical tasks, that what they should cry out for in their final passion was a number to crank onto a gunsight. The yelling came out of a different world, a world where I didn't belong, a world where men felt different courages and despairs and were moved by emotions that were inexplicable to me. In the confusion of the battle, half-choked by oil and deafened by the noise, I listened to the voices and thought how strange it was that I had finally found human beings who believed in something beyond preserving and cherishing their own selfish existences.

Finally a voice on the bridge heard them and yelled something back. But the voice was interrupted almost immediately by the shattering crash of the guns. The firing went on raggedly and intermittently. In between the explosions there were confused voices: "Go ahead, take it, don't wait for them." "... target." "Are you on? Goddam it, are you on?" Then there was a direct hit on the top of the bridge, scattering debris and burning fragments, and the whole surface of the sea seemed to spring up convulsively around me.

I was surrounded by continuous din, water, noise, blackness. I sank and turned slowly somewhere under the surface, beaten on all sides by the thud of concussions. This time I knew I had to stay under for a long time and I fought to keep from rising, my lungs pounding and the blackness mounting to my head. At last the thudding stopped. When I came up to the air again everything was so strange that it might have been a hallucination. There was no gunfire and everything was silent. The forward end of the destroyer had disappeared and only a few feet away from me the enormous bulk of the stern was slowly rising up and capsizing. Ponderously the propellers and then then keel rose out of the water, and the black shape went on turning like some enormous and precise machine. Men in orange jackets were clinging to it and dropping off one by one into the sea. Two feet away from me a startling apparition rose out of the water; an oil-blackened face with two white surprised eyes. It hung there mutely for an instant and then disappeared in the smoke. The oil in the water was burning all around me, and it was only by beating with my hands that I could keep it away from my face.

The broken stern was still turning slowly on its axis. An odd shape sank towards me through the flames, four-petaled with a curved arching shadow over it. It was a moment before I grasped was it was: a propeller with its curved guard, upside down and out in the air where a propeller should never be. As the hull turned the curved bar of the guard came slowly downward. I stretched for it but it was still too high; it was a stupid and irrational impulse but my strength was almost gone and I was sick from the oil and I felt I had to hold on to something solid, at least for a few seconds until my strength came back. The next time, lunging up out of the water, I reached it and gripped it with both hands.

I couldn't let go. A spasm raced through the palms of my hands, and I hung for an interminable moment while the skin loosened like wet paint and slid off onto the metal. I felt the glow of the hull now on my whole body. At last the metal freed what was left of my hands, and I fell blindly downward.

Under the water was darkness, coolness, the agonizing pain of my hands. I was no longer aware of anything except my agony and a sick rage and disgust over the stupidity of what had happened. I was beyond vanity, beyond irony, seeking only oblivion and escape from pain. And yet the pain went on, past the moment when I thought it had become intolerable and into other moments when it increased tenfold, then a hundredfold. I thought I had touched bottom more than once before in my life but I hadn't; this was it. When the skin slid off my hands onto that incandescent metal I sloughed off everything with it: ego, name, identity, the ink that still clung from the fingerprint room in San Francisco, all the scars, passions, bitterness, humiliation, the lingering odor of failure like stale cabbage that had sunk into my flesh in all those years of cynicism and apathy. I no longer had any idea whether I was dead or alive, underwater or in the air. My hands pulsing, I sank naked through the blackness.

When I became aware of myself again I seemed to be hanging in space. Everything throbbed. A part of my mind, the passive consciousness, was quite lucid. I remember hearing very clearly a voice explaining that the depth charges were armed and would explode when they reached a given depth, I think fifty fathoms.

Other voices talked but I didn't connect the sound with any meaning. Someone was trying to push me up onto something, a raft or a piece of floating wreckage; the hard edge of it was digging in my ribs. I understood that these voices that were talking about me thought I was one of them and wanted to preserve my life; I felt like telling them not to bother, that they were making a mistake, but it didn't seem worthwhile explaining it to them. I didn't want them to push me up on a raft or do anything to me, I just wanted them to go away and leave me alone with my pain, above water, underwater, anywhere. But against my will, working patiently against my recalcitrant arms and legs, they lifted me out of the water where it was death to stay and into the air. And I knew that, even though passively and unwillingly, with the compliance of my body I joined together with those unknown hands against the common enemy, not the Japanese ships but pain, weakness, death. "Jack, hang on, God damn it, I cain't hold you," a flat Texas voice warned me patiently.

But without my hands I couldn't hold on and I slid back into the sea again. The first depth charge exploded far underneath; I had the sensation of water forced with a hammer blow into all the openings of my body. "Git your carcass *up* there, now, go on," the Texas voice insisted. The hands pushed me up again (I wish I knew who he was, this lunatic who went on patiently trying to save me while the depth charges exploded around his own testicles) and finally I was sprawled on a hard surface out of the water. Everything rocked: bump, bump, bump. I felt the shock of the board I was lying on against my teeth. I was conscious for a while and when I woke up I was retching, the nauseous taste of fuel oil in my mouth. There wasn't any pain anymore and the vomiting seemed only a mild annoyance, something that prevented me from going back to sleep. Once I had the impression there was somebody else with me on the broken raft: perhaps a corpse, perhaps a hallucination. Or possibly it was my own body I was dreaming of, strangely aware of the touch of my limbs against the boards as though they belonged to somebody else. There were no more voices, and with a sensation like floating I felt myself slipping back into the coolness of sleep.

Oblivion, dream, hallucination. When I opened my eyes again it was because a light was shining on them, so strong I could feel it through the lids. A round eye of white stared at me and there were disconnected noises. Talking, lights; I was suspended in the air by my armpits, then with a swoop I was lowered. I was in a litter; I could feel the reticulated pattern of wires under my body. The pain had not stopped as I had thought; it was still there but too big for my brain to grasp. It had become simply the fact of existence, reality itself. Now the needle slipped in and the pain was washed away in a cool flood, and I realized how immense it had been. I felt alternatingly chilled and covered with sweat; I dozed. Somebody pried my teeth apart with a finger and stuck in a glass tube, and I drank. I heard the soft throb of propellers. When I tried to move my arms I became aware of the two balls of my hands, swathed in soft cotton. It was not the propellers that were pulsing but the hands, a soft almost audible throb at the ends of my arms. *Pough, pough* like the big blades cutting the water as I slept, the insides of my eyelids were coated with phosphorescence, the wake swarmed and whorled across them. Another needle, more sleep. The sun was shining uncomfortably hot and bright; I lay on a dock while a black man who smelled of coconut oil waved away flies with some rags on the end of a stick. Then somebody must have given me a really terrific injection because I slept for a long time, dreaming of soaring and vibration, a reassuring sound like a cataract, warm and continuous, playing over my nerves. The next thing I remembered was lying in a base hospital, looking straight upward with a very still and hypnotized curiosity into the arched ceiling of a Quonset hut.

I had lost all contact with the passing of time. The corrugated walls bulged and dimpled as though they were made out of water, the sounds came to me undulating in the disconnected logic of a dream. Now and then I woke up and heard people talking around me, impersonally, as though I were an object. From the words I gathered, I was in Noumea and I remembered that this was where they had taken Kammerath ashore. Somehow I knew that he was dead now and this seemed strange; it had not struck me before that a man who was not alive, who had no emotions and gave nothing to others, could die. While the walls rippled around me I pondered over this, with a kind of delirious and lucid clarity.

Someone changed the urinal now and then and asked me if I wanted anything. No one had time to take any special interest in me. Every four hours they would give me a shot, and once a day they would change the dressings on my hands. For the most part I kept my eyes closed. I wasn't blind, it was just that the eyes were scorched or perhaps inflamed from the fuel oil and it seemed more comfortable to keep them shut. When I opened them, if it happened to be daylight I looked detachedly at the hands that lay on the sheet on either side of my body. I could feel nothing in them and they hung at the ends of my arms like two inert animals, their tentacles coiled into a ball. Once somebody took off the bandages and tried to straighten out the fingers. I let out a piercing yell and that was the end of that. The cracked skin oozed fluid and the corpsman had to mop it up with a piece of cotton. After that they left me alone.

It was the third or fourth day. A Navy doctor who needed a share, in khaki shirt and pants, was standing by the bed, and behind him was a corpsman with a clipboard.

I opened my eyes, stared at him for a few seconds, and shut them again.

"Name?"

There was nothing there; around me everything rippled and the sound hung in a void.

"Service number? Wake up now."

It was like listening to a radio program tuned in idly. The silence followed and nobody answered. *"What's your name, your name, your name?"* My brain turned the phrase over. I was aware of the significance of the words, but they didn't seem to have any relation to me or even any abstract importance. The doctor seemed to agree; his voice was flat, unemotional, and impersonal.

"Is he still on Demerol?"

"We can take him off if you want."

"No, leave him alone."

They hung a bottle of glucose from a kind of a hat-rack and stuck a needle in my forearm. I felt the nutrition drip, drip, drip in the vein. My bladder was uncomfortable and I began mumbling and keening peevishly. Finally the corpsman brought a urinal. The fluid dripped in one end of me and leaked out the other. I was a conduit, a hydraulic system.

I woke up and the voices were talking again. This time they were at the other end of the room but they were moving slowly toward me. It must have been a couple of days later.

"These two stay."

"Right."

"This one we'll ship out, send him to CincPac[1] and enter it on the jacket."

"Check. No, listen Commander, I got him on the other form." The voices came closer.

"This one's okay, we'll keep him. What the hell's wrong with you anyway, *son?* You start eating and get some flesh on."

"These are the three from Tulagi, these three here."

"Compound fracture, can't move him. The burn case to CincPac." He was standing now by my bed.

---

1 Acronym: Commander in Chief, Pacific.

"I got no BuMed[1] jacket on that one, Commander. What do I write?"

"Unidentified, off the *Marcus*"

Somebody tied a string around my wrist with a cardboard tag attached to it. The voices went on.

"Com Twelve for medic discharge."

". . . all right, check."

Toward nightfall I was loaded into a plane. I opened my eyes once: I was inside a metallic cave painted yellowish-green with litters arranged inside like bunks. The litters were stacked three high but not all of them were occupied. There were perhaps eight or ten other wounded. One of them was moaning in what seemed to me an affected and unconvincing way, as though he had learned how to do it from a bad war movie. The engines barked, missed, barked again and caught. We began moving, bumped across the runway, then my head lifted and I was horizontal; I realized that before I had been lying on a slant. The plane banked and climbed, then it settled back to the level and the note of the engines lowered a little. We flew all night. It was dark except for a small light up forward where the corpsman sat. We landed several times. Whenever the noise of the engines stopped I could hear the man across from me moaning. When we were in the air I lay half-conscious listening to the boom of the engines, which had a pleasant lulling throb, and now and then the corpsman in white pants and a T-shirt would come and give me another shot. Then it was daylight again. "Hickam in ten minutes, I heard somebody yelling over the noise of the engines.

---

1   Acronym: Bureau of Medicine and Surgery.

Chapter 9

.-- .... --- .- -- ..   .- -- .... --- .- -- ..   .- -- .... --- .- -- ..   .- -- .... --- .- -- ..

In the naval hospital in Pearl Harbor I stayed for three months. I don't remember very much about the first week; I was feverish and under heavy sedation and I slept most of the time. People came and looked at me and went away again, but except for changing the dressings they left me alone. I ate nothing because of the nausea. Night and day a glucose needle dripped into my arm. There didn't seem to be any reason to think, and in the brief intervals when I wasn't asleep I lay quietly listening to the messages from my hands. It was like a telegraph system in an unknown language: little flashes, throbs, and arrows ran up the nerves to my brain where I examined them with interest. Some raced with incredible rapidity and others drifted quite slowly up the arm, little balls of aching that gathered shape as they came. I lay there by the hour wondering about the meaning of these curious messages from the ends of my arms. Were they trying to tell me something? Were they friendly or hostile? I thought that probably they were hostile and they had their reasons, but I was perfectly indifferent to them. The fact that the messages they sent were called pain didn't prejudice me against them. I didn't particularly want the pains to go away, nor did I want anything else. I would wake up and lie quite benignly for an hour or so with my eyes closed, listening to my hands and opening my mouth obediently when they stuck a glass tube in it for me to drink. Then they would give me another injection and I would sink away with a swoop into sleep. I would still hear the propeller blades going *pough, pough* underneath and it was only in my more lucid moments that I recognized the sound as my own pulse. Something about the fever made the bed tilt slowly and then turn back the other way; I could hear the soft wash of the water slipping by alongside. No more watches no, no more sweat and no goulash and it was permanently cool, like the breeze off the mountains in Utah. Sometimes it was dawn and the leaves would rustle outside the window, and I would hear a dog bark and the morning paper strike the porch with a slap. A voice would wake me up: "Temperature." I would open my mouth and the thermometer would go in. At other times the sedation would go deeper and it seemed I was underwater; the sensation wasn't unpleasant, only a cool blackness in which I revolved slowly, head over heels first and then spirally around the axis of my body. There was nothing strange in any of this and it seemed quite natural and simple. was not aware of myself; instead the events and sensations took place in a kind of a void, they simply *were* without the necessity of being perceived or understood by a consciousness. At times I cogitated (vaguely) over whom this was happening to. I was aware that there were words like *me* and *I* but for the present their meaning lay elusively just out of grasp, like a telephone number that has slipped your mind. And were they really important, these words? It was as though the pieces of my personality had been fractured and there was no particular reason for them to settle back into place again, and for a while it was uncertain what form they would take when they did.

The brief periods when it was necessary for me to become fully awake were when my dressings were changed. The hands were the worst, but there were dressings on my face too and one long pad of gauze along the side of my chest, fastened down with tape that stung and pulled off skin when they removed it. On my head, it seemed, the hair was singed off and there were other raw places from the irritation of the fuel oil and salt water. All this had to be unwrapped and redressed once a day. In Noumea they had put Vaseline on it, but it seemed the theory of medicine was different in Hawaii and they used tannic acid packs. It took three men to do it: one to turn me over, one to squirt tannic acid at me with an atomizer and then apply the wet packs, and the third to hold my bandaged hands so I wouldn't roll on them. I lay limply as they turned me, my mind quite calm but the nerves jumping as the pains shot along my arms. I was mildly surprised that my nervous system could still feel this indignation after all that had happened to it. Usually I kept my eyes shut while the dressing was going on. "Feel that?" somebody asked me once when he accidentally dropped my hand onto the bed. Yes I could, I got the message. I didn't say anything. If he was interested in the subject he should have talked to the hand.

After about a week of this they put me on a little cart ("Easy, watch his arm, now lower him") and rolled me off to another ward. As I lay in the new bed I began to gather from words and scraps of dialogue that I was in the plastic surgery section.

I opened my eyes and for a day or so I just watched what happened to go by in front of me, without turning my head. There were a number of people in this ward in grotesque predicaments. One man would come down from surgery with his forearm sewed to his thigh, another one would be doubled up with flaps from his leg stitched onto his chest. The doctors took quite an interest in it. Whenever an unusual case came down from surgery they would all gather around and make comments.

"There's a good trick, he used the pectoral flap."

"Yeah, but where are you going to get the circulation?"

"Well, he should know what he's doing, he specialized under Kramer."

"Oh well, hell, he was a Mayo man. They always did it that way at Rochester."

While the discussion went on the object of their curiosity would look at the ceiling. It was possible to learn a great many interesting facts about the circulation of the blood, the anatomy of the epidermis, and so forth by listening to what went on in this ward, in case you were interested. It was here for the first time that I saw my new face in a mirror. They had taken off the dressings except for the one on my chest and the balls of gauze on my hands, and I was propped up to be shaved with an electric razor. I was too weak to do anything but stare; with an effort I could move my eyes around the room a little. There was a mirror hanging on the folding screen at the foot of my bed. My eyes were already trained in that direction and out of inertia I went on looking. I saw a pinkish mottled face, very lean and absolutely expressionless. The eyes lay at the bottom of two pools of shadow, and the flesh had a curious rubbery-chemical look, as though it had been flattened with a hot iron. Starting at the temple and covering most of one cheek was a suppurating splotch of pink skin, shiny with some kind of medication.

The other deep facial burn, at the left corner of my mouth, was smaller but deeper; it hadn't formed any new skin yet and it was a mass of purple bubbles, shrunken at the edge and pulling my lips a little to one side. This sardonic lifting of my mouth was the only alive thing on the face; the rest of it was a mask. Out of curiosity I made a faint effort to work the muscles of the face, but nothing moved. Meanwhile the corpsman shaved me, skirting carefully around the blistered spot. I felt nothing.

The surgeon in charge of the ward was a naval commander named Waldbach. He was supposed to have been an eminent specialist in civilian life, a member of the Columbia medical faculty and a worldwide authority on burns. I don't know what a surgeon that good was doing in the Navy. Maybe people didn't get burned often enough in civilian life to suit him. In any case he didn't look like a naval officer; he was stocky and middle-aged, with a neat mustache and a brisk way of speaking, and he had a way of glancing at you skeptically as though he was trying to decide whether you were worth patching up or not and on the whole thought not. Still he was friendly in his rather autocratic medical-professor way; he never showed annoyance and he treated everybody in exactly the same way, enlisted men and officers alike. He had no patience with all the military nonsense, disliked uniforms, and went around the ward in a white linen jacket and a surgical cap, both antiseptically clean. Just the same the corpsmen were careful to call him Commander.

After I had been in the plastic ward for two or three days Waldbach came to look at me, accompanied by another younger officer in khakis with a neatly pressed necktie. This was Lieutenant Baroni, the group intelligence officer attached to the hospital, whom I was later to get to know much better. At this first interview Baroni did most of the talking, while Waldbach checked me over to see whether I was worth saving from the scrap heap.

The corpsmen had taken the dressings off my hands and they lay neatly on the sheet on either side of my body, each one resting on a clean square of gauze with the fingers clenched up tight to the palms. They were the color of boiled lobsters, and the fingers were barely distinguishable in a mass of suppuration. "These are a nice mess," Waldbach remarked, prodding them with a swab. "What have you been doing to them?" There was no insistence in the question and I didn't bother to answer; he was just making conversation. Skillfully he lifted the thumb with the swab to look underneath, I hadn't realized I still had a thumb, and I watched him with considerable curiosity as he separated it from the mass of coagulated flesh.

It was Baroni who asked the real questions, the ones that were supposed to have answers. In contrast to Waldbach he was energetic and impatient and his voice had a keener edge. I lay listening to the voice the way you listen to the sound of rain or some other noise outside your bedroom window. "You see," he explained while Waldbach worked, "it would help us a lot if you could remember what happened. The doctors think the burns on your hands might have been made by some kind of a cylindrical object, a pipe or a tube. Maybe you grabbed a hot gun barrel, or tried to pick up something burning and throw it over the side. Do you remember what it might have been? What were you doing when the ship sank?"

I said nothing, and he watched the hands while Waldbach worked on them with the swab. After a while he said, "You know, most people who have these things happen to them can remember something if they don't try too hard. The thing is to relax and let it come out by itself. Sometimes you have to approach it obliquely. Let's take your first name, for instance. Or a nickname; what did they call you on the ship?"

I glanced at him and went back to staring at the wall across the room.

"Well, he's still got a little fever," said Waldbach, who was shining a flashlight onto my left hand and lifting an edge of the skin with his swab. A flood of urgent signals arrived from the hand, but he assured me, "This positively doesn't hurt. Nerve endings all cauterized. Those imbeciles in Noumea didn't straighten out your fingers soon enough. If they had they'd have saved us a lot of trouble."

They tried, I felt like telling him, but they didn't know how hard I could yell. But this was rather complicated with a burned mouth so I went on looking at the wall. Baroni had brought a clipboard and a pencil with him, but so far he hadn't written anything. He put the clipboard down on the bed and his manner became casual, almost friendly. "You see, there were only a couple of other survivors off the *Marcus*. They were Marine passengers going to Tulagi and they didn't know anybody on the ship. They couldn't tell us much, and anyhow they're still in Noumea. You're the one we're counting on to find out what happened to the ship, especially in the last two hours. Now let s start with your name." Unobtrusively he had picked up the clipboard again and was pretending to fill in something at the top of the sheet.

I lay passively with my hands on either side of me, still staring across the room. After he had waited for a few seconds he did a curious thing, something that was quite natural but at the same time seemed oddly callous. He reached over and with both hands turned my head toward him, as though I were an inert marionette or some kind of a machine for talking that had temporarily balked.

"Now, just try to pay attention. I know it's hard, but it's absolutely necessary. Afterwards we can leave you alone."

From the bed I gazed at him without curiosity and without hostility, the way you look at things when you first open your eyes in the morning, accepting what you happen to find in your frame of vision but making no effort to judge it or even comprehend what it is. Wall, window, man, clipboard: I was aware that there were objects in my vision but I didn't feel any need to identify them by name. It was they who wanted to put a name on things, with their clipboards and their questions. Could anyone really believe that a name, the verbal formula that other people had used to identify me a long time ago and in other places, was of any importance? I wouldn't have lifted a finger to establish it, let alone go to the muscular effort of forming a word. The subject bored me. I couldn't see why anyone else got so worked up about it when it was so meaningless to me. The name—the identity, the events, the things that had happened—were there, lying like pebbles in a path, but there was absolutely no reason to make the effort of turning them over. And if I did? Perhaps there was nothing underneath them.

"Well, let him alone," suggested Waldbach. "Wait till we make some hands for him, then we can think about a mind."

But the next day Baroni came back again, and now the struggle started in earnest between my apathy and the dogged and tireless insistence of a bureaucracy that everything must have a label. It wasn't really that Baroni was interested in what happened to the ship: the ship had sunk, everybody on it was dead. What really drove Baroni was that he stood for Intelligence, and for Intelligence there are no mysteries. He was going to have my name if it took three wars and six clipboards. There was a blank place on his form: out with it! Everything must have a label! Intelligence confronts the sullen beast in us all.

Well, wasn't all this sulking rather childish? Why wouldn't I tell them what they wanted to know, these intelligent fellows with their pressed khaki shirts and their clipboards? I didn't quite know why myself. I had no objection to facts and labels in principle. Let them find out the facts, let them write labels all day if it gave them pleasure. I had no facts to give them, that was all. I had stopped believing in facts the way an atheist stops believing in God. I was in the water and then it had all been burned away—past, ego, identity, memory. There was something left, evidently. Something was thinking. But what?

During those long weeks as I lay in bed I worked it out. Most people believed in a body and also in a soul, or whatever you wanted to call it, an ego. But it was more complicated than they thought. They thought of the ego as a kind of a foggy pear-shaped essence inside you that stayed the same no matter what happened to the body: aware of other people and different from them, knowing its name, preferring coffee with cream, disliking warm beer. It didn't matter what you did with your body, tattooed yourself blue, became a hashish addict or fell into a sausage machine, you were still you and inside there was an unconquerable soul that went marching on. All this was probably true and I had had an ego like that once too. But what they couldn't get through their heads, Baroni and the others with their clipboards and their questions, was that this part of me had been burned away too that night in the water. They thought the burns were only third degree (charred skin, some tissue damage) but they had gone deeper than that. Or perhaps my ego had been closer to the surface than most people's, out in the skin where the fire could burn it away. Anyhow it was gone, disappeared with the fingerprints that had slid off on the hot metal and dissolved in the sea.

Then who was lying in the hospital bed looking at the wall? I didn't understand this very well myself, but somehow I felt that under the ego there was something deeper: a thing without any name, formless, elusive, yet it was *the thing that I was*—not identity or I-ness but being itself. When you burn something living, an oak tree or a pine, for a while the husk is dead and then from inside something green pushes out. It isn't the same tree anymore, the form and shape are different, only the life inside is the same. There I lay for three months in a hospital bed, an inert network of pains, discomfort, smells. Inside was nobody. There was only a nexus of existence, buried very deep and only gradually working to the surface. Out of habit the body when on breathing, eating, excreting, being awake and connected to its eyes and ears. Inside lay the awareness, and was magnificently uninterested in everything that went on outside.

Waldbach, that skillful man, was working on me now, slicing off skin from one part of me and stitching it onto another. Once a week or so I would go up to surgery. My hands had been straightened and were kept taped flat on boards, like two small planked steaks. They were fixed to the boards with their backs up, since for the time being they lacked fronts. Meanwhile Lieutenant Baroni came to see me every afternoon, bringing his clipboard and a constantly increasing pile of intelligence material from the Southwest Pacific. He was always the same, precise, lucid, and objective. He was a Princeton man and if he felt any resentment toward me he was too well-bred to show it.

"Now let's go through it again," he would say patiently, spreading the papers around on the bed. He had everything, maps, combat reports, even the names of the Japanese ships. "You were on the *Marcus*, sunk at 0140 hours by *Suzuya*, *Nagara*, and four destroyers that were coming back from hitting *Chicago* and *Vincennes*. *Marcus* was detached from the group at 1150 hours because she was afire and couldn't maintain steam pressure. They were trying to make Tulagi with her, but the Japanese column ran over them on its way back. This much we've established with a fair degree of certainty. We've got to find out from you exactly how it happened, what you were doing, what you remember of it."

After three or four days I finally thought of an answer to this. I said, "Why?"

"Because," he explained quite lucidly, "if we can establish the details of what happened to the *Marcus* we can fit them into the whole intelligence pattern of the action that night, and then we can hand the whole thing over to the tacticians and let them make their conclusions. For example, the last thing heard from the *Marcus* was a message at 0115 that she had a submarine contact. We think she might have armed her depth charges and when she sank they detonated; perhaps that's why there were so few survivors. Maybe this means that ships that are damaged shouldn't arm their depth charges. In any case, as long as there are some pieces that don't fit together the pattern is incomplete. You're the only one that can give us those pieces." I had my eyes closed. "Never heard of any *Marcus*."

"The *Marcus* was a destroyer. Do you know what a destroyer is?" There was absolutely no irony in the question; Baroni was a technician and did not indulge in irony.

"Ship," I admitted.

"How long is it? What's its tonnage?"

I pondered over this but no inspiration came to me.

"Where did you sleep on the ship? Forward or aft? Where did

you stand watch? On the bridge? In the engine room? What was your battle station?"

A blank.

"Do you remember the fire? How did the fire start?"

"Never been on a destroyer," I apologized with my eyes still shut. And then I added, although talking hurt my mouth, "I was in the water. That's all."

It seemed to me that I was being remarkably, even excessively, loquacious in making this lengthy statement, but Baroni wasn't satisfied. "How did you get in the water? Did you fall or did you jump? Was the ship dead in the water when you jumped or still moving?"

"I was in the water."

And so on, day after day. Baroni was infinitely patient and never showed the slightest sign of annoyance, he seemed in fact to have no personal feelings or nerves, but after several weeks of this he understandably began to feel he wasn't getting anywhere. I was repeating myself like a broken phonograph. He couldn't think of any more questions to ask and I knew all the old ones. By this time Waldbach was finished with me, although it would take a few more weeks for the surgery to heal. From things I overheard I knew I was going to be transferred to another ward. One afternoon a new corpsman I had never seen before came in followed by three orderlies, and without a word the four of them lifted me up and put me on the little wheeled cart. I had no possessions; they threw the medical chart which was my only document onto the wagon and wheeled me out of the ward.

We went down a long shiny corridor while they talked and I watched the lighting fixtures going by in the ceiling.

"Where's he going?"

"Psychiatry, fourth floor."

"Take the big elevator, the long wagon won't go in the other one." In the elevator I amused myself by idly reading the pink transfer form stuck into the blanket near my chest, the end of which explained; *Unidentified, combat fatigue, amnesiac w/poss. neural lesion due to hyperpyrexia.*

On the fourth floor the corpsman stopped at the ward deck. "Where do you want this one?"

The duty nurse was a squarely built woman in her fifties, with cropped gray hair and strong hands like a man's. She picked up the transfer form and looked at it without even glancing at me. "Four sixty-two." She stuck the form back in the blanket.

Chapter 10

In plastic surgery I had been in an open ward but in psychiatry I enjoyed a certain degree of luxury, a semi-private room with a tiled shower and flowered cretonne drapes. There was a steel grill over the window behind the drapes, but I didn't notice that for a while. The other bed in the room was occupied by an ensign named Bledsoe, a Navy pilot who had also been transferred to the fourth floor from the plastic ward. It seemed he had overshot the runway one day, coming in on Ford Island in an F4F, and when he went through the chain-link fence at the end of the field he smashed his face on the instrument panel. This was why you were supposed to fasten your shoulder harness, as his squadron commander pointed out to him one day when he came to visit him. The surgeon had gone to a lot of trouble on the face and had achieved what everybody said was a remarkable improvement, but evidently Bledsoe wasn't satisfied with the results, because twice he had tried to go out the window in the plastic ward, so now he was in psychiatry with a steel grill on the window and a corpsman sitting outside the door on a chair. It seemed that a desire to end an intolerable existence was considered evidence of insanity. It was really a philosophical question.

I never got around to discussing these interesting matters with Bledsoe, since he never talked to me and I didn't feel I had anything to say to him that he didn't already know. He had a bandage over one eye, or over the place where the eye had been, and he lay all day on his back with the other eye searching restlessly over the ceiling. Once every four hours the corpsman brought him the urinal, and this tinny tinkling between his legs was the sole event in his existence. When his dinner came usually he didn't pay any attention to it. If I felt sorry for Bledsoe it was only in a quite abstract way, as a symbol of the human predicament. I felt the only useful thing I could have done would be to help him out of bed and open the window for him, and I couldn't do that because of my hands. We were ideal roommates, two nice quiet psychos.

It was in this room, 462, fourth floor, east wing, that Lieutenant Gore used to come every day to see me. The first day I didn't realize he was a psychiatrist; when he walked in the room I thought he was the chaplain come to slap me on the back and give me Zane Grey novels. It was impossible not to like Gore, since he was not only an excellent psychiatrist but a basically likeable person and an indefatigable optimist. He was also intelligent; he had graduated from Western Reserve (cum laude, Kappa Sigma) and then gone through the medical school of an Ivy League university and done his residency in psychiatry in the naval hospital at Bethesda. He told me all this once, perhaps as part of his therapy or perhaps out of sheer friendliness. Just by looking at Gore you could see that he had been a red-blooded American boy in Terre Haute, Indiana and now he was a clean-cut young American psychiatrist, the kind you read about in women's magazines. He didn't believe psychiatry was infallible, since this wouldn't have been scientific, but he thought it was a beautiful thing and capable of solving most if not all of the problems with which the human soul is afflicted. He smelled of shaving lotion, which was a pleasant change after the smells in the surgical ward.

Gore took a liking to me from the first. This was partly because he liked everybody, but he was particularly interested in me, or rather in my case, because he liked challenges. The more difficult and stubborn a neurosis was the better he liked it. Bledsoe's case, for instance, was quite simple and therefore not very interesting. Bledsoe didn't like his face and he wanted to go out the window. It was banal. But me, what was wrong with me? Imagine, here was a fellow who didn't even have a name, who refused to have a name! He was born out of the sea, naked, like Aphrodite! It was a psychiatrist's dream. Usually the patient keeps pestering you, trying to tell you who he is and what *he* wants. I didn't want anything. I was a blank slate.

Gore began with me in the scientific-palsy manner he had learned in medical school, or perhaps in the fraternity house, then gradually the wrinkles in his forehead became more genuine, and finally he ended up hostile. But this took a long time, almost seven weeks. He remained cheerful almost to the end; he shared not only Baroni's intelligence but also his patience.

The mornings in room 462 were usually taken up with making the bed and changing the dressings on my hands, which healed only slowly. In the afternoon Gore would come and stay, usually, for an hour, sometimes bringing Baroni with him. After a few days his confident voice, his clean intelligent face, his hair which stuck up in a little cowlick in the back no matter how carefully he brushed it, became as much a part of my life as the succession of meals or the spots on the ceiling. "Hallo there, old fellow, thought of any names? You know, I'm getting curious; maybe you're Judge Crater, or Ambrose Bierce. Well now, what did you have for lunch?"

He would inspect the remains of my tray, which usually had not been taken away. "Roast beef? Great Scott, I'm going to move over here. In the BOQ we get hamburger steak." In addition to being facetious he was strenuously, in fact dogmatically, democratic. It was only an accident that I was lying here with a steel screen on the window and he was walking around as free as a bird. "You needn't be depressed because you're here, you know. As a matter of fact if you examined a thousand people off the street you'd probably end up locking up nine hundred of them." He said this with an earnest if jocular candor, as though he really believed it himself. This was perhaps the secret of his success as a psychiatrist; he had an effortless command, not of sincerity exactly, but of all the gestures of sincerity. The key to his method (or rather to his personality, the whole Gore-Gestalt that went along with his cheerfulness and his cowlick) was that he began by recognizing me (or pretending to) as an intelligent human being and dealing with me (or trying to) as an equal.

"Now, to some extent amnesia is essentially a rejection of one's self," he would explain to me. "In other words, frankly I'm not convinced that your loss of memory is entirely of traumatic or organic origin. The traumatic shock you suffered was probably only the trigger which set off the fugue state followed by loss of personal identity. For instance I've been checking in Ribot, the classic authority on the subject although he's getting a little outdated now, and he points out that in the typical fugue state there is not only a loss of identity accompanied by a lack of interest in the surroundings, but a single idea tends to possess the thought processes of the patient and direct his behavior. This is why you keep saying, 'I was in the water.' Now the therapy has to take account, to some extent, of the fact that your loss of memory is only a surrogate for your more basic rejection of your entire identity. In other words the layman would start out looking for the Self, as you might call it—the thing that is lost—but the analyst starts in another way, by setting out to discover the reason for the rejection."

These interviews, or rather monologues, went on by the hour.

"Now I'm just thinking out loud, so to speak, but I wonder if perhaps we can throw some light on the basic rejection through the Rorschach response." He knew every test in the textbooks and the Navy bought him all the testing equipment he wanted. The next time he came he brought the Rorschach cards and we began going systematically through them. "Now just give me your snap impression. No, no, don't think—just whatever comes to you off the top of your head."

I stared at the ink blots without interest. "Croquet mallet."

He would make a note, in cipher so I couldn't read it.

"And this one?" (A large balloon-shaped circle with a row of teeth in the middle).

"Navy psychiatrist."

A good-natured smile. "And?"

"Giraffe balls."

"And?"

"Chinese short-time towel."

"And?"

"Teddy Roosevelt."

Out of boredom I would sometimes tell him the whole pack of cards from A to Z looked like women's genitals, at other times water faucets. Or sometimes, when I was tired of talking and my mouth hurt too much for a long word, simply "Turd," which was what they all looked like to me. Conscientiously he filled his notebook. If it gave him any clues as to why I had rejected myself he didn't let me in on the secret. After two weeks, however, he had shown me every Rorschach card ever printed, and no sweeping revelation seemed to have been made. Perhaps a slight tendency to coprophilia.

"Well, maybe we've reached the point of diminishing returns with that approach," he admitted. "I'm just thinking off the top of my head now, but suppose we try word associations."

This kept us busy for several days.

"*Sister,*" he would exclaim suddenly, his pencil poised.

"Brother," I would drone. After the first day I knew them all.

"*Black*"

"White."

"*Blood.*"

"Circulation."

"*Grape.*"

"Nuts."

"*Excrement.*"

"Navy psychiatrist."

"Well, you're getting your sense of humor back, anyway. To that extent we're making progress. You see, the amnesia is really only a kind of psychic defense reaction to the organic damage, or rather to the narcissistic blow the organic damage necessarily entails. I mean that ever since your hands were burned you just inwardly don't want to think. This results in a more or less irreversible syndrome of autistic thinking—you refuse to take cognizance of stimuli lying outside your somatic field, or in other words your mind rejects the effort of dealing with external realities. Actually, you see, the ego is simply a set of accumulated memories from the external environment. So a rejection of external reality results automatically in amnesia and loss of personal identity. So you see, your problem is very simple if you look it square in the face and don't try to retreat from it."

But this was only the beginning. The next time he came he explained to me that I was suffering from the Korkasow syndrome. "Although that's just picking a term out of the air," he admitted. "To be frank, diagnosis is largely a matter of semantics. The Korkasow syndrome is characterized by a lack of affective feeling, along with a breakdown of imagination and thought-production. The key to it lies in a failure of registration of sensory stimuli. The patient is aware of his environment, but he sees each event around him as isolated and meaningless."

Now he was getting closer. It was as though I were up in a tree watching a beagle sniffing around looking for a rabbit-hole. I knew more or less where the rabbit was, although it didn't matter to me whether he found it or not, and I took only a mild interest in it as Gore thrashed around in the underbrush. Closer—he's got it! no, he's off the scent again.

"These disturbances—and I think this is particularly pertinent to your case—start on the level on which memory functions are formed. As Buerger-Prinz puts it, the patient's somatic needs and emotions are no longer driving forces. He lacks spontaneity and he is apathetic to external stimuli—which I must say frankly is a good description of your attitude—and his autistic thought-processes dominate the field until he can no longer do anything on his own. Now, for example, the corpsmen tell me you could very easily get out of bed and go to the bathroom by yourself. It would save them a lot of trouble, and frankly I think it would have a salutary effect on your outlook." At this point he was still amiable, although I thought I could detect a slight note of stiffness creeping in.

It was Baroni who made the only real discovery of those first weeks. He would come in once in a while with Gore but he seldom said anything; he would simply sit at the foot of the bed and watch me as Gore talked. Then one afternoon, after a long silence, he announced out of a clear sky, "He was an officer."

Gore looked at him, puzzled. "It's possible, although to be frank the Rorschach and the other tests don't show any particular sense of responsibility—"

Baroni got the lamp from the bedside table and took off the shade. He held it a little above my head and to one side, throwing my face into half-shadow. He was speaking to Gore, but as he talked his glance tacitly included me in what he said. "You see that crease across his forehead? Here—starting high on the right and slanting down to the left. It's faint, but you can see it in the shadow from the lamp. It's the mark of a cap with a hard band. He was an officer or a warrant officer, and he habitually wore his cap over his left ear. You've got a crease like that too; we've all got one. His is deep enough to show through the burns. He must have worn the hat for a good many months." For the first time he spoke directly to me. "Do you remember wearing a cap?"

"I might have."

"We know the officers who were assigned to the *Marcus*, and that narrows it down quite a bit. We have a lot of other data. We even have a chart of your teeth. No fillings, one cracked molar, upper wisdoms slightly impacted. That molar ever hurt you?"

I shook my head.

"Do you remember anything else about your health?" He was still holding the lamp over my head and examining my face. "Your nose has been broken, incidentally. How'd that happen?"

When I seemed unimpressed by this piece of information he got a hand mirror and held it up so I could see. I stared at this asymmetric bump in the middle of my face—it was strange, I still had the same nose! the one the cop in San Pedro, an innocent man who probably loved his wife and was kind to his dog, had fractured with his nightstick for listening to the voice of liberty: "When in the course of human events—" Smack!

"I guess it might have been broken. Anyhow it's a poor excuse for a nose," I muttered through my stiff mouth.

"Why do you say 'pore' for 'poor?'" Baroni wanted to know now. "You came from west of the Mississippi."

If he had gone on like this he might have found out more interesting things about me, for instance that I said creek for stream or that I jerked a little if you yelled "Full astern!" at me suddenly. But the war went on, he was busy now with the survivors off the *Chicago* and he didn't have much time for me. Gore still came every afternoon to give me my lesson in Psychology

1. By this time it was obvious to both of us that he was making very little progress, and a querulous note was beginning to creep into his ebullience. "You know, old fellow, to some extent I fail to understand your attitude. A certain amount of resistance to the analyst is normal, but you reach a point after a while where the patient has to make some slight effort to come to grips with his own problem."

I conceded with my silence that this might indeed be true.

"In fact your very apathy," he went on, "is extraordinary and perhaps revealing. It may be the clue to your whole rejection of identity."

He pondered, and then craftily began stalking the rabbit-hole from another direction.

"Now let's approach it this way," he suggested, assuming his friendly-offhand manner again, "by asking a very simple question. What are you?"

If he could find this out, I thought, he would win my genuine respect. I didn't know, so I looked at him.

"You're a naval officer," he answered for me. "That is, you belong to a service with a long tradition of honor, and a certain code of conduct has been instilled in you. It's become a part of your nature. In a certain sense the Navy, or rather the authority it represents, performs the function of a father figure in your subconscious life. Now, if there is any one tendency running through the Rorschach and the other tests you've taken, it's your rebelliousness or your refusal to accept authority. Your hostility to psychiatrists and your preoccupation with coprophilia, for example, are a part of this pattern." (He *was* annoyed about my calling him a piece of excrement.) "This, to my mind, indicates a deep-seated Oedipal disability. For example, your identification of one card in the Rorschach series as the genitals of a giraffe reveals your subconscious resentment of a long-legged, tall, genital-bearing animal which is easy to identify as a father figure."

He seemed particularly pleased with this item in his demonstration.

"Unfortunately," he went on, "we know nothing about your family history, especially in the infantile stages. But assuming, then, that at the bottom you suffer from a deep-seated Oedipal guilt, how is this involved with your relation to the Navy? Obviously your guilt is transferred to this more immediate manifestation of the father authority. Superficially you respect and obey this authority, as you did your father, but subconsciously your attitude is one of rebellion. Now suppose we put you in a situation of pressure—the sinking of the ship on which you were supposed to behave as an officer and therefore a model of courage and ethical conduct. But in the moments when the ship was sinking, what happened? Perhaps under stress, your latent rebellion asserted itself in some way—and you did something that was not strictly honorable."

He allowed this to sink in for a few moments. When he spoke again it was in a lower tone, friendly and almost conspiratorial, as though he and I shared a secret.

"You see, under conditions of great stress anyone—even an officer of the finest character—might do something he was later ashamed of. He might repress the incident—especially if it had a neurotic origin—and drive it down into the subconscious. But it's still there, and later it may cause a massive psychoneurotic disability. Don't you see—nobody really cares what you did on the ship in those last minutes, but if we could find out it might make you well. The first step is to stir you out of your apathy somehow—to get you to feel *some* emotion—any emotion—over this incident in order to flush it from its hiding place." In his earnestness he forgot to add "so to speak" after this metaphor.

During this long speech Ensign Bledsoe, in the other bed, was following a fly around on the ceiling with his one eye. For some reason this made my face itch. I began wishing my hands weren't bandaged so I could scratch it. The thought occurred to me that probably Gore would scratch it for me if I asked him, but probably also it would annoy him to be interrupted.

"Don't you see, old fellow? Frankly, it's even possible that you were, well, a coward, so to speak—but that isn't important, is it? What's in a name? The important thing is to get it out."

"Oh, go screw yourself," I growled finally.

"Ah, now we've got it. Splendid!" he said enthusiastically. "Do you know, that's the first emotional response you've made since you entered the hospital."

That was the high point in Gore's exploration of my soul. But the scent was false, and he never succeeded in establishing whether I had hysterically struck my superior officer on the nose as the *Marcus* went down or trampled several enlisted men in my anxiety to get to a lifeboat. To tell the truth I don't think Gore had ever been on a sinking destroyer and had very little idea what it was like, that destroyers have no lifeboats, for example. The funny thing was that both he and Baroni were right about me from the beginning, insofar as they came to any conclusions at all, but they were never able to bring it all into focus and see the meaning of what they themselves had discovered because all their thinking was built on one single fact that was incorrect: it never occurred to either of them to question the basic assumption that a man found floating in the water after a ship had sunk must have been a member of its crew. And in the strange world where I lived, contemplating the spots on the ceiling and only half-listening to the voice of Gore in the distance, it began to seem somehow that they were right, that I had belonged to the *Marcus* and shared with her crew something deeper and more basic than I had shared on the ship that had really been mine, even though they had never known my name or I theirs. I had shared pain with them, and they had pushed me up on the raft. Why? Because human life is very precious, with a preciousness apart from the personality it happens to be attached to. They had recognized this instinctively, and they had saved me not because I was a shipmate but because I was a fellow human being and weaker than they were and less able to fend for myself. They might have done the same for the Japanese officer if he had been there, the aviator I had killed in the clearing. What was this strange thing, my life, which those strangers had valued so highly arid which I valued not at all?

As I became more interested in this problem Gore became less interested in it, or at least a slight cloud began to gather on his enthusiasm. I don't know whether it was his idea or Baroni's, but the week after I had invited him to commit an indecency with himself he changed technique radically. One afternoon instead of Gore there arrived a photographer, an enlisted man with a cigarette in his mouth who told me he had worked for a New York daily in civilian life. I sat up in bed holding my cracked face gingerly and he took several shots of me with a Speed Graphic: front face, profile, three-quarters. Then he folded up his camera and went away. For the time being nobody told me what the photos were for. Gore didn't come back for several days. Instead Baroni came in one afternoon, sat in the chair and said he just happened to be passing by and thought he would see how I was getting along, asked me how the food was, and finally said, "You know, I've been looking at those word-association tests that Dr. Gore made."

I waited to see what he was getting at.

"First I had to learn the code he uses to write them down. But I got interested in it, and I noticed a couple of curious things. For example, he tested you three times on the word God. Twice you came back with 'damn,' and the third time 'poplar.' What do you suppose that means?"

I might have mumbled something facetious about only God being capable of making a tree, but I didn't feel in a facetious mood and so I didn't say anything. My face hurt when I talked anyhow. Probably Baroni hadn't traveled very much in the west and he didn't know there was a tree called the Mormon poplar that grew in every desert town from Idaho to the Sierras. Even if I had pointed this out to him it wouldn't have helped, probably. It didn't really explain what the trees had to do with God, or why even now in the hospital sometimes as I went to sleep I would hear the leaves rustling outside the window of the room I thought I had forgotten, the room where I hadn't slept for eight years. But it did seem to me funny that it was Baroni who had noticed this word: what did Intelligence have to do with God?

After two or three days Gore came in to tell me that the photographs had been sent to various people in the States who had lost relatives on the *Marcus*. "You see, we're getting somewhere now, at last. We've got it narrowed down to a half a dozen names. There's one enlisted man, Ellerton, a quartermaster who has relatives in Abilene, Kansas—" (he had never fully accepted Baroni's theory about the crease in my forehead) "and two junior grade lieutenants, Kale and Davenant. Then there's McGuire, an ensign, grew up on a farm near Tacoma. Now do any of these names mean anything to you?"

I was (almost) genuinely sorry that they didn't.

"There is also Preston, the executive officer, who was approximately your height and weight, but frankly I don't see you as an Annapolis man. There are certain character qualities that are missing in the tests, as well as, I might add, in my personal subjective evaluation of your character. Next week," he revealed in conclusion, "we're going to start flying some people out from the States to look at you. I want you to think about this, and try to put yourself in a slightly more cooperative frame of mind than you have in the past."

Obediently for a week I concentrated on these faceless relatives. I had surrendered myself passively to everything that was done to me in the hospital, from changing the bedpan to the

Rorschach cards, and this didn't seem to me any more pointless than the rest. Everything was unreal and yet logical, like a dream in which events, people, fragments of language succeeded each other without any particular connection or significance. Very well, now I was a zoo animal and they were going to charge admission to look at me. When my first visitors arrived one morning they were a pair of rural middle-westerners, the husband with a sun-burned neck and a collar that made him look uncomfortable and the wife in a print dress and a round straw hat set exactly on the middle of her head. These two portraits by Grant Wood came into the room escorted by Baroni, stood looking bleakly at me for a moment, and went away. Nobody ever introduced them to me; I think they must have been the Ellertons, the parents of the enlisted quartermaster. Three or four more people came during the same week. There were two women together, the wife and sister of the gunnery officer Kale, and a stocky fleshy woman with red arms, a cousin of a warrant officer who had no other relatives. There was an enlisted man who had known Davenant, the communications officer, in basic training in San Diego. He had been flown from his ship in the Third Fleet and he was still in dungarees. Out of uniform and surrounded by officers, he felt uncomfortable and didn't know what to do with his hands. He stood in the middle of the room staring at the riddle of my burned face; probably he realized now that it had been a long time ago and he didn't remember his old division officer very well anyhow. Finally he said tentatively, "Lieutenant? Lieutenant Davenant?"

I didn't move so much as a muscle of my face. There was an awkward pause, and finally he raised his shoulders in a kind of gesture of helplessness, as though he didn't know what was expected of him. When Baroni asked him a point-blank question he had to shake his head, and they led him out.

There I lay, wrapped in surgical gauze in the Department of Unclaimed Packages, while various people who had lost things came to look at me. The last ones to arrive that week came a couple of days later. I think they must have been the Prestons, the parents of the executive officer who had been an Annapolis man: an old gentleman with a lean face and a shock of white hair like Bertrand Russel, and a black-clad old woman, pale and dry-eyed. When they came in the room Baroni had fallen a few steps behind them, and at first they turned uncertainly toward Bledsoe's bed. Baroni shook his head and indicated the other bed where I was laying propped up on pillows. This time Gore had come along too. He stood a little behind in the doorway; I could see he was watching not the Prestons but my own face. The Prestons moved slowly towards the middle of the room and stood facing me. The woman was nervous and pale; her lips formed a word. She came a step close to the bed and then she stopped and said softly, almost apologetically, "Son?"

The husband looked at Baroni and swallowed once or twice, saying nothing. After his wife had stood there a long time he took her gently by the shoulders and led her out of the room.

When they were gone Gore took a deep breath and began pacing I back and forth on the linoleum. "You see, old fellow, this is all very hard on people, on everybody concerned. If you could only take a more positive attitude and try to cooperate a little—"

"I'm sorry. They were nothing to me."

"Still, you might try to look a little brighter, you know, and more cheerful. Nobody wants to claim a corpse."

"I'm not asking to be claimed."

"That's not the point, is it? The point is this. Either your subconscious resistance to the therapist and toward your rejected identity is phenomenally strong, due to some undetected cause I haven't yet stumbled across, or you are faking. I don't feel that you have a positive attitude at all toward the course of treatment or toward these people who have made a long trip to try to help with your identification. Frankly I have been very disappointed

in the results. After seven weeks we seem to be getting nowhere."
He had never spoken in such brief and admirably lucid sentences.
"Now let me give you a summary of where we stand at present.
First there is McGuire, grew up on a farm near Tacoma, unmarried.
His mother and father refuse to make positive identification. The
parents of Ellerton, the quartermaster from Kansas, say definitely
no. Kale and Davenant, the two JG's. Kale's father says you're positively not his son but the uncle—" (I had forgotten him, I couldn't
keep all my relatives straight) "thinks you might be and wants to
look again when your face is healed. The enlisted man we flew
in didn't know what to say, and Davenant's parents rejected you
outright from the photographs. Now for the last time, do any of
these names, places, or associations strike any kind of a chord of
response, even, so to speak, subliminal?"

I didn't even bother to shrug this time; I was getting rather tired
of the gesture and besides it hurt the burned place on my chest.

"And there is Preston the executive officer," he went on in a
voice that began to rise a little, "who was about your height and
weight, but I don't really see you as an Annapolis man. Anyhow
we've gone over all this before. I'm going to run down every lead
to the end. But you've got to help, God damn it!" Suddenly and
unexpectedly he began to shout. "Listen, do you understand,
seven weeks I've spent on this, and you just lie there. Will you
try to appreciate the trouble and expense that people are going
to over this, while you're not doing a God damned thing? We fly
sailors in from the Third Fleet, we bring parents and relatives.
I have a file a foot thick on you and all the things we've done
for you. Meanwhile you haven't come an inch to meet us. I'm
going to try drugs next, sodium amytal or pentathol, and if that
doesn't work we'll try insulin shock. It jolts the psychic patterns
and breaks up mental blocks. It also breaks bones sometimes;
you have to be held down by four strong orderlies. We have a lot
of things we haven't tried yet. There's another woman coming

next week, a wife. But frankly I think we've reached the point of diminishing returns on relatives. As long as you refuse to accept your identity, you won't *become* yourself, so to speak, and nobody is going to recognize you."

This was quite philosophical, for Gore. Perhaps the experience was doing something for his own psychic patterns. I said I was sorry to cause so much trouble, and I'd be glad to leave as soon as my hands were well, if they'd give me some clothes to put on. He told me he'd had about enough of my sarcasm.

In conclusion he uttered a pithy word. "We've all got to be somebody, McGuire. You can't lie here the rest of your life without an identity, so to speak, getting three meals a days. That's too easy."

I don't know why he called me McGuire. I think by then he had reached the point where he had to call me something; he was used to a world where everything had a name and after those weeks of groping for phantoms his own sense of reality had reached the threshold of shattering, as a fine glass can be shattered by a soprano singing a high note.

Chapter 11

.-- .... --- .- -- ..   .-- .... --- .- -- ..   .-- .... --- .- -- ..   .-- .... --- .- -- ..

Over the weekend Gore left me alone. On Saturday morning they took the dressings permanently off my hands. The scar tissue had begun to form, and in a basin of tepid water I stretched the fingers tentatively and felt the muscles work under the stiff and thickened skin. Before lunch Waldbach came in to look at the hands. "They'll be stiff for a while. You'll have to exercise them in hot water—not lukewarm like that—hot, as hot as you can stand it. It'll be six months, probably, until you have full movement." The rest of my burns were almost healed now; he scarcely glanced at them. Only the bad place on the cheek was still tender, although the whole face still looked like a lump of something you find in a butcher shop. I wasn't surprised that nobody wanted to recognize it; I didn't recognize it myself. Luckily I had never particularly cared for my face anyhow, so I didn't feel any desire to go out the window like Bledsoe. In any case my life didn't seem important enough to me to go to such efforts to end it. Before you could even swat a fly you had to be annoyed at it, and I seemed to have forgotten how to feel even the most rudimentary emotions, the ones that for most people are like reflexes. I didn't particularly care: would I be any happier with emotions? And what emotions would I feel if I felt any?

Sunday and Monday I spent mostly sleeping and working my hands in the basin of hot water: clench, open, clench, open. I could get out of bed now with the corpsman helping me, but my hands were tender and it was painful to hold on to things. After the weeks in bed I was feeble and I had forgotten how to stand up. Shakily, the corpsman holding me under the shoulders, I walked as far as the bathroom. It was better when I was back in bed, weak and a little dizzy under the cool sheets.

For some reason now I was sleepy all day. Perhaps it was a symptom of convalescence. It was hot in the room and they had opened the windows so that a light breeze came through the steel grill. As I lay half asleep I could hear the planes warming up their engines on Ford Island a mile away, and once in a while the hoarse shaking of a ship's whistle. I wondered if Bledsoe could hear the planes and whether he remembered everything that had happened, or whether he had retreated into a land of unreal timelessness like me where the past and present were all the same and nothing was very important. I thought probably he hadn't, that he still remembered and thought about things, and I had no desire to come out of my phantasmagoria and be as he was, alert, conscious, and agonized. It was better as I was, except when Gore came around and I had to answer questions. I dozed, woke up now and then, and went back to sleep. When they woke me up for meals I ate everything they brought and drifted off to sleep again as soon as they had taken the tray away.

I ended by losing track of the days. It must have been Tuesday when the corpsman on duty came in and woke me up, leaving the door open behind him. I thought he had come in to crank up the bed and get me ready for dinner, but after him came Gore, and then unexpectedly someone else appeared in the doorway. I was still half asleep and at first all I was aware of was a woman in a tailored linen suit with a scarf. Then I saw she was young and I noticed the striking darkness of her eyes against the white face. She walked in the room and looked around at everything as though she were being shown her suite in a hotel (the corpsman played the bellboy, Gore the assistant manager), then she saw me across the room and, pulling off her gloves, said quite casually, "Hello, darling. I thought it was you." A moment later she was bending over the bed and I felt the light touch of her lips on my forehead; I caught an elusive scent of linen and perfume. Even then I was not fully awake. And yet in those few seconds when everything hung on a knife edge I committed myself by my silence. I felt words forming in my mouth, but I couldn't arrange them properly; the time passed when I might have spoken and still I said nothing. I had never lied before, to Gore or Baroni, but now the seconds raced away and with each second the implication of my silence became more concrete and fatal. I knew I had made a decision; in that moment when I might have spoken I had *chosen* silence, even though it had been mostly out of apathy, and in doing so I chose for myself a certain reality over all the other possible forms of reality. After that first moment I was committed permanently to the words, the gestures, everything that followed. Inside I felt something precious and irretrievable slipping away from me: my right to nothingness. And somehow she, this stranger, had succeeded, merely by walking in the room, where Gore after seven weeks had failed.

For a while neither of us spoke. She put her handbag on the bed and I lay looking at her while she smiled. She was not a woman I would ever have noticed in a crowd. Her head was large with a slender, rather nervous neck; long black hair that seemed too heavy for the rest of her fell carelessly over her forehead. But at first you didn't notice these details; instead you saw only her eyes, which were large, dark, and sagacious and seemed to take everything in without making any particular effort to be observant. In spite of her outward calm she had a gesture of pushing the hair back from her forehead with a motion of her hand, as though the weight of it hampered her when she was trying to think or deciding what to say. She made this gesture now, and started to say something but changed her mind and was silent again.

Gore was still standing awkwardly in the middle of the room behind her. "Mrs. Davenant—" he ventured finally.

She turned with mild surprise as though she had forgotten him and then smiled at him too, but it was a quite formal and impersonal smile, the one you make to the assistant manager when the room is perfectly all right and you don't need him anymore. Now that Gore had finally attracted her attention he found he didn't know what to say, and as he hesitated for a moment he found himself overwhelmed by her placid assurance. In the end it was she who spoke instead. "Now we'll have to see about getting him out of here. I hope it isn't too complicated? I hate red tape."

"Well, I really don't know. He's still convalescent psychically as well as physically, you know, and his hands—"

"He doesn't walk on his hands, and there are doctors in California." He turned to me. "And do you, Lieutenant—" (he almost called me McGuire again) "do you, do you—" It was too much, he couldn't say it. He lifted his shoulders resignedly and left, muttering, "You people would probably like to be left alone."

"He was trying to say, 'Do you take this woman?'" she finished for him after he had gone.

I started to laugh, and then I remembered that this hurt my mouth and I stopped. I think I made a kind of a lopsided smile. We were silent. She got a cigarette out of her handbag and lit it, waving out the match, looking around through the cloud of smoke for a place to put it and finally dropping it on the floor. After a while she said, casually but with a kind of a diffident hesitation, "You don't remember anything?"

I made a faint negative motion of my head.

"That's what they said. They said it would probably begin to come back when you got home. You know, they only sent the photographs last week. You were in here for three months and this idiot Navy never told us anything. First they said you were missing, then definitely dead. But they wouldn't pay the insurance or send the discharge papers, and there was something queer about it. An intelligence officer from San Diego came up to see us twice. Finally they said there was one survivor off the ship but they didn't think it was you. Then they sent the photos. What imbeciles!"

She paused. "Although I must say I hardly recognized you in the photos. I think it was because your hair was burned off." She was looking at my face but there wasn't a trace of uncertainty in her manner now; her expression was curious and a little fastidious, as though she were looking at a burn on her own face and found it rather unpleasant but something she would probably get used to in the end. She sat talking for another ten or fifteen minutes, mostly about trivialities, asking me whether the food was good in the hospital and whether I needed anything. She talked in short assertive sentences, in a manner that seemed slightly flippant and superficial at first but was only one of her mannerisms. I lay on the pillow looking at her, and when she asked a question I would think what the answer was and nod rather vacantly or shake my head. When my dinner came they asked her to leave. She said she would come back that evening, in the regular visiting hours.

I ate my dinner, feeling nothing in particular, or rather not able for the moment to grasp exactly how it was I felt. I could hold a spoon after a fashion now, although my fingers were still too cramped to handle a knife and fork. I was intent on getting my lamb stew into the spoon and for the time being it didn't occur to me to reflect that I had acted in some other way than I should have acted. That this brisk young woman who seemed so sure of herself was mistaken was a fact of no interest to me, or rather it was a meaningless assertion. A silence, I knew, could be a lie, yet I hadn't represented things as other than they were, since I had given up believing that things were any particular way. The way things were was simply determined by the way people acted toward them. If Gore treated me as insane, a coward, a malingerer, I was these things, just as for Waldbach I was a moderately interesting medical problem and for Baroni a cipher, an annoying broken cog in an intelligence system. As far as I was concerned I was totally uninterested in the problem; I was content to let others make of me what they wanted. To myself, for the present, I remained something inchoate, nascent, self-sufficient. It seemed that in the darkness, blundering around in a marsh, I had wandered across some kind of a Rubicon. For the moment I was more interested in the lamb stew; it (like talking) hurt my face but at least it was solid and you knew what it was. What the hell, I was getting better, I was aware of what I was eating! With cautious voracity I consumed a dish of Jello.

But Gore was right; we all have to be somebody. How did you do it? The idea of having an identity that belonged to you seemed mysterious now and I had forgotten the trick. But I felt that in some elusive way it was connected with having a name, and now I knew why names had been invented: not so that people could be told apart, but so that each person would know who he was. After you had a name you moved through the world constantly aware of your identity: not that you went around saying the name to yourself, but the name lay there in the dark of your mind, forming your sensations, marking each experience with its stamp. With each event in your consciousness you knew: *this is happening to me*. I had been this way too once, but something had slipped away and I no longer believed in a me; I simply existed, hovered like a spectator in a universe of abstract impressions, aware not of *this is happening to me* but simply of *this is happening*. Thus it seemed—not natural since nothing seemed natural anymore—but perfectly unremarkable for the dark-eyed young woman in the tailored suit to stand by my bed and call me by a name that was not mine, or even to bend over and kiss me on the forehead. It was Gore, Baroni, *the others* who had found her and brought her to the bed. In the queer unreal dreamlike mental state of the hospital room even her scent as she had bent over the bed seemed familiar and normal, like something remembered out of a previous existence. And so, lacking any particular reason to do otherwise, I had performed my simple act of affirmation: my silence. If someone had come along and told me, "You are Pope Innocent the Third, you are Amelia Earhart's copilot Fred Noonan," it would have had exactly the same reality as Gore telling me I was a Korkasow's Syndrome or a malingerer. They were the ones who said it and I was ready to be whatever they wanted, as long as it required no particular effort, and above all no talking.

For the moment I was content to be an alimentary canal. After I finished my dinner I just lay digesting it for a while, oddly serene and not thinking about anything in particular. A little after seven that evening *she* (I didn't even know her name!) came back. She sat in a chair with her legs crossed and for a while didn't say anything. She hadn't even greeted me. She opened her handbag and began looking through it.

"Do they let you smoke?"

"No."

"Why not?"

"Hurts my face."

"Have one anyhow."

She put the cigarette between my lips and lit it. The heat of the match burned my cracked lips, but the taste after the months of not smoking rose pungently into the back of my mouth. It was a kind of cigarette I had never heard of before, mild and faintly perfumed, with an ivory tip. I lay savoring the novel and yet familiar flavor and watching the smoke curling over the bed.

"I have space on the *President Jackson* on Friday."

"What day is this?"

"Tuesday. First I have to get you out of this damned hospital. There's a lot of red tape but it seems I can get you transferred as an outpatient to the naval hospital in Long Beach. They say they can't release you because you're a psychiatric patient and still deranged."

"Maybe I am."

"I'll worry about that. We'll go to Laguna first and stay for a while before we get involved with the hospital, so you can get some rest. You must have had enough of hospitals anyhow. Do you re-member the house in Laguna?"

I shook my head.

"It's on the cliff, over the beach. The bedroom faces the sea and you can hear the surf at night. It'll all begin to fit together after a while. Leo will be there; I cabled him this afternoon and told him we'd be home around the tenth. And Suzanne is living with us too now. I don't think you knew that Carl is in North Africa. Before they shipped him out they made him a Pfc. and Suzanne went around telling everybody as though he were a general, the dear girl. But of course she's always been totally irrational on the subject of Carl. She's anxious to meet you. Of course she and Carl were away in Georgia before. She said Benning was awful, incidentally."

I reached up for the cigarette and found even this faint glow was painful to my hand. She took it out of my mouth, knocked the ash off onto the floor, and put it back in again.

"In Laguna we'll be close to Long Beach in case they want to look at your hands or X-ray your brain or anything. Do you know what that precious idiot Dr. Gore told me? That the tests showed you were above average in intelligence but psychopathically irresponsible."

"He's probably right."

"I brought a suitcase full of clothes. I don't know if they're what you would have wanted." For the first time I noticed it standing over against the wall, a worn but expensive pigskin weekender with Mexican travel labels all over it.

"Did you get that purse in Mexico?" I ventured. It was my first spontaneous sentence.

"This?" She glanced at the tooled-leather handbag she wore over her shoulder. "Of course. You bought it for me in Cuernavaca. Don't you remember the shop with the woman who looked like an authentic Aztec and turned out to be named Monogan?"

She stood up and wandered toward the window with her cigarette; she acted as though she was getting a little bored with the hospital. "My God, they've got bars on the windows—you'd drink you were a criminal. If you need more things, clothes or anything, we can buy them in Honolulu. I brought a pile of money, all cash. You always used to disapprove of that. You said I ought to carry a checkbook. When I bought the return passages the ticket agent was shocked. I began taking the money out and it was all fives and tens; it made a heap on the counter a foot high. I think he thought I was a streetwalker."

The orderly was in the room sweeping the floor, and this time she made him go out and get her an ashtray. She crushed out the cigarette.

When the orderly had gone she said, "For a while it'll be odd, your not remembering anything. In a way it'll be easier; we'll be starting over. Everything we do will be for the first time. At first when I thought about it the idea scared me a little, but then I decided this was what everybody wanted—a chance to start over. You know, we were awfully young, and we made a lot of mistakes. In a way your parents were right. But it wasn't," she insisted, "just because I was young. The fact is they simply didn't approve of me, and I don't think they do even yet."

Here she made one of her serene pauses. The conversation

(or rather monologue, I didn't say anything) was filled with long silences which neither of us seemed to find awkward. She went on telling me that the house next door had been rented by a Marine major, that because of the gas rationing they had decided to keep her Ford instead of trading it for a larger car. I accepted these small pieces of information naturally, as though she was talking about something I knew. I didn't feel it necessary to make any comment; I sensed that she was talking most of all to reassure me, to bring me back into the world of familiar things. I lay quietly watching her, I noticing now the strong and yet somehow fragile line of her throat, the expensive cut of her suit, the way she stood with her feet apart in a casual fashion-model slouch that was not particularly like any woman I had ever encountered before. I remember looking at the tailored jacket and thinking that her breasts were probably not much, and wondering whether she was more nervous than usual or whether she was always this way. But her nervousness wasn't the kind that made others nervous; it was a kind of animal awareness under the surface that she controlled with a deliberate outward calm.

She moved quickly but with precision, her head with its heavy hair ' somehow languid in spite of the quickness of her eyes. I lay there watching her while she talked, answering now and then in monosyllables and hardly paying attention to what she was saying, absorbing the newness and yet the odd familiarity of it, like the half-forgotten taste of the cigarette she had given me. She chatted on about the big Hawaiian ferns in the hospital foyer which she had never seen before and about my alleged skill at tennis which would perhaps be impaired by my burned hands. Finally she said, at the end of a long speech, "I don't want to tire you. I'll come back tomorrow. It'll be in the afternoon, though. In the morning I have to go see a while procession of admirals about getting you transferred. I'll wear something décolleté." She kissed me on the forehead for the second time that day, a brief domestic gesture, and left. On her way out she stopped at Bledsoe's bed. "Don't you have any kith or kin to visit you?" I heard her asking blithely. He shook his head. "I'll bring something the next time I come. Perhaps a little calve's-foot jelly." The miracle was that Bledsoe smiled.

I lay for a while looking at the half-darkened empty room and the suitcase standing against the wall. After I had thought about it for a long time I finally pushed myself upright in bed and gingerly lifted the sheet off my legs. Then I swung the legs around, inch by inch, until they were dangling over the side of the bed and with infinite precautions lowered them to the floor. It was the first time I had got out of bed without the corpsman. I couldn't hold on to anything with my hands, and because my legs felt weak I was afraid of falling, but somehow I made my way across the room to the suitcase. It wasn't locked. I tried to open the catches with the backs of my hands, but it was no good and I saw I was going to have to use my fingers. The sharp metal edges dug into the half-healed flesh; I set my teeth and finally managed to pry open the catches. I felt rather foolish, and it would be even more awkward if anyone came in the room and found me going through the suitcase like a child taking a peek at his Christmas presents, but I positively had to see what was in it and I had to do it now, while she wasn't watching. I had an odd feeling that the secret of everything was inside the suitcase, that the clothes I put on would impose their form on me, sink into me somehow and in the end determine what I was going to be. The future was there inside the suitcase—something concrete, not merely a revery or a possibility but a *reality* in which I would have to live and move and assume a reality of my own. Well, for hell's sake, all this philosophizing about lifting a lid? What did I expect, snakes? Inside there would be clothes, you put them on and forgot about them. Kneeling down, I raised the lid gingerly with my fingernails. From his bed Bledsoe watched me silently with his single eye.

No snakes, just clothes. On top there were some flannel slacks and a pair of tailored Bermuda shorts. A half-dozen handkerchiefs, monogrammed "BD." A pair of tan loafers, some sport shirts in conservative solid colors. Sunglasses, underwear, an electric razor with its cord, socks in Argyll plaids. Strapped into the top of the lid was a carefully folded sport jacket, a soft tweed in a dark bluish gray. Everything was expensive, conservative, and carefully packed. These things were mine now, I thought, or rather *I belonged to them*. I wondered whether something would change in me when I put them on and I would feel different, or whether it would be the other way around, my essence that would sink into the clothes, gradually wearing away their strangeness and making them familiar. For that, of course, you would have to have an essence. On the whole I would have preferred to stay as I was in the anonymous hospital pajamas. But the clothes were mine now for better or worse; I had passed the point where I could choose or reject them.

I lowered the lid carefully and latched it. On the long and precarious journey back to the bed I caught a glimpse of myself in the mirror. It was the face of a stranger, a patchwork in various shades of red, expressionless except for the left side of the mouth still pulled a little upward by the shrunken muscle. The leanness was skull-like; growing out of the scalp there were meager tufts of brown hair. You're an ugly brute whoever you are, I told the face in the glass. But I knew who he was; he was the owner of the clothes in the suitcase. For a few seconds that afternoon I had balanced on the razor edge, and then I had chosen and now the clothes were mine, or rather they *were myself*, a new human being I would have to study and master. For an instant I felt the vertigo of empty space: where was I going? I realized I was still sick and I got back in bed.

I lay in bed and thought about it in a muddled feverish way. Did I still have a fever? Whether or not it was logical this is what I thought. The child doesn't will to be born. He lies passively in the womb until the muscles squeeze him out, and from that moment he gets involved in an elaborate chain of things that are beyond his control. He can cry or not cry just as he pleases, but for the rest he can't choose: time and place of birth, name, sex, rhythm of feedings and excretions. He is the object of pressures inside him and out that are none of his doing. Well, but isn't man free? Yes, but the child's freedom is still something to be won. Nobody gives it to him; only gradually does he free himself from the things that have made him and create his unique nature, his self. He does this by making choices. For a long time he just lies there accepting everything, but then he starts discriminating: he swallows Cream of Wheat but spits out strained prunes. This way he makes his personality. And in choosing between A and B he creates his own freedom, because freedom is simply the state of being able to make decisions.

But somewhere back in the past I had given up this right to make decisions. Perhaps it was the night I was burned in the water, or perhaps it was some time much earlier, when I had let life do what it wanted to me and just drifted along not giving a damn, like most of the other people I had known. At any rate in the hospital I had become a foetus again. I liked it that way and so for three months I had been content to lie there in a state of embryonic irresponsibility. Things were done to me, I allowed them to be done, it was warm in there under the covers and if I wanted to urinate or eat these things were provided for. There was safety in darkness; Gore and the others could prod the outside of the womb if they wanted but I wasn't coming out. But what I didn't know was that this only lasts for nine months at best and in my case not even that long. Something pushed me or pulled me and out I came: Benton Davenant, Lieutenant (j.g.) USNR, cum laude University of Washington and Kappa Phi, connoisseur of monogrammed handkerchiefs, wearer of tan loafers and flannel slacks. I felt suddenly cold, there was space out here, too much of it, and things were not provided by osmosis anymore, not simply absorbed into your skin. Out here things had to be seized and grasped, choices had to be made. When do we eat? When do we excrete? Do I wear my shirt open at the neck, my belt notched in the third hole, carry my change in my right-hand pocket? It was incredible that all the others, those who didn't live in hospitals, had to go around making decisions like this all day. And I knew that with each decision I would define myself, each decision was infinitely crucial. With my tongue I felt the strange hardness of my teeth, wondering whose they were. My body was as strange to me as my clothes. I held up my right hand before my eyes, ordered the forefinger to move, and it moved. When I lowered the hand it came to rest between my legs, and I broke out in a cold sweat. My body was bad enough, but that other body, the dark eyes, pale forehead, boyish breasts in the tailored jacket, what was I supposed to do about that? Everything we do will be for the first time." And suppose you did it wrong, would there be another chance?

It was all unreal. My mental state was confused, febrile, nightmarish, yet in a curious way crafty and alert. She came back the next afternoon and I found out her name by an ingenious ruse. I lay face down with my eyes closed, pretending to be drowsing, although I wasn't so sleepy now anymore. Sound of the door opening, heels on the linoleum floor, the now familiar odor of linen and perfume.

"O, you sluggard."

"Who is it?"

"Me."

"Nurse? go away."

"No, me. Ary."

I rolled gingerly over and opened my eyes. The same suit, the same Mexican handbag. She sat down and talked and I listened more to the sound of her voice than to the words. The décolleté had worked on the admirals and she had orders in the handbag transferring me to outpatient section, USNH Long Beach. When my hands were healed they would give me a medical discharge with compensation for partial disability. There was some holdup, however, about the Purple Heart.

For the first time I noticed what she was saying. "What did I do to get a Purple Heart?"

"You got your hands burned. I think it's more or less automatic. Anyhow, didn't you hold up a drowning comrade or commit some similar heroism?"

"I think somebody held me up. At the time I didn't care whether he did or not. I wish I knew who he was."

She was getting a cigarette for me out of her bag. "You're beginning to remember," she said offhandedly as she shut the bag and lit the cigarette for me.

And I was. But what was it I was beginning to remember? I wondered if somebody had told her to make that remark, that casual question that had led me so easily into a minor confession. Because it was a confession; I accepted myself for what she and the others had told me I was and yet in some lurking uneasy part of my mind I knew I was not. I was like a sleepwalker who suddenly becomes partly awake and is aware of the space all around him. One false step and I would fall off the roof. What had I said? It was more than I had ever told Baroni or Gore. Well, somebody *had* held me up! The line between memory and fantasy seemed suddenly blurred, elusive. I lay for a moment thinking, as though extracting something from the darkness. And suppose the memory was an illusion, only an ephemeral shadow after all—if I were as helpless as the others to establish the plain neat reality of what had happened? The past was formless and fluid, a kind of a cloud that was already evaporating at the edges. For the past to exist it would be necessary for somebody to believe in it. And suppose I chose to believe in something else instead, the pastless reality before me in the suitcase?

You're beginning to remember. Fine, now we're getting somewhere; but what did I remember? "Only that moment, in the water. Somebody pushed me onto a raft. Before that, nothing."

And even as I said this I realized it was true; before that there was only a kind of a limbo, unpeopled and eventless, a past I was aware of in the way you remember a book you have read a long time ago and then forgotten the plot, the title, the characters, everything except a dim recollection that such a book existed. This was what amnesia was; and I knew now it was possible beyond any malingering or fakery to *choose* amnesia, the way you might choose suicide, or heroism, or going into a religious order. It was against nature and it was a land of obliterating your own essence but so were all these other things. These things also had in common that they were all irreversible. "Hell, what does it matter?" I muttered half to myself and half to her. "Remembering or not remembering, it doesn't change anything."

She had lit the cigarette and now she took it out of her own mouth and put it between my lips. She held it out with her left hand and I noticed for the first time the wedding ring, a plain band of white gold; there was no engagement ring.

"And Leo? The house in Laguna? The Mexico trip?"

I shook my head.

"It'll come back. It's a matter of time."

"Is that what Dr. Gore told you?"

"No, that's what I told Dr. Gore. He told me you preferred amnesia and would probably never come out of it."

"He's a good psychiatrist. He told me I subconsciously rejected my past."

"Why not? I reject mine too. The past is a very boring subject. Everyone who is intelligent rejects his past."

It was odd and a little uncanny in that conversation that she said things and I said things and I couldn't keep it straight in my mind which of us said them. It was as though we only had one

204

consciousness between us and these ideas floated around through it hanging like a kind of a cloud over both of us at once. Probably this was all part of the hospital-phantasmagoria or passive unreality I had been living in for weeks; I seized onto her mind the way you cling reflexively to the shoulders of anybody, even a stranger, who is trying to lift you out of bed when you are weak. Was it she or I who had said there was no past? "And so there's just the future?"

"No, just the present."

I heard myself making another stab in the dark. "I don't remember you as quite so philosophical."

"Perhaps I've gotten more so lately. You see, you were dead for three months. I had to accept that and go on from there. Once the first shock was over I sat down and thought things out. And then after a while I saw that the present was all there was. There was no point in feeling grief or remorse or wishing things had been some other way. And it was impossible to live in the future, because it was something that didn't exist yet, it had to be created moment by moment. After that I just went on as I had before, cooking meals, brushing my hair, listening to music. If Leo had been an ordinary father he might have reproached me with 'not being faithful to your memory' or some other such boring remark. But he didn't say anything. I think he understood what it was that was going on inside me and knew there was no point in interfering, that it might even be dangerous and tip me over some kind of an edge. Then the pictures came, and the last telegram. I packed your clothes in the suitcase and came. I hadn't driven you into the grave with my grief, you see, and so I didn't have to resurrect you. It was as though nothing had happened and you'd been there all along."

I remember the easy natural way she had come into the room that first time, and then I remembered the suitcase. "I'd never thought about wearing clothes again. It's an odd idea."

"I had thought about getting everything new, to make a new start. But you can't get very good things now because of the war, the pants have no cuffs and so forth. Anyhow I wasn't sure of your size—anymore." Later, much later, I remembered that slight pause before the end of the sentence. At the time I was too busy being astute in my devious invalid's way.

"What shoes did you bring? The tan loafers?"

She nodded, with an expression I hadn't noticed before, a kind of subdued smile at the corners of her mouth. I lay watching the line of her cheekbones and the dark hollow at the base of her throat. It was her energy and movement, I saw now, that gave her face its vivacity; in repose her leanness was shadowy and a little tired under the surface poise.

"When can I put on the clothes?"

"Any time. Right now, if you like."

"Will they let me?"

"You're in my custody. I'll flaunt the papers," she said, touching the handbag.

In the presence of her calm I began to feel a kind of vertiginous confidence. I pushed myself up weakly in bed and handed her the half-smoked cigarette.

"Can you get out of bed by yourself?"

I couldn't see Bledsoe, but I could imagine him listening behind the screen. "No. Or I don't think so."

I swung my feet over the side of the bed and she slipped her arm under my shoulders. I stood up, feeling the pressure of her arm and the firmness of her body against my side, and made my way across the room to the suitcase.

"You'll have to open it. I can't work the clasps."

She lifted the suitcase onto a chair and opened it for me. Then she turned quite naturally away and stood looking for a moment out the window. I pulled the drawstring of the hospital pajama pants and stepped out of them. Tottering on one foot, I managed to get into a pair of underpants. She turned and glanced at me, not offering to help. I finished dressing by myself: the flannel slacks, the socks, loafers, then I pulled off the top of the pajamas and put on a dark blue sport shirt with short sleeves. The shoes were a little loose but the rest of it fitted me perfectly.

I was suddenly tired. I sat down in the chair.

"So much for the first lesson," she said. "A for effort. It is customary in refined society, however, to zip the fly."

On Friday I dressed again, taking off the hospital pajamas for the last time. The corpsman brought me my breakfast and I ate it sitting up at a little table. Around ten o'clock Ary arrived with Gore, the head nurse on the floor (the formidable square-jawed one I hadn't seen since the day I came into the ward), and an orderly with a chromium wheelchair. I got in and allowed myself to be wheeled along the corridors. At the ambulance entrance Gore started to shake my hand and then instead gave me an awkward pat on the shoulder.

"Good luck, Lieutenant. To some extent I think you're much better. Although frankly I think you have some problems ahead of you. I've spoken of them to Mrs. Davenant, and—well, never mind about that now." He didn't know how to go on and instead he turned and stalked off. It was the last I ever saw of him. The weakness you get after weeks in a hospital is funny and I felt a little twinge of something like sadness, or perhaps it was regret, as he disappeared down the corridor. Before I came he had been as happy as a boy scout and as pure as St. Francis, and I had made him lose his temper. I was sorry now it had happened.

With the orderly helping me I lowered myself carefully into the taxi, holding my hands tucked under my elbows so they wouldn't get hurt. The suitcase was put in the trunk behind and Ary's baggage was already at the pier. The taxi pulled out of the drive and went down a boulevard full of traffic; the tropical sun hurt my eyes and I leaned back on the seat squinting. Taxis! streets! the city was full of people hurrying somewhere, people who had appointments, jobs, friends, complications, projects, crises. All this had gone on just as usual while I was lying in the white room and I had forgotten it. The emotion and intensity of it bewildered me, and the thought that I was going to have to live and move in this world and hurry around like these people made me tired. I lay back on the seat, not answering when Ary spoke. She didn't seem to notice, or if she did she didn't comment on it.

At the pier I looked out the taxi window and saw an oddly familiar silhouette: the bridge and the two funnels of the big President liner sticking up over the shed, looking strange now because it was all painted a toneless gray. It was a ship I had seen a hundred times, the big black hull with the white superstructure moving out through the Golden Gate or coming up over the horizon in mid-Pacific, but all that had been in a different universe, *before*, and I couldn't connect it with this gray bulk I now saw rising up behind the warehouse. This was fresh, new, hard, palpable, and other seemed like a fuzzily remembered dream. Still a little dazed by the sun, I allowed myself to be led out of the taxi, across an expense of asphalt crisscrossed with railroad tracks, and up a gangway. Most of the other passengers going aboard were dependents of service men being shipped back home; there were a few other wounded heroes like me with assorted slings and bandages. It was the first time in my life I had been a passenger on a ship. These long decks full of chattering women seemed to have nothing to do with the kind of ship I had known, with machinery, boilers, a crew who had to work. In an obscure part of my mind I recognized familiar sounds, the chatter of cargo winches, a deep-throated hum from under the deck which meant that the watch below was turning over the turbines to warm them up: back a hundred turns, stop, then ahead a hundred turns. But it didn't really register and the ship remained for me what I imagined it seemed to the other passengers, a more or less palatial hotel where we would sleep for a week while a crew whose business it was carried us to San Francisco. Ary had managed to get a good cabin on A-deck, large, with two portholes and a lot of arty leather furniture. We inspected everything and then went to eat lunch in the dining room. She cut up my meat and I practiced holding a fork, gripping it solidly in spite of the electric shocks it sent up my arm. I was nervous, and she noticed it. After lunch she suggested going to the bar.

The bar was paneled in leather and the lights were dim. Here I felt better; I realized that one reason I had been edgy was that all morning the sun had been hurting my eyes. I remembered the sunglasses in the suitcase and made a mental note to put them on the next time I went outside. I had never worn sunglasses in my life.

The barman looked up expectantly.

"You used to like Alexanders," she reminded me.

I hesitated.

"But I can't remember," she added, "whether it was gin or brandy."

"Two brandy Alexanders," I told the barman impulsively.

Like her cigarettes the drinks were something for women: frappe, delicately pungent, elegant. I made a second mental note, to announce that my taste had changed to bourbon and water. Or was this considered vulgar? We sat silently at the bar sipping. There was a muffled vibration from underneath and then three long blasts from the whistle; the ship was backing out of the berth. Our glances met very briefly, but neither of us said anything.

When we finished the Alexanders we had another round (tomorrow would be soon enough to announce my conversion to bourbon) and then we went back to the cabin so I could rest. According to Waldbach I was supposed to get plenty of sleep, and besides my weakness and the alcohol I wasn't used to anymore had made me a little feverish and everything seemed buzzing and slightly fuzzy. In the cabin she pulled the green baize curtains over the portholes. It was dark and cool, as though the light came from underwater, and through the portholes you could hear the rhythmic washing of the wake as the ship moved out from Diamond Head. I kicked off my shoes and painstakingly, working methodically at each button took off my shirt and pants. She turned back the covers and I slid sideways into bed. When she bent to pull the covers up over me her face was near and in the half-darkened cabin I was conscious of her fragrance, the heavy shadow of the hair that hung downward toward me, the coolness of her hands. The thing I did in that moment as she hung over me was half automatic and yet quite conscious and willed: I reached up with my useless hands and crossed my wrists under the dark hair, pulling the shadowy fragrance downward and then rolling sideways to crush it and merge with its softness. It was important that handless and crippled as I was, weak, sleepy, only half desiring, I still willed this first gesture and reached to her myself, and perhaps she understood this too and wanted it to happen that way.

Chapter 12

.- .... --- .- -- ..   .- .... --- .- -- ..   .- .... --- .- -- ..   .- .... --- .- -- ..

In San Francisco she took care of everything. At the dock she ordered everybody briskly around, found a place for me to sit down when there was a delay with the baggage, and miraculously procured a taxi. Hotel rooms were hard to get because of the war but she had cabled ahead to the Mark Hopkins. I let her do whatever she wanted; I couldn't use my hands anyhow and I accepted the role of a passive invalid that had become a habit with me in the long months in the hospital. At the hotel we went up in the elevator and walked along a carpeted corridor, and the boy showed us into a room with dark red drapery. There were two small sofas, a coffee table, and chairs in pale gold. I wondered if we were going to sleep on the sofas. Then the boy opened another door and showed us the bedroom. I had heard of suites but it had never really struck me before what the word meant. I suppose I had imagined politicians smoking cigars in them, or Greta Garbo giving interviews. It all seemed perfectly natural that we should have a suite; it was just that I had the feeling of waking up in a strange place and not knowing for a moment where I was, except that instead of lasting for just a moment the sensation lasted all day.

They were bringing in the bags, and she automatically opened her purse. I knew they would wonder why she took care of the tip instead of me, but it occurred to me for the first time that my pockets were empty, and that even if I had money I wouldn't have known how much to give them, a nickel or five dollars, because I had never stayed in a decent hotel before in my life. I turned and looked out the window while she dealt with this problem. It was a clear day with a light haze, and you could see all the way across the bay to; the Berkeley hills. It seemed strange to me that I had been in this city before. It was the same city but there was something about it that was not right; I recognized the shapes, the Ferry Building, Coit Tower, the Bay Bridge, but from a window in the tenth story of the Mark Hopkins it all had the glossy unreal quality of a travel brochure. Down in the bay off the Embarcadero a Navy tanker was backing out of a slip. It moved slowly until it reached the open water, then a tug came up and began pushing at its bow to turn it. It was a toy: two toys, the tanker and the tug, revolved on the polished toy surface of the bay. I left the window and turned back into the room.

She had gone into the bedroom to change. I went silently through the door and watched her from the rear as she pulled on the only other dress she had brought with her, a black cocktail dress with a low neck. She didn't see me at first, and I stood waiting for her to make the gesture all the other women I had known made, the vulgar waggle of the bottom to shake the skirt down. But she only smoothed the skirt deftly with the palms of her hands and then turned toward me. Evidently there was more than one way to put on a dress.

"Do you like the hotel?"

"It's fine. Can we afford it?"

She smiled. "Why do you ask that?"

"It's just that I don't know how much we have, that's all, so I don't know where we stand."

"Enough to get home. Don't worry about it."

"That's not what I mean."

"What do you mean?"

I still felt a little annoyed about the bellboys and I was determined to get to the bottom of this thing about money, although I didn't know quite what it was I wanted to know or how to go about finding it out.

"I mean are we rich or what?"

She laughed. "Now what am I supposed to say to that?" She reached up with both hands to fasten the snap behind her neck. "We have enough to stay at the Mark, if that's what's bothering you."

I realized she had been right to laugh; it was a naive question and there were some things you couldn't ask but only find them out day by day, the way ordinary people come to know whether they are rich or poor, beautiful or ugly. I had known before I said it that it was something I shouldn't have asked, but I was like an actor reading a part who hasn't quite got the feel of the play yet and reads his lines mechanically, trying to work out the natural gestures. To be natural was something that should have been easy, but now it seemed to me the most difficult thing in the world. I was not well yet, my mind was not well and my body was not well, and everything made me incredibly tired. I had to decide how to tip bellboys, whether to put on the bottoms of my pajamas first or the tops, how to get rid of the dishes after we had had lunch served in the room. I had been to the movies and this last was fairly easy: "Room service? Will you—" etc. But five minutes later I made another blunder. It was after lunch and we were in the bedroom; she was lying on the bed with her ankles crossed, reading a magazine, and I was standing by the window looking out at the city. I was a little bored and thinking of nothing in particular, whether married people made love only at night or whether an occasional

213

matinee was allowed, and wondering what I was supposed to do while she was reading her magazine.

"Where did you learn that trick?" I heard her asking.

"What?"

"I suppose there's nothing wrong with putting your finger in your ear, but when you look at the finger afterward to see if you've got anything on it, it makes it fairly obvious."

She went back to reading her magazine. I didn't know whether to answer or not. Finally I wiped my finger covertly on the drapes, and then I went in the bathroom and slammed the door. She scarcely glanced up. Well, and what did the idle rich do when they had wax in their ears? Tell the servants to take care of it?

In the bathroom, still half angry, I turned the water noisily into the washbowl and went to work on Waldbach's exercises: clench, open, clench, open, in water so hot it scalded the half-healed skin. The fingers were good enough now to clean your ears with but still stiff; the muscles pulled when I flexed them. Well, hell, I decided to straighten the stupid things out. With my teeth clenched I pressed the right hand flat against the side of the washbowl. The skin pulled and little cracks of pain ran around on it. Flatten out, you bastard! Who's running things here, you or me? Then the left hand. Now I was getting somewhere; there was a smear of blood on one palm but at least they were starting to look like hands and not boiled shrimps. I went back to the exercise: clench, open, clench, open. I was supposed to do this for an hour a day. Then I realized I didn't have a watch. I dried my hands, leaving pink smudges on the towel, and unlocked the door and went back into the bedroom.

"Listen, have you got a twenty?"

"Of course."

She put down the magazine, got up placidly off the bed and went to the dresser for her handbag.

"I need it to buy a watch," I explained, although she hadn't asked me.

"What happened to the Rolex that Leo gave you?" "Same thing that happened to the skin on my hands, I guess." She gave me two tens and I stuck them in my pocket loose (I didn't even have a billfold). Then I put a jacket on over my tieless shirt and went downstairs in the elevator, still a little angry at something, at my hands, I suppose. There was a gift shop in the lobby but all the watches were a hundred dollars. Instead I went outside and walked down Powell Street until I came to a drugstore, and went in and bought a watch for fourteen dollars, pigskin strap included. I also bought some cigarettes, a cheap imitation-leather billfold, and a paperback Evelyn Waugh novel to read in the hotel room. If I was going to be a member of the leisure class I might as well start reading some of their books. There was a dollar and some change left and I put it in my pocket. It occurred to me that I had gone around with a lot of women in my life but I had never taken money from them before. It still didn't feel like my money; it seemed to weigh more in the pocket than it should have. I had an impulse to throw it away, but you didn't throw away quarters and dimes in the middle of a sidewalk in San Francisco; if you did they would probably take you away to the hospital for observation and I had had enough of that.

When I got back to the room she hardly glanced at the watch. The change in my pocket didn't last long, and the next day I had to ask her for another twenty. She never gave me any money spontaneously, but when I asked her she always opened her bag and handed it over quite simply, as though I had asked her for a match. She agreed with the same simplicity, the same placid and faintly ironic smile, when I indicated I wanted to go to bed with her. Except for my expedition to the drugstore we never left the hotel during the two days we were in San Francisco. We had our dinner sent up that night and breakfast and lunch the next day. The rest of the time we loafed in the bedroom and read. I did my clenching exercises twice a day in the washbowl, and once that afternoon we made love under the gold damask bedspread. In bed with her I forgot to be careful of my hands and they gripped her body like two small hungry animals, stinging with pain. I was aware of the pain but indifferent to it, as though it were a telephone ringing in the next room; it was only later that I realized how much the hands had hurt. And perhaps it was really this that brought back their strength and their assurance, and not the exercises in the hot water. Once a couple of weeks later after we had made love I looked at them; in the cracked skin tiny, almost invisible threads of blood had appeared, as though new fingerprints were growing where the old had been smoothed away.

Toward evening that second day we checked out and took the night sleeper to Los Angeles. Our roomette was four or five cars from the diner, and when we went to dinner that night she had to open all the doors for me as we went from car to car. She made a half-humorous ritual out of it, opening each door and then waiting almost with a little bow for me to walk through. I was beginning to feel a vague annoyance, not at her but at my hands, the train doors, my whole predicament. In the hospital I had not minded other people doing things for me, but now I felt stupid and some-how emasculated. It seemed that in order to be a complete man not only certain glands were needed but also hands. What was I so annoyed at? It was getting complicated. Always before I had simply opened women's legs without bothering to open doors for them too. But in those days, I remembered, I had paid them, and now if she was not paying me at least the money came from her. When we reached the dining car she started to come around the table to pull out my chair but I stood in her way, as if by accident, and the waiter did it for me.

I paid for the dinner out of my new twenty. The bill was a little over six dollars, and when the change came I found I had thirty-seven cents in coins. I was damned if I was going to give the waiter a dollar. I shoved the thirty-seven cents across the table and ignored his patient contempt as he picked it up penny by penny and slipped it into his white jacket.

She seemed to find this amusing. "Don't scowl at the poor fellow so," she said. "You'll frighten him with your ferocious scars."

"Come on," I told her.

We got up and walked back through the cars to our roomette. I went ahead and when we came to each door I put the back of my wrist against the handle, set my teeth, and shoved. Somehow the door opened. She walked through each door solemnly, without a trace of a smile, and then waited for me to follow.

In the roomette she took off the jacket of her suit and stood before the mirror in her blouse, watching me lazily in the glass as she brushed her hair. I knew she was ready to make love again if I wanted. Instead I waited until she was finished at the mirror and then I turned the hot water on, this time so hot it steamed, and stuck my hands in. I had a watch now so I could tell when the half hour was up. Clench, flex, clench, flex. They would open doors or I would boil the skin off of them, the hypersensitive pansies. Clench, flex! While I exercised she lay in the berth quite primly reading my Evelyn Waugh novel: it was *Vile Bodies*.

At nine o'clock in the morning we were in Los Angeles. At Union Station we walked through the long tunnel under the tracks, and in the waiting room a stocky middle-aged man came toward us, smiling broadly. Except for the dark patches around his eyes he looked nothing at all like Ary; he was compact and barrel-shaped, with a broad chest and a head that seemed too large for the rest of him, and his stiff gray hair was clipped close to the skull. He was wearing a sport shirt open at the neck and a pair of rumpled trousers that hung a little too low on his hips. He threw both arms up into the air while the grin became even broader, and then he brought the arms back down again and put them around Ary's shoulders. When he had kissed her he turned to me and started to offer his hand.

"No, wait, hell, I forgot, you can't shake. Let's see."

I showed him my hands and he glanced briefly at them. "That's a rotten thing," he told me. "What were you trying to do, be a hero? Let's get out of here, there's no point standing around in the station. Where are your bags?"

He seized our three suitcases from an intimidated redcap, jammed one under his right armpit, and walked off carrying the other two in his hands. We followed him. So far I hadn't said a word. I was still a little confused by the noise and activity of the station and I simply walked along looking at the back of Leo's neck, concentrating on not losing him in the crowd. We came out into the hazy sunshine of the parking lot and I absorbed the new feel of the city, the smell of something pungent like cottonseed oil or Mexican cooking, the fake Spanish architecture, the haze that hurt your eyes and gave a faint mauve tinge to the air. Perhaps things seemed unreal because I had the sunglasses on now and through them everything was the color of syrup. It was strange that I had been to Long Beach and San Pedro a hundred times and had never bothered to come in to Los Angeles, although it was only a forty-minute ride on the streetcar. We found the car-, it was a big Chrysler station wagon, no longer new. Leo heaved the suitcases in the back, opened the front door, and helped me in, gripping my elbow almost gently in his big hand.

"Okay, Tiger. Are you all right? You sit in the middle. Want a cigarette? Want a drink? We haven't got a drink. Well, never mind, we'll be home in an hour if God wills." He started the motor, twisted around to look out the rear window, and backed out in one long curving swoop. "I've got to get gas. No, I guess we've got enough to make it. Tiger, you watch the needle, and if it gets absolutely to the bottom let me know."

We drove the sixty miles to Laguna sitting three in the front seat. The car had been an expensive one when it was new, but now it was full of rattles and the woodwork needed varnishing. There was a head of lettuce on the floor under Leo's feet, and there seemed to be a wine bottle or something rolling around in the back. Ary noticed the lettuce too; it was a wilted brown head that had evidently been in the car for some time. "For God's sake, Leo," she said tolerantly. She picked the lettuce up, examined it briefly, and threw it out the window. It rolled across the street past a cop directing traffic, who glanced at it dumbfounded and then stared after the car.

Leo only snorted and waved his hand negligently, as though he couldn't be bothered about anything as minor as a head of lettuce. "I bought three carloads like that from a fellow in Visalia and it was all frost-bitten. I finally sold it to an Armenian in Saugus who has a horse farm. I saved that one head to show to the fellow in Visalia, and he told me there was a war on. How do you like that, Tiger— there's one for your buddies out in the Pacific." He drove carelessly but skillfully through the traffic, talking in a steady stream. Somewhere in the suburbs a woman driver lurched at us backward out of a driveway and he jammed on the brakes; the bottle in the back clunked against the seat. "Now that shows real intelligence. Do you know what Aristotle says? You, you charming feminine creature," he told Ary, reaching behind me to ruffle the hair on the back of her head.

"What does Aristotle say?"

"He says woman is the highest animal in nature to lack an organ of reason. Of course there's one theory that Aristotle lacked a few organs himself. Well, we've all got to get along with the organs we have. Oh, you're a darling." (A truck stopped dead in front of us in the middle lane.) "Oh I see, he's unloading a side of beef. Well, that's logical." He shifted into second and pulled around the truck. "He's probably quite bright in other ways. We're all a little meshuggah nowadays. It's a weird century. You have a little trouble remembering things, and a hundred million Americans didn't notice Hitler was building gas ovens. The other day I started to brush my teeth with shaving cream. You take this charming creature, she refuses to understand automobiles. She's got a mental block about them. I've told her about forty times to pull the choke out just a little and then shove it back in when the car starts. Instead I think she uses it to hang her purse on."

He talked like this all the way to the beach, while Ary looked placidly out the window. I sat between them taking everything in a little vaguely: the traffic that seemed to shoot down the highway at a terrific speed, the oil wells in Huntington Beach, some white cows in a pasture near Costa Mesa. There were too many new things for one day. We drove through Laguna, a little resort town full of shops and hotels, and a mile or so out of town we turned off the highway onto a road lined with pepper trees. The house was at the end of the road in a grove of pines. It was a big old-fashioned bungalow-style house with overhanging eaves, finished in redwood siding weathered gray by the salt air. The sun was shining through the beach haze and the house smelled of pines and the faintly musty odor of redwood. In the driveway Leo unloaded the suitcases and carried them off into the house, leaving the door open behind him. Ary slipped her hand under my arm and led me toward the door. Inside it was cool and shadowy and it took a moment for my eyes to adjust. We seemed to have come in through a side door; there was a service porch and then a kitchen. Then we went through into the living room, large with a high ceiling and windows looking out over the sea. In the shadows across the room another woman was waiting for us, and when we came in she smiled. She was younger than Ary but obviously her sister, slender and inconspicuous, with the kind of timid alertness of a small quiet animal. She was dressed quite simply in a summer dress with big pockets, her hair pulled smoothly back and knotted at the back of her neck, and as we came in she smoothed her hands a little nervously on the sides of her skirt. "This is Suzanne," Ary was explaining matter-of-factly. "She was away at Benning when we were here before. Hi, darling."

Suzanne came forward and timidly offered her hand, then she remembered my burns and hesitated rather awkwardly.

"Oh, for heaven's sake, darling, don't be so formal," Ary told her. "That's not the way I act with Carl."

Suzanne laughed, laid one hand flat on each of my ears, and kissed me on the forehead. "That's what Ary does to *my* husband." Then she added quickly, "I've got to see about lunch. If you want to rest I've fixed up the bedroom." She disappeared unobtrusively and I was alone with Ary.

I looked at her but she said nothing. After a moment I crossed the living room and went silently down the hallway beyond. Two or three doors opened off the hall, but somehow I knew that the last one on the left, a room that evidently faced the sea, was our bedroom. The notion struck me that she had told me this in those afternoons in the hospital when I was half asleep, that the words had left no impression at the time but somewhere inside was the shadowy recollection of what she had said. I pushed open the door and went in, sensing that she was coming on slowly behind me. The room was finished in a dark royal blue. Facing the sea there were high small windows with mahogany shutters, and to the left was a door leading to the bathroom. Through the mahogany shutters the sound of the surf came up faintly through the pines. The furniture was white, and the big double bed was white with a dark blue bedspread. I turned and saw she was still watching me, saying nothing, as though she were waiting to see what I would do next. I went into the bathroom. In the holder over the washbowl there were two toothbrushes, one red and one ivory. The red one was hers, the burgundy color of her lipstick and the scarf she wore with the end pulled through the buttonhole of her jacket. I looked at the other toothbrush; it was worn and a little frayed and it hadn't been used for some time. In a kind of unreal slow-motion I opened the medicine cabinet. Inside were various feminine jars and flasks, some aspirin, a vial of mercurochrome, and a bottle of scented aftershave lotion: Old Spice. It seemed that somebody liked to perfume himself. When I shut the medicine cabinet the face that swung to meet me in the glass, motley with the new skin growing in patches, had an expression I didn't recognize. It was a frown of concentration, the look of a man doing something terribly difficult and at the same time trying to understand what it was he was doing. It was as though I had sleepwalked out onto a ledge where there was no going back, and now suddenly I found myself awake. As soon as I saw that toothbrush I knew I was not the man it belonged to, and I knew that she knew it too. Usually the more we know about people the more we understand them and this realization should have made things simpler, but instead an enormous ambiguity sprang up about her and I didn't understand anything anymore, myself or her or the meaning of these walls that I could have reached out and touched without moving from where I stood. How was it that a man's existence, his very being or ceasing to be, could depend on these things, doorways, toothbrushes, the shape of a window? And then suddenly I felt a kind of visceral emptiness, and I wanted to sit down or lie down or get in bed and pull the covers over me and go to sleep. It was easy enough when you were lying in a white room with your veins full of sedatives to live in a dream world and believe you could soar without wings or become another person, but this was real, hard, palpable, these objects around me were ironic and skeptical. For the first time it really struck me that I was sick and I ought to be back in the hospital instead of standing in this bathroom with its chrome fixtures and its dark blue towels.

I turned and went back into the bedroom. She was still watching me. I went to the windows and opened one of the mahogany shutters. You couldn't see the beach because it was directly below, under the cliff, but you could see the pines and through them the flat blue line of the horizon softened by the California haze. The path down the cliff, I knew, would start at the other end of the house, under the porch. And the place on the beach where you found abalones would be off the rocks at the end of the cove, rocks I could hear now rather than see as the surf washed gently over them.

"Did we stay here very long?"

"Not very long. When we were first married you were on duty in San Diego and you used to come home weekends. Then you had a leave and we went to Mexico. When we came back we stayed here for a week. Then a little after that your orders came."

It made me uneasy for us to stand looking at each other as she said this, because what she said was not true and for me to meet her glance as she said it made me participate in the untruth in a way that for some reason, for the moment, I didn't want to. I went back to the window and looked out at the pines. I wanted a cigarette but I didn't have one with me and it didn't seem to be the time to ask her for one. Most of all I wanted to go to sleep so that the empty feeling in my viscera would go away, or at least so that I wouldn't be aware of it anymore. I didn't know what to say and finally I said, "I know it and yet I don't," oddly feeling for some reason as I said it that there was a kind of truth in it.

She smiled. "Yes. It's a little strange to me too. I expected you would be half a stranger when you came back—I told myself it would be that way. But it's odd, still." She seemed perfectly calm.

"I'm a stranger?" I said after a moment.

"It's just that—there are moments, certain slants of light, when I look at you and there's something I don't recognize. I thought perhaps it was because of the hospital, and it would be the same again when we got home. But even here, now, there's something different —a kind of awkwardness about our being together, as though something about us doesn't quite fit yet. Don't you feel it? Maybe it's just me—it's because of those silly burns I haven't got used to yet, and they're only on the outside. But the outsides are all we can know of people. In the end that's all we can know of anything, just what we can see and feel and touch. And the outsides change. Even if people haven't been burned they can become strangers when we're separated from them for a while; everything that happens to them that we don't share changes them a little. You can't make them back the way they were before. And perhaps we wouldn't want to if we could."

She seemed to be looking at something across the room as she talked, and finally I followed her glance. There was something there on the dresser I hadn't noticed before, a picture in an ebony frame. I didn't want to go any closer. Even from a distance I could see it was a photograph of a naval officer in summer whites, wearing an obviously new cap with slightly self-conscious pride. We resembled each other, the two of us, like cousins. We had the same lean, slightly aggressive face, the same immature petulance around the mouth that suggested a lingering impatience with the world and its imperfections, yet something was missing. The face in the photograph wasn't mine; it was the face of an intelligent college boy, well-mannered, pleased with himself, proud and a little solemn to find himself an ensign in the United States Naval Reserve.

"Do you remember when that was taken?"

I lifted my shoulders vaguely.

"It was before we were married. You'd gone home for a few days and you sent it from Seattle. It's the only picture you ever gave me. You always detested having your picture taken."

"I still do."

I didn't, in fact, like the photograph. It wasn't that the face in it belonged to somebody else—with due allowance for burns, new bitterness, the passing of time, it resembled me enough to be a passing likeness—but that I felt the photograph was somehow a

224

false representation of something, I wasn't quite sure what. There he was, with his solemn intelligent face, this young officer just graduated from college and keeping himself pure for the girl he was going to marry—and then I realized why I disliked the picture so much; I had refused to accept my own past and now it seemed to me the photograph committed me, condemned me, to his. This solemn ass of an ensign in his black picture-frame! I dropped the picture into a drawer and shut it.

"Have you got a cigarette?"

She gave me one and lit it with the lighter from the nightstand, touching my hand to steady the flame, and then lit one for herself. When I looked at her I saw she was smiling, and I stared at her stonily for a minute and then I smiled a little too.

As he had promised, Leo fixed a drink, a highball with good scotch. At lunch nobody talked very much; Suzanne was too shy and Leo was busy eating, and as usual Ary was not very loquacious. I was tired from traveling, and all that afternoon I slept in the blue bedroom. It must have been around five o'clock when I woke up. I lay in bed lazily for a while, and then I realized that what had wakened me was the sound of voices from the living room. Someone was playing the piano and somebody else was singing:

I can't give you anything but gin, baby—
That's the only thing that I take in, baby . . .

There was laughter, some skeptical jeers, and the clinking sound of glasses. It was pleasant and a little strange lying in that quiet cool blue room and listening to this as though it were a radio program coming from the house next door that had nothing to do with me. Then I realized it was not in the house next door and I would have to get up, or sooner or later somebody, probably Ary, would come in to wake me up, and I didn't like the idea of her finding me lying fuzzily in bed in my underwear at five o'clock in the afternoon when she had just come from a room full of people who were drinking and playing the piano. I was tired of being sick while other people were walking around fully dressed, but I was a little annoyed too that she had invited people to the house when I didn't want to do anything but rest and above all not talk. I got out of bed reluctantly and put on the checked blue shirt and the slacks I had worn ever since Honolulu, then I went into the bathroom, wet my hands, and smoothed down the straggly hair on my scalp. It stuck up the back but I still couldn't use a comb because the skin underneath was too sensitive. The socks I had traveled in were a little ripe and I didn't have any others, so I put the loafers back on my bare feet. As I came out of the bedroom I could hear voices from down the hall.

"I think he's awake, I heard gurgles from the bathroom."

"Oh, why not let the poor dear sleep?"

The room seemed to be full of people but there were only three new ones: a man around forty with a mustache and an exaggerated British accent, and an arch and rather reserved couple in their fifties. Ary came toward me and took my arm. "You remember Maurice, don't you, darling?" The term of affection struck me as a slightly false note, as though she were saying it for the others and not for me. "The Redmans I don't think you've met," she went on smoothly. "He can't shake hands, everybody, you'll have to excuse him."

"I can shake," I said a little defensively.

I offered my hand to Maurice and he took it with care, as though it were a rare piece of Ming porcelain. "Actually,'" he explained, "you might *not* remember me. I only came once or twice, and in those days you were somewhat preoccupied, being newly wedded." Ary was explaining that he was a set designer for MGM and did some really smashing things, and I could believe it, because I had never seen anybody quite so phony outside the movies. I stared at the hound's-tooth jacket with the lemon-colored handkerchief, the impeccable mustache, the long hair carefully brushed over the temples. I wasn't sure whether I was supposed to take his drawling manner as arrogance or humor. Before I could decide I was pulled away and introduced to the Redmans. It seemed that Oliver was a poet and professor of creative writing. He was owlish and serious with a long narrow jaw, and he shook my hand casually, almost negligently, without saying anything. His wife Kelly, who "painted and did clever things," was a lean middle-aged woman with a kind of nervous vitality and a blasé way of speaking, as though she viewed everything with a somewhat jaundiced eye. I saw her looking at the burns on my face with the slightly morbid curiosity people have when they look at wounds or disfiguring scars, her eyes resting a moment too long on the twisted place by my mouth, but she only said simply, "So nice to know you." From across the room Suzanne was smiling her usual shy smile. Leo was fixing drinks at a kind of buffet that served as a bar and he didn't even turn around when I came in.

"I say, really, someone give the poor fellow a drink," suggested Maurice to break the awkwardness. "What will you have? Scotch? Manhattan? Or what is that new thing with vodka and orange juice? It's very nutritious."

"Screwdriver," muttered Leo, busy with his bottles.

"I refuse to say that word," said Maurice flatly.

"The fact is that he is not supposed to drink," Ary pointed out. "There was this doctor in the hospital, a most intelligent young man but a kind of a—what was he like, Ben?"

"A YMCA director."

"Exactly, an intelligent young YMCA director. Anyhow the Rev. Gore said Ben was not to indulge in alcohol for some time, because he ought to avoid anything that would affect his sense of reality."

"Why on earth should he have a sense of reality?" protested Kelly. "That's the last thing any of us need."

"In any case it's essential that the home-turned Odysseus should quaff at least one festal flagon," insisted Maurice, pressing a large highball into my hand. "Although as a mattrafact you just got back to Ithaca in time, old fellow. Your Penelope was getting just a touch lonely, you know, and I got in the habit of hovering around helping her weave her rug. Perhaps when you learn the facts you will pierce me through with arrows."

"Oh, Maurice," protested Kelly. "Penelope was a terrible old drag. Odysseus only came home to her because he needed his shirts pressed. I see Ary more as the Circe type, or no—the other one, what was her name? Calypso."

"Thank you, Kelly, that's the first compliment I've had for months. Ben's idea of a compliment is, 'Do you think it's too early go to bed?'"

"And is it?"

"Never has been," said Ary imperturbably.

"I think that's a splendid compliment. Now Oliver never says that."

"After thirty years?" protested Oliver.

"I say, what frightful negligence," Maurice defended her gallantly. "Of course," he conceded, glancing at his watch, "it *is* too early now, Kelly darling, but bring the matter up again around eight o'clock, will you?"

"Oh, quiet, you're shocking poor Ben. And besides, if anybody is to go to bed with anybody he's the guest of honor."

"I think it was the Duke of Marlborough," Suzanne broke in when she found a place in the conversation, "who came back from the wars and his wife later reported—oh no, I really can't say that."

"Come on! For shame!" everybody encouraged her.

"Well, in her memoirs his wife reported that he 'pleasured' her three times before he took his boots off," she finished, blushing furiously.

"A good story, only it was the Duke of Wellington."

"Oh, it wasn't Wellington, he was a horrible old Victorian."

"How could Wellington be a Victorian if he fought in the Napoleonic Wars and Victoria ascended in 1837?"

"Oliver, if you start giving history lectures out you go."

"In any case we ought to be going in a minute, darling," said Kelly. "We promised to take Maurice to dinner. Or Maurice promised to take us to dinner, I forget which."

"Out of the question. You've drunk all our liquor and now you must stay here and eat. If you went away what would we do all evening?"

"Same thing Marlborough did."

"Three cheers for Marlborough! Three, I believe, would be the appropriate number."

"Exactly, three cheers with boots on."

"No really, this is serious now. You must all stay. We'll have a feast in honor of Ben. A saturnalia, insofar as that is possible in Laguna Beach."

"Of course there's nothing in the house, you irrational feminine creature," said Leo.

"Isn't he a charmer? I'll go out and get something."

"What will you get? Before we stay we demand to be presented with all the alternatives."

"I'll get everything—ambrosia, nectar, peacocks, ladyfingers. I won't be long; there's a delicatessen just down the highway. Now you must all not go away—do you promise?"

She went off and we heard her car scattering gravel in the driveway, and she came back in a quarter of an hour with her arms full of paper bags. "Peacocks—Kelly love, do you want to heat them up in the oven? There's more in the car." Leo went out to help her and came back with two magnums of champagne and a sack of cracked ice, and she carried in another bag of groceries and an enormous mass of flowers wrapped in waxed paper. All, she explained, from the local Saturnalia Supply Store. While Suzanne unobtrusively began setting the table with red napkins and white Danish dinnerware, Ary ripped open the waxed paper and began strewing the flowers among the plates: marigolds, zinnias, poinsettias. There were too many and she threw the others around the room, on tables, on the floor. We sat down to eat amid the heaps of flowers. There were roast chickens from the delicatessen, cold artichokes, a jar of Greek olives, French bread seasoned with garlic. Leo twirled a magnum in a bucket of ice, cut the wires, and held the bottle over the glasses as the foam gushed out.

Maurice raised his glass. "To—well really now, to what?"

"To Marlborough."

"Oliver—"

"Very well, to *Lady* Marlborough."

"No, really now," suggested Maurice. "How's this? To the home-turned Odysseus: may it never be too early to go to bed."

"Well, let's compromise—to Odysseus, understood to include in an allegorical sense the Duke of Marlborough."

"Shut up and drink the bloody toast," ordered Leo. They all drank together. I started to drink and then I realized I wasn't supposed to drink a toast to myself and I stopped. I felt awkward and ill at ease; I understood that this feast was in honor of my homecoming and that these people wanted to be my friends and wished me well, but I had no idea how to act with them, how to talk, how to hold my hands or what to say when I was spoken to. I might as well have gone into a village of Zulus as among these people. Kelly asked me a question, whether I was home for good or whether I had to go back to the hospital, and I muttered something inaudible. Maurice was talking to Oliver about the wine. "Actually, you're right, but still it's hard to get now with the war, you know, the real *brut*." It might have been Sanskrit to me; I thought he was talking about brew. I wasn't sure I approved of Maurice anyhow; I couldn't see what he was hanging around for and what he had to do with Ary. All I knew about his type was that if he showed up around the waterfront he was likely to get his face pushed in. He seemed perfectly at home in the house, chattering to everybody, helping himself to the food, filling the others glasses for them. It was probably all perfectly natural and I didn't have any reason to resent it; I was the one who was the stranger. And in spite of his affectations he was basically friendly and it was impossible not to like him. He saw that my plate was empty and leaped into action. "A bird—a piece of a bird—a peacock-knee for the hero."

"Thanks, I've had enough."

They heaped my plate up anyhow. We had finished the first magnum and were on the second. Kelly was twirling a poinsettia in her fingers and gazing over it, moody but content. There were cherry tarts; they passed the bakery box around and we each took one. Nobody felt like going in the kitchen for forks and we ate them with our fingers. When we had eaten everything on the table we scattered around the room, some on the two big sofas and some on the floor. Through the windows the sun had set and the sea was black, but the sky above it was still a milky gray. Somebody put a record on the player, a Vivaldi concerto. Ary produced a bottle of Courvoisier, passed out balloon glasses, and began pouring. I stared puzzled at what Kelly was doing. She cupped the glass in her palms and rolled it back and forth, and now and then raised it to her nose and sniffed. I had never heard of warming brandy with your hands and I thought perhaps she had some rare gastric disease and had to inhale her liquor instead of drinking it. But finally the ceremony, whatever it was, was over; she took a long sip. I stopped staring and drank mine too.

"Who put that record on? It's all wrong, wrong mood," declared Ary. She stopped the player and put on something dark, Spanish, and smoky: Albeniz' *Iberia*. Then she pulled Maurice up from the floor and they began dancing to it in a slow grave parody of a tango. There was laughter; the others began clapping in time to the music and somebody shouted "Ole!" I sat on the floor with my drink between my legs, awkwardly watching. I didn't know what I was supposed to do, get up and dance with her or just sit there and clap with the others. She had never seemed so much a stranger, so unattainable, even that first day when she had walked into the hospital room and I didn't even know her name. These friends with their glib conversation, this slightly affected theatrical manner of hers when she was with the others, isolated her from me like a wall. The whole room seemed to buzz and I sat there stony-faced and reticent staring straight ahead of me; I realized now I had drunk too much. Gore was right about drinking, I was only cling- ing to reality by a tiny thread and alcohol was bad for me. Nobody seemed to notice, or at least they left me alone and didn't ask me any questions. The only one who ever looked at me was Suzanne, and when she caught my eye she would just smile without saying anything. I began to suspect that they had talked about me earlier that afternoon, when I was asleep, and Ary had told them I would act rather strange for a few weeks and not talk very much. They played records all evening, first *Gâité Parisienne* and then popular dance music, Goodman and Artie Shaw. Maurice was dancing with Kelly, Oliver with Suzanne. Ary, warm and excited from dancing, went around with the cognac again and filled the balloon glasses. When she finished she sat down on the floor next to me; she didn't touch me or say anything but I could feel the warmth of her body against my leg. The records succeeded each other and the bottle of cognac gradually disappeared. About midnight the others left; it was a weeknight and they all had to work the next day.

Suzanne had disappeared as unobtrusively as usual; she seemed to melt into the air when there was no longer any need for her in a room. Leo was sitting on the sofa across the room with his feet on the coffee table, looking quite calm and thoughtful in spite of the fact that he had been drinking all evening. His shirt was unbuttoned and he was scratching the stiff hair on his chest.

"Hairy old progenitor," Ary told him, "good night."

"Sweet dreams," he said a little abstractly. He seemed to be thinking about something and not paying any attention to us. As we left the room he looked up briefly, then he picked up his glass and took a sip and went back to his thoughts.

The house was quiet. In the blue bedroom only the small night light was on and the room was almost dark. Through the shutters you could hear the lazy crushing of the surf: a soft intermittent rhythmic sound. Ary was undoing the buttons of her blouse, her face a white patch in the gloom. Even from across the room I could sense the subdued glow she still felt from the music and the dancing, a kind of excitement that lingered just under the surface and that she held in only by a conscious calm. I was tired but I didn't feel like sleeping; I didn't know what I did feel like. Something in my head was working like a machine that was trying to start up but couldn't because the voltage was too low and the gears wouldn't come together and mesh. I took off my shoes and lay down on the bed on my side, looking not at her but at the dark wall in front of me.

"You're depressed about something?"

"No."

I heard her clothes fall, then she came around the bed to get her nightgown out of the dresser. I reached out and took her wrist, and she turned, looking at me calmly, expectantly, but with the shadow of a smile at the corners of her mouth. Lying there on the bed I clung to that wrist with a kind of insistence, not really out of desire but because everything around me that night seemed strange and incomprehensible and she who had been a stranger only a week before was the only thing that was familiar. It seemed to me that I had known her an age, an infinity, compared to the elusiveness and ephemerality of everything else, that only by seeking out and possessing again the familiarity of her body could I reestablish even that tenuous flimsy reality I had hung to before, a narrow island of consciousness where I could go on existing until

I found the strength to build a stronger place to stand on. For a few seconds I held her wrist like that while she looked at me with her questioning half-amused expression. Finally she sank down across the bed, and from the moment we touched it was the same as before. The brittle and actressy affectation she had put on when she was with the others was gone and in its place there was only darkness, calm, the wordless quickening urgency of her own need. Afterwards she went to sleep almost immediately and I lay for a long time thinking in the dark. As soon as I no longer touched her the reality began to turn queer. Even Leo now, the house, Suzanne, seemed to me strange and yet in another way things that I had always known. How had I come here, to this place? Wasn't it possible that I might have gone somewhere else? It seemed to me as I lay there awake that my existence and everyone else's was a part of an intricate pattern that underlay everything and that we would never know, that now and then we saw where two threads crossed and this made us realize the intricacy of it and the hopelessness of ever understanding more than a small fragment of the significance of our own lives. But the threads had to cross before they could make a pattern, and that was why every thread was important. All this was obscure to me and probably always would be, it meant that in some way I was important to other people, that everyone was important to everyone else, even those they never met. I felt I was hovering very close to the edge of some intricate and important truth, but it was too hard finding my way to the center of it and I had never been very good at untangling ideas like that even when I was well. And if was not well now; I realized that now even more than I had that morning, when I stood for the first time among these strange and familiar things that seemed to be trying to speak to me in a language I couldn't understand.

Chapter 13

.-- .... --- .- -- ..   .-- .... --- .- -- ..   .-- .... --- .- -- ..   .-- .... --- .- -- ..

Those early weeks in Laguna were a funny time, a new kind of unreality after that other blurry dream-world of the hospital. Everything seemed vivid but fragile; the things around me were real but I felt they might break like an eggshell if I reached out for them. Somewhere inside my head the pieces of my mind were healing slowly like a broken bone. I made a lot of blunders and for a long time I did things that were unaccountable, not only to other people but to myself, but I knew it didn't matter because at least for a while it would all be put down to my sickness. I would sit in the sun, wide awake but not thinking, for hours on end; I felt physically keen and mentally anesthetized. I had nothing to do but eat, sleep, loaf on the beach, and get well. The numbness gradually wore off and green shoots began to come through. Then I began to get a little bored sitting around all day on the beach with my brain softening in the sun, and probably this boredom was the first sign I was getting well. I began to notice things going on around me: Leo, Ary, Suzanne, this house they lived in and the way they lived. But even then I didn't try to think anything out to the end, because I knew that if I did my thoughts would begin to clog as though my brain was stuck full of molasses, as it had been now for months. I must have been a spooky character, floating silently around the house with my burned face and hands like something out of an old Boris Karloff movie. Nobody said anything; they just smiled at me in that reassuring, tolerant, slightly patronizing way you smile at people who have been sick and are now getting better. Leo was away most of the time on business trips, and when he was gone I was alone in the house with Ary and Suzanne. They lived impulsively and without any particular schedule. I discovered you could go for days without looking at a clock, make love in the morning, skip lunches, go swimming at dawn, make a meal of cheese and fruit and wine after midnight when other people were asleep. I realized now that before I had always lived a life rigidly controlled by time; there was a time to work and a time to sleep and you always knew what to do down to the last minute. I couldn't get used to a way of living where you did things easily and impulsively simply because you felt like doing them. For a long time the casual untidiness of the house seemed strange and almost immoral; it seemed to me that things were strewn around all over the place and when people got done with things they just dropped them on the floor. Then gradually I began to see that this disorder had a reason. I had been used to the filth of all the fifth-rate ships with their odor of stale food and sweaty underwear, the deliberate dirtiness of people for whom dirtiness was a part of their fake ball-scratching virility, but this was different. Here in this house all the things that never got put away—cigarettes, records, wine, books piled on tables, sweaters hanging on doorknobs—were there so they would be at hand when you wanted to use them. Ary and Suzanne never seemed to plan anything and yet everything they did had a reason. For a long time I wondered why they kept an old avocado pit sitting around in a glass of water, and then one day just as I was about to ask about it, it sprouted into a tree. The house was like the universe, untidy but purposeful. And then I began to understand that the life I had led before had been the opposite: neat, wily, and meaningless.

It took me some time to understand all these things, because at first I had the impression Leo was some kind of a millionaire and this wasn't my idea of how people with money lived. I suppose I had got most of my ideas of millionaires out of old Fred Astaire movies. In that world people never wore anything but tuxedos, rode around in long shiny cars, spent most of their time in nightclubs and had everything done for them by servants. When Fred Astaire took off his gloves (pearl-colored, suede) he just tossed them into the air and there was a valet in a striped jacket to catch them. Leo didn't wear gloves and had probably never been inside a night club, and his station wagon looked as though he had bought it second-hand from a Japanese gardener. It was obvious they had a lot of money and didn't mind spending it, but Leo's shoes were run over at the heel and Ary dressed so casually that it was a long time before I realized how much her clothes cost.

It all seemed as plausible, in its way, as the Fred Astaire movies and after a while I just stopped thinking about it and surrendered passively to the way they did things. As spring came on and it got warmer we spent more and more time on the beach, which was almost deserted at that time of the year. Usually in the morning when it was foggy the three of us would walk down the beach or explore the rock pools, then in the afternoon the fog would burn away and it would be hot. For long hours I would lie face down on the beach with my eyes closed, listening to the buzzing of insects and the crisp foaming of the surf, the sounds coming to me muffled and yet somehow magnified by the heat. When it got too hot I would swim, wading out waist-deep in the glassy water and then kicking my way lazily out to the rocks a couple of hundred yards offshore. Suzanne would usually come with us on the morning walks, but often in the afternoon she would take Ary's car to go to Laguna or Newport Beach to shop. Ary would go swimming with me (she swam languidly, hardly making any effort, yet she seemed to move through the water quicker than I did), then she would sit cross-legged reading a book under a large Mexican straw hat. Sometimes in the afternoon we would go up to make love in the blue bedroom, closing the mahogany shutters and then afterwards lying drowsily in the darkened room until the evening breeze came through the shutters to move across our naked bodies and wake up. After a week or two these things were as familiar to me as my own body, with the familiarity of a half-forgotten taste or the pain of an old wound: the odor of the pines baking in the sun, the muffled sound of the surf, the coolness of Ary's body, the shadowy blue room where the light from the sea played dimly on the ceiling.

I gained weight and lost track of the calendar. Like everything else she seemed familiar and yet at the same time strange, and for a long time the strangeness didn't go away. One part of me felt easy and relaxed with her, but another part, the reasonable and conscious part, would wake up now and then in a blurry way and make me realize the precariousness of what I was doing. I knew, as I had known from that morning I first entered the house and sensed her watching me as I moved uncertainly through the bedroom, that *she knew* (but what was it that she knew?) and yet neither of us spoke about it and it seemed that we never would, that we would go on pretending this strange dark place was not there and yet skirting carefully around it whenever we talked. I knew that there was no question of my becoming anyone that I was not, that even if I were letter-perfect in the part I would have given myself away a thousand times, that earlier when I had imagined I could do this I was simply lost in the hallucinatory non-logic of the hospital world. And yet if this wasn't what I was doing I didn't quite know what I was doing. Somehow I sensed that whatever it was I was doing she was on my side, and probably Leo and Suzanne were too, but why they were or what was going on in their minds was a mystery, an enigma that my thought processes were not capable of coming to grips with. The fact was that in spite of the precariousness of my whole existence I didn't think very much about it at all. It was like the other basic questions, why God created the world and then put evil in it or what happens to us when we die. Most people believe in a part of their minds that these questions are very profound and important and have a crucial significance for them, that they are important above all other questions, and yet they don't think about them very much because they don't believe there are any answers to them, or perhaps because they are afraid of what they might discover if they thought them out to the end. In this way my situation was a kind of a metaphor of the whole human predicament; I sensed I was balancing over a chasm but I preferred not to look down. And probably I was right; now that I had walked out over the chasm what good would looking down do?

The thing was to stop worrying about it and simply relax and be natural. But how the hell did you do it? In the situation where I found myself, being natural seemed the most difficult and intricate thing I had ever had to do. I thought I had been around a lot, I had been on my own since I was seventeen and I had wandered around over half the world, but I had never ordered a bottle of wine in a restaurant, made love to a decent woman, seen a play on the stage, listened seriously to music, or paid any attention to the food I was putting in my mouth. I was getting better now, and I couldn't blame all my blunders on my sickness. When I began to grasp the complexity of what I had to do I felt like a trained baboon trying to play a cello. At every turn it seemed there was a new decision, probably crucial, although I could never be sure. What did I want for dinner? Which necktie should I put on? Did you wear a necktie at all to go to the Coast Inn at eight o'clock for drinks? Before a rack of neckties I was in a cold sweat. I knew enough not to say ain't, but did you say, "the man who came" or "the man that came?" "I am different than you" or "I am different from you?" When you broke wind in public and there was some doubt as to whether this accident had been noticed, did you say nothing or murmur some apology?

This was nothing compared to the bafflement caused by a wine list. What the hell were *crus classés* anyhow? I bought a book on wine and studied it covertly, the way I had read dirty magazines in Spanish Creek. Instead of explaining what *crus classés* were, it was full of other French words and I was thrown into despair. Holy Moses, have pity, I had never studied so hard for my license! And wine wasn't enough, it seemed that there was more than one kind of cheese. To me cheese had always been just cheese, it was a yellow stuff that tasted cheesy and you put it between two pieces of bread. Now it seemed there was Bel Paese, Brie, Camembert, Edam, Gruyère, Liederkranz, Mozzarella, Muenster, Port Salut, Romano, and Roquefort, and there was a time to eat each one or you were a yahoo. Swiss cheese, it seemed, was called Emmenthal. The kind of cheese you put in mousetraps was called Cheddar. I wondered if the mice knew it was called Cheddar and whether they preferred it to Pont l'Evêque. I almost decided it would be easier to give up eating, and all this was before I discovered that gravy was called bordelaise sauce.

One evening in March or April Leo had just come back from a trip and the four of us were sitting down to dinner: filets, asparagus hollandaise, a bottle of Beaujolais. I took a preliminary bite of my steak and then I got up and wandered off toward the kitchen. When I couldn't find what I wanted I came back into the dining room.

"What are you looking for?"

"Catsup."

"What for?"

"To put on my steak," I said, feeling the first premonition that something was not quite going right.

The three of them looked at each other.

"I think there's some A-1, or some Worcestershire," said Suzanne.

"What's the matter with catsup?"

"Nothing, nothing."

"All right, skip it."

"I think there *was* a bottle somewhere," said Ary. She got up and went off toward the kitchen, I heard cupboards opening and closing, and in a few minutes she came back with it. The three of them stopped eating and watched me while I socked the bottom of the bottle and spread this stuff on my filet mignon.

When I saw they were all watching I put down the bottle. "All right, what do you have catsup in the house for if you're not supposed to use it?"

They looked at each other again. "For hamburgers, I suppose," said Leo.

I noticed now for the first time that there was a bowl of sliced lemons on the table. I went on cutting up my filet and chewing for a while, and then I slowly scraped off the catsup with my knife. Leo silently passed me a lemon and I squeezed on some juice.

"It's just that," Ary remarked, "some things kill taste and others enhance it." So I finally understood why we used to put catsup on the goulash on the *Chileno Cape*. But I was still a little annoyed; I felt I was being maneuvered and these people were trying to educate me without my realizing it, and I wasn't having any of this and I didn't understand what was going on in their minds anyhow. I was ready to have it out with them right then and there and tell them to mind their own damned business because I liked catsup on my steak. But I didn't, partly because I still felt uncertain and defensive and partly because the steak was better with lemon. Instead I went on meekly eating, with lemon on my steak mixed with the traces of the catsup I hadn't been able to get off. Besides it was impossible to be annoyed with them for very long because I sensed their good will and because they themselves took the whole thing so casually, as they took everything else. After a while Leo remarked, "Joe Gould when he was living in the Village always used to pour catsup out on his plate and eat it with a spoon. He didn't like the stuff but he said it was the only thing in a Village diner that was free."

"Who was Joe Gould?" I demanded, still a little truculent.

"A philosopher," was all he would say. A philosopher who ate catsup? That night after the others had gone to bed I locked myself in the study and looked him up in Baldwin's *Dictionary of Philosophy* but he wasn't there.

For a long time I went on this way, feeling more or less like a passenger in an airplane who had grabbed the controls when the pilot had died of a heart attack. I was staying up in the air somehow but I wasn't quite sure how I did it. Small crises, like downdrafts and puffs of wind, would hit and I would hurriedly make some readjustment. The plane would go along smoothly for a while, and then there would be a lurch. I would have to think fast: what was I doing wrong? Putting catsup on my steak, applauding between movements at the symphony? I pulled the levers blindly, waiting for the time when I would accidentally pull the one that made the bottom drop out. I was so busy with this that I never really thought out my basic situation or what I was trying to do or who the hell it was I thought I was kidding. All I knew was that I had finally found a world to which I would like to belong, even if it meant cheating and misrepresenting myself and living all the time with the ghost of an unexamined reality hanging somewhere just out of sight in the back of my thoughts. One morning that summer there arrived in the mail a letter from the Eleventh Naval District. I opened it and found a check for my back pay as Lieutenant (j.g.) in the United States Naval Reserve. I stared at this document. In addition to the amount payable, which was in four figures, it contained an admonition not to fold, spindle, or mutilate along with a pithy warning not to commit any kind of a fraud.

In the desk in the study there was a pigeonhole full of old papers belonging to me. (So to speak, I heard Gore adding.) Ary had suggested a couple of weeks before that I look through this and "throw away what I didn't want anymore." I suppose by this she meant that she wanted me to clean out the desk and throw everything away; it was one of those vague double-entendres we used to exchange with each other in that time without ever really saying what we meant. I locked the door, sat down at the desk, and went through the papers. Finally I found a sample of my alleged signature. Holding a pen in my stiff fingers, my tongue between my teeth like a second-grader, I practiced the art of forgery. I wish I could have seen my face; it must have had a look of concentration as though I were inventing something terribly difficult, like the telephone or the double-entry bookkeeping system. When I was done I examined the results. A poor thing but my own, or a reasonable facsimile.

Meanwhile breakfast was ready; Ary and Suzanne were in the kitchen and hadn't noticed the study door was locked. With the evidence of my crime in my pocket I sat down and ate my first shirred eggs Grand Marnier. They tasted queer and I couldn't figure out what they had put in them, marmalade, lemon extract, or a good grade of whiskey. By this time I knew that if I kept my mouth shut I would sooner or later find out by accident what it was, so I simply said nothing and ate it.

After breakfast I walked the mile into Laguna to the bank and opened a checking account. There were no hitches, although the whole thing made me slightly nervous. Everyone in the bank kept calling me Mr. Davenant and inquiring whether I wanted a joint account with my wife, which would merely be a matter of adding my signature to the account she already had. I smiled and agreed this would be the simplest. I walked out with four hundred dollars in cash making a lump in my back pocket, and a great deal more in the checkbook. Fraud! Embezzler! It was strange, I felt nothing. I had no desire to write a check. Or to buy anything; I had plenty of cigarettes and enough clothes for years. On the way back I stopped out of impulse at a shop and bought a jade pin for Ary. It was a big massive silver pin with a green stone mottled with black streaks. My God, jade cost money! A hundred dollars for a piece of stone? Well, at least I found one way to spend it. I even bought a scarf for Suzanne: four dollars plus California sales tax.

I felt reckless, a master criminal, but this was only the start. The next week I had to go with Ary to the Long Beach Naval Hospital to get psychoanalyzed again, have my urine examined for albumin, and various other rituals connected with my final severance from the Navy. This went more easily; I was an old hand now in duplicity, or rather in half-statements and ambiguous silences, and I sat in a chair and answered their questions without turning a hair. At the end I even smiled a little at them. It was not necessary to make a public display of mirth, but I felt I ought to indicate at least that I was beginning to feel more normal.

The psychiatric examination was a pure formality. There were two psychiatrists. The younger one was evidently some kind of an intern or apprentice and said very little. The other was a full commander with wrinkled jowls and a wise and ruminating manner, like an old bird dog. He sniffed at me without very much interest as I answered his questions. Obviously he considered me a rather common sort of psychopath. I told him it was beginning to come back my life with my wife, the house, the things we had done together. About the time before that, Seattle, college, nothing. Another blank for the night in the sound off Tulagi.

"Normal, perfectly normal," he said indulgently. "You're back home, and the places recall the experiences. For a total amnesiac you're coming normally. How long is it now—let's see—" he consulted the file—"a little over eight months? Well, you are coming a little slowly, but you're progressing. Anxieties? Bad dreams?" He seemed impatient to go to lunch.

No anxieties, no nightmares.

"Sexual relations?"

Well, yes, I confessed, a little confused. What he wanted to know, however, was whether they were the same as before, i.e. normal. I glanced at Ary, lifted my shoulders noncommittally, and the commander put something down in his notes. Perhaps that I was bashful, a good sign. "Normal, normal, a typical traumatic amnesia." It was a quarter after twelve and from somewhere inside the commander were coming faint audible noises indicating hunger. "A textbook case." The interview was over. He folded up the file, handed the notes to the yeoman to be typed, and disappeared with the younger doctor in the direction of the officers' club. Ary and I sat for a while listening to the yeoman clacking away at the typewriter, and finally he looked up. "You can go, Lieutenant," he told me. "They'll send you the papers from Com Eleven."

This was the last thing I ever had to do with the United States Navy. The papers came in about a month from San Diego: partial disability with a small pension, referred to Veterans Administration for continuing post-surgical and psychiatric treatment. There wasn't very much to the post-surgical treatment; at the outpatient clinic of the Veterans Hospital they told me to continue Dr. Waldbach's exercises. For about six months more I went on working my fingers in hot water for an hour every day: flex, clench, flex, clench. The brain was supposed to recover its resiliency by itself.

The Navy was only an institution, and like all institutions it was easy to deceive. What institutions wanted out of you was a conventional response, something that could be put down on a form. If there was anything unconventional about your case they preferred not knowing about it. Telling them the truth was something like pouring sand in the gears. Everything grated to a stop and they started yelling at you. I learned that in San Quentin, the only institution of higher learning I ever attended, and it was a valuable piece of wisdom which served me well the rest of my life.

With human beings it was not so easy. Ary seemed to accept me casually and naturally, and yet I had no notion what was going on in her mind or what she was thinking to herself. Sometimes I would accidentally do the right thing and she would accept it without comment. Other times I would make blunders, like ordering red wine with fish or wanting to make love without taking off my socks. (Making love in the morning, it seemed, was spontaneous, making love with your socks on merely crude.) Sometimes she would laugh, at other times she would make some mildly ironic comment. What was I supposed to do, laugh too? It didn't seem to make much difference, because by this time both of us were committed to this thing we were doing together and neither of us could back out. But I couldn't go on doing queer things forever; sooner or later I was going to have to start acting more like myself. *Like who?* I thought. I didn't know who I was until I saw how I was going to act. Secretly and half unwillingly I tried to keep all the rules in my mind. Once in a while I tottered on the tight wire I was walking on, flailed for balance, and almost fell. Toward the middle of the summer she told me, "I've written to Seattle."

It wasn't difficult for me to assume the proper expression, since I felt exactly the uncertainty I was supposed to feel at this remark. I waited, mute and cautious, for her to go on.

"I wrote about a week ago. This afternoon an answer came. I didn't know whether to tell you about it or not. Finally, when you were down on the beach, I called Dr. Keller and talked to him about it."

"Who?"

"The psychiatrist at Long Beach." It was the bird-dog commander. "He thought you ought to know about it. You're well enough now and there's no reason why you can't face realities, even when they're unpleasant." She hesitated. "The fact is that your mother didn't even answer my letter. Your father wrote for her. You know she's always been nervous and unstable, and it seems that last winter, when the photos came from the Navy, she had some kind of breakdown. She's still under a doctor's care, and the doctor doesn't want her to talk about it or even think about it. And your father ends the letter by saying he doesn't want to think about it either."

She paused, while I looked at her and waited for her to go on.

"You see, in a way they had a shock almost as bad as yours. First they were told you were dead, and then they sent those gruesome photographs. All this happened to me too, and I understand the emotions they must have gone through. It's just that I'm younger and more flexible, but for them it was too much. When the news came their son was dead they couldn't comprehend it; it was like being struck an overwhelming blow. For a while you're numb, and then gradually you learn to accept. Or not to accept, exactly, but to *understand* what has happened. Finally they understood, they bore the pain the way you accept a surgeon's knife going into you, because you know it must be borne and it's the only way. It's like surgery too, because afterwards you're numb, a kind of paralysis, and then there's a long period of convalescence."

"All this happened to you?"

"Not as badly. Or perhaps worse, I don't know. Anyhow I came out of it and they didn't. After the ship was lost they knew they would never see their real son again and so they lived with the dead one—the school pictures, the letters, the memories. For them this remembered son became the real one. So you see, when the other photos came from the hospital—"

"They wouldn't believe it," I broke in harshly. "And they don't believe it now." I didn't like this conversation at all, I felt it was leading us into an area where neither of us would have anything to say without breaking into the dark place we had tacitly agreed not to go, the place that above all it was important to keep intact. Besides there was something else, something physical; the more she went on talking the more I felt a kind of intangible vacuum forming under my feet, as though the ground were slowly softening and dissolving and leaving me no place to stand. It was a kind of a malaise, a vague unpleasant physical feeling, and I didn't like it because I sensed that if we went on this way something even more unpleasant would happen. "All right," I told her, "They don't believe it. Let's just drop it."

But she seemed to need to go on and explain it, as though she were explaining something not only about them but about herself. "Don't you see—at one point you say to yourself: at last it's happened, the worst thing, somehow I've come through it and at least it can't happen again. For them it's too much, now, to wipe away all that grief as if it never happened and start again. If they accept you now all their grief would have been false, all that pain would have *gone* for nothing. And so they're being asked to do something they're utterly unable to do—to kill the son who lives in their memory and accept a new son, a son who is—"

"Disfigured. Go ahead, why don't you say it?"

"Whose face is not the same," she said quietly.

"Why the hell should it be the same? It's not the same, I've been burned, I look like something you scare the kids with at Halloween!"

She was silent for a moment, and then she began again. "I know how you must feel—"

"How the hell do you know how I must feel?" I got up and paced around the room. The sick feeling inside me was growing as she talked, and it seemed to me that for some reason she wanted to drive me into a corner, she wanted to inflict pain on me or wrench some secret out of me no matter what it cost or how much it hurt. "You're so damned omniscient, as though you know everything that's going on and how everybody's feeling and thinking. Nobody knows how anybody feels, do you understand? Nobody knows anything and we can't help each other, so let's not try. All right, I'll tell you how I feel. I'm supposed to feel some reaction at the word mother, tears are supposed to come in my eyes or something. I tell you I feel nothing, nothing, and I can't fake it!" I hardly knew what I was saying. "I'm tired, tired, I want to be myself, I want to be natural! I'm tired of faking!"

Her voice had begun to rise too. *"Nobody is asking you to fake anything!"*

At this we suddenly stopped and were silent, as though we had said too much and frightened ourselves, and for a long moment we looked at each other across the room.

After a while she regained control of herself, and when she spoke again it was in her usual blasé and faintly amused manner. "Anyhow," she told me, "your pose of indifference isn't very convincing, you know, because there are tears in your eyes."

"Like hell!" I said furiously. But she was right; I was seeing things through a blur. "Well, what's wrong with that?" I asked her hotly. "Don't you ever cry?"

She was still looking at me calmly, and then she turned away with a casualness that I thought was a little forced. "Occasionally. I just arrange to do it when other people aren't around."

"Well, I'm an exhibitionist."

That was the end of the matter. She didn't show me the letter, and we never discussed it again. But I still didn't know what the tears had been for: do people weep for strangers?

Chapter 14

.-- .... --- .- -- ..   .-- .... --- .- -- ..   .-- .... --- .- -- ..   .-- .... --- .- -- ..

All that summer and into the fall I was content to loaf there on the beach. My hands lost their stiffness only slowly and it was a long time before I could do anything. During the week we lived mostly by ourselves, and on weekends people would come down and we would have parties that sometimes lasted all night and ended with going down to the beach to swim at dawn. When Leo was gone on his business trips we didn't see as many people and we lived like hermits, sleeping and swimming when we felt like it and eating at odd hours, and then when he came back the house would be full of people over the weekend. Gradually I found out what the business was: he bought carload lots of tomatoes and lettuce in Imperial Valley and shipped them east, and he had an interest in some orange ranches around Fullerton. Once in a while he would make a trip north to buy produce in Fresno or Visalia. For some reason it always seemed to me an odd business for Leo to be in, and actually it seemed that he had got into it more or less by accident. He had come from a typical orthodox family, back in Philadelphia or somewhere, but when he was about twenty he decided he wanted to be a poet. This caused the usual family crisis; his father thundered old-fashioned patriarchal threats and his mother fainted, and finally Leo went to New York by himself and rented a furnished room off Sheridan Square. He wrote poems at night and in the daytime he worked in a vegetable store on Seventh Avenue. The poems were not very good but one of them was published in Harriet Monroe's *Poetry*, I looked it up once and it was the typical kind of free verse they were writing in the Village in those days, a kind of imitation Sandburg. In 1917 he joined the Army and spent twenty months in France. When he came back the first thing he did was get married. His wife was a French teacher in a high school in Queens and before that, when she was a girl, she had won some kind of a local beauty contest and had her picture in the paper. I saw the clipping once with her photograph: a rather prim girl with an ethereal and fragile kind of beauty, much like her daughters except that her eyes were blue and her hair was lighter. Leo's family never forgave him for marrying a Gentile and I don't think they even wrote to him after that. He went back to work in the vegetable store, but he saw he couldn't support a wife that way, especially when it turned out almost immediately she was going to have a baby. Instead he came out west and with a little money his wife had saved up he went into the brokerage business in Imperial Valley. For several years they lived in El Centro and the two girls were born there. Leo had enough sense to see that he was a bad poet but he could be a good produce broker. He made a lot of money in the twenty years he had been in the business; he had gone broke two or three times, I think, but by the time I knew him he was a millionaire. He bought the Laguna house in 1930, in the middle of the Depression. He had always liked the Monterey pines that grew native along the California coast, and he bought the Laguna place partly because the soil was right for them there and because there were already two or three on the cliff. He planted more pines, and everything else that was tough and hardy and would grow without much care: manzanita, live oak, sumac, sage, wild grape. Now it was like a miniature forest on the hillside, the trunks of the pines twisted and gnarled by the winter storms. When Leo got home from a trip the first thing he would do was turn on the sprinklers, the big rainbirds that threw a stream of water a hundred feet or more, and then when he had everything soaked he would wander around the rest of the afternoon smacking the pines with the flat of his hand and jerking at the branches to see if any had been broken by the wind. When you looked out through the window, especially on a misty day, it was hard to tell Leo from the pines; he looked as though he was built out of knots and as strong as living wood and his short stiff hair was like pine needles. He even smelled like them, although probably this came from socking the trees with his hands.

Leo made a lot of money mainly because he enjoyed making it, but he was never quite sure how to spend it. He liked to eat well and he bought a car about once every five years, but he didn't know what to do with the rest of it and for years he turned it over to his wife and forgot about it. Whatever his relatives in Philadelphia thought, she was an excellent wife for Leo in at least two ways: she was attractive and she was very good at spending money. She used to stay at the Del Coronado on San Diego Bay for two or three weeks every winter, and she visited Europe once a year and bought her clothes in Paris. Her French was perfect; in Paris nobody took her for a schoolteacher and in Coronado they took her for a European. This was partly because her one affectation was signing her name in the French manner: Mme Madeleine Halévy. I saw it once written on a letter she had never sent, in violet ink in a fine precise hand. You might say it was a slight affectation too to name her elder daughter Ariane, although this soon got shortened to something more breezy and a little less Proustian. On the whole, from what I could gather, it was a very satisfactory marriage. She died in 1934, however, and after that Leo had to count on his daughters to spend his money for him. He saw to it they had a good education so they would have expensive tastes. Ary went to Scripps in Claremont and later to the University of Grenoble; she learned to ski at Cortina and to ride in England. All this got rid of quite a lot of the money, although not as fast as Leo had hoped. "My God, the stuff is like moss on a ship's bottom," he told me once. "Even giving it away is hard work. It takes a woman to get rid of it. I don't know how they do it, but they're damned clever at it."

This was in one of our muscatel dialogues. That summer whenever he was home we would sit out in the pines drinking California muscatel and talking about women, science, and how to get rid of money. I found him easier to talk to in a way than Ary or Suzanne. He seemed to take a liking to me; I think he had always wanted a son, probably so he would have somebody to leave his pine trees to, and besides he didn't know anybody else who would listen to him while he talked about these things. When Maurice and the others were around he growled good-naturedly in monosyllables, countered their kidding, and never said what he really thought. In a way he was closer to his daughters than most fathers are, but he didn't really understand women very well. "I tell you, Ben, they reason like a corkscrew, it's impossible to teach them how to drive a car, and they wear their coats with the fur on the outside. It's beyond the grasp of a mere male. Do you know, I lived with my wife for sixteen years and I never found out what she did for two hours every night in the bathroom. Sometimes I think she had an artificial leg."

I had my own stories about the inscrutability of women, but they weren't stories I could tell Leo, at least not yet. "Would you like it any better if you understood them?" I asked. "You could always have bored a hole in the bathroom wall."

"They wash their faces with cold cream instead of with soap and water," he went on cheerfully, "they always lose one glove but never two, and they produce magic wounds in the rhythm of the moon cycle, exactly twenty-eight days. At least I think they do, I've never really understood it. I guess that's why we have to have them; without them everything would be too neat and reasonable. Can you imagine living in a world without women?"

"Yes. I lived in one once," I told him. I wondered if I had said too much and I was afraid he was going to ask me what I meant, but he only lifted one eyebrow as he always did and went on drinking wine, as though we agreed perfectly between males that they were charmingly batty, or as he put it, pre-Aristotelian, and there was nothing you could do about it. "Madeleine," he told me, "Madeleine could never find her key to the front door but she had a power like seventeen sorceresses. She only had to unfasten one snap of her dress and bang, the guard of honor came to attention." This made him sad, thinking about it, and he filled up his muscatel glass again.

Leo had never seen the inside of a university but he was an educated man, the first one I had ever met. The house was full of books, and he seemed to have read everything from Talmudic philosophy to mathematics and modern physics. It was he who told me about Heisenberg's Principle of Uncertainty and what this had to do with muscatel, women, and the human predicament in general. Back in the nineteenth century the scientists used to think that everything in the universe was predictable. Everything went around in circles and followed laws, and if you wanted to know where any particle in the universe was at any particular time theoretically you could just look at a logarithm table. But Heisenberg proved that there were some particles you couldn't pin down exactly. There was one formula for their velocity and another one for their position, but you couldn't apply them both at once. In the end the universe eluded mathematics. "I tell you, Ben, if the physicists can't even keep track of a particle how can you keep track of a human mind? Freud, Pavlov, the behaviorists, they're trying to unscrew the inscrutable. St. Teresa did better." I had read Freud but I had to make a mental note to look up Pavlov and St. Teresa.

"Have you ever read the *De Rerum Natural?*"

I admitted that it had been a long time ago. "Lucretius had the same idea. There's nothing but atoms and void. The atoms are falling through space, but some of them swerve as they fall, and that's how everything starts. They only swerve a little, and Lucretius doesn't explain why they do it, in fact he says he doesn't know. But it all comes from that." This was the land of atoms, he thought, that women were made of.

Lucretius, I found from Baldwin's *Dictionary of Philosophy*, was an Epicurean, and after a while I began to see that this was what Leo was too. He left stoicism to anybody who wanted it, and when he felt like having emotions he had them. I never saw him angry, but he could start laughing at something he had thought of, sitting all by himself in a room. When he felt grief he didn't bother to hide it any more than he would hide the pain of cutting his hand with a knife. Once we had a freak rainstorm in July and I looked out through the window and saw him sitting in the rain with the tears pouring down his cheeks, looking out at the sea. You couldn't tell the tears from the rain except that he kept knocking them away with his hand, the way you would never brush away raindrops. Ary told me later that her mother had died in a summer storm like that; the telephone wires were down and that was why they couldn't call a doctor. Summer storms are very rare in California, and probably the time I saw him out weeping in the pines was the first time it had rained in July since 1934. Once I figured out that I had run away from home in Utah almost on the same day that Leo's wife died, the day he had known he would never have a son. I had started looking for him at the exact moment he started looking for me. What kind of atoms were these that worked in their orbits so purposefully? Heisenberg should investigate astrology, or perhaps he should look into the ways of that ingenious old ironist, God.

Most of the other houses near us on the beach south of town belonged to Los Angeles people who came down only on weekends and in the summer. Maurice had a large place with an unlimited number of bedrooms and he almost always had guests on the weekends, Hollywood people or the kind that Ary called Cadillac bohemians. Often he would bring these people over for dinner, or for drinks later in the evening, At first I couldn't see why he was always "hovering around," as he himself put it, and then I began to understand that he liked our house for a number of rather complicated reasons. Ever since he had been coming to Laguna he had always been mildly sentimental about Ary; they were old friends now and he felt easy and relaxed with her. In a way he seemed to know her better than I did. All week he had to deal with the egomaniacs and stuffed shirts and fairies in the film world, and we were the only people he knew outside of Hollywood. He liked Leo because he had the impression Leo was a practical man and did something concrete; he wasn't quite sure just what it was Leo did but he thought of him vaguely as having his fingers in the good black earth and making things grow. ("Yeah," said Leo, "I've got a callus on my ear from phoning long distance to New York.") He was interested in me for the same reason, because I was "real" (there was a joke) and had been out in the Pacific in the real war, not the one they hooked up on the Fox lot. Maurice had enough insight to see that everything in Hollywood was more or less fake, including himself, and we were his non-fakes. After a while I found out that everybody in Hollywood needed this; some of them bought ranches in Montana, some of them picked up hitchhikers on the highway and some went to skid-row bars and got beat up by jackrollers, but they all had a terrible hunger to know what the "real" world was like.

Anyhow Maurice himself was about as real as the papier-mâché sets he designed but he was harmless and I found that I liked him too. I even got so that I enjoyed the weekend parties, and began to learn what sounds to make at them and how to act with the others. Often on the weekends Oliver and Kelly would sleep in our guest room; Oliver was a college teacher and didn't have any money, and they were the only ones in our gang of steady friends who didn't have a house on the shore. No one seemed to notice whether Oliver had any money or that his car was ten years old, and he and Kelly stayed with us on weekends and ate our food (I thought of it as my food too now) without any particular self-consciousness. I used to spend a lot of time talking with Oliver, although if anyone had suggested to me five years before that I had anything in common with a creative writing teacher I probably would have socked him in the nose. We used to argue about Henry Miller; I admired him and Oliver said he was a pornographic Booth Tarkington. In this way we got along fine.

There were a lot of different people that summer and some of them I forgot almost as soon as I had met them, others I remembered. One Saturday night we were having cocktails with Oliver and Kelly, and around eight o'clock Maurice appeared with a couple called the Widdisons and an extraordinarily pretty girl we had never seen before. The Widdisons had already been down once or twice; it seemed that Janet Widdison had a little money and ran a small avant-garde theatre off La Cienega Boulevard, and her husband Keene experimented around making surrealistic films and off-beat documentaries. For a long time I thought that he was just a dilettante amusing himself with his wife's money, and then I found out that some of his films had won international prizes in Europe, at Venice and at Cannes. In any case Widdison didn't look like an artist; he drove a Cadillac and he looked like a parody of a capitalist in a left-wing newspaper. As for the girl, Maurice introduced her as Marta but he wouldn't tell us her last name. He claimed we only wanted to debauch her. She looked very young to be going around with Maurice.

"How would it debauch her if we know her last name?"

"Oh well, you know, you'd ring her up on the phone and start asking her places. This way only I know where to find her."

"And what is your name, my dear?" Oliver asked her.

"Kopnick," she admitted candidly.

"But don't go looking for it in the phone book, old chap. The studio thought up a much better one."

"You see," Kelly put it to her practically, "the question is, would you rather be debauched by us or by Maurice?"

"Well, Maurice *is* very nice, but the studio said if I wanted a romance they would find me a Van Johnson type and clear it with Hedda first."

"Gad, what self-sacrifice. If only we had had that singleness of purpose when we were young. All right, go off and drink Coca-Cola with the freckle-faced boy if you must. Heartless nymph, I was counting on you to console me in my old age."

"I'd love to console you, Maurice darling, but there's a clause against it in my contract."

"You'll never know what you've missed. *Si jeunesse savait...*[1]"

"Don't forget the rest of it, old boy," Oliver reminded him. "*Si vieillesse pouvait.*[2]"

They went on like this through several rounds of margaritas. Leo was gone on a trip so I was acting as barman. When I wasn't fixing drinks I amused myself by looking at Marta, who was really spectacularly pretty. We all sat admiring her, in fact, until it was absolutely necessary to do something about dinner. Oliver wouldn't go to the Victor Hugo because he had on his old corduroy jacket with chalk on the elbows, and Janet Widdison

---

1   French: If the young knew.

2   French: If the old could.

refused to go down on the beach and cook steaks because she was wearing a cocktail dress. Finally it was decided we would go to Delie's, a kind of rathskeller and German restaurant on the highway outside of town. The great advantage of Delie's was that it was only about a quarter of a mile away and we could walk, which avoided misunderstandings with the state highway patrol. We set off in a procession down the lane that ran along the cliff a block or so from the highway: the Widdisons and Kelly ahead, Oliver with Marta, and the rest of us bringing up the rear. Ary, who was walking with Maurice, was trying to find out exactly what the situation was with Marta. They had both had several margaritas and the conversation was slightly oblique.

"But I thought she came with you," I could hear her saying behind me.

"Came where?"

"I mean I thought she was *with* you."

"Oh, you mean in the Biblical sense. Well, it's sort of *comme ci comme ça*, darling."

"But still, why do you let her walk with Oliver?"

"Darling, what would I say to her? I'm terrified of the child."

They fell a little farther behind and I couldn't hear them. Ahead of me Oliver was telling Marta about Herrick, who was a country parson and thought you ought to gather rosebuds around the time you were twenty. Marta seemed to find this an enchanting idea.

Somehow I had paired off with Suzanne. "You know," she was telling me, "I used to be the ingenue around here until that infant arrived."

"Well, we all have to grow up sometime. Besides she is spectacular."

"You too?"

"I mean objectively."

"Let's take it subjectively."

"Subjectively," I had to admit, "she's still spectacular."

It was a mild summer night, dark except for the starlight, and absolutely calm. After ten minutes down the lane we found ourselves at Delie's, where we all ordered sauerbraten and potato pancakes with dark bitter German beer. After dinner, slivovitz, which I had never had before and which tasted like vodka slightly flavored with prune juice. On the effects of this stimulant Oliver, Maurice, and Widdison got into an involved argument about Rene Clair.

"What do you mean, who is Rene Clair? I'll tell you who Rene Clair is. He's just the Chaplin of France, that's all. No, that's sacrilege. Chaplin is the Rene Clair of America."

"All right, tell me one thing. Do you know a picture called *A nous la liberté*?"

"Of course I know it. Where do you think I've been all these years?"

"All right. Did *A nous la liberté* come before or after *Modem Times*?"

"What difference does it make which came before?"

"I'm just asking you which came before, that's all."

"Well, it's an asinine question. Clair made *A nous la liberté* at a time when—well, at a time when the possibilities of surrealism had hardly even been explored for the cinema. He also made a picture which, for all your erudition, you probably haven't heard of, called *Sous les toits de Paris*—"

"What about Cocteau?" Maurice interrupted him.

"Well, what about him? Who the devil is talking about Cocteau?"

"Well, I mean to say, you talk about the possibilities of surrealism hardly having been explored and all that, whereas as a mattrafact Cocteau made *Le sang d'un poète* back in—I think it was '25—"

"Oh well, that was just an experimental."

"Well, what the blazes is *A nous la liberté* if it isn't an experimental?"

"I'll tell you what the blazes it is. It's a good film, that's what it is. A good film with no arty Cocteauesque pretensions, and a lot more subtle than anything Chaplin ever did. Chaplin was a good clown, maybe the greatest clown, but he couldn't direct other people and he never understood sound."

"Well, why should he understand sound? What's so wonderful about sound?"

"I know, a silent-film crank. I've met a million of them. Sound is just the fourth dimension of the cinema, that's all."

"Oh brother, when people start talking about fourth dimensions. . . And what do you use words like cinema for? Why don't you say movies like everybody else?"

At this point a small but very loud German band began playing right in our ears. There was nothing to do but dance. Oliver paired off with Suzanne and Maurice with Kelly, and I was given a polka lesson by Marta. I was a clumsy dancer and I felt rather foolish, but still it was pleasant feeling rather foolish while a pretty girl taught me something I didn't know. Marta smelled like fresh linen and strawberry sherbert, and sang me my instructions: "Left left left. Plink plink plink. Now we shift to *right*, plink plink."

By this time the evening had taken on a thoroughly Teutonic tone and Oliver was getting nostalgic about his student days at Gottingen. He began singing lieder in a spurious baritone:

Ich weiss nicht was soli es bedeuten,
Dass ich so traurig bin.[1]

He really had a surprisingly good voice, even though it was an octave lower than he normally spoke. Everybody turned to look at him, and finally he was enticed up to the platform to sing with

---

1   German: I wonder what it presages, I am so sad at heart. From "Die Lore-lei" by Heinrich Heine.

the band *"Du bist wie eine Blume"* and several other pieces of *Gemütlichkeit*. It was only with difficulty that we pulled him off the platform and got him out the door into the night air. He had drunk more slivovitz than we thought.

"I thought when I married a poet," Kelly was complaining, "I would spend my life with somebody quiet and retiring who would not make a public spectacle of himself."

"Now lay off poor Oliver," I defended him. "He was wonderful. Professor, your talents are wasted in education."

"Ja, weil ich Gesangvogel bin,"[2] he said modestly.

"Oh, don't encourage him. Next he'll want to stand on his head."

"I wouldn't dream of standing on my head. I am perfectly familiar with the distinction which Aristotle makes in his *Poetics* between art and spectacle."

It was decided that what we needed was something bracing to neutralize all that Mitteleuropean slivovitz. "Black coffee for you, songbird," Kelly told Oliver. We went back down the lane toward the Coast Inn, which was on the highway only a few hundred yards from the house. Myron, the barman, recognized us as soon as we came in and began setting up brandy-and-benedictines with coffee, our usual nightcap. After the first round of these Oliver told him to skip the coffee. It was the middle of the vacation season and Saturday night, and the room was full of city people and Marines from Camp Pendleton. We couldn't get a table and there was barely elbow room for us at the bar.

"Mr. Davenant, is that little girl over twenty-one?" Myron asked as we were passing Marta her third drink.

"Of course she is. Are you over twenty-one, dear?"

"I'm almost sure I am, but all the records were destroyed in the San Francisco earthquake."

"Mr. Davenant, I'll have to see some identification."

---

2   German: Yes, because I am a songbird.

Amid a great deal of confusion Janet Widdison's driver's license was passed behind backs, brought to the front, and shown to Myron. Janet had been born in 1902 in Green Bay, Wisconsin.

"Okay, Mr. Davenant," said Myron. "I have to check, you know."

It was almost two o'clock. Most of the crowd in the room had been drinking all evening and one group of Marines over by the door was getting a little loud. Three of them looked like recruits and the fourth was a little older, a sergeant with a lean tanned face and a collection of battle ribbons. Over the noise in the room I caught several words I hadn't heard recently, and I wondered if the others noticed. They did. After the next obscenity there was a silence, and then Kelly inquired quite innocently, "I wonder what *that* one means."

"Haven't the foggiest," said Ary.

Myron went over and told the Marines to quiet down.

"Go screw yourself, Gwendolyn," we heard one of them telling him. He was a short cocky kid who didn't look old enough to be out of high school, but he had a face like Jimmy Cagney and the mannerisms to go with it. It was obvious he had been drinking more than he was used to.

"We'd better leave," said Janet.

But the sergeant was talking to Cagney. He didn't look very much older than the other three, but they seemed to respect him, or at least they listened when he talked. Evidently he was giving Cagney a lecture on etiquette. Cagney with elaborate contempt lit a cigarette and blew the smoke out of the corner of his mouth, as though he wasn't paying any attention, but at least for a while he quieted down.

It was almost closing time and the crowd was beginning to thin out. Janet and Marta went off to the powder room, and on their way back the trouble with the Marines began again. This time Cagney reached out and took Marta's arm as she went by.

"What's your hurry, hey? Lissen, you going around with those squares?"

One of the other Marines, a red-headed boy who hadn't been drinking so much and was still cheerful, began trying to start a conversation with her. "What's your name, huh? Lissen, I'll bet you're an actress or something."

But Cagney was in no mood for amenities. He wanted to get to the point, or perhaps he just wanted to start a fight. "Come on, Agnes, let's go upstairs and kick the gong," we heard him saying.

Maurice set down his glass and went over with his most Mayfair manner. "Old chap, I'm sure it's inadvertent, but you seem to have hold of the young lady's arm."

"Beat it, Clarence."

I put down my glass and started over too. The sergeant was trying to hold Cagney but he jerked his arm free. When I was still a few feet away Maurice raised his hands in an ineffective girlish gesture and Cagney knocked him flat. Oliver and Widdison were coming too but they were too far away. Another Marine was moving in on my left and Marta dealt him a shrewd kick on the shin; he stopped and began hopping on one foot. Cagney stepped over Maurice's legs and swung hard at me. I bent and seized the wrist as it went by and twisted it, and down he went; he was drunk and off balance anyhow and ready to fall. He and Maurice were together on the floor in a heap. "There, smart ass," I heard Ary say calmly in the confusion.

Before Cagney could get up the sergeant had hold of one of his arms and Myron had the other. It was all over. Myron pushed all the Marines outside. For the first time I realized how much I had hurt my burned hand; it was stinging like fury and I began massaging it with my fingers.

"Whyncha let me at that one sonabitch?" Cagney was complaining. "The one with the scars, I'll get him when he comes out if I hafta wait all night."

With an odd emotion I watched them yanking and pulling this small fierce animal out the door. I was perfectly sober now.

I hadn't had time to get angry or even feel any particular hostility, instead I felt a great detachment, a kind of clarity, as though a part of me were doing this and another part standing by and watching. I remembered the night I had swung at Victor in his cabin, and how easily he had seized my wrist and thrown me to the floor: "Agh, before you hit an old man you'd better go learn how." I knew that for Cagney I was just a Babbitt, smug and soft, with money in my pocket and women to go to bed with; I had forgotten a lot of things but I hadn't forgotten how it was to be twenty years old and violent and bitter and resent the fat and privileged, the ones who had it made. I had an impulse to follow Cagney out the door and say something to him, but I decided not to. What was it I wanted to tell him anyhow? That the world was out to get you? Or just not to lead with his left so high?

"Riffraff," said Myron. "Those are from Camp Pendleton. The ones from El Toro, they're not so bad."

"What the hell, Myron. They were probably just lonely and looking for a girl."

But Myron was a barman, and he divided all humanity into those who were likely to break his glassware and those who weren't. "Pardon me, Mr. Davenant, but you've probably led a rather sheltered life. I mean, you've gone to college and all and met a lot of people, but living like you do there's a certain side of life you don't see. What I mean is, you spend your time mainly with nice people and you're more or less isolated from the other side of it. Now you take these kids, they're just riffraff, they belong down on the waterfront. That's a part of life you probably haven't seen very much of." I think he wondered why I grinned so much.

It was time for Myron to close anyhow and everyone was leaving. When we went outside Cagney had disappeared, but the sergeant and another Marine were still waiting for us. The sergeant stopped us and began embarking into a long-winded and rather emotional apology. "Sir, I'm sorry about what happened and I don't want you to hold this against the Corps. You understand, these kids are just recruits, they're not combat Marines. They've hardly got the milk off their chins yet." He was around twenty-two himself. "I'm ashamed of the way they behave. I told them they were a disgrace to the uniform. Listen, sir, I want to tell you something." He had his hand on my shoulder in case I tried to get away. "I want to tell you something now, I fought in the Corps all the way across the Pacific, I was with the First Division on New Guinea and Guadalcanal and I never saw a combat Marine insult a civilian, I don't care, gooks or anybody. We weren't fighting for our sixty-five a month, we were fighting for the honor of the Corps."

It was impossible not to believe in his sincerity; he had tears in his eyes. "Sir," he went on, "I think the Corps owes an apology to the young lady and to all of you. I wish it never had happened. Sit, I hope you understand me, I've been around myself and I've got nothing against raising hell and having a good time. But I wouldn't ever make a remark like that to a decent girl and I hope nobody in the Corps would. So sir, I hope you'll forget all this and the honor of the Corps won't be stained by what happened tonight." He went on about the honor of the Corps for about fifteen minutes. He was wonderful; Kelly wanted to take him home with us but he wouldn't come.

We walked back down the lane to the house, Kelly still saying in the dark, "That sergeant was a cherub. I could have eaten him up." In the kitchen we found Leo, who had just got back from his trip and was malting himself a meal out of cheese and a big loaf of sheepherder bread. Kelly and Janet were hungry too, so we all started eating cheese and Ary made some coffee.

Maurice and Oliver were explaining to Leo what had happened. "It was a deuce of a row. Here was Marta being violated by this enormous soldier, and Ben and I plunged in with bared fists."

"The soldier was a Marine of less than average size, and he knocked you flat."

"Well, I said it was a deuce of a row, didn't I? My God, it was like an old Bill Hart serial, with everybody hitting people with breakaway chairs and falling over the bar. I was lying doggo on the floor, you know, to stay out of the strife, and the next thing I knew this particularly enormous soldier flew over me and his head struck the wall with a sickening thud."

"The only sickening thud I heard was your ass hitting the floor." It *was* impressive," said Kelly. "Ben darling, where did you learn that trick?"

"I took judo at the University of Washington."

"I tell you, Ben was wonderful. I'm glad one of us boozehounds has some character."

"I'm not sure that a barroom brawl is the final test of one's character," Ary remarked carefully. "In fact some people might feel that to be too good at it casts doubt on one's breeding."

"Speaking of breeding," I told her, "it seems to me that at the height of the excitement I heard you use a very vulgar expression." This quieted her for a while, but the others went on talking about it for a half an hour.

"Tell him about the sergeant," said Kelly. "O, that sergeant was an Easter egg."

Leo couldn't get it all straight. "So as I understand it, the two of you set on this one unarmed Marine?"

I kept trying to explain that the one Marine was just mixed up and the rest of them were perfect gentlemen. "The one Marta kicked was just going over to the cigarette machine. It was a misunderstanding."

Marta denied kicking anybody, and Oliver claimed he had been in the thick of it from the beginning.

"Ah, you're a bunch of drunks," Leo told us. "Why don't you all go nude swimming or something and sober up?"

This was considered a brilliant idea, and in the end Leo came with us. It was a moonless night, the beach almost invisible in the faint starlight, and the water was warm. But it was not warm when you came out, it was cold as hell, and we all wrapped up in towels while Leo built a fire. Widdison was smoking a cigar and with his towel draped around him he looked like a kind of parody of a Roman senator. On the other side of the fire Marta was explaining that she wanted to play serious parts and didn't see why they kept casting her as an ingenue. "You're absolutely right," Oliver was telling her. "You're absolutely right."

"That Sergeant was a lollipop," sighed Kelly for the tenth time.

"All right, but I don't know why Myron lets them come in there anyhow. They cause nothing but trouble. The Coast Inn used to be a nice place before all that gang started coming up from Pendleton."

"Where do you want them to go, Widdison?" I asked him.

"Why don't they just drink beer on the base? They've got their clubs and everything."

"Wait a minute." I wasn't quite sure why I was defending the Marines, but Widdison was acting a little pompous and I felt it was important to show him where he was wrong. "Let's look at this thing fairly and stop acting like a lot of smug Pillars of Society. Those kids don't want to be Marines; they're in the service because there's a war on. I don't know if you've heard about this up in Hollywood. If they weren't in Laguna the Japanese Marines would be—would you like that any better? Sure, they're just a bunch of kids and they probably don't come from very good families, but those same kids are fighting right now, tonight, out in the Pacific and in North Africa so we can go on enjoying the Coast Inn and spending our money." I must have sounded like an OWI broadcast with lyrics by Norman Corwin. "And what were we doing tonight? Getting drunk and singing German songs. I'm no militarist, believe me, but if we had any sense of fairness instead of asking Myron to throw those kids out we would all sing the Marine Hymn."

"I'm sorry, Ben," said Widdison. "I forgot you were a veteran."

"I'm not talking about me, goddam it. Anyhow what I did out in the Pacific was not very much, and I probably caused more trouble than I was worth. I'm a civilian now like the rest of you. We're lucky. Those kids aren't so lucky—of those four who were in the bar tonight, one or two won't come out of the war alive. Sure, it's too bad Marta was insulted. I was twenty years old once too. Were you?"

There was a silence. Finally Janet said, "He's right, Keene. My God, when I think of that sergeant apologizing to us—that boy who was on Guadalcanal while we were riding around in our Cadillacs and drinking black-market scotch—"

They all agreed with her in a chorus, sounding like the sextet from *Lucia*, and Widdison even apologized to me—to me! everybody was apologizing to me tonight. I had convinced them without even half trying. Who was I to teach these people things, these people who had gone to college and had their names on screen credits? I had always been wrong before, I had been wrong for so many years I had almost got used to it and it seemed like the normal side for me to be on. Now here I was on the side of all the right ideas, and the others listened to me and agreed, a little ashamed. It felt funny, being one of the right-minded. I didn't quite understand why I was coming out for patriotism and courage and idealism anyhow, unless it was out of some obscure feeling that I was the one who ought to apologize to the sergeant, this idealist with tears in his eyes who had fought in the jungle across the sound those long nights when I lay asleep under the pandanus tree. It was too much for me and perhaps it was a mistake to get sober. I went up to the house and got a bottle of cognac and some paper cups.

"To the honor of the Corps," proposed Oliver.

They all drank and I drank with them. I didn't say much after that, but the others went on drinking the cognac out of paper cups and talking for another hour until it was almost dawn. It felt good, sitting there by the fire listening to them and feeling Ary's warmth next to me, that night after I had eaten and drunk well and defended beauty and innocence with my fists and then made my little speech and convinced the others, but I still wasn't sure whose side I was on. The sergeant's? The Pillars of Society? Cagney's?

Chapter 15

.-- .... --- .- -- ..   .-- .... --- .- -- ..   .-- .... --- .- -- ..   .-- .... --- .- -- ..

At first the burned places on my face and chest wouldn't take the tan, and stayed pink and peeled away one layer after another. But gradually the skin hardened, and the outlines of the scars merged with the healthy skin. The burned places never tanned as dark as the rest, but by October there was only a kind of mottled effect here and there in the brown skin. It was only when you came close that you could see my face had been patched together like a clumsily made rag doll. For a long time the palms of my hands stayed pink, like a Negro's.

Ary was in the sun as much as I was, but she hardly seemed to tan at all; instead her skin seemed to turn from ivory to a translucent olive without darkening, as though she somehow absorbed the sun through her pores. When we went up in the afternoon to make love in the blue bedroom I would have a rather foolish stripe of white around my middle, but she was the same color all over. Her shoulders and legs were only slightly darker; along her breasts and flanks the amber shaded imperceptibly into a shadowy ivory, lightly fragrant and cool to the touch. Why her skin didn't show the marks of her bathing suit I didn't know. Like Leo, I had stopped trying to understand women and I was content with what I could touch and possess on the outside.

It took me a long time to get used to these two strange beings, my body and hers, and the way they felt when they were together. For over a year I did almost nothing but walk, swim, lie on the beach, eat, and make love. Make love: I pondered over this expression. Make: to create. Love—to desire? To wish someone else well? It wasn't quite either. Then I (we) would perform the ritual again to see if I could solve the mystery. It was not that I wanted that badly to go on repeating this same set of gestures over and over, but I felt somehow I had to go on doing this thing until I grasped the secret of it that seemed to hover elusively just out of touch. It wasn't this way at first; at first I just accepted, but then as my brain began to work again I got sex in the head and I thought about it all the time. I thought about it from all angles, and the more I thought about it the less it seemed I understood. Sometimes I used to get angry with myself for thinking so much, and at other times I blamed it on her, because it seemed to me that if I had never met her I would have gone on the rest of my life understanding women perfectly. I had never had any difficulty understanding all the Claras and Connies; you simply spread their legs and there was nothing more to understand. Then there was the other kind, the brisk efficient ones like the nurses in Pearl Harbor. I could deal with them all right too but there was no question of sex; it would be like going to bed with a file cabinet or a typewriter.

I had always classified women in these two groups (receptacles and machines) and at first I couldn't figure out which Ary was. In her tailored suit, dealing with Gore and the others in the hospital, she had been brisk and efficient. Then in bed that first time on the ship I had discovered another side, a sorcery that had sharpened something quick and insistent in me I hadn't even known was there. While I was still puzzling this out we arrived in Laguna and she slipped away from me unexpectedly into a world of Hollywood friends, laughter, brandy in balloon glasses, Albeniz, and owlish allusions to Homer. It wasn't enough for her to have two sides, it seemed she was some kind of a polyhedron. Then as I came to know her a little better I saw that all the sides were one, but this didn't any easier to understand. For a long time I didn't like the tangoing, flower-strewing, slightly affected Ary, and I fought against it and tried to pull her away from that world. When we were together again in the blue bedroom it would be the same as before and I would think I had won, then the next night the house would be full of friends and she would be a stranger again. When I got to know the friends better that side of her seemed less mysterious, but by that time I had discovered other sides I hadn't even suspected. The more I knew her outwardly the more something inward and secret in her seemed to elude me. Who was she anyhow? I was the one who was supposed to be a mystery! By now it seemed I knew everything about her past, what she had studied at Claremont and how she had gone to bed with a teddy bear named Orestes when she was seven years old, but there was still something that seemed to slip away elusively when I reached out for it. For months the whole point of my existence seemed to center in those brief moments in bed, and yet these were the times when I seemed to understand myself and her the least. Something was working in me all that time, a new and obscure land of understanding was forming in the blood almost beyond my will. It was different from the kind of understanding that forms in the mind, and somehow it was connected with the physical act of love and the difficulty of comprehending what it was and how it really happened. Sometimes after we had made love and she had gone to sleep I would lie there contemplating her for what seemed like hours on end. There the two long amber legs came together, the even swell of the stomach tapered away between them, and deeper there was only shadow, mute and chthonic. What was I, some kind of a voyeur? The more I looked the less I understood. But I was looking in the wrong place for the mystery. I began to realize finally that it was not in her body, in this simple concave mechanism which was designed to receive a convexity, but in myself.

And after all what was so complicated about myself, about this part of my body that had always been nothing more than a subject for crude jokes before? It had its needs, everybody knew that, and everybody knew what to do about it. I had thought I knew everything there was to know about this need and the gesture that satisfied it, the gesture that the people I had lived among described with a single ugly word. And for what they had done, and what I had done, the word was precise and expressive. It was simply a matter of gratifying my own body, or rather the small part of my body where the need seemed to be concentrated and which demanded its own way before it would leave the rest of the body at peace. Now I began pondering over the way this part of my body was made and studying its design (what the hell, I was an engineer!) and it struck me for the first time what its real purpose was: to give pleasure to others. This was the only possible way of accounting for its shape; otherwise it would merely by a vague sensitive spot I could propitiate by myself. And this discovery led me at last to the definition—love: to give yourself. Make love: to create through giving yourself to others. And it had taken me twenty-six years of my life to understand this? No wonder I spent all those first months at Laguna brooding over this thing which to most people, those who love and give themselves simply and freely, is as natural as the coming of spring.

Perhaps it was worth the time I spent learning it. Anyhow this is what I did from January of 1943 to late February of 1944. It was not a time when most people could devote themselves to their private education. I hear several moralists inquiring whether I spent the worst months of the war, one of the most critical periods in history, contemplating my private parts and making love in a blue bedroom to a woman who was not my wife. I'm afraid that's about the way it was. I didn't know whether it was admirable or not, but I had never been either a moralist or a patriot and I didn't worry very much about it. It was only sometime later (perhaps about the time I made my little Norman Corwin speech to Widdison) that I began to realize the world had been saved and me along with it, that other people had died so I could enjoy my private happiness, like the unknown sailor with the Texas accent who had used the last of his strength to push me up on a raft and then drowned without a word. To tell the truth we didn't take a newspaper, and except for the rationing we almost forgot the war was going on. Once in a while I would remember they were still fighting out in the Pacific or hear on the radio about the landing in Sicily, and it would seem strangely unreal, a kind of drama written daily by the script-writers in the radio stations that had nothing to do with my own war hidden in the blurry scraps of recollection somewhere in the back of mv head. As for other people, it was agreed on all sides that I had done my part by getting sunk, and nobody asked me for anything more. If anyone wanted to see my documents as a noncombatant I could show them my hands.

For a long time I was content to go on this way, but later I understood that this period of my life was only a prolonged convalescence, a kind of limbo. Or perhaps the right word was purgatory; I wasn't much of a theologian. Dostoyevsky said that hell was the state of being unable to love. I had got beyond hell, I knew what love was now, but I didn't know who it was I loved because I didn't know who *she* was yet. Most of all I didn't know who I was. This was the question I had viewed with such a fervent indifference when I was in the hospital and for a long time afterwards, the secret that Gore had tried to help me find out, as though we were two tots sitting happily down together to solve a jigsaw puzzle. Poor Gore, he didn't know what he was asking, and so he never found out what it was that would cure me. But perhaps he had an inkling when he had threatened me with shock treatment: "It jolts the psychic patterns and breaks up mental blocks. It also breaks bones sometimes. Old fellow."

In that winter of 1944 there was a warm spell in February, and the high school kids from Santa Ana used to cut classes in the afternoon and come to the beach to swim. One afternoon I sat on the beach watching four of them trying to launch a boat in the surf. It was an ordinary flat-bottomed skiff, the kind you rent in city parks, and even the gentle breakers at Laguna were enough to capsize it. The four big bronzed kids in skimpy trunks would push it out and all pile into it at once, and the first wave that came along would swamp it. Then they would dump out the water and start over. Finally they managed to get it out beyond the surf line. The rest of the afternoon they rowed clumsily around bailing it out with a tin can. I almost offered to help them when they were trying to get it launched, but then I remembered they were only seventeen or eighteen, and I was almost twenty-seven now, a middle-aged war veteran. There were too many of them for the boat anyhow and it was the wrong kind of a boat for the surf, you would need a dory or something with sides high enough to vault over the breakers when you were pushing it out. But it was a long time since I had seen anybody having that much fun, and that night I asked Leo if they had ever had a boat on the beach.

"A boat? You can't use a boat in the surf."

"You could if it were the right kind of a boat."

"Okay, you're a sailor, I'm just a vegetable clerk from Seventh Avenue."

I didn't say anything more about it that night, but the idea was still in the back of my mind. The fact was that I was getting a little bored lying around on the beach and wanted something to do with myself. The next afternoon I borrowed Ary's car and went to look around in the boat shops in Newport and Costa Mesa. In Newport all I could find was a nine-foot dinghy, probably originally built as a tender for a small yacht. Because of the war the dealer wanted two hundred dollars for it. In the old days I would probably have told him where to put it; now I just said politely, "Thank you very much," and drove away. There was nothing in Costa Mesa or Balboa either except a few of the Snowbird-class sailboats the kids used for racing in the bay. On an impulse I decided to drive on to Long Beach; it was only about an hour on the coast highway and I would still get back in time for dinner. Somewhere beyond American Avenue I got lost and ended up in Wilmington, on the road that led out to Terminal Island. It was the first time I had ever been in the harbor district in a car and I was a little confused about the streets. I thought I remembered there was a yacht harbor and some boat yards somewhere near the foot of Avalon Boulevard, and I drove around trying to find them. Finally I saw some inflatable rubber boats sitting in a yard with a wire fence around it. It wasn't the kind of a boat I was looking for, but I stopped anyhow. The place was a kind of junk yard that had bought up a lot of used Army boots and defective parachutes and now called itself a war surplus store. The yard in front was full of wooden crates, old airplane wings, and various kinds of junk. In the back was a tin warehouse with a sign: "L. Pollbock — Surplus. Plumbing Fixtures. Parachutes. Boots and Weather Gear. Camouflage Cloth. AU Govt. Contract Material at Fraction of Case."

I went in through the gate and walked over to look at one of the rubber boats. It was getting rotten from standing in the sun and it was not what I wanted anyhow. I didn't quite understand why I had gotten out of the car. I stood for a while in the thin winter sunshine looking at the boat and then I realized that I didn't feel very well; I didn't know what was wrong with me but it was an unpleasant empty feeling that seemed to be partly in the viscera and partly around me in the air. And yet I couldn't turn away; I went on standing there looking at the boat and the little puddle of dirty water in the bottom and the instructions printed on the side in black letters that wouldn't quite come into focus. Finally I managed to walk away and get in the car. I drove for about a block and then I realized I didn't know where I was driving or how I had got there. I was on a road that ran along the Terminal Island channel; on one side, the beer parlor on the corner, but the only thing I couldn't figure out was why I was in the car and dressed in these clothes, and why I seemed to be getting sick and had a vague inchoate feeling that I didn't belong here. I stared at the beer parlor for a long time, and finally I opened the door of the car and got out and walked toward it, across the white sidewalk in the piercing white sunlight.

It was a typical waterfront beer joint, dark inside with a cool dank smell, and coming in from the sunlight I couldn't see very well. I sat down at the bar and saw the white blur of the bartender's shirt coming toward me.

"What's yours?"

"Beer."

"Draught, Lucky, Budweiser?"

I had to think for a minute what I wanted. Finally I ordered a draught. When my eyes began to adjust to the light I saw the other customers in the place were looking at me, probably wondering what I was doing in there in those clothes. There were a couple of longshoremen at the other end of the bar and some merchant seamen sitting in a booth at one side. The bartender was an old bull-shaped character who looked as though he might have been a longshoreman once himself. He was giving me the once-over too, and then I wondered if he could see what was happening on the inside of me, if any of it showed on the outside. I didn't know what was happening myself. These people, this place, it was all familiar and yet the familiarity wasn't reassuring, there was something disquieting about it. I had an odd sensation of doubleness, a feeling of being there and yet not being there, as though a part of me were about to float away and leave my corpse sitting there on that bar stool forever. When my beer came I realized I was thirsty and I finished half of it at one swallow. I thought perhaps I was just thirsty and the sun had hit me a little and I would feel better when I had drunk the beer. I didn't feel much better, however, and the beer was probably bad for me because it made the floating sensation a little worse. The bartender was mopping up the bar with a beery old rag. It was a small place and you could hear everything anyone was saying. The two longshoremen at the other end of the bar were talking about boosting whiskey and Swiss watches out of the cargo. I realized that I was listening to them with a vague sense of wrongness, of guilt, and yet with fascination, die way you might listen to the intimate conversation of a married couple from the next room.

"Ole Hymie, I seen him drop a case yesterday. He didn't know how to drop it and he damn near bust his foot. You could smell the stuff a mile. Ole Hymie, he started stuffing it in his shirt."

"You drop a case of them watches and you might as well throw 'em away. Hell, there's better ways than dropping."

"Yeah, I seen you the other day, prying 'em with a crow. Ole Fairbanks was around, you know the shapeup man. He ast me what you was doing, and I said you lost your watch and was trying to find out if it was time to knock off. He didn't say nothing."

Then one of them glanced down the bar and made a motion toward me with his head, and they stopped talking. For a few minutes the place was silent. The bartender got out a dry rag and began polishing his whiskey bottles, standing behind the bar and looking at me.

"You work along the front?" he asked me after a while.

"In a way.

"I floured maybe you was an engineer or something. You over at the Moore yards?"

"What's eating you anyhow? What do you take me for, a cop?"

"I don't take you for anything. I was just talking, that's all."

I had finished my beer and I felt now I wanted to get out of that place and into the daylight. But the daylight was bad for me, the daylight had made me giddy and ill and that was why I had come in here in the first place. And yet I knew that wasn't the reason. But what was the reason? I remembered my car then and I wanted to be in it, driving along the road. I felt that as soon as I was in my car again I would be alright. But I didn't want to leave right away because everyone in the place was watching me now and they would think I was leaving because the bartender had started asking me questions. In the mirror I could see the two merchant seaman in the booth. One of them had a queer kind of a bulging forehead with a crease in the middle of it that somehow seemed familiar, and I had an irrational feeling that he recognized me; there were hundreds of people I had sailed with and I couldn't remember them all. I picked the beer glass up again, found it was empty, and set it down.

"What do I owe you again?"

"Fifteen."

In my pocket I only had a nickel and a few pennies in change, and when I felt around in the back pocket for my billfold it wasn't there. With deliberate calm I looked for my checkbook and found it in the other back pocket.

"Listen, can I give you a small check?"

The bartender looked dubious. "How much?"

"Say five?"

He made a vague noncommittal gesture. I unfolded the checkbook and began writing the check, and then I came to the line for the signature. I hesitated, the pen making slow circles in the air over the check, and I had no idea what I was going to write. I didn't know what was the matter, but it was as though something inside my head was the part that I thought was healed was still paralyzed, and what was paralyzed was the part where I knew how to move the pen. The bartender had stopped polishing bottles and was watching me curiously.

I turned the checkbook over and found the name where the bank had printed it on the outside. Then, forcing myself to act slowly and methodically, I wrote it on the check syllable by syllable: Ben . . . ton. Da . . . ve . . . nant.

"You got some identification, something with your name on it? Driver's license?"

"I'm sorry. I seem to have lost my billfold. That's why I had to write a check."

He turned the check over dubiously in his hands. Finally he handed it back to me. "Skip it. It's only a beer. Take care of it the next time you come in."

Everybody in the place had stopped drinking now and they were watching to see what I would do. Mechanically I stuck the check in my pocket and walked to the door. Out in the bright sunshine, the light rising in waves from the pavement, I found the car and got in it. When I opened the door I saw the billfold lying on the seat; it had simply slipped out of my pocket when I was driving. I didn't go back to pay for the beer and I didn't bother to pick up the billfold. I found the key and put it in the ignition, but then I took my hand away and sat quietly, fixedly, looking at something I saw out through the windshield. A hundred yards away a ship was going down the channel, a grimy British freighter with a deck load of gray-painted bombers for England. The deck gang was stowing the cargo gear for sea, and I could hear the voices and the rattle of winches as the booms came down into the cradles. A cook was standing in the galley door in his undershirt, looking at me as the ship went past. Then a plume of steam formed over the funnel, and an instant later came the sound of the whistle, a deep hoarse blast that went through my bones and shook in the sill of the car door under my hand. It went on for a long time, and as I listened to that bass shaking I felt something inside me, my entrails, stirring and pulling me helplessly toward it. And then I knew that the sickness that had been hanging over me all that day had finally found a weak place to enter. I knew that the thing that pulled me was a parr of myself, a part of me that was sick, and yet I had no power to resist it. I knew the meaning of that cook who had looked at me silently from his doorway, and what he had wanted to say to me. In that moment I could have opened the door of the car and walked away, leaving the billfold with the money and the driver's license and all the documents neatly on the seat. The person I had pretended to be would simply never have been, and yet I knew if I did that, if I obeyed the sound of that whistle and followed it, something vital would be broken in me and there would be no going on, I would cease to exist. Finally the deep shaking stopped. It came with a sense of relief, but it was as though a knife had been withdrawn from my flesh and left the wound behind.

Somehow I started the car and turned it around on the road. I wasn't conscious of turning onto the coast highway or of going through Long Beach; I only remember putting the car in the garage and carefully shutting the garage door, even checking afterward to be sure it was locked. Then I went into the house and walked down the hall to the bedroom. Ary heard me from the kitchen; I heard her call "Hi." I shut the door of the bedroom, and at that moment something pulled loose in me and I was no longer aware of my body or had any control over it. Although I was not conscious of falling I was lying on my back looking up at the ceiling. I knew I was sick but it wasn't the way it had been before, in the hospital. There everything had just been a blur and it didn't seem worthwhile to bring it into focus. Now I knew I was on the point of madness because something I had pretended was not there suddenly appeared before me in perfect clarity, like a ghost in broad daylight. I saw everything, everything I had tried to forget, the degradations and betrayals and deceits, magnified a thousand times and precise in every detail.

Even the objects around me had a terrifying kind of precision, as though I was seeing them through a microscope. I had never understood that madness was just this kind of lucidity, this seeing things too clearly. Something was wrong with my body too, my throat gradually tightened as though a hand was gripping it and the rest of me lay in a kind of slack paralysis. While this was going on I lay there conducting a quite rational conversation with him; it seemed perfectly natural for him to be there, even though I had never worked out in my mind exactly who he was. I think I talked to him for a long time, although perhaps it was only for a few minutes, and I think I talked to him aloud, although I may have been mistaken about that too. I don't remember very much about what we said, except that I felt awkward and vaguely guilty because I refused to admit I knew who he was, and we both knew that I knew who he was. I remember at one point he told me I was hooked on something, I forget what, and when I told him I wasn't he said *Get up off the floor if you're not hooked*. But he was right, I couldn't get up. off the floor, and when I told him again I didn't know him he said *You know who I am, kid. Quit faking. How can you tell so goddam many lies?* After a while I didn't answer anymore, and the voice went on talking to me while I looked at the ceiling. I knew if I made an effort I could kill him. I didn't have to stand up and strike him, I could do it lying there; it was only necessary to will to do it. There wasn't any particular emotion involved, it was simply a practical question whether I should kill him or not. But my mind was operating quite clearly and I realized that killing him or myself or anybody else was not the answer, that people for whom life is too complicated always want to pull a trigger or press a pillow over a face and imagine that in some way that will make things simpler. But instead of solving the problem it only makes it more complicated, or it ends everything. There wasn't any simple way; I would just have to take it complicated. I knew now that the only way to make the voice stop was to kill myself, because this was what killing him would mean. He was inside me and he was not going to get out, and if I wanted to go on living I would have to live with him.

I lay for a long time thinking of this. Then Ary came in and found me lying on the floor. My face was wet with perspiration and when she spoke to me I couldn't answer. She tried to help me up, but my arms and legs were heavy and I had no will to move myself. Finally she got me onto the bed.

"I don't want to anymore," I told her. "Let me alone, I'm tired. I don't want to try anymore."

"Don't talk."

"I'm tired of trying, it's no good."

She went away without saying anything, and after a while she came back with an enormous highball. When she handed it to me I looked at her. Her face showed nothing and I couldn't tell what she was thinking.

"Did you hear what I was saying?"

"Drink it."

She had something else in her hand, a capsule, and I put it in mouth first and swallowed it. Then with my hands that were still heavy and clumsy I raised the glass and began sipping. Gradually my throat loosened. She sat across the room watching me.

When I had finished half the drink I relaxed and began to feel a little foolish. I was still covered with perspiration but it was cool sweat now; I could feel it trickling under my armpits. "I guess this is what you call a nervous breakdown," I said after a while.

"For the moment you have what is called an alcohol deficiency. Drink."

I began trying to explain, rather incoherently. "It's as though— you know, some people have been hurt and they have hunks of metal inside them that the doctors don't find. I guess one of them worked loose. It's stupid, I'm sorry."

She didn't seem to take it very seriously. "We've all got our problems. If you have hunks of metal inside it's probably better for them to work loose. I suppose there are a lot worse problems to have. Some people are born without any arms or legs, although that's never very much of a consolation, for some reason."

She said this matter-of-factly and without even any particular sympathy in her voice, as though we were discussing the fact that her fingernails broke or my hair was falling out. This was the only discussion we ever had about my fit or trance, or whatever it had been. I didn't know if the voices had been real or whether she heard them too or what it was that she was thinking. But at least I was grateful she hadn't acted like most women, running off to call a doctor and asking me how I felt and badgering me with a lot of questions, and instead had just sat there quietly so there would be somebody with me while I worked it out for myself. After a while she went away and got herself a whiskey and soda too, and sat there sipping it while she watched me. I remember thinking it must have got to her a little after all, because she never drank in the daytime. Then the capsule worked and I went to sleep.

Chapter 16

.-- .... --- .- -- ..   .-- .... --- .- -- ..   .-- .... --- .- -- ..   .-- .... --- .- -- ..

I slept the rest of the afternoon and all that night without waking or even moving, my limbs in the same position when I woke up as when I went to sleep. The next morning when I woke up it was a little after dawn, and I got out of bed quietly and went down to the beach. I felt stronger and my head was clear, as though something foggy had been washed out of it by a storm. There on the cool beach at six o'clock in the morning when everybody else was asleep I saw what had been wrong before and what it was I had to do from now on. My mistake had been that I had never really thought it out and come to terms with what I was doing. I had thought I was trying to be something I was not or change myself into an image of something I had only a rather vague notion of, a kind of a half-baked Platonic form of what I thought I was supposed to be. For a while this had gone fairly well, so we in fact that I had got a little cocky on success. The others had accepted my blunders and mistakes as part of a sickness that took a long time to get over, as though the glue in my head was still soft and might come unstuck once in a while. But with myself it was not so easy. You could only fool yourself up to a point; that was why voice had said *how can you tell so goddam many lies?* Before that little crackup when all my mistakes piled up on me I thought it made, but it wasn't really made yet; the hardest part of it was still to come. It wasn't really the others I had to convince but and it didn't matter whether I selected the right cheese or which necktie to wear with a Harris tweed jacket. I saw now I had to forget the cheese and come to grips with the really important questions that lay ahead of me, the questions that in the end would determine what I was going to be. I wasn't a matter of convincing these people or anybody else that I was something I was not, or even of trying to make myself into something they wanted me to be. It was a matter of making myself into something *I would decide*; of asking myself what was the best I had and what I could made with it and then working as hard as I could to make it.

So far I had been lucky, but my luck was not that I was alive when other people were dead or even that I had fallen into a good thing. The luck was that so far I had managed to avoid falling off the tight wire and I knew now that I happened to have the two or three qualities I needed to do what I had to do. I had read enough books now to make the proper noises when somebody mentioned the postimpressionists or Molly Bloom's soliloquy, and my senses were better than average: I could pick out stars in broad daylight, read the label on a spinning phonograph record, hear the minute mistakes of the cello player in the Boston Symphony record of the *Eroica*. For the first time in my life I began to see myself as I really was, intelligent in my way with a foxy kind of alertness, fairly good at concealing my feelings from others and even better at deceiving myself. I had never particularly thought of myself as superior or inferior to other people, and I didn't now; these were simply my sins or my virtues, whichever way I chose to treat them. I had done a lot of dark things in the years I had kicked around the world, I had gone to prison and I had killed a man with my bare hands, but my real sin had not been dishonesty or embezzlement or cowardice or even murder. My real sin had been apathy, the kind of cockeyed contempt or everything I had learned from the others on all the bad ships I had sailed on in all those pointless wandering years. I had never known a name for this until I read Dante; it was called acedia and it was one of the seven deadly sins, and the Church knew what it was talking about. You couldn't spend your whole life just standing on a throttle platform and watching the gauges, four on and eight off, because that wasn't life. In order for it to be a life, you had to make something even if it wasn't something very important, so you could feel that your being around and breathing and taking up space in the world made at least a little difference.

I didn't know what I could make, but I thought I had an idea of where to start. For a couple of days I did nothing; I sat on the beach and answered in monosyllables when people spoke to me, feeling relaxed and more or less benign but not particularly wanting to talk. The third day after breakfast I asked Ary for the keys to the car again. The remarkable thing was that she gave them to me and let me back out of the garage and drive away, even though she could see I was still acting strange and a little preoccupied. Maybe she felt that people over twenty-one were free to do as they pleased, or perhaps she simply sensed in some way that I was different from the way I had been three days before and stronger, and nothing was going to happen. I drove down the coast highway through Long Beach and straight to Wilmington. The streets confused me a little and it was as though I had been there twenty years before instead of only three days, but finally I found L. Pollbock Surplus again. I walked through the gate into the yard full of junk and began looking around. I didn't bother with the rubber boats this time because I was interested in something else, something I remembered seeing out of the corner of my eye the last time I had come. It was still there, a gray-painted Navy crate with the specifications stenciled on the outside, "Multiphase generator Mk VIII 110/120 v. 10 w.," but when I looked at it closer I saw it was empty. There were two or three other similar crates lying around. Either L. Pollbock had sold the generators or he had them in the back somewhere. Everything else in the front yard was rubbish, unless you had a use for old airplane wings.

I walked back to the warehouse. At first there didn't seem to be anybody there, and then back in the rear I found a bald squat man in steel spectacles counting a pile of aircraft flares. He looked as though he might have been a plumbing wholesaler or a used-car dealer before the war, or perhaps he had just sold second-hand pants. Now he was in the surplus business and you could tell he thought he had a good thing. He was shrewd and garrulous and began giving me a great sales line about everything, but after I had talked to him for a few minutes I saw he didn't know anything about the stock he was selling and was just trying to turn it over as fast as possible for what he could get out of it. He was trying to sell 1917-model gas masks for four dollars apiece, although nobody in his right mind would pay fifty cents for them even if he needed a 1917 gas mask, and surplus tank periscopes with precision-ground prisms for two dollars when the prisms alone were probably worth twenty. I didn't happen to need any prisms, but the place was beginning to look interesting.

I walked around the warehouse with Pollbock following me, giving me a steady stream of misinformation about the stock. He told me a coil of uninsulated antenna wire would be fine for house wiring, and that you could make boat sails out of old parachutes. I didn't bother to contradict him; I just wandered around and looked at things for myself. On a shelf in the back I found some of the generators I was looking for, still in their crates. They were high-quality equipment and what the Navy had surplussed them for I didn't know. Probably nobody in the Navy did either, or perhaps it was just that this screwy country was overproducing war material so fast they didn't know what to do with it and had to sell it for junk.

"What are those?"

"Those? Those there are electrical motors. Navy contract material, never been used. I can let you have them for ten, twelve dollars. Say ten."

They had probably cost the Navy seventy-five or eighty dollars each. "Have you got any more marine electrical equipment?"

He began rooting around in a pile of junk and pulled out a secondhand Navy handybilly, a portable fire pump driven by a miniature gas engine. "This here is a wonderful thing. This is a little fire pump, it's got an engine on it that you can take off and use it in a boat. You've still got the pump left, and the pump alone is worth what I can sell it to you for. Say thirty dollars. That little engine, it's got four cylinders and it's built just like an automobile engine." He had a great air of knowledgeability about him, this man who didn't know a generator from an electric motor, and an unbounded confidence in the worth of his stock. I knew the handybilly was no good for a boat engine because it didn't have any thrust bearing and the cooling system wasn't designed for salt water, but I bought it anyhow, for twenty-five dollars. I had only a vague idea what I was going to do with it. I think I brought it mainly because Pollbock didn't know what it was. I also bought one of the generators for eight and a half dollars, and paid for them both with a check. This time I didn't have any trouble remembering my name, and Pollbock put the check in his pocket without even looking at it.

"Have you got any more like that?"

"Those there electrical motors? I've got what you see here. Fifteen or twenty of them."

"I mean the handybilly."

"Oh, that there fire pump." He scratched his head, which had a long strand of hair combed across it and dangling over the opposite ear. "You know, that'll make a fine engine for a boat, or you can make a little car with it for the kids. I haven't got any more now, but I can get you some. How many would you want?"

"I don't know. It was just an idea."

"I'm going to go down and bid on a bunch next week in San Diego. You want to take fifteen, twenty I can make you a better price."

I told him I had to think about it. The idea I had was probably half baked anyhow. He and a boy loaded the stuff in the car for me and I drove off with it. When I got back to Laguna I had to take the generator and the handybilly out of the car by myself. My hands were almost healed now, but it was the first time I had lifted anything heavy since I had been in the hospital. My muscles were soft, and even a slight effort left them aching a little. I set the equipment out on the garage floor and measured everything and made some sketches. Then I got back in the car and went to Newport Beach to a tool-and-machinery place to rent a welding outfit. I spent the rest of the afternoon and most of that night out in the garage cutting and welding, with half an hour off to eat around seven. In the middle of the afternoon Ary came out to see what I was doing.

"I'm taking a correspondence course in safe-cracking. Don't look at the torch, it's bad for your eyes."

"Where did you learn to solder?"

"Weld."

"What are you making?"

"I don't know yet."

She walked around, turning over the junk with her foot and looking at it as though it was quite natural to find I had set up a welding shop in the garage.

"What about your eyes?"

"I've got goggles."

"They won't do any good up there on your forehead."

I pulled the goggles down without answering and went on working. She stood around watching me for a half an hour and then she got bored and went away. I finally quit that night about midnight. The next day I had to go out and buy some more parts: a voltmeter, a pair of vee-belt pulleys, and a fan belt from a gas station. By four o clock I had the pump out of the frame and installed the generator in its place, and I had built a small portable generating unit powered by the gas engine. I thought it would put out about a kilowatt of power, but I wouldn't know until I tried. To test it I connected it up to the house current in place of the city power, and when I started the engine the first thing it did was to blow out every fuse in the house. Ary came out again to see what I was doing, remarkably calm considering that I had blown out the fuses while she was trying to cook a roast in the electric range, and I explained to her that all it needed was a governor to keep the engine from running away.

"Perhaps we could just go on using the electricity from the Edison Company."

"If Edison had been married," I told her, "we'd still be using oil lamps."

"Edison was married."

"Edison was a lifelong bachelor. Have we got any more fuses?"

She helped me find the spare fuses and put them in. The second time I started the engine I kept the RPM down, and the generator lighted the house perfectly.

The next month I worked harder than I ever had in my life. From our occasional trips to Los Angeles I thought I remembered a small machine shop and welding place on the highway outside Santa Ana, and one morning I put the generating rig in the car and took it up to show to the owner of the shop. He was a long lanky Arkansan named Prentiss, lazy and slow talking, with a small round belly like a melon in the middle of his overalls. I got out the generating rig by myself and set it on the ground, and he looked dubious before I even started talking.

"Can you make these?"

"Listen, with this war on you can't get anything, welding rod, nothing."

"I'll get you the welding rod."

He looked at the generating rig skeptically. "Who made this here?"

"I did."

"You ain't much of a welder, are you?"

"Can you make them or not?"

"I ain't got the help. A man quit on me last week."

"All right, suit yourself. How about giving me a hand to lift it back in the car?"

Later I often wondered whether Prentiss took the job just to get out of lifting a heavy weight. He was no athlete; he may have been a machinist once but now he had a pot belly and belonged to the managerial class. We went in his office and he broke two or three stubby pencils, used up a half-dozen sheets of paper, and finally agreed to build the units for thirty dollars apiece, welding rod extra.

I left him the model I had made and drove back to Laguna. I hadn't washed for two days and had hardly eaten; my face was grimy and I had a hole burned in my shirt sleeve from the welding torch. I found Ary sitting on the sofa looking cool, in a persimmon-colored jersey and a pair of linen slacks. It was eleven-thirty in the morning and she was reading a novel by Dorothy Richardson.

"Listen, how much have we got in that checking account?"

"Why?"

"I want to buy something."

She closed the book and lit a cigarette, regarding me thoughtfully. "How much do you need?"

"Two thousand, maybe twenty-five hundred."

She let me wait while she shook out the match and set the cigarette carefully in the ashtray.

"Well, this is a new development, isn't it?"

"I never asked you for anything before. Now I'm asking you for this."

"Well, don't make such a drama out of it. After all it's our money. Take what you need."

"It's not our money!" I shot back a little angrily. "Why should we pretend it is? It's your money, we both know it, and I don't like asking you for it. With all your famous sensitivity I shouldn't think you'd like it either. I've been loafing around here for a year now, and every time I want a pair of shoes or a cigarette I have to ask you for it—"

For some reason this produced the usual ironic smile at the corners of her mouth, and then I realized I had automatically picked up her pack of cigarettes and was taking one out as I talked. I threw the pack across the room and the cigarettes scattered.

"The hell with it! I don't like those things anyhow, they've got no taste." After a while I calmed down a little and said, "I don't know, I guess I'm just not cut out to be a gigolo, that's all."

She left the cigarettes where they were, scattered over the rug. "You could be a fine gigolo if you put your mind to it," she told me. "I think it would be a gallant gesture, though, if you washed your face before lunch."

It was an odd feeling, getting back in the habit of work. I didn't go swimming as much now and I slept only five or six hours a night. I couldn't explain it to the others or even to Ary, because I wasn't sure myself what I was doing or why I was doing it. What I did understand was that everything I did and every step I took helped define what I was going to become. I wasn't sure what this was yet, but I knew that even the invalid who had come to this house a year before was a stranger to me now, and that every decision I made was crucial because it somehow hardened an identity that was gradually taking form out of a blur. Was I easy-going or shrewd? Hard-working or lazy? I couldn't tell yet; I acted half by instinct and half by plan, almost as though I was watching myself to see what I would do next. I sensed that Ary was watching me too, but she made no particular comment and hardly seemed to notice what I was doing. Once I cracked my finger when a monkey wrench slipped and she was properly sympathetic, kissing it first and then wrapping it up for me. "Didn't they teach you to use a monkey wrench at the University of Washington?" she asked me.

I was too busy to psychoanalyze her anyhow because I had other things on my mind. The next week I went down to the auction at the San Diego naval depot and outbid L. Pollbock for the fire pumps. He looked a little startled, especially since my bid was only about half of what he had offered to get them for, but he didn't seem to hold it against me and later he sold me the generators at the price he had quoted. I began to see another side of Pollbock. It was true he was ignorant and didn't know anything about the merchandise he was selling, but he had an instinct for what could be bought and sold, and in his own way he was honest. He could be as sharp as a razor in a deal, but once he had given his word you could count on him delivering exactly what he had promised. He even showed me things about the business I never would have found out by myself.

"Ain't you a veteran?" he asked me when I talked to him after the auction at San Diego.

"Why?"

"You're entitled to a ten percent discount, only you got to apply for it on a form eighty-five. These here supply officers would never tell you about it if you fried them in lard. You ought to read the code, it's a very interesting book."

I was in the middle of Kierkegaard but I put it away and read the 1942 *United States Code* instead, especially the section on military surplus. In addition to the one he mentioned I found several more laws that were worth money and that the supply officers would never have told me about. It was also Pollbock who showed me how to figure out whether you were in the red or the black: you wrote down what you paid for things and what you sold them for, amortized your tools and equipment at the depreciation rate, subtracted the interest on your capital, and put the rest in your pocket. Pollbock was my business school; in a month I learned enough about merchandising from him to last me the rest of my life. It was he who got me the welding rod, from a shipbuilder in Long Beach who had a priority but didn't need it because his contract had been terminated. He didn't do this for nothing because Pollbock didn't do anything for nothing, but even taking out his commission I still got the rod at a little below wholesale.

I spent most of that month driving all over Southern California in Ary's car, sleeping when I got the chance and hardly stopping to eat. Gasoline was still rationed, and when I ran out of coupons she began borrowing for me from Leo's supply. By March Prentiss had finished the first of the generating units and I signed a contract with an electrical supply house in East Los Angeles to market them. The purchasing agent for the company couldn't figure out where I had got the generators; he had been trying to buy some for two years and couldn't find them. I had taken the Navy specification plates off the generators and I said something vague about connections and priorities. Electrical equipment was still in short supply and the units sold very quickly; people used them as portable power supplies for mountain cabins and boats. The Navy even bought four for some patrol boats they were building in Long Beach. In June I was contracting with Prentiss for a second lot of three hundred. My own unit, the first one I had welded up out in the garage, was sold in a lot along with the others.

By summer I had my own checking account and the balance was up to four figures. To reward myself a little I bought a car: a 1936 Ford V-8 coupe with radio, price-controlled at three hundred and sixty dollars. For some reason I became very fond of this car and used to spend all my spare time polishing it and tightening up nuts and bolts. One morning I went out and found some kids from the neighborhood playing around on the running board, and I chased them off. "Don't you know this is private property?" I told them sternly. The kids stared at me, and after a while I started laughing. My God, but I was getting bourgeois! I wondered why I was so attached to this car, and why I enjoyed working on it and would go out in the morning before breakfast like a kid to see if it was still there, and then I realized it was the first thing in my life I had ever owned except my clothes.

That summer I had my last encounter with the law, in which it turned out that I was innocent. I was working in the study one afternoon and Suzanne came in and told me "a man from the government" wanted to see me. I had never given my address to anyone but Pollbock and Prentiss, and I had a slight cold feeling in my chest. But it was only an agent from the War Production Board, somewhat overdressed for Laguna in a business suit and shiny black shoes. I was in shorts and sandals with no socks. He began by apologizing for disturbing me in my home. "I wonder if I could ask you a few questions. You've been selling generating units on the open market."

"Yes."

"Where did you get the priorities for the materials?"

I showed him the receipts from Pollbock and the auction invoices from the San Diego naval depot.

"You mean all of this material is declared surplus?"

"That's right."

I didn't mention the welding rod, since this was only a minor item in my cost accounting schedule (I was learning the jargon). He looked over all the papers and couldn't find anything wrong with them. I even had a bill to show that the V-belts were synthetic and not on the priority list. He pulled the lobe of his ear thoughtfully and then shook his head.

"I don't know, either I'm crazy or somebody in Washington has got a screw loose. Did you know that your jobber has been reselling some of these units to the Navy?"

"So I've heard."

'In other words, you've been buying the material surplus and making the units for—let me see—" he began figuring on a scrap of paper—"about seventy-five dollars apiece including labor, you sell them wholesale for a hundred and twenty-nine seventy, and the jobber retails them to the Navy for a hundred and eight-five dollars."

"After all, this kind of initiative is what made America great."

"Sure, sure."

"Have a drink?"

"Don't mind if I do."

I made him a gin Collins and fixed one for myself. "You know," he said, "I've looked at a lot of books but I never saw a business like this. Don't you have an office?"

"What for?"

"To keep your secretary in, I guess."

"What do you need a secretary for?"

"To take care of your office. What do you do when you want to write a letter?"

"I've only written four or five, and I go into Laguna to the steno service."

"You know, when the report came in the office you were running this business out of your home I thought we had something. There are a lot of fly-by-night operators using black market materials. But as far as I can tell you seem to be on the level."

"Look at it this way. One end of the Navy needs these units, and the other end has got the materials in surplus and doesn't know it. It's worth my markup of fifty-four seventy to show their left hand what their right hand is doing."

"Sure, sure."

At this point Leo drove in the driveway, and I fixed him a drink and made another for myself. The WPB man wouldn't take a second; he said he couldn't risk it during working hours and he had three more firms to visit that afternoon. He was the most likeable bureaucrat I ever met. "Jesus, I wish I could go around wearing shorts like that," he told me as he left.

Leo never seemed to feel there was anything extraordinary in my becoming a minor manufacturer, and neither did anyone else. It didn't even seem extraordinary to me, except once in a while when a pair of wires would cross in my mind and I would see something out of the past, something I thought I had forgotten, with an unexpected and vivid clarity. But after that afternoon on the bedroom floor these little visions didn't bother me anymore; I knew where they came from now and they no longer had any power to harm me, because I was no longer pretending to be anything I was not. I still had the sensation I was playing a role but it didn't bother me anymore, because I knew now that everybody else played a role too; it was just that some played them well and some badly. For example Firmín had been a bad imitation of a captain, and Maurice was a good imitation of an Englishman, all the more impressive when you knew he had been born over a delicatessen in Soho and spoke Yiddish before he spoke English. In a way it was lucky all this happened in California where nobody has any past and everything is more or less artificial; we were all fakes together. Nobody had ever asked Mike Romanoff for his credentials, and nobody asked me for mine.

Anyhow, what was a human being if not just a role with a consciousness inside? That night at dinner, after the WPB man had left, we got into a funny conversation: we talked about identity and how you know who you are. Leo had been reading Chinese philosophy, and he said that according to Confucius it was all a matter of names. A father was one who fitted the name of a father, a soldier was one who fitted the name of a soldier, and so on.

"Maybe the WPB man was a Confucian," I pointed out. "For him a businessman is somebody who has an office and wears a business suit. I didn't have an office and I didn't wear a business suit, but I seemed to be in business. This baffled him, and he had to have a drink while he figured it out."

"What do you think he decided?"

"I think he decided I was a non-business-man who for some reason had got into business." And this, I thought, was fairly astute of him after all.

"On the other hand," suggested Leo, "suppose you had a business suit and an office, but you didn't have any business? What would the WPB man think of that?"

"He would probably decide you were a crook and want to look at your tax returns."

"I think this whole conversation is silly," said Suzanne. "I don't think you have any control over who you are—it just happens. Sometimes in the morning I wake up and don't know who I am. I have to get out of bed and open the closet door, and then I think, oh yes, I'm the girl in the red dress."

While this symposium went on we were devouring several helpings apiece of sole marguéry with Napa Valley sauterne. Probably the wine made the ideas sound better than they really were. Anyhow Leo and I defended the Confucian theory of names and Ary agreed with Suzanne that it was mainly a matter of clothes; probably this was a typical feminine point of view. "And that is why," she concluded, "we go on putting on clothes and joining things and having our calling cards printed—to remind ourselves who we are."

"I haven't joined anything yet," I told him, "but the other day I got a letter asking if I didn't want to join the State Manufacturers' Association. That shows you what happens when you go out in the garage and start fooling around with a welding torch. I'll probably end up joining the Lions' Club and the Chamber of Commerce."

Ary said, "In time you may even join the PTA."

Leo looked up and glanced at her a little curiously, and then he went on eating again. But he had known her longer than I had, and there at the dinner table it didn't strike me she had said anything out of the ordinary. It was only later I remembered that even her most casual remarks were never totally pointless or offhand and that when she said something, even something trivial, it was exactly what she wanted to say and not merely the first thing that came into her head. Then I felt like a dense male: I began to put things together and it occurred to me that her three-day interludes of untouchability, which she conveyed with such impeccable tact, had not happened for some time and that lately her Gioconda smile seemed to have taken on certain new nuances of private wisdom. I began to see what Leo meant by living with women for years and not understanding them. I had thought I knew her body, its intricacies and needs and secrets, as well as I knew my own, but now it seemed I didn't know the first basic thing that was going on inside it.

But what really interested me or befuddled me or gave me food for thought was not what was going to happen to her, or was already happening to her, or in her (calm down now and get this straight, I told myself), but what was happening, or going to happen, to me. This was a role I had never imagined myself in, and on the whole I didn't feel I had any real talent for it. I wasn't even sure I had a paternal instinct. But perhaps it all came together; it was a package deal. There were a lot of other instincts I had never known I had until the time came to use them. (I was trying to convince myself.) I imagined myself as a father robin, fiercely defending the nest from ferrets, tree snakes, yellow cats, etc. But the effort of the imagination didn't really take, and, as I argued to Leo when we were sitting out under the pines after dinner, admitting in an abstract sense that reproduction was necessary or even inevitable for a large proportion of the human race, it really wasn't fair of women to make this decision inside a dark womb without telling you anything about it and then expect you to accept the consequences. It ought to be something you could join, like the State Manufacturers' Association.

"I don't object to it, you understand. For the moment I just have the slight feeling I'm being used."

"Used by what?"

"I don't know, biology, I guess. Or maybe just women."

"In the culture I came from we like to feel that we're using them," he told me, holding the muscatel bottle up to the light to see how much was left. "They're entitled to their opinion, but for us a woman is just a kind of an incubator we use to keep our sons in for the first nine months, until they're ready to come out and fend for themselves. This is a very important matter. It's a philosophical question, in fact, it's the only philosophical question. You see, the Jews never believed in an afterlife, so for us a son is the only immortality you have."

"What, now you're a Jew?"

"'What am I, a Hindu?"

"I thought they excommunicated you or unfrocked you or whatever they do, when you ran off and became a poet."

"Fine, but you don't throw off nine thousand years of history just by going off to Greenwich Village. What do you want me to believe, that Luther and John Knox are up there playing harps and waiting for me with open arms?"

"All right, don't get sore."

"Who's sore? We're having a philosophical discussion. I'm just telling you that you're mortal, goddam it, we all are, and if you don't want to die out completely you've got to recreate yourself in the only way the human race has figured out to recreate itself so far, and that means accepting all the consequences, including your wife having a mysterious smile which soon turns into a fat stomach. Who's using whom? The two of you are using each other. And maybe there's something that didn't occur to you, damn it—I'm using you too."

I remembered now how he had said a son instead of children, and how he had lived all his life in a house full of women.

"Sons, that's immortality? I never thought you were so mystical," I told him, "or the Jews either."

"What do you mean mystical? I'm talking about something perfectly literal and scientific. You don't have to go to the Old Testament, all you have to do it look at a good book on cytology."

"On what?"

"Well, it's not so very mysterious, it's just the study of cells. The chromosome is the kind of cell you pass along to your children, and the chromosome tissue is absolutely and literally immortal. Each chromosome keeps its identity from generation to generation; the same germ plasm is living in your body that was living in your ancestors' bodies a thousand years ago. In fact you might say the germ plasm is just using your body as an instrument to perpetuate itself. When you mate you're just doing what the chromosome wants you to do; the male chromosome knows that it needs to find a female cell to unite with or it will die out. All the rest of it comes from this—love, literature, the Trojan War, Tristan and Isolde, and the bulge in the middle of your wife. You're being used all right," he concluded, "but you just didn't understand by what."

There was a pause while he filled our glasses again and I looked at him.

"And the funny thing is," he went on, "that even though the chromosome is immortal it can't exist by itself and can live only inside the human body. Without you it dies in a few hours. So it needs you too. You might say the human race is a way the chromosome has invented for staying alive. But the poets knew that before the cytologists: '*Alles was Leben hat, lebt durch etwas ausser sich?*'"

"What's that?"

"Goethe," was all he would tell me.

I had got used to doing my homework in secret, behind a locked door. Before I went to bed that night I went in the study and translated it for myself from the dictionary, word by word:

Alles: all
was: what
Leben: life
hat: he, she, or it has
lebt: he, she, or it lives
durch: through
etwas: something or somewhat
ausser: outside or out of
sich: himself, herself, or itself, reflexive.

"All that lives, lives through something outside itself."

It was almost midnight and when I went in the bedroom Ary was undressing. The mysterious smile was still there but there was no sign of a bulge yet. I didn't feel particularly amorous but I felt like being there with her somehow, and I sat in the armchair watching her while she took off her blouse and then her skirt and hung them carefully over a hanger. I remembered that first night in this room when I had reached out and seized her impulsively and almost desperately with a need that transcended eroticism and ended in something metaphysical that even I didn't understand, as she had gone past the bed to get her nightgown, and clung to her as though not only my existence but the existence of everything depended on it, and that other time on the ship when I had no hands and had to pull her awkwardly down toward me with my wrists. Probably there never was such a determined set of chromosomes in the history of cytology.

"Well, did you and Leo get it all settled?"

"It's all right," I told her. "You can go ahead. What do we do next?"

She looked at me calmly and almost patronizingly, with only a trace of amusement. "Wait," she told me. "For six more months."

I had enough to keep me busy while the chromosomes worked their mysterious ways, because now I was in the manufacturing business, although still a non-member of the State Association. When Prentiss failed that fall, mainly through sheer laziness, I bought him out and started making marine electrical equipment. I would design something and build it up myself in the shop in Santa Ana; when it wouldn't work I would redesign it, until finally I would have something that somebody would buy. In this way I made a simple float alarm to warn when a hold was leaking, and then a portable cleanout rig to free clogged pipes. By the first of the year I had three employees and a part-time girl to type invoices. The things we made were small and simple, but when there was a need for them they would sell and make a little profit. Prentiss' shop was badly organized, all the space taken up with broken-down machinery that was never used, and I cleaned it out and replanned it. Then that spring I got interested in the problem of cargo pumps for small tankers. Ordinary pumps were all right for crude oil and diesel, but for gasoline they were dangerous because of the spark hazard. There were several gasoline pumps on the market but none of them were very satisfactory; the good ones were too expensive and the cheap ones were no good. I spent several months trying to design a pump that would do the job. My idea was to make a single compact unit, motor and pump, sealed in rubber and submerged in the tank with the gasoline all around it. It was a good idea in principle, but the trouble was that the gasoline rotted the rubber. Around this time a lot of synthetics and plastics were coming on the market, and I experimented with about forty different compounds trying to find something that would stand up to the gasoline. I got a fifty-gallon steel drum full of aviation gas and we used to test the pumps in that. We were lucky we didn't blow ourselves up. In the fall of 1945 I finally solved the problem and made about thirty of the pumps. But meanwhile the war had ended, and when I tried to market them I found a Swedish firm had got into tire field ahead of me and was already selling better pumps for two-thirds of what I could make them for.

It was my first failure. Who were these Swedes anyhow? I began to understand the mentality of tariff cranks. I hired American citizens and used domestic materials, then these foreigners started shipping in cheap merchandise and put people out of work, and so forth. If they didn't stop this it could wreck this economy. The only one I ever tried this speech on was Leo, and he laughed at me. "You sound like an NAM press agent," he told me.

"Why not? I'm a manufacturer."

"All right, if you can't make a living manufacturing, quit. But stop griping."

"That's easy to say. Wait till you're faced with the problem yourself."

"I am. I was raising tomatoes in Imperial Valley, and then I found out they were growing them in Mexico for half the cost."

"What did you do?"

"I started buying tomatoes in Mexico."

"So you put American labor out of work."

"All right, they're out of work, but they eat tomatoes awfully cheap. Anyhow there's a shortage of farm labor in the valley. What are you, a nationalist or something?"

I thought about this. Who was I to start complaining about foreigners anyhow? I had been a foreigner all my life, I had never belonged to anything but myself. Besides it was a question of who was in charge, me or this tinny little shop that would fall down if I kicked it hard. Was I going to change my opinions now and build my whole philosophy around a balance sheet? Here I was hating these Swedes because they had built a better pump than I had and left me in the red for a few dollars. Dollars! Next I would be talking about a preventive war against Sweden.

Instead I bought one of the Swedish pumps and took it apart to see how it was made. It was a beautiful design, simpler and more efficient than mine. I had worked all afternoon and evening taking it apart and it was after midnight; I sat and contemplated it, in the back room of my shop in Santa Ana, and remembered again how fine and clean and precise machines were when they were well made and kept in order. I had felt that when I first started going to sea, but then gradually I had begun to resent the machines, all the resentment of my own life was focused on them and they were nothing but greasy junk that smelled of oil and broke at the wrong time, and I was their slave who had to lubricate them at stated intervals. Now, contemplating the Swedish pump, I saw it was the other way around after all, that machines signified the whole human domination over the world of matter. As long as we made them precisely and used them well it was we who owned the machines and not the machines that owned us. It was late at night and I was getting, perhaps, a little sentimental. Anyhow I saw clearly that I could never make as good a pump as the Swedes, but it didn't matter because basically we were on the same side, the human race against the indifference and intractability of the universe. The fact that they had made the pump so well was good for everybody, Swedes, Americans, the last Zulu going down a jungle road with a gasoline popper on his bicycle. The next day I bought two hundred of the pumps from Göteborg by cable, and I had them all sold before the shipment arrived. In November I sold the shop to a Greek named Hercules Pappas who wanted to use it to make bathroom fixtures. He gave me a little more than I had paid Prentiss for it, and from then on I was in the import business.

I rented an office in Long Beach, on the fourth floor of the Kelton Building, and now I was really operating, with a real secretary and a button I pushed when I wanted her to come. If I forgot

who I was I could always look at my letterheads: Benton Davenant, Imports, 516 Ocean Avenue, Long Beach, California, cable
address Bender. I didn't have any illusions about the superiority
or grandness of this new personage I had created; I knew I was
just a businessman and not a very important one. Like Pollbock,
I simply bought things for less and sold them for more. I was a lot
more complicated than I had been before and I lived on a higher
level of awareness, but most of that was luck. I didn't even have
any vanity about making money, although I made more in a month
now than I had made in a year before. I knew now how easy this
was, that it came as an accident usually because you got interested
in something and worked hard at it for the sheer kick, and then
one day you realized that money was coming in faster than you
could spend it. The office in Long Beach had a washroom, and
in the washroom was a mirror: sometimes I would go in there
and look at it and think of all the mirrors I had looked into in my
lifetime—for a man who disliked his face I seemed to have spent
an extraordinary amount of my life looking into mirrors—and it
seemed to me even now that it looked more like the face of a third
engineer on a fourth-rate ship than an importer who sent cables
to Yokohama and Milan. But there it was, if you didn't believe it
you could go back and look at the letterheads again. My secretary
was named Gogo, and she only worked in the afternoon; she was
still going to business school in the mornings.

Chapter 17

.-- .... --- .- -- ..   .-- .... --- .- -- ..   .-- .... --- .- -- ..   .-- .... --- .- -- ..

For a while after we had Sid I didn't know what you were supposed to do with him, and when Ary was asleep I would sit by the crib watching to be sure he didn't stop breathing or anything. When you thought about it, it was terribly precarious, breathing, and I wasn't sure a baby could do it. And the heartbeat! Something pulsed feebly in the fat region under his neck: what if it stopped? I went on standing watch this way for about a month. Then I began to see he could breathe by himself, and after that I went to sleep at night and let him take care of his own physiological processes. I still wasn't sure how I was supposed to act around him, however, and it was a long time before Sid and I found any use for each other. I accepted his value in the abstract as a bearer of chromosomes, somebody to pass along the baton to in the cosmic relay race, but it wasn't easy to be friends with someone who seemed so blase and so unimpressed with all the affectionate remarks made to him. Then one day when Ary was out of the house I had to change him. I went to work at this and it was a clumsy and heavy-handed business, like shoeing a horse. How could you fasten a rectangular piece of cloth on a bifurcated animal, especially if he wouldn't hold still, the fat worm? When he felt the strange hands it startled him and he began to screw up his face in indignation, then he opened his eyes to see who it was and looked at me quite calmly: oh, it's you. He recognized me! After that the normal instincts began to assert themselves and I even got, I think, a little fatuous. When nobody was around I would look at him covertly and think: my kid, look at the intelligence in the face, and he's got a chest like a brass boiler. The proud progenitor! What next? It was the last conformity. It was the winter of 1945, then Christmas and we had to buy a new calendar. I had lived in this place for three years. I was a commuter, a proper papa with the evening paper under his arm like the ones in the funny papers, and Ary was different now too, or rather the rest of her was still the same but the irregular polyhedron had taken on yet another side. (It was about this time that I learned that if you went on adding sides to a polyhedron eventually it became a circle, the shape of absolute simplicity, but that didn't make it any clearer.) It was not so much that age could not wither nor custom stale the infinite variety of her charms, but that she was so inexplicably adept at disembarking from the Nile and turning in five minutes into a competent nursemaid, complete with talcum powder and brisk no-nonsense manner. ("If you spit it out once more I'm going to put the bottle away. You'll get hungry eventually, I imagine.") I wondered if I seemed as complicated to her. Probably not, since she never showed any surprise at anything I did. But then, I reflected, I never showed any surprise (outwardly) at anything she did. We were a couple of artful deceivers, ideally cast in our parts: she Garbo or rather Katherine Hepburn (long legs, slightly coltish manner), I George Raft with scars. Various supporting players: Cagney, Kelly as Zazu Pitts, Maurice as a slightly spurious Leslie Howard, Leo as Wallace Beery, etc. This was life? Pass the popcorn.

One day a postcard came for her in the mail, and she read it and handed it to me with a funny smile. On one side, in gaudy colors, a square lined with medieval buildings: Grenoble, Place Victor Hugo. On the other side was a finely-written paragraph in a spidery hand; I couldn't make much out of it because I couldn't decipher the French script very well, even if I had known French. It was apparently intended as a Christmas card, a month late, and it said something about Noel and *"les meilleurs voeux pour la nouvelle année, de la part de vos amis de la Pension Fleurie*[1]*."* Then there was more I couldn't read, and at the end I made out, ". . . *nous avons toujours regretté que vous avez dû partir si précipitement*[2]." I handed it back to her.

"Why did you depart so precipitately?"

"Oh, something came up."

"It was when you were a student?"

She nodded. "It was a good boarding-house and they were nice people. Almost the only friends I made in France, really."

It occurred to me now that this was a part of her life I had never really thought very much about. I knew she had studied in Grenoble but now for the first time I began to wonder about the year she had spent in that town among people I didn't know, made friends, taken courses, sat in cafes probably in that same Place Victor Hugo arguing about Rimbaud and Lautreamont— when was it? 1938, around the time I had sat for my license. It was odd that I had never really imagined her as being a student and learning things, or thought of her as ever having been any different from the way she was. She was the land it was hard to imagine as a child, the kind who seemed to have been born adult and mature and a little ironic.

---

1 French: The best wishes for the new year, from your friends at Pension Fleurie.

2 French: We always regretted that you had to leave so hastily.

But now I had a funny curiosity about it. "What happened in Grenoble?" I asked her.

"What happened? I went to school."

"No, something else happened. Something about your having to leave suddenly."

She looked at me for a moment. "Well, you are keen today, aren't you?" Then after a pause she remarked, as though it had some kind of a connection with what we were talking about, "Grenoble was a very dull town. There was really nothing to do there."

"Then why did you go there?"

"I don't know that there was any particular reason. They had a special course at Grenoble for foreigners, and most of the American students went there. I came through an international foundation for exchange students, and they decided where I would go anyhow. They arranged for my passage and the course of study and everything, and found me the boarding-house. Of course I was very young. The Foundation thought it was better for girls not to go to Paris because they might get in trouble. They never actually said this, but you got that impression."

"Didn't any get in trouble in Grenoble?"

"A few."

Here she made one of her serene pauses, and after a while she went on. "I was trying to be very French; I had my hair cut straight with bangs over the forehead and I always carried a pack of Gauloises around with me when I went to a cafe. Girls that age are rather affected anyhow and I think I must have been a particularly silly child. I went around speaking my third-year college French, very correct, with audible accent marks over all the vowels. I thought I was terrifically sophisticated, and of course the very first thing I did was to fall in love with a soldier."

I grinned.

"Well, it wasn't funny at the time. He was an officer from the cavalry barracks, and he was almost as young as I was. But he had had a lot more experience; he was French and he came from a very old family, and it seemed tremendously romantic to me at the time. Probably I was mainly in love with his riding boots. The trouble was that from the beginning we were having a slight misunderstanding. I thought we were going steady or something, the way you do in America, and he was under the impression he had a mistress. He immediately began making passionate Gallic overtures, and of course I was quite virginal and confused by all this. It was all an international misunderstanding out of Henry James. I was like Daisy Miller and he played Giovanelli or whatever his name was."

"So he took you to the Roman ruins by moonlight, and you caught a fever?"

"No, he took me to the circus. I don't know what a circus was doing in Grenoble at that time of the year; it was a silly little provincial circus anyhow, with two old lions and a skinny elephant. But the acrobats were remarkable. They were Italians and they were about as young as we were. They looked hungry and their costumes were coming out at the seams, but they did incredible things, and always with a wonderful kind of desperate grace, as though you thought every time they weren't quite going to make it and then they did. At the end the ringmaster came out and announced with great pomp that there would be a *salto mortale*—I suppose you would translate that a death-defying leap. When I saw what this crazy Italian boy was going to do my heart almost stopped. They brought out a ring no bigger than a barrel hoop, and soaked it in gasoline and set it afire high up in the air. The Italian got up on top of the trapeze and stood for a while biting his lip and looking at the burning ring, and then he simply swung out into the air and let go. He turned over three or four times and doubled up to go through the ring, and it seemed he just barely caught the trapeze on the other side with his fingernails. The whole audience gasped and my heart flopped completely over."

She picked up her pack of cigarettes, found it was empty, and set it down again. "Anyhow, after the circus we—he and I—started talking about Nietzscheism and risking yourself and living dangerously. I told him I thought the Italian was out of his mind. He asked me 'Why does he do it then?' I said for the money, but he was still crazy. He said, 'No, I don't think so.' He was very serious and I could see it somehow meant more to him than just a stunt in a circus.

"Finally I asked him why he thought people acted this way, and he told: *'Parce que, à l'autre côté, c'est soi-meme.'*[1] You have to make the leap at least once, because on the other side is yourself, and this is the only way of finding out what it is. It wasn't just a matter of proving your courage to yourself or anybody else. The important thing was letting go of the bar when all your instincts were against it. I think he meant you would never know what you were until you let go of everything that was comfortable and secure—your family, your background, everything you had been as a child—and went out into empty space. The thing was that you had to have faith there would be something on the other side—another bar to meet your hand—even if you didn't know what it was."

For the first time I realized that what she was saying applied to me as well as to her, and I wondered if this was in her mind too as she said it, but I couldn't tell, even when she stopped at this point and waited for just long enough for me to have spoken if I had wanted to. I didn't say anything, and after a moment she went on. "Well, it was just a good line, perhaps. At any rate it worked. Of course it was that night that he took me to a hotel. Actually it was just a little inn outside of town, a few miles down the river. We went there quite often after that and it went on for three months, all the way into the spring. I didn't go to lectures or prepare for my exams and I hardly ate. I felt as though I had a fever during the whole time; I never thought about anything else

---

1   French: Because, on the other side, is you yourself.

even when I was asleep. I didn't expect it to last, and I knew he wouldn't marry me. He was perfectly honest from the start. He had known a lot of girls and when he was eighteen or nineteen he had an affair with an older woman, a friend of his mother."

"And what happened?"

"Nothing, it just ended. It wasn't much of a mortal leap, and if it was I sort of slipped and fell on my face. I suppose the real *salto mortale* in my life was something else. But at least after it was over I was entirely different from what I had been. As soon as Leo saw me, when I came home that summer, he knew what had happened. I walked and talked differently, I thought differently, I even sat in a chair differently. The reason I came home was that the Foundation got wind of what was happening from the other students and packed me off on the first train. Their precautions hadn't worked; the might as well have sent me to Paris. It didn't really matter anyhow because it was 1939 and the students were all sent home that summer the war started in the fall."

"And the officer?"

"I never heard from him again. But I hadn't expected to and after a while I got over it; I wasn't a child anymore. Then, afterwards, I began to understand a lot better the things that he had told me. About leaping and finding yourself on the other side, for example. I hadn't quite made it that time, but the next time I had to leap I would know better." She stopped, thought for a moment, and then said in another, quite matter-of-fact voice, "Anyhow that's what happened. Do you care?"

I didn't know whether I cared or not. It was a new and disconcerting idea, that she owed something I thought of as uniquely hers— something that seemed almost her very nature—to a Frenchman whose name I didn't even know. (For some reason I had begun to think of him as George.) Perhaps I was a little jealous, not of the officer but of her, because I had never been lucky enough to be in love when I was nineteen years old. Or perhaps I already half understood what she meant by saying the real *salto mortale* in her life had been something else. And if so, perhaps, it was George who should be jealous of me.

"Was he the one who taught you how to make sole marguéry?"

She smiled. "No. We didn't eat very much. Neither of us had very much money, and we spent it all on rooms at the inn. Usually we would just buy some cheese and wine there, out in the country where it was cheap. To tell the truth he wasn't very much interested in food. He was rather limited in his way and actually he was only interested in one thing. But he was very good at that."

For about a week I brooded over it and tried to imagine her Frenchman, George with the riding boots, and the inn where they had gone to eat cheese. Did it rain while they were in the room, and did they drink the wine out of glasses or just take turns with the bottle? Did the room have a window over the river? It was the first time in my life I had ever really thought deeply about anybody's life but my own, and after a while I began to see how much Europe, or Grenoble, or George, had had to do with making her what she was. I began to realize too that whatever it was I had discovered this house, something that had changed me and made me more aware of myself and others and the nuances and vividness of everything, was something like the Europe she had discovered that year when she and George spent all their money on inn rooms, except that she had been younger and so it had made deeper changes and fixed her the way she was going to be for the rest of her life. But Europe wasn't exactly the right word; it was a way of looking at reality, or rather feeling it, and you could discover it in Des Moines or Ogden if you happened to be lucky. Anyhow, I saw now that whatever it was that George had learned from his mother's bridge partner he had given to her, and then she had passed it along to me. I could think of several words for what this was, but most of them were sentimental and the rest dirty. It wasn't important what you called it anyhow; the important thing was that being alive was all there was, and the more deeply you could savor and know things, the roughness of sand or the smell of rain or making love, the more fully you were alive. Probably it was not a very profound discovery and other people had made it before, but at least I saw now it was she who had taught me.

Anyhow George, the *salto mortale*, Grenoble and the rest of it must have started some kind of a ferment in my head, because that week all sorts of funny and hitherto unprecedented things started going on inside it. One night when we were going to bed I did a queer thing. The bedroom, the dim light, the clothes I was taking off, everything was the same, and yet for some reason that night I broke into the chain of habit and did something impulsive and a little irrational. Like most people I had a habitual sequence for taking off my clothes: first the shirt, then the shoes, then the pants. The shoes were loose and I could kick them off without even bending over. They were the same tan loafers she had brought to the hospital room in the suitcase, three years before. All the other clothes had worn out and been thrown away, and the loafers were all that was left. I hardly ever wore them. They were good shoes but they had always been a little large and I didn't like them; they had a way of half coming off when I lifted my foot from the ground and this annoyed me. This time I took them off and looked at them there on the bedroom floor, and then I picked them up and dropped them in the wastebasket.

"What did you do that for?"

"I don't like them. I never have."

She looked at me, mildly curious, "They're hardly used."

"Besides they don't fit me."

"You never mentioned it before."

"Why should we get into a quarrel about a pair of shoes?"

"Why indeed?" She turned away indifferently to brush her hair as though she didn't think it was very important either. And yet it still hung in the air; we both sensed that there was more to it than we had said and that if we went on it would lead us into a region that was unknown to both of us and perhaps perilous. It seemed to me that she didn't want to do this, that she preferred to brush her hair and let sleeping dogs lie, or even that she wanted to warn me by her feigned indifference that there were some things you didn't have to look at, like Orpheus who was forbidden to look back at his wife but turned and looked anyhow, and lost her for good.

But I went on. "Let's put it this way. Why do you want me to wear them?"

"Why do I? I don't understand."

"Yes, you do." I was calm and yet I felt a kind of recklessness, as though I was finally going to do something I had always known I would have to do but had refused to face, out of a kind of fear that was perhaps really only laziness or rationalization. "Let's forget the shoes; they're not important. But there are other things that are. You know the things I mean; we both do. You're no good at pretending you're stupid when you're not, and we're both too old to play games. Besides telling lies is too much work. How old are you now, twenty- six? And I'm even older. We've got to live the rest of our lives together; we've got to become old, old people until we wear away all the sharp comers and have no more secrets between us."

"We don't have any now."

"I can tell you one we have. My shoes don't fit."

For the first time in my life, it seemed to me, I looked straight at her. She met the glance steadily but there was an uncertainty in her expression; I had never seen her like this before and I watched as she thought what she was going to say next.

"Then why don't you throw them away and forget about them?" she said with a casualness that rang a little false.

"If they were mine I would have thrown them away a long time ago, but they're not."

"Then whose are they?"

"You know that better than I."

She hesitated for a long time and finally she smiled, the small and half-reluctant smile of someone who is finally confessing something she had thought the others didn't know.

"Yes. You see, I knew from the first he was dead. I didn't believe it when they said he wasn't, because he wasn't the kind who was capable of amnesia. Ben—the other Ben—always knew thoroughly who he was. He was a bit fatuous about it, I'm afraid."

"And yet you went to Hawaii."

"Yes, I went. I don't know if I can explain it. I knew he was dead, and I had accepted it. When the photographs came from the hospital I knew it was all wrong and they were making a mistake. And yet I had to go; I had to see for myself, to be sure. It was a way of ending it, don't you see, of wiping out the last of the uncertainty. So they put me on a plane and I went, and all the way over I wondered about that nameless man in the hospital bed and who he was. It was a sort of a riddle, and I felt that somehow I had to find the answer. Then at the moment when I walked in the hospital room it suddenly came to me that it didn't matter. And then I finally knew what *he* had meant, in the circus in Grenoble, about finding yourself on the other side. Those were strange times, those months, and I think we all lost our grip on reality a little. It wasn't that I thought the matter out; I didn't *think* at all, really. It was just that somewhere below my thoughts there was a logic operating, the logic of life itself. I understood simply that the man I had given my life to was dead, and that in this room was a man who was nobody, who would be whatever I had the courage to call him. If I turned and left him, went out of the room, he would have no name and he would die."

So she had known even this too. I watched her now steadily to see what she would say next.

"And so it was simply a question of which I wanted to choose, life or truth. Anyhow we never have time; it was a matter of seconds. In those seconds it was perfectly clear to me what I had to do; I chose life. But this meant that we both accepted a lie, and we had to work back toward the truth only very slowly. It was harder for you, because you were doing it in the dark, but I knew what we were doing."

"And what was I doing? Impersonating a ghost?"

"I thought so for a while. Now I don't know."

I began to remember a look I had seen on her face in those first months, sympathetic and yet a little ironic: it was the expression of a director watching an inept pupil from the wings, a pupil playing a part he doesn't really understand and making small clumsy mistakes as he feels his way through it.

"And did I succeed?"

"Not very well. But perhaps it wasn't worth doing."

"Wasn't worth doing? How?"

"It's just that—to tell you the truth he wasn't particularly worth modeling yourself on. You see, I was still quite young when I married him and I did it rather in a rush, and it didn't work out exactly as I had expected. He was very attractive in his way, but he was weak I soon found out. And he was vain, and a little priggish."

I thought of the picture in the ebony frame, the picture I hadn't liked, and how we had put it away in the drawer and never taken it out again.

"I don't mean that I didn't feel grief, real grief, when he died. I was still young and I loved him terribly, or I thought I did, the way we love people even when they have weaknesses. But later, with you, it seemed simpler to start from the beginning. Probably you had faults of your own to get rid of. There was no point in piling all of his on top of it. I didn't see that at first; it took me a little while to think it out. But after I got to know you a little I realized that, whatever it was that you were trying to make, it wasn't the other Ben."

"Then what was it?" I asked, more than anything else out of a kind of curiosity to see what she would say as she tried to put into words something I had known for a long time.

"I don't know. Something that you yourself had to make, I suppose. It was strange; I myself didn't know what it would be until it happened. And I felt that this human being that was taking shape existed, really, only as long as you and I believed in it. And you felt that too; I could sense it."

And I knew she was right; we had both believed in it. And I saw now for the first time that what we had been making was not one human being but two; I had been necessary to her as she had been necessary to me, all those long months we had been clinging to each other so we wouldn't drown. And all that time we had gone on pretending to each other that one of us was someone else and the other didn't know it. I smiled. "You told me a hell of a lot of lies.

"Because we couldn't have both life and truth, you see. At least not for a while."

Then something else occurred to me. "And Leo?'

Again she was uncertain and it was a moment before she spoke, with the same tentative smile. "It's odd, but I simply don't know. I went away to Hawaii and came back with you, and we never talked about it. He's a funny father in a way; he's always been more like a friend than a father. Even when I was very small he would never scold me or reprimand me, he would just let me go on doing things my own way. When he met us at the station that was the time for him to say something; I was watching him. But he just gave you one look and then he picked up the suitcases and walked off. I never knew what he thought. And yet there was something he said once that I thought about afterwards. It was a week or so after you had come home—I was going to bed, and when he kissed me he said, 'You know, I never did trust guys with kiss-curls.' "

"What did he mean by that?"

"I wasn't sure. But you see *he*, the other Ben, had hair that was straight like yours except that there was a wave over each temple. Actually it was attractive in a kind of a Byronic way, but the trouble was that he knew it, and after a while it became a little affected.

He had a gesture he made of patting the two curls into place when he combed his hair. I often wondered whether he didn't roll them up on curlers after I had gone to bed."

"While you waited?"

"I would go to sleep. Because the truth was, you see, that there wasn't very much to wait for."

So this was what I had been imitating, those queer spooky days on the ship and in the hotel in San Francisco, when I still thought I was the Master Impostor. I smiled, and so did she a little. It was nothing very much to smile at, perhaps, and yet I knew she could tell me this now only because it was something that no longer mattered very much, something that had happened a long time ago and might have happened to somebody else. It seemed to me I knew more about her now than I had ever known about anybody, even more than about myself, but it didn't mean that I knew what she was, or finally saw her stripped naked down to the soul the way you see people in novels or in the case histories in psychology books. If you went on adding sides to a polygon it eventually became a circle, and a circle was harder to grasp, perhaps, than anything else in geometry. But I no longer felt it was so important to grasp this, because I knew that even she herself was helpless to sort out all the complexities and contradictions in her own life and see the pattern that lay behind it, and that everybody else was the same way. Know yourself! It was easier to understand a spiral nebula a million light years away. You could tell what happened to you on Wednesday and how you felt on Friday but when it came to making any sense out of the thing or saying what it all really meant you might as well ponder over the Mystery of the Trinity or how many angels can stand on the head of a pin. It was an ontological problem, and like all ontological problems it was insoluble.

Thinking over all these weighty matters I had fallen into a silence, and finally she said almost blithely, "Well, don't you have any more tremendous questions?"

"I've never been very inquisitive. Besides questions are pointless anyhow."

"Pointless?"

"When you ask a question you think that when you have the answer you'll see something, and instead all you have is a fact."

"What do you expect to see? If you close your eyes it's hard to remember the shape of your own face."

"Even if you wanted to remember it."

"And don't you?"

"Not very much."

"Sometimes I can't decide whom I understand less about, you or Leo." And then she said, not smiling anymore now but with a kind of gnomic, almost clairvoyant calm, "That afternoon when you were sick, and lay on the floor in this room. Are you afraid of that now?"

"No."

"You talked to somebody. I think it was somebody you used to know. Somebody out of your past."

I didn't say anything, and waited for her to go on.

"Who was he?"

"Myself."

"And who is that?" she asked quietly.

It was the first question she had ever asked me, and I knew it would be the only one, and if I didn't answer she wouldn't ask it again. I had got beyond that foxy shallow cynicism when I thought that revealing anything inward about yourself was a sign of weakness, and I knew there was no point in concealing anything from her now or telling her anything but the truth. But the truth was an infinitely dark and complicated thing; it was not merely a name she wanted to know because she already knew that, and if I had known the answer to what she asked I would have known the answer to everything and I would have been God. But I was not God and I had never felt so human and so mortal,

and all I could do was to stand there naked before her with my
hands turned out like a saint of Piero della Francesca showing
the stigmata: "I don't know."

Chapter 18

.-- .... --- .- -- ..   .- ..-- .... --- .- -- ..   .- ..-- .... --- .- -- ..   .- .... --- .- -- ..

That winter Suzanne's husband was finally released from the Army and I drove her to the station to meet him, the same Union Station with the palm trees where Leo had come to get me three years before. Carl came toward us through the crowd not knowing whether to grin or not, carrying a faded khaki barracks-bag over his shoulder by the drawstring, a tall shy soldier who looked like a rather studious American college boy until you noticed the lines around his eyes and at the corners of his mouth. He was still a corporal after four years in the Army. He and Suzanne fell into each other's arms without a word and it was about ten minutes before I could get them separated and into the car. I didn't like to break up what was so obviously a display of genuine feeling, but we were supposed to get home in time for lunch.

At first Carl was self-conscious with me and didn't have much to say, as he was with everybody for a while, but after a few days he got over it and began to talk a little. He was always uncomfortable around other people like Maurice and the Hollywood crowd, but he seemed a little more at ease with me, perhaps because my scars were a kind of a handicap too, something to balance his shyness. For the first few weeks he didn't know what to do with himself. He had two years of college before the war and he thought he would go back and finish, but the academic year had already started now and he would have to wait until summer. He told me he wanted to study marine biology, or at least he thought he did, but he wasn't sure. Perhaps he would go to business school. As it happened I bought a new car a week or so after he came home, a black Continental coupé with red leather upholstery, and I think it was when he saw the car that he got the notion that maybe he ought to be a businessman instead. It was also about this time that I moved into a new office—the old one was all right but the agent told me I owed it to myself to have one with plate-glass doors and oak paneling—and when I took Carl to see it he was visibly impressed by the teletype, the buffet with swingout bar, the secretary, and the other accessories. It was that day in the office that he began telling me his doubts about marine biology.

"I don't know, Ben. It's a long time to go to school—three more years for a master's—and I'm tired of marking time. The Army was four years out of my life, and now this is three years more. And then there's Suzanne; don't you see, I have—"

"Yeah, I know, responsibilities."

"Well, I do. You know, Leo has always been well off and she's had everything she's wanted. She's been waiting a long time for me to come home. Now I don't see how I can ask her to go and live in some furnished room for three years, or probably a lot longer. Even as a biologist I probably wouldn't make much. I've been thinking that perhaps what I should do is just take an accounting course or something for six months, and then get into something like you do," he concluded, looking around again at the oak paneling.

"You mean you'd rather be a businessman when you could be a scientist? You must be out of your mind."

"I beg your pardon?" he said politely as he always did.

"Look, Carl. Wait, have a drink, for God's sake." I pushed the button and gave a practical demonstration of the swingout bar. "Look, I've got no business giving you advice, or anybody else either, but it seems to me you've got a bad case of inferiority complex. Good God, we only have one life. I'd give my right arm if I had the chance you have, to go to college and make something useful of myself. Gogo! There's no ice, run downstairs to the drugstore, will you?"

Gogo took a half-dollar out of petty cash and left on the run.

"Listen to me, Carl. You must be out of your wits. You're intelligent, you already have two years of college, you know what you want to study, and on top of that there's the GI Bill and the government will pay your tuition. And you want to be a junk dealer like me?"

"Well, I don't even know if I would be a good scientist, Ben," he objected half-heartedly.

"Why not try? What can you lose?"

"It's just that it's no fun being poor, that's all. Especially for a woman. I can't ask Suzanne to do that."

"Have you tried asking her?"

He didn't answer, because we both knew she would do anything he wanted.

"Look—it isn't that money isn't nice to have. I've lived without it and I've lived with it, and believe me, with is better. It's just that you've got a chance of becoming what I can never be—somebody who is really important in the world—and it's discouraging to listen to you sitting there and saying you want to be like me because I've got a secretary and a little bar that pops out when you push the button. A biologist! What are five bars and nine secretaries if you can be a biologist? If you think it would hurt Suzanne's feelings to live in a furnished room, I'll lend you the money. Or better, let Leo lend it to you; he's got more than I have anyhow. Here, for

God's sake," I told him, "Don't drink gin without ice, you'll ruin your stomach." He allowed some ice to be put in his glass; he had been too polite to ask for it before. He didn't drink very much anyhow, and afterwards Gogo poured half of it down the washbowl.

Carl was easily discouraged but he was also easily undiscouraged. I think he believed me when I said I would give my right arm to be a biologist, and there was no reason why he shouldn't have, because I believed it myself. A week or so after our talk he enrolled at UCLA for the summer session, and then he and Suzanne stayed with us at the beach for the rest of the spring. But he never got over his somewhat boyish respect for me and I became, probably, his best friend. It was a little goofy, the idea of my being anybody's best friend. He admired me for the wrong reasons anyhow: because I had been an officer when he was an enlisted man, because I had made a little money, because I could handle after my fashion the particular land of repartee you needed to keep up with Maurice and Oliver and the rest. I think he even envied my face with its scars, although he knew as well as I did that getting hurt in a war was either an accident or your own fault, the result of some stupidity. Once when he and I and Suzanne were down on the beach he explained to me his theory that there were some people in the world that "things" happened to, and other people who were immune. Nothing ever happened to them, at least nothing big, either good or bad. They might get caught in the rain or catch cold, but they never got struck by lightning in the rain or won the Irish Sweepstakes. It was the others who had appointments with destiny. "For examples, do you know how Aeschylus died? He was out walking one day, and an eagle mistook his bald head for a rock and dropped a tortoise on it. This is the way the gods took him to themselves. Can you imagine that happening to me?"

"But Carl was wounded too," said Suzanne. "Tell him about how you were wounded."

He offered a sample of his usual deprecating smile. "In Normandy I went in on Omaha Beach on D plus one. It was always D plus one, you see; I was never in the first wave. When we were disembarking I crushed my finger between the boat and the side of the ship. They always told us to keep our fingers out of there. I took it to a dressing station on the beach and the doctor told me, 'What the hell are you bringing me that for?' He had a tent full of people who were shot through the stomach. I told him, 'I'm sorry, this is the only wound I've got.' I was really only trying to apologize, but he got mad as hell and told me to clear out or he'd have me court- martialed for shirking duty. I wrapped the finger up myself and went back in the line. We had forty percent casualties in my company the first week in France, and I caught a cold."

"Would you rather have been one of the forty percent?"

"I just don't know," said Carl.

"I had a tortoise dropped on me once too. Believe me, it's better to have nothing happen." But I was really like Carl; I didn't know whether it was better or not.

"At least I had read Eliot in college and knew what people like me were called—Prufrocks. There's some advantage in having an education."

'What do you call the other kind?"

"I don't know. Heroes, saints, martyrs," he said a little awkwardly.

One Saturday afternoon in April that spring Carl and Leo and I went abalone-fishing off the rocks at the end of the cove. Oliver and Kelly were down for the weekend too, but Oliver was not a great athlete and he stayed on the beach reading Montherlant while we fished. It was before the days of elaborate skindiving equipment, and we had nothing but face masks and some old tire irons to pry the abalones loose. It was a calm cloudless day and the sea was glassy. When the weather was like this the water was very clear and you could see the abalone shells ten feet under the surface, camouflaged against the rocks that were almost the same color. The trick was to slip in the tire iron and pry shell and all off the rock with one quick motion, because a second later the muscle contracted and you couldn't get the iron under it. In a couple of hours we got a half a basket of abalones, more than enough for our dinner. Just before we quit Carl made one more dive and came up with a beautiful lobster that must have weighed three or four pounds. "I thought I saw him the last time I went down," he told us. Whether or not he would make a good biologist he understood the psychology of lobsters; he knew which holes they were in and when they were likely to come out, and how to take them in his fingers without getting pinched. The others went in to change, and I went to the shed behind the garage to find a bucket to boil the lobster in; I thought I would cook him right away and then we would have him cold with the cocktails before dinner. There was a small gas-plate out in the shed, and I put the bucket of salt water on it and left the lobster to wait in a basket until the water was hot. When I came outside again the others had disappeared into the house. My shorts were almost dry and I pulled on a jersey, feeling the evening breeze beginning to move through the trees. The sun was setting and the sky was an intense platinum blue, the pines dark against the light sky. There was nothing for me to do in the house until the others had taken their showers, and I sat on the broken stone wall behind the garage to smoke a cigarette while I waited. I could hear a lizard scratching around in the wall and the sound of the surf under the cliff, and once in a while the leaves rustling in the trees over my head. I sat for perhaps a half an hour smoking and watching the sky darken, lazily aware of these small familiar sounds. Then I heard another noise, the gritting of leather as someone turned uncertainly on the cement walk beyond the garage.

I knew what it was: somebody had come down the walk from the street and was trying to find the entrance to the house. The mailbox with Leo's name on it was out in front, but the door was kept locked and overgrown with vines and we almost never used it. All our friends knew you had to come to the side door, which led in through the kitchen. But people who came for the first time always wandered around outside for a while until they found out how to get in. I thought it might be one of Maurice's friends or somebody Leo had invited. I got up off the wall, dropped the cigarette and stepped on it, and walked up to look through the grape arbor to see who it was. Through the leaves I saw an old man with a splotched face, peering puzzled at the house trying to find out where the doorbell was. He was wearing an old trench coat with shoulder straps and a fedora with a brim turned down.

In the twilight he seemed very small, almost a child. I felt a strange sensation; it was not exactly like seeing a ghost, but a kind of dislocation of reality, as though something had been thrown into the wrong gear, into reverse, and the whole machinery of logic had got of hand. It was like a dream in which you go up to the coffin at a funeral and look in and see the dead man is yourself; you try to defend yourself with logic, telling yourself that it is impossible, but the logic dissolves away before the vividness of what you see. There was never any doubt about what I was seeing, but it was a kind of recognition that grasped only the externals, and it was a few seconds before I could understand the significance of what had appeared before me and bring myself to do something about it. In those seconds I simply stood motionless behind the grape arbor and watched him as he circled furtively around on the cement walk like a bird looking for a place to light.

Inside the house I heard somebody turn the water on and then off again. He was moving now toward the side of the house; in a moment he would find the doorbell. When he had first appeared, only a few seconds before, he had been something like a hallucination, but as the moments passed it was he who seemed real and the house, the people, everything in it had become thin and transparent, as though any moment it might evaporate and dissolve just as easily. He had seen the door now and he was stretching out his hand for the bell in his shaky old-man's way. It was then finally that I called out to him in a voice that sounded strange, disembodied, even to myself: "Victor, wait, I'm over here."

He followed me around behind the garage without a word. I saw him taking everything in as we went: the path that went down to the private beach, the Lincoln in the driveway, Oliver's Chevrolet with the sticker on the windshield that said, "Occidental College Faculty." We sat down on the old broken wall. We were behind the trees here and I knew no one would see us from the house. It was almost dark now, the pines were black, the first star had come out and hung faintly in the western sky.

For a while he didn't know what to say. Then he cleared his throat and said, "I saw your picture in the paper, kid. You're a businessman now."

Then I knew how it had happened; the Long Beach paper had sent a photographer around when I opened the new office, a few weeks before, but the picture had never turned up or at least I had never seen it, and I had decided they weren't going to use it.

"You gave me a funny feeling, Victor. I thought you were dead."

"I know, I saw your hands."

But it wasn't what I thought; he hadn't noticed the scars in the twilight, and it was just that my hands had a funny tremor. I picked up a stick and began breaking it idly, dropping the pieces on the ground as he went on talking.

"I figured you thought that," he told me, "but it's harder to drown an old man than you think." Everything was the same, he still talked in the old way, looking not at me but at something off to one side. "Agh, listen, what do you think? I went to sea for thirty years. Those other vags, they all lost their heads."

This was all he ever said about that night in the gulf and what had happened to the ship. There was another pause, and he took off his stained fedora and looked into it. His hair was white and he was shrunken and emaciated, the flesh thin over his teeth; he seemed a frail doll-like imitation of himself. My God, what had happened to him! I wondered how old he could be; surely only seventy or a little more, I had never known exactly how old he was. But something had happened, something had dug or wormed its way inside him and sucked the life out, and then I knew what it was; Victor was mortal, like Kammerath and like the rest of us, and this was the secret he had wanted to conceal. I wanted to tell him *Victor, Victor, you're old, what the hell have you done with your life*, but instead I asked him if he was still going to sea. He said he had quit a few years back. He had a shack in San Pedro on the side of the hill and he was living off beans and canned willy. He was doing all right. He had a little arthritis that bothered him. He showed me his fingers; they were yellow and shrunken and he couldn't straighten them out. He looked around at the house and the cars again and then he put his hat slowly back on. "It looks like you fell into it, kid."

I didn't turn to look at him but I knew the expression he would have, wise and furtive, like an old jackal sniffing carrion in the distance and pretending not to look.

"Who's Halevy? I saw the name on the mailbox."

"My father-in-law."

"I figured that was probably it. You're in with them now, eh?" He scratched his head, pushing the hat up in the back. "You're smart, kid, you always had a head on you. There's no use fighting them, the only way is to get in with them." There was no irony in his voice and I saw at last that he wasn't really antisemitic; why should he hold it against the Yids for doing what he would have done himself if he had the chance? It happened to be a fact that they ran the whole world and he thought it was a good con. He almost admired them for it.

"Agh, you know," he was saying, "it's funny how things turn out. I saw the house, the cars, all this stuff. I didn't know whether you'd remember the old man." He squinted through the trees as a light went on in the kitchen window. "Sure, you changed your name, kid, I can see you worked the whole thing out. But when I saw the picture I recognized you right away. It gave me a funny feeling, you know, like you said about me. At first I didn't know what to do, but then I decided to come down and talk to you. I didn't know whether to or not, but I figured you shipped out with the old man for a long time, you'd want to play it square with him now."

I waited for him to go on, but he was in no hurry to come to the point.

"The other day I got to thinking about it, kid. We sailed together on a lot of ships, and we were always pretty good–" he stopped dead before the word friends– "you know, we sort of stuck together in our way. You remember I got you that berth when you came out." He didn't say come out of what, and he didn't mention why I had gone in. "Hell, sailing with all those spics and people, we had to stick together. Agh, it's even worse now. A white man can whistle for a berth. You went on the beach at the right time, kid, it's gone downhill since. You know, I always figured that Firmín would crap out with his stomach and I would get a command. That's why I signed on that pisspot, and instead he ran it into a torpedo. Thirty years, thirty years, kid, I went to sea and I never got a ship of my own. Then I got this arthritis. Last fall that Cap American outfit folded and I went back to the *Lucknow*, you know, but they had no use for an old man who couldn't even hold up the binoculars. You know what they told me? How come you quit during the war when we needed people and we could have given you a command? Agh, I'll tell you, you can't win, they're out to get you, kid, the whole system. I told you that from the first, I always played it square with you. When you came out in '42 I even lent you some money. Maybe you've forgotten that now."

"I didn't forget, Victor."

It was dark now and we had been sitting out there a long time. I wondered how long it would be before somebody came out to see what I was doing all by myself, or heard the voices. I could have tried to lead him away down to the beach, or into the garage, but it wouldn't make any difference; in the end he would go where he wanted to go and find out what he wanted to find, just as he had always found out everything. I started feeling for a cigarette and then I realized I was still in my shorts and didn't have any, and besides the light might be seen from the house. Somehow just by coming he had made me a fugitive again, an outsider.

I knew what was going to happen next, and I had already formed in my mind the sentence that I would speak, the sentence that had to be spoken in exactly the right way, casually and almost with a kind of a smile, to show there was no hostility in me and I had nothing against him for being the way he was: "Victor, you wait here, and I'll go in the house and get my checkbook." And I knew what would happen afterwards; he would pull his hat down over his ears and go off down the walk with the piece of paper, looking back once, furtive and expressionless, at the house, and after a few days he would come back. I would always sit there on the broken wall in the evening, waiting to hear the gritting of his shoes on the pavement, until the arthritis finally got him and he died. And in a part of my mind I resigned myself to paying him, perhaps out of some obscure feeling that I owed him something, or perhaps just because I would be paying for the right to be different from him, the right to be what I had become.

"I thought you'd remember, kid. You know, we know a lot about each other, there's all those things that happened that we still remember. That's why when I saw your picture in the paper I thought I'd come down and talk to you. I figured you weren't still sailing or I would have heard of you."

"What do you want, Victor?

"It's like I said, it was just for old times, I came down to see how you were getting along."

"Let's quit the kidding, Victor. You didn't come all this way to look me. You could see my picture in the paper."

He smiled, and in the darkness I caught the faint yellow gleam of his teeth. "You want to lay it on the line, don't you? You always were that way. It's like this, kid. I came to ask you to make it easy on the old man. I figured I'd come to you and put it to you straight before you found out for yourself. You know, you're in with all these—" he made a vague motion of his head toward the house— "you know, these other guys, and I figured sooner or later you'd hear about it and tell them, and they would make trouble about the insurance. I wouldn't blame you in a way; I know that when you're in with them you all have to stick together. But I just came to ask you to remember some of the times we used to have, in the old days."

I stared at him. "What are you talking about?"

"I'm talking about us, kid."

"What insurance?"

"You remember, we wrote it to each other, that last trip. You made out your policy to me and I collected the five thousand. It probably doesn't seem like much to you but it was a lot to me. This shack I'm living in now I bought with that." He was talking in a funny tone I had never heard him use before; it was the quick and not very hopeful spiel of the panhandler who is afraid he is going to be interrupted. "I never asked you for anything, kid, you know I used to lend you money in the old days. All you've got to do is say nothing and the old man can live a few years in his own house. It doesn't mean anything to you."

He stopped; he didn't have anything more to say. He was looking at the ground in front of him, but I could tell he was watching me out of the corner of his eye to see how I was taking it.

I said quietly, "What guys are you talking about that I'm in with, Victor?"

"You know, all these—" you could tell her was thinking Yids but wondering now if he ought to say it— "you know these Halevys and all, Wall Street and all that gang. I know you all stick together. But I just wanted you to think, maybe the insurance company doesn't need it as bad as the old man."

I didn't know what to tell him. Finally I said, "Victor, why would I do that?"

He hesitated. "I was thinking about the time in the Italian place, when I went out the window. You know, I saw those two guys in the corner. I knew who they were."

He waited for me to say something.

"Victor, I used to drink a lot of your whiskey. Let's forget what happened, everything."

He nodded; I couldn't see his face very well in the dark. He got up and started to go, pulling his hat over his ears. "I thought I'd explain it to you," I heard him say half to himself.

It was then that I spoke the sentence I had worked out in my mind earlier, it seemed like a hundred years ago, before I knew what it meant and how I would say it. "Listen Victor, you stay there and I'll go in the house and get my checkbook."

We were walking down the cement walk toward the street. "Keep it, kid. I never asked anybody for anything. Anyhow you can use it yourself, you've got a—you know, a son now." He seemed to speak the word awkwardly, as though he had never used it before. I don't know how he knew that anyhow; they must have said something about it in the story in the paper. I stood there not knowing what to say to him. I had lived with him for years almost without speaking and now at last I knew who he was: of my three fathers perhaps the one who had changed me the most, an old man who loved the sea and had been betrayed by it, and who lived by himself in a shack now and was going to die soon.

"How did you get here anyhow? At least wait until I go in the house for the car keys, and I'll drive you back to San Pedro."

"Nah, there's a bus takes me right into Long Beach where I can get the short line."

"The bus stops a mile from here, down at the cafe."

"I know that, kid, that's where I got off."

I watched him go off down the highway with the old foxlike gait, a little stiff now because of the arthritis. Except for that he was the same; the trench coat was too long and struck him half-way below the knees, exactly like the old Navy coat he had worn before the war. It was really too warm for a coat anyhow, but it was early in the season and he had always been cautious.

Standing there on the cement walk after he had left I felt a funny subdued kind of wisdom that was also a sadness, like a birthday when you are getting old. What was I supposed to do, light a candle in the church? Send out announcements to my friends? I should have gone in the house; they were waiting on me and probably wondering where I was. Instead I went down to the beach and sat for a while listening to the sound of the surf and the wind in the trees overhead. I suppose I must have sat there for a half an hour; I didn't have any cigarettes or anybody to talk to and so I just sat. I wondered why it was that all the events of my life were somehow so connected with the sea, the same sea that that touched the mud flats of Oakland, the barnacle-crusted pilings in the Chilean nitrate ports, the Solomons where the monsoon would be coming now and the leaves and vines would wash out of the rivers into the gulf. I didn't know the answer and I knew there were a lot of things I would never understand, but I did know that this sea that had once been my enemy, the sea I had tricked and cajoled and hated, the same sea that had burned the flesh I had never understood until I had suffered in it, had somehow become my friend, like the other things of the earth I had finally come to accept. It had happened so slowly I hadn't noticed it; the sea was the same but I had changed. Was I any better now? I didn't know that either, and perhaps there wasn't any point in talking about whether people were better or worse. They were the way they were, and the things that changed them came from the outside as much as from the inside; sometimes it was the things they wanted least, the sufferings and defeats, that changed them the most. I had changed but I couldn't really take the credit for it, even if I had chosen and worked to make myself the way I was. We were all free and we were all responsible, but in the end the changes we could make in things were very slight and the best we could hope was to understand ourselves a little. On the whole I had been worse than most people, I had killed and betrayed and degraded myself and others, and even after a second chance I hadn't done anything to make the world a better place for anyone but myself and my family. But I saw now that however cheap and dishonest I had been, how many lies I had told to myself and others, the worst thing I had done was not to call myself by a name that was not my own. That was a crime only for the people who believed in names; the bureaucrats, I supposed, and the police. The philosophers knew better. I wasn't a philosopher and I didn't exactly grasp the secret of the universe, but at least I knew now what I believed in: the earth, and other men. I had got over wanting things to be any different from the way they were, and I was content merely to sit on the beach and feel the rough wet sand against my haunches. Perhaps that was a cockeyed kind of religion; my religion. I didn't know what the absolutes were; maybe when the time came I would send for the priest or possibly the rabbi, but not yet. After a while I got up and climbed back up the path to the house.

Afterword

by Steven G. Kellman

.-- .... --- .- -- .. .- .... --- .- -- .. .- .... --- .- -- .. .- .... --- .- -- ..

"You don't seem like yourself," Taylor Coates tells his son Julian in *Tenth* (1984), MacDonald Harris's eleventh novel. A professor of music, Julian has abruptly tossed the student papers he was grading into a trash can, walked out of his university job, and taken a young, attractive student home to live with him. "Il faut changer la vie" (You must change your life), insisted Arthur Rimbaud, and Julian does just that, transforming himself from an unexceptional academic into a creative imposter, someone who dares complete a dead composer's unfinished symphony. His presumption resembles Nils-Frederic Glas's attempt, in Harris's fourteenth novel, *Hemingway's Suitcase* (1990), to pass off his own confections as Ernest Hemingway's famous lost stories. In the Harris universe, characters cannot seem like themselves, because the self is fluid and elusive, a moving target.

"Who am I?" This epic – and Socratic – question that, appearing at the end of its second paragraph, launches *Mortal Leap*. It's an enigma that also animated the French Existentialists who, in

345

1964, the year the novel was first published, were still à la mode in America. The narrator's conviction that "a man is simply the sum of his acts" echoes Sartrean doctrine that existence precedes essence. The attack of nausea that, in Jean-Paul Sartre's novel *Nausea*, jars Antoine Roquentin into a realization of the happenstance of his own has its counterpart in young Larry Backus's reflections when he wanders tipsy at night along the vacant Oakland waterfront after losing his virginity to a prostitute. "I felt an odd sense of vertigo," he recalls. The epiphany that he is alone in a universe indifferent to whoever he is will eventually lead to an Existential conviction that "freedom is simply the state of being able to make decisions." Larry Backus exercises that freedom when he decides to get off his hospital bed and become Lieutenant Benton Davenant.

Mortal Leap begins with an epigraph from Blaise Pascal that ponders the meaning of personal identity. If smallpox – or something else – eradicates every trait of your beloved, who is it that is now the object of your affections? The New York Yankees are a baseball dynasty, but, since a team is the sum total of its players and every player is eventually traded or retired, the Yankees do not exist except as a fiction of continuity. If, after seven years, every cell in the human body is replaced, must we periodically apply for new Social Security numbers? Or is there an essence – a soul? – that persists despite physical alterations? By the end of Chapter Eight, a wartime catastrophe in the South Pacific reduces Larry Backus to nothing. The rest of the book is the fascinating story of how, like a Method actor performing in a Chekhov play, he becomes the new part that he plays.

For MacDonald Harris, the fictionality of personal identity begins with his byline. Born Donald Heiney, in 1921 in South Pasadena, he adopted MacDonald Harris as his nom de plume for his first published novel, *Private Demons* (1961). Having earned his PhD in comparative literature at the University of Southern

California in 1952. Heiney became a respectable – and respected – academic, a professor of English at the University of Utah until 1965 and then, from 1965 to 1991, at the University of California at Irvine, whose prestigious creative writing program he co-founded. Heiney published numerous scholarly studies, while Harris was a prolific creator of fiction – seventeen novels and one collection of short stories. Heiney died suddenly at his home in Newport Beach in 1993; Harris lives on in the bookshelves of discerning readers.

When the editor of a literary encyclopedia asked him about his pen name, Heiney explained: "The use of a fictional pseudonym, which I began with my earliest stories, has provided a convenient form of controlled schizophrenia which has enabled me to cling to an artistic temperament and a creative outlook even though I've lived most of my life in a banaly [sic] bourgeois atmosphere. The problem for a writer in those circumstances, I think, is to resist the forces that attempt to make him normal and to remain a little crazy. In this, at least, I think I have succeeded."

Mortal Leap is not nearly as crazy as some later Harris works, such as *Bull Fire* (1973), whose narrator is the son of a man-made bull, or *The Little People* (1986), in which an American visiting rural England cavorts with a race of ancient, mischievous creatures only he can see. But its peculiar premise is that a man can expunge every vestige of his existence – his face, his fingerprints, his memory – and then appropriate another man's life. How likely is it that a plebeian seaman named Larry Backus could pass for the well-heeled bon vivant Lieutenant Benton Davenant? However, life anticipated Harris's art in the case of Wallace Ford, a character actor who appeared in more than 150 films, including *Shadow of a Doubt* and *Spellbound*. Before his death in 1966, he revealed the fact that he was not really Wallace Ford. Born Samuel Grundy Jones in Lancashire, he grew up in a succession of orphanages and foster homes in England and Canada. He was sixteen when he and a friend ran off to ride the rails in the United States. After his companion slipped and was crushed by a train, Jones appropriated for himself his dead friend's name, Wallace Ford.

Harris may or may not have known about that case of impersonation when, in Rome on a grant from the American Council of Learned Societies, he wrote *Mortal Leap*. A more recent example of passing for someone else is Don Draper, the lead character in *Mad Men*, a TV series that aired from 2007-2015. Flashbacks gradually reveal the fact that Draper – played by Jon Hamm – was really Richard Whitman. During the Korean War, Whitman switches dog tags with his commanding officer, Lieutenant Don Draper, and assumes his identity after Draper is killed in combat.

Trying to pass for Ben Davenant, the anxious narrator of *Mortal Leap* confesses that he "felt like a trained baboon trying to play a cello." Elsewhere, he likens himself to "a passenger in an airplane who had grabbed the controls when the pilot had died of a heart attack." Part of his challenge is a matter of putting in a convincing performance of the customs that define caste. Within his new social circle in tony Laguna Beach, the upstart must repress his inclinations to put catsup on filet mignon, drink red wine with fish, and applaud between movements of a symphony. He studies the myriad varieties of cheese as if they were conjugations of a foreign language he is obliged to learn. When sophisticated friends of Davenant's wife, Ary, gather to offer her husband a convivial homecoming, he confesses that: "I had no idea how to act with them, how to talk, how to hold my hands or what to say when I was spoken to." Although the man he would replace was a polished graduate of the University of Washington, the usurper is keenly aware that a California prison is "the only institution of higher learning I ever attended."

However, more fundamental than its account of extraordinary, abrupt social mobility, from a bunk in a ramshackle freighter to the posh Mark Hopkins Hotel, is the novel's challenge to the integrity of personal identity. Backus/Davenant contends that "my situation was a kind of metaphor for the whole human predicament." What accounts for the book's enduring fascination is its exploration of what it means to be "me" and not "you." Its unsettling suggestion is that the lines that define us are porous and unstable. Each of us is a tissue of contingencies. At any moment, each of us could be other than what we are. And each of us is not who we seem to be.

Imposture is a Harris signature. Larry Backus passes himself off as Ben Davenant. In *The Treasure of Sainte Foy* (1980), Patrick, a disaffected American art historian in cahoots with Occitanian terrorists, signs into his hotel as Professor Adrian Proutey to reconnoiter the medieval French church he intends to loot. In *Pandora's Galley* (1979), Jean-Marie de Fontenay is a French secret agent pretending to be a music student in Venice. In *Yukiko* (1977), Angelo, the navigator on an American military mission against Japan in 1945, is a double agent. And the narrator of *Trepleff* (1969) recounts how, faithful to Stanislavsky's Method, he becomes the Chekhov character he portrays in a stage production.

In *Mortal Leap*, identity is not only arbitrary; it is also a kind of incarceration. Victor Gamoff, a cunning, cynical Russian sailor, becomes the narrator's tutor in the ruthless ways of the world. After Victor allows the younger man to take the rap for a crime he himself committed, Larry learns a philosophical lesson. Although it means twenty-two months in San Quentin, he emerges from confinement bitter over something more disturbing than a friend's deceit: "The resentment I felt inside was not hatred for being imprisoned or for Victor who had betrayed me but something deeper: a rebellion against the very way of things that condemned men to be imprisoned within their own identities." Much of the Harris oeuvre testifies to the arbitrariness of those prison walls.

In Harris's world, the other walls used to enclose and define us are just as flimsy. Pondering his attraction to the ambiguously named Syd, the narrator of *Trepleff* states: "I had thought I was clear on the difference between the sexes but she confused me a little." In *Herma* (1981), a similar challenge to binary sexual categories comes through the title character, a diva who is able at times to project herself as the male Fred Hite (Herma + Fred Hite = hermaphrodite), a fusion of what to the binary mind is usually thought distinct. Nor are species isolated in the Harris universe. In *Bull Fire*, Nino is a half-god, half-demon who aspires to be human. The boundaries of time itself are erased in *Screenplay* (1982) when its protagonist, Alys, finds himself propelled back six decades to the Hollywood of the 1920s.

Mortal Leap, which begins with an admonition to be attentive, locates its story precisely within the wartime 1940s. "By paying attention to the little things," we are told, "we finally come to notice things that are deeper and more elusive, things that are invisible to ordinary eyes." The things that the novel bears convincing witness to include daily routines aboard a rusty, leaky freighter, medical procedures within the ward of a navy hospital, and the business of buying and selling vegetables. In *A Portrait of My Desire* (1993), we are told that for the novel's protagonist, Harry, the owner of an art gallery, "the world was divided into two classes of people: those who fixed their own cars and those who hired somebody else to fix them." Harris is repeatedly drawn to characters who fix their own cars and relishes the opportunity to show how they do it. Taking the initiative to construct generators and cargo pumps out of military surplus and merchandise marine electrical parts, the narrator of *Mortal Leap* is one of many Harris tinkerers.

Just as Donald Heiney, who graduated from the Merchant Marine Academy, spent the final years of World War II as a naval officer in the Atlantic, Mediterranean, and Pacific, and remained an accomplished and enthusiastic sailor, MacDonald Harris writes knowingly about Larry Backus's resourcefulness as third engineer of the ramshackle merchant vessel *Chileno Cape*. In other novels, Harris shows the reader how to navigate a yacht (*Private Demons*), a gondola (*Pandora's Galley*), and a submarine (*Yukiko*). Harris's characters pilot vehicles that include a helicopter (*The Treasure of Sainte Foy*), a balloon (*The Balloonist*, 1976), and a Curtiss June Bug biplane (Herma). The motto of the eccentric Franciscan monk Fra Mauro in *Pandora's Galley*, *"etiam vir sanctus scientam non abhorret"* (even a holy man does not abhor knowledge), applies to many Harris characters. However, their knowledge cannot avert disaster. For all his seafaring skills, Larry almost dies in a wreck off the Solomon Islands, just as, in *The Treasure of Sainte Foy*, Patrick's expertise in medieval art does not prevent plans to plunder an old French church from going fatally awry.

The trajectory of *Mortal Leap* is defined by the narrator's two mentors. When he ships out on his first deepwater vessel, the *Emil Lucknow*, Larry Backus bonds with its second mate, Victor, a crusty older man who teaches him never to trust anyone. Because everyone – even, and especially, Victor – is indifferent to his existence, he has to look out for himself. Victor, a drug smuggler who describes himself as a "realist" – by which he means someone who sees through naïve illusions of a benign universe – becomes a surrogate father for the eighteen-year-old *ingenu* who has left his biological father back in Utah. Victor is, according to Larry, "my father and enemy who stole from me and gave me good advice." That advice is to remember that "the world is out to get you and that it was better to be a live jackal than a dead lion." That advice helps explain Larry Backus's emergence from a hospital bed as Ben Davenant.

Victor is a prickly anti-Semite who is convinced that the world is controlled by a cabal of malevolent Jews. So it is significant that Leo Halevy, who becomes the narrator's father-in-law and mentor in his new life in southern California, is Jewish. A failed poet who made a fortune selling produce, Leo is a stark contrast to Victor, although he, too, takes a liking to the younger man, who reasons: "I think he had always wanted a son." Leo, who finds it much easier to make money than to get rid of it, is generous, tolerant, and thoughtful. In his spare time, he reads Heisenberg, Freud, and Confucius. The novel never resolves the question of whether Leo ever becomes aware that the man now calling himself Ben Davenant and sharing his daughter's bed is an imposter. But the implication is that, even if he knows, Leo does not really care as long as the arrangement makes everyone happy – and produces a grandson for him.

It is appropriate that, in the final scene of the novel, Victor reappears, to announce that he has scammed an insurance company out of money due for Larry Backus's death. Larry/Ben acknowledges that Victor was "of my three fathers perhaps the one who had changed me the most." He has abandoned forever his stern, Mormon biological father. But now, a father himself, he recognizes that he has outgrown the aging misanthropic sailor, who wanders off alone, "an old man who loved the sea and had been betrayed by it, and who lived by himself in a shack now and was going to die soon." Leo remains.

Leo's daughter Ary is, of course, the catalyst in Larry's transformation and, ultimately, the transfer of his filial bonds from Victor to Leo. The novel's turning point comes when Ary Davenant bends over a badly disfigured stranger lying in a naval hospital bed in Pearl Harbor. "Hello, darling," she says. "I thought it was you." Larry remains silent, but when Ary (whose name rhymes with Larry) tells Lieutenant Gore, Larry's psychiatrist, "Now we'll have to see about getting him out of here," the fiction of their marriage is spun. Ary only much later reveals she has been conscious of Larry's imposture all along. Their relationship ripens amid Jamesian intricacies of awareness, in which each puzzles over what the other is thinking, even over whether the other is puzzling, too.

Among much else, *Mortal Leap* is an intricate love story, the convergence of a man and a woman in an enduring relationship of mutual trust. Ultimately, Ary and Ben model 2.0 remain mysteries to each other, but the willingness of each to respect and embrace the mystery of the other is what generates love, something that, under the sway of Victor's egotistical cynicism, Larry never knew. Toward the end of the novel, Ary recounts how, while visiting a circus in Grenoble many years ago, she witnessed an acrobat execute a perilous jump from a trapeze through a ring of fire and back onto the trapeze. This *salto mortale* – mortal leap, from which the novel derives its title – is clearly a metaphor for the dire risk that Ary and Larry each take in hurtling into the other's life. It is also an emblem of the perilous gamble that living fully often demands.

Reading, similarly, requires a leap of the imagination, an eager submission to the power of another's words, trusting that we will sail safely from front cover to back cover and emerge on fire but unburnt. Harris's fiction usually rewards that trust. It is hard to begin a Harris novel without being drawn in. Yet the same contingencies that bedevil the narrator of *Mortal Leap* generate the vagaries of literary reputation. "In the end there's no justice: the universe is not an auditing firm," says the narrator Ben. His observation could legitimately apply to the haphazard way some authors are adulated and others underrated, even ignored.

Early in his academic career, Donald Heiney published a survey titled *Recent American Literature*, a breezy overview of hundreds of literary figures. About the author of *Jurgen* (1919) and other narrative fantasies that were once highly regarded, Heiney wrote: "Yet [James Branch] Cabell is a writer of great talent, perhaps even of genius, and it may be that another literary generation will come back to his work as the generation of the Thirties came back to Melville. Cabell is the kind of an author who is likely to prove durable, whatever temporary disfavor he may happen to fall into as public taste changes with the years." That prophecy has not (yet?) been fulfilled. Nor, despite the fact that *The Balloonist* was a finalist for the National Book Award and its author a recipient of the Award in Literature from the American Academy and Institute of Arts and Sciences, has MacDonald Harris maintained the wide public or scholarly following his exquisitely crafted work deserves.

In recent years, several Harris novels – *The Balloonist*, *Herma*, *Screenplay*, and *Yukiko*, in addition, now, to *Mortal Leap* – have been brought back into print. The world has changed dramatically since 1964, but Harris's deft sparring with questions of change and self stands the test of time. More than just a literary entertainer – though he was certainly that – Harris devised sophisticated and enduring philosophical fiction not out of place in the company of Umberto Eco, Milan Kundera, Iris Murdoch, and even Fyodor Dostoevsky.

An autodidact who reads two or three books a week, Larry Backus has little patience for works that do not sustain his interest. If a book does not hook him in its first ten pages, he tosses it overboard. *The Forsyte Saga* ends up at the bottom of the Pacific because of his distaste for its author, John Galsworthy. "Galsworthy was a gentleman," he concludes, "and no gentleman would ever write a good book."

Donald Heiney was a gentleman – an inspiring teacher and a generous colleague. For many, Heiney is best known as the supportive professor who secretly submitted to his agent a manuscript by one of his writing students, Michael Chabon, thereby facilitating publication of Chabon's first novel, *The Mysteries of Pittsburgh* (1988). He favored me, a junior colleague at UC Irvine, with an excursion into the ocean on his private sailboat.

Nevertheless, his doppelgänger Harris managed to write many, many good books. Appearing early in his career, *Mortal Leap* received national attention only from *Kirkus Reviews* and, improbably, the *New York Times Book Review*. *Kirkus* concluded its brief, anonymous notice by stating: "The story is well told, with convincing characters and a sense of purpose." However, writing in the *Times*, Elizabeth Janeway, herself a novelist, sneered: "MacDonald Harris, a good writer, has written an almost good book."

Six decades later, Harris's novel has aged more gracefully than Janeway's oafish gibe. Despite the audacity of its premise, reconstructing a human identity after reducing an adult to a blank slate, *Mortal Leap* is not as overtly inventive as later Harris works involving time travel and other supernatural phenomena. Its cast of major characters is limited to four, only one of them a woman, but string quartets generate glorious sound. "I am convinced that the universe is terribly ironical," declares the narrator in his opening paragraph. And the wonderful irony is that Harris's deftly crafted novel of rebirth in the 1940s is finding readers who can treasure it in the 21st century.

Mortal Leap
By MacDonald Harris (pseudonym of Donald Heiney)

First published in this edition by Boiler House Press, 2024
Part of the UEA Publishing Project
Mortal Leap copyright © Estate of Donald Heiney, 2024
Introduction copyright © Jonathan Coe, 2024
Afterword copyright © Steven G. Kellman, 2024

Proofreading by Ava Cline

Photograph of MacDonald Harris and cover photograph by
permission of Paul A. Heiney
Endpaper photographs courtesy of the Library of Congress

Cover Design and Typesetting by Louise Aspinall
Typeset in Arnhem Pro

ISBN: 978-1-915812-10-0